SPOILER
ALERT

Also by Olivia Dade

Lovestruck Librarians Series
My Reckless Valentine
Mayday
Ready to Fall
Driven to Distraction
Hidden Hearts

Love Unscripted Series
Desire and the Deep Blue Sea
Tiny House, Big Love

There's Something About Marysburg Series
Teach Me
40-Love
Sweetest in the Gale: A Marysburg Story Collection

SPOILER ALERT

A NOVEL

OLIVIA DADE

AVON

An Imprint of HarperCollinsPublishers

SPOILER ALERT. Copyright © 2020 by Olivia Dade. Excerpt from SLOW BURN © 2021 by Olivia Dade. All rights reserved. Printed in the United States of America. No part of this book may be used or reproduced in any manner whatsoever without written permission except in the case of brief quotations embodied in critical articles and reviews. For information, address HarperCollins Publishers, 195 Broadway, New York, NY 10007.

HarperCollins books may be purchased for educational, business, or sales promotional use. For information, please email the Special Markets Department at SPsales@harpercollins.com.

FIRST EDITION

Designed by Diahann Sturge

Thumbs-up emoji on page 68 © FOS_ICON / Shutterstock, Inc.

Library of Congress Cataloging-in-Publication Data has been applied for.

ISBN 978-0-06-300554-9

20 21 22 23 24   LSC   10 9 8 7 6 5 4 3 2 1

To everyone who's ever doubted, as I did: Someone who looks like you can be desired. Someone who looks like you can be loved. Someone who looks like you can have a happy ending. I swear it. ♥

1

BETWEEN TAKES, MARCUS DID HIS BEST NOT TO ACKNOWL-
edge the obvious: this was a stupid-ass way to die.

Still, at the director's call of action, he let out a guttural howl
and rode amid the chaos of warfare once more, adrenaline metal-
lic on his tongue as he galloped through choking smoke-machine
clouds. Bellowing stunt performers on horseback whizzed past
while his own horse jolted rhythmically between his thighs.
Mud—or some foul combination of mud and horseshit, from the
smell of it—splattered against his cheek. The special rig raced
ahead of him, the camera on the SUV's rushing arm capturing all
his determination and desperation.

He didn't love this season's script, true. But he loved *this*. The
physicality of it all. The way their show's big budget bought those
enormous smoke machines, wired the spider camera tracking
overhead, hired those stunt actors, and paid for his training on
horseback. That money reserved acres and acres of Spanish coast-
line for the sole purpose of the series's final, climactic battle, and
it allowed them to rehearse and film for weeks and weeks and
endless, miserable *weeks* to get just the right shots.

And it was miserable. Often. But because their behind-the-
scenes crew of almost a thousand consummate professionals had
set the scene so thoroughly, so convincingly, he didn't have to

pretend quite so hard, didn't have to fight to lose himself in the moment. The hazy, chaotic landscape around him helped him drop into character, even as the literal and metaphorical choreography of a successful show and this particular scene came to his hand like a well-trained hound.

There was no cut when Dido—Carah, his talented colleague of more than seven years now, ever since pre-production for the series began—appeared through the fog at exactly the place they'd rehearsed, sword aimed directly at him. The showrunners had specified long, continuous takes whenever possible for this battle sequence.

"I have come for my revenge, Aeneas the Betrayer!" Dido shouted, her voice raw and cracked with rage. Real-life exhaustion too, he imagined.

At a safe distance, he brought the horse to a standstill and swung down. Strode up to her, knocked aside her sword in one swift motion, and gripped her shoulders.

"I have come for *you*, my beloved." He cupped her face with one dirty hand. "As soon as I heard you lived once more. Not even the return of the dead from Tartarus could stop me. I care nothing for anyone or anything else. Let the world burn. I want you, you alone, and I would defy the gods to have you."

If those lines in the script contradicted seasons' worth of character development, not to mention the books that had inspired the series, he wouldn't dwell on that. Not now.

For a moment, Carah softened against his touch. Leaned into his palm.

By this point in the long filming day, she stank. So did he. So did everyone else. So did the entire horseshit-strewn field. Mud had burrowed into places he didn't care to consider. Portraying misery and perseverance against all odds wasn't much of a stretch.

Dido shoved him away.

"You *are* a demigod," she reminded him with a sneer. "Married to another, and an adulterer besides. You lay with my sister, and she fell on her sword in disgrace at such a betrayal upon word of my return from Hades. I can only hope she too rises today and takes her own revenge."

Shame, so easy for him to muster, bowed his head. "I thought you lost forever. Lavinia may be my wife in name, but she has no hold on my heart. And Anna—" His brow furrowed, a plea for understanding despite his seeming betrayals. "She was a tarnished mirror of you. Nothing more."

The thought appeared unbidden. *Unapologetic Lavinia Stan is going to fucking* detonate *when she sees this scene.*

"You've betrayed mortals, and now you betray the gods as well. *Pius Aeneas* indeed." With a swift, crouching swipe, Dido reclaimed her sword. "I'll have my own revenge first. All others will have to settle for your torment in the afterlife."

Her grip was sure and steady on the weapon, and she brandished it easily. Despite a heavy bronze handle, the sword's blade was blunt, lightweight aluminum for the safety of everyone involved, exactly like his. Still, the impact of metal against metal rang out as they began the dance they'd been learning for weeks now.

His movements flowed without much thought, the product of endless planning and repetition. The fight coordinator and choreographer had carefully planned each motion to emphasize the one-sidedness of the battle: Dido was trying to hurt him, but he was attempting to disarm her and avoid wounding her in the process.

After driving him back with a sudden, violent surge, she rasped, "No man will defeat me!"

More horses galloping past. Partially obscured by the smoke, escapees from the underworld bit and kicked and swung and aimed discarded weapons at their mortal and immortal foes, who were attempting to drive them back to Tartarus. Groans and death and shouts surrounded his own fight.

Precise footwork, back toward Dido. Precise. Precise. Block her wild swing.

"That may be true." He offered a smile, sharp and predatory. "But as you just reminded us both: I'm more than a man."

A clumsy callback to the famous lines in both the second *Gods of the Gates* book and the second season of the series, when Dido had murmured in his arms that no man could seduce her. *I'm more than a man*, he'd returned, and then they'd paused filming to incorporate Carah's body double for the rest of the scene.

More swings of the sword. Some connecting, most not. And then the fatal moment came: He fended off her last, impassioned attack, inadvertently shoving her onto the green-tipped rubber sword of one of his own men.

The VFX department would fix the sword and blood later. The audience would see a fatal wound where only muddy silk existed now.

Tears. Final, whispered words.

As he knelt in the field, she died in his arms.

When she was gone, he took one last, wet-eyed look at the battle all around him. Saw that the forces of Tartarus were losing, and his men no longer had need of him. Then he gently laid her on the ground beside his own sword, a cherished gift from Dido from their time in Carthage, strode into the chaos, and allowed himself to be fatally stabbed by one of the dead.

"In the Elysian fields, I'll see you once more, my beloved," he murmured with his final breath.

For that extended stretch of time, Marcus was gone. Only Aeneas, disoriented and desolate and dying and hopeful, existed.

"Cut!" the director called, the order echoed by other crew members. "I think we got everything we needed this time. That's a wrap for this scene!"

As the director and production manager turned away to discuss something, Marcus surfaced, blinking back to himself. His head floated above his shoulders, buoyant and uncluttered, as it sometimes did after he'd truly slipped his own skin and lost himself in a character.

Bliss, in its own way. For so long, the sensation he'd lived and labored for day by day.

It wasn't enough. Not anymore.

Carah recovered more quickly than he did. Levering herself up out of the mud and to her feet, she heaved a heartfelt sigh.

"Thank fucking Christ." She held out her hand to him. "If I wanted mud in my ass crack, I'd pay for one of those full-body detox treatments, and that motherfucker would smell like tea tree or lavender, not horseshit."

He laughed and allowed her to steady him as he stood. His leather armor seemed to weigh as much as Rumpelstiltskin, the Friesian the horse master was now leading away. "If it's any consolation, you have a healthy, just-been-stabbed glow."

"A goddamn shame they did all the close-ups in earlier takes, then." After sniffing her armpit, she wrinkled her nose and gave a resigned shrug. "Shit, I need a shower *pronto*. At least we're done for the day."

Carah generally didn't require much response. He simply nodded.

"Just one more scene for me," she continued. "Back at the studio, later this week. My sword-training montage. How about you?"

He sounded out the words in his head, checking for falsity.

Somehow, they were true. "No. This is it. They filmed my immortality scene before the Battle for the Living."

This scene would be his own last memory of filming *Gods of the Gates*, but for the television audience, Aeneas's ascension to full-god status would be their final glimpse of the character. Ambrosia and nectar and a healthy swallow from the river Lethe, rather than blood and filth and despair.

After said swallow, Aeneas would forget Dido and Lavinia both. Poor Anna too.

And after the final season aired, fans were going to slaughter R.J. and Ron—the series's head writers, executive producers, and showrunners—online and at cons. For a multitude of reasons, since the abrupt reversal of Aeneas's character arc was only one of many storytelling failures in the last episodes. Marcus couldn't even estimate the number of pointed, aggrieved fix-it fics that would appear after the finale.

Hundreds, definitely. Maybe thousands.

He'd be writing at least one or two of them as Book! AeneasWouldNever, with Unapologetic Lavinia Stan's help.

Squinting through the residual smoke, he eyed the swords on the ground. Bits of torn costume. A plastic water bottle hopefully hidden from the camera's view, behind a dummy dressed as a dead member of Aeneas's fleet.

Should he take something from the set as a memento? Did he even want to? And what on this filthy field could both encompass more than seven years working on the show and smell acceptable enough for display in his home?

Nothing. Nothing.

So after a final, heartfelt hug for Carah, he headed empty-handed toward his trailer. Only to be stopped by a palm clapped on his shoulder before he'd gone a dozen steps.

"Hold on, Marcus," an all-too-familiar voice ordered.

When Marcus turned around, Ron beckoned several cameras closer—they were rolling again, somehow—and called back Carah and all the nearby crew.

Shit. In his exhaustion, Marcus had forgotten this little ceremony. In theory, a tribute to each main series actor at the end of their last day on set. In reality, a behind-the-scenes extra to tempt their audience to buy physical copies of the show or at least pay more to stream the special content.

Ron's hand was still on his shoulder. Marcus didn't shrug it off, but he tipped his face toward the ground for a moment. Gathered his thoughts and braced himself.

Before he could finally leave, he had yet another role to play. One he'd been perfecting for most of a decade, and one he'd wanted to leave behind with greater fervency as each of those years ticked past.

Marcus Caster-Rupp.

Friendly. Vain. Dim as that smoky battlefield surrounding them.

He was a well-groomed golden retriever, proud of the few tricks he'd miraculously learned.

"When we began looking for our Aeneas, we knew we had to find an athletic actor. Someone who could portray a leader of men and a lover of women. And above all else . . ." Ron lifted a hand and pinched Marcus's cheek, lingeringly enough that he might have felt the flush of sudden rage. "A pretty face. We couldn't have found prettier, not if we'd searched for another decade."

The crew laughed.

Marcus's stomach churned.

Another pinch, and he forced himself to grin smugly. To toss his hair and shed his armor so he could show the unseen audience the flex of his biceps, even as he moved out of Ron's reach. Then the showrunner and the crew were urging Marcus to say something, to make a speech in honor of all his years on the series.

Impromptu speaking. Would this fucking day never fucking *end*?

The role, though, surrounded him like an embrace. Familiar. Comforting, if increasingly claustrophobic. In its confines, he knew what to do. What to say. Who to be.

"Five years ago . . ." He turned to Ron. "Wait. How many years have we been filming now?"

Their boss chuckled indulgently. "Seven."

"Seven years ago, then." Marcus gave an unembarrassed shrug, beaming toward the camera. "Seven years ago, we started filming, and I had no idea what was in store for all of us. I'm very grateful for this role, and for our audience. Since you needed"—he made himself say it—"a pretty face, I'm glad mine was the prettiest you saw. Not surprised, but glad."

He arched an eyebrow, settling his fists on his hips in a heroic pose, and waited for more laughter. This time, directed and deliberately elicited by him.

That bit of control settled his stomach, if only a little.

"I'm also glad you found so many other pretty faces to act alongside." He winked at Carah. "Not as pretty as mine, of course, but pretty enough."

More smiles from the crew and an eye roll from Carah.

He could leave now. He knew it. This was all anyone outside his closest colleagues and crew members expected of him.

Still, he had to say one last thing, because this *was* his last day. This *was* the end of seven damn years of his life, years of endless hard work and challenges and accomplishments and the joy that came from doing that work, meeting those challenges, and finally, finally allowing himself to count those accomplishments as worthwhile and *his*.

He could now ride a horse like he'd been doing it his whole life.

The sword master said he was the best in the cast with a weapon in hand and had the fastest feet of any actor she'd ever met.

At long last, he'd learned to pronounce Latin with an ease his parents had both acknowledged and deemed a bitter irony.

Over his time on *Gods of the Gates*, he'd been nominated for five major acting awards. He'd never won, of course, but he had to believe—he *did* believe—that the nominations didn't simply reward a pretty face, but also acknowledged skill. Emotional depth. The public might believe him an acting savant, able to ape intelligence despite having none of his own, but he knew the work he'd put into his craft and his career.

None of that would have been possible without the crew.

He angled away from the cameras to look at some of those people, and to obscure the change in his expression. "Finally, I want to thank everyone behind the scenes of our show. There are nearly a thousand of you, and I—I can't—" The sincere words tangled his tongue, and he paused for a moment. "I can't imagine how any series could have found a more dedicated, knowledgeable group. So to all the producers, stunt performers, location managers, dialect coaches, production designers, costume designers, hair and makeup artists, VFX and SFX people, and so many others: Thank you. I, um, owe you more than I can express."

There. It was done. He'd managed to say it without stumbling too much.

Later, he'd grieve and consider his next steps. Now, he simply needed to wash and rest.

After a final round of embarrassing applause and a few claps on the back and hugs and handshakes, he made his escape. To his trailer for a quick wash at the sink, and then to his generic Spanish hotel room, where a very, very long and well-deserved shower awaited him.

At least he thought he'd made his escape, until Vika Andrich caught up with him just outside the hotel lobby entrance.

"Marcus! Do you have a minute?" Her voice somehow remained steady, even though she was jogging over from the parking lot in sensible heels. "I had a few questions about the big sequence you're filming now."

He wasn't entirely surprised to spot her. Once or twice a year, she'd show up wherever they were shooting and get whatever on-site impressions and interviews she could, and those articles were always especially popular on her blog. Of course she'd want to cover the end of the series's filming in person.

Unlike some other reporters, she'd respect his privacy if he asked for space. He even liked her. That wasn't the problem.

The other qualities that made her his favorite entertainment-blogger-slash-paparazzo also made her his least favorite: She was friendly. Funny. Easy to relax around. Too easy.

She was also smart. Smart enough to have spied something . . . off . . . about him.

Offering her a wide smile, he stopped inches short of freedom. "Vika, you know I can't tell you anything about what's happening this season. But if you think your readers want to see me covered in mud"—he winked—"and we both know they do, then feel free to take a picture or two."

He posed, presenting her with what he'd been told was his best side, and she got a couple of shots.

"I know you can't tell me anything specific," she said, checking the images, "but maybe you could describe the sixth season in three words?"

Tapping his chin, he furrowed his brow. Playacted deep thought for long moments.

"I know!" He brightened and turned a pleased grin on her. "Last. One. Ever. I hope that helps."

Her eyes narrowed, and she studied him for a beat too long.

Then, confronted with the blinding gleam of her own innocent smile, he had to blink.

"I guess . . ." She trailed off, still smiling. "I guess I need to find one of the other actors to ask about how the show's ending deviates from both E. Wade's books and, of course, Homer's *Aeneid*. Aeneas ended up married to Dido in both those stories, but the show might have taken a different approach."

Homer? What the fuck?

And Dido was long, looooong dead by the end of the *Aeneid*. By the final page of the third *Gods of the Gates* book, she was alive but decidedly no longer interested in Aeneas, although he supposed that could change if Wade ever released the last two books in the series.

Somewhere, Virgil was probably uttering Latin curses as he shifted in his grave, and by all rights, E. Wade should be side-eyeing Vika from her lavish compound in Hawaii.

He pinched his forehead with a thumb and forefinger, absently noting the dirt beneath his nails. Dammit, *someone* needed to correct such grievous misapprehensions.

"The *Aeneid* wasn't—" Vika's brows rose with his first words, and her phone was recording, and he saw the trick. Oh, yes, he saw it. "The *Aeneid* isn't something I've read, sadly. I'm sure Homer is very talented, but I'm not much of a reader in general."

The last bit, at least, had once been true. Before he'd discovered fanfic and audiobooks, he hadn't read much besides his scripts, and he'd labored over those only until he'd learned them well enough to record them, loop the recording, and play the words back to himself over and over.

She tapped her screen, and her own recording ended. "Thank you, Marcus. It was kind of you to talk to me."

"My pleasure, Vika. Good luck with your other interviews." With a final flash of a vapid smile, he was finally inside the hotel and trudging toward the elevator.

After pressing the button for his floor, he leaned heavily against the wall and closed his eyes.

Soon, he was going to have to grapple with his persona. Where it chafed, how it had served him in the past, and how it served him still. Whether shedding it would be worth the consequences to his personal life and career.

But not today. Fuck, he was tired.

Back in his hotel room, the shower felt just as good as he'd hoped. Better.

Afterward, he powered on his laptop and ignored the scripts sent by his agent. Choosing his next project—one that would hopefully take his career in a new direction—could wait too, as could checking his Twitter and Instagram accounts.

The only thing that definitely needed to happen before he slept for a million years: sending a direct message to Unapologetic Lavinia Stan. Or Ulsie, as he'd begun calling her, to her complete disgust. *Ulsie is a good name for a cow, and* only *for a cow*, she'd written. But she hadn't told him to stop, and he hadn't. The nickname, one he alone used, pleased him more than it should.

He logged on to the Lavineas server he'd helped create several years ago for the use of the lively, talented, ever-supportive

Aeneas/Lavinia fanfic community. On AO3, he still occasionally dabbled in Aeneas/Dido fanfic, but less and less often these days. Especially once Ulsie had become the primary beta and proof-reader for all Book!AeneasWouldNever's stories.

She lived in California, and she'd still be at work. She wouldn't be able to respond immediately to his messages. If he didn't DM her tonight, though, he wouldn't have her response first thing in the morning, and he needed that. More and more as each week passed.

Soon, so very soon, he and Ulsie would be back in the same time zone. The same state.

Not that proximity mattered, since they'd never meet in person. Only it did matter. Somehow, it did.

Gods of the Gates (Book 1)
E. Wade

The Literary Tour de Force That Inspired a World-Famous TV Series

E-book: $8.99
Paperback: $10.99
Hardcover: $19.99
Audiobook: $25.99

When gods play at war, humanity loses.

Juno has watched Jupiter dally with mortal women too many times through the centuries—and when she leaves him in a righteous fury, his own godly temper takes hold. Heedless of the consequences, he heaves thunderbolts so mighty that the underworld itself cracks open in fissures reaching all the way down to Tartarus, home of the wicked dead. Freed from eternal punishment, they would return to Earth, challenge Jupiter for power—and doom humanity.

To preserve his cruel rule, to save the mortals he beds but does not respect, Jupiter tasks his fellow gods with guarding the new gates to the underworld he's created in his reckless rage. But the immortals, as always, care more for their eternal feuds than duty. If humanity is to be saved, demigods and mortals will have to guard the gates too.

Unfortunate, then, that Juno has her own reasons for wanting Tartarus unguarded. Humanity be damned.

2

DIRT. MORE DIRT.

This particular dirt would tell a story, though, if April listened hard enough.

She squinted at the site's final soil core through her prescription safety glasses, comparing the different shades of brown to her color chart, then noted the sample's water content, soil plasticity and consistency, grain size and shape, and all the other relevant data on her field form.

No discoloration. No particular odor either, which didn't surprise her. Solvents would emit a sweet smell, and fuels would smell like—well, fuel. Hydrocarbons. But lead would simply smell like dirt. So would arsenic.

After wiping her gloved hand on the thigh of her jeans, she jotted down her findings.

Normally, she'd be talking to her assistant sampler, Bashir, about their most egregious coworkers or maybe their most recent reality show binge-watches. But by this point in the afternoon, they were both too tired to make idle conversation, so she finished logging the sample silently while he filled out the label for the glass sample jar and completed the chain-of-custody form.

After she filled the jar with soil and wiped her hand on her jeans again, she labeled the container, slipped it into a zip-top bag, and placed it in the ice-filled cooler. One last signature to confirm she was handing off the sample to the waiting lab courier, and they were done for the day. Thank God.

"That's it?" Bashir asked.

"That's it." As they watched the courier leave with the cooler, she blew out a breath. "I can take care of cleanup, if you want to relax for a few minutes."

He shook his head. "I'll help."

Other than their thirty-minute lunch break, they'd been on task and focused since seven that morning, almost nine hours ago. Her feet hurt in her dusty safety boots, her exposed skin stung from too much sun exposure, dehydration had her head throbbing inside her hard hat, and she was ready for a good, long shower back at the hotel.

Her cheek also itched, probably from a stray smear of dirt. Which was unfortunate, because soil-to-skin contact was, in technical terminology, an exposure pathway. Or, as April would put it, a fucking bad idea.

Uncapping her water bottle, she wet a paper towel and swiped until her cheek felt clean again.

"You still have some . . ." Bashir's finger scratched at a spot near his temple. "There."

"Thanks." Despite her headache, her smile at him was sincere. She could count the number of genuine friends she had at her current firm on one hand, but Bashir was among them. "Good work today."

After one last swipe and Bashir's affirmative nod—she'd gotten rid of all the mud this time, apparently—the paper towel ended up in the same garbage bag as her used gloves, and good riddance.

The soil was dirty in more ways than one. Until midcentury, a pesticide factory had operated on the site, polluting the facility's surroundings with lead and arsenic. Because of that history, April had spent the last several weeks gathering samples of the soil to analyze for both chemicals. She wanted neither directly on her skin. Or on her jeans, for that matter, but paper towels were just a pain in the ass at the end of the day.

"Did I tell you?" As she gathered their paperwork, he slid her a sly grin. "Last week, Chuck told that new kid never to drink water in the exclusion zone. Because it's bad practice, and goes against health and safety guidelines."

Together, they turned to stare at their red cooler filled with water bottles, which she'd placed on the tailgate of their field truck that morning.

"Chuck's a self-congratulatory twenty-two-year-old prick who's spent almost no time on actual job sites." At her flat statement, Bashir's eyes widened. "He doesn't know what the fuck he's talking about, but is happy to tell everyone how to do their jobs anyway."

At that, Bashir snorted. "Not just our jobs."

"Oh, Jesus." April rolled her eyes skyward. "Did he lecture you about hummus *again*?"

"Yes. Even though I don't eat much hummus, or give half a shit about chickpeas. I guess he just assumes I do, because . . ." Bashir waved a hand at himself. "You know."

Together, they began carrying the paperwork to the company truck.

"I know." She sighed. "Please tell me he wasn't telling you to try—"

"The chocolate hummus," Bashir confirmed. "Again. If you'd like to hear about its fiber and protein content, or perhaps how it's a vast improvement over more traditional versions of hummus—*the hummus of your people*, as he put it—I've been well informed and would be delighted to share my newfound knowledge with you."

He opened the passenger door for her, and she tucked the paperwork inside the latching case of her clipboard.

"Ugh. I'm so sorry." She grimaced. "If it's any consolation, he also has very definite opinions about how his few female colleagues should dress to score more jobs."

In a small private firm, consultants like her had to hustle for clients, woo them over lunches and at professional meetings, draw them aside at conventions and conferences about remedial technologies. Convince them she should be taken seriously and they wanted to pay her company for her geological expertise.

To remain optimally billable, she had to look a certain way. Sound a certain way. Present herself in the most professional light possible at all times.

Billable had become an epithet to her in recent years.

Reputation in her industry could be a fragile thing. Could be damaged. By, say, the revelation that a seemingly serious and practical colleague liked to play dress-up as her favorite pretend TV character and spent most of her free time discussing fictional half gods.

Bashir rolled his eyes. "Of course he has opinions about women's clothing. You told management, right?"

"Literally five minutes later."

"Good." Bashir walked by her side back toward the sampling table. "Hopefully they'll fire his ass before much longer."

"He knows nothing. Less than nothing, if that's possible." A pluck of her fingers at her shirt demonstrated how it clung damply to her. "I mean, look at how much we sweated today."

"Copiously." He glanced down at his own sweat-soaked orange shirt. "Disgustingly."

Stopping by the table, she shook her head. "Exactly. Someone needs to set that new kid straight. Unless she wants to end up in the hospital for dehydration, she needs to bring water."

Bashir inclined his head. "You would know."

"I would know."

And she did. Up until now, almost a third of her work hours as a geologist had been spent staying upwind of drill rigs like the one on this site, poring over soil samples to be logged and shoved into jars and sent off for lab testing. For a long time, she'd loved the processes and the challenges and even the physicality of doing fieldwork. Some part of her still did love it.

Not all of her, though. Not enough of her.

As they flipped the table on its side and folded its legs, Bashir paused. "You're really leaving, huh?"

"Yup." This was her last day visiting a contaminated site in her current role, her last week as a consultant at a private firm, and her last time washing dirt from her jeans. "I'll miss you, but it's time. Past time."

In less than a week, she was moving from Sacramento to Berkeley. And in less than two weeks, Future April would begin her new job at a state regulatory agency in Oakland, overseeing the work of consultants like Current April, which would mean more meetings and document analysis, and less time in the field.

She was ready. For so many reasons, personal and professional both.

Once she and Bashir had all their supplies back in the truck, she changed into her regular glasses and removed her other personal protective equipment. With a sigh of relief, she untied her dusty boots and deposited them in a plastic bag, then put on her battered but clean sneakers. Beside her, he did the same.

Then she was done. Finally, blessedly done, and desperate for a shower, a cheeseburger, and approximately a gallon of ice water. Not to mention some more Lavineas fanfiction, group chats on the server, and DMs with Book!AeneasWouldNever. Hopefully BAWN had written while she was working.

First, though, she and Bashir needed to say their goodbyes.

"I don't know if you already have plans for the weekend, but Mimi and I would love to treat you to dinner. To celebrate your new job and say farewell." Even after several years of working together, he was still shy enough to fidget while issuing the invitation. "She knows you're my favorite colleague."

As he was one of hers, and she considered his wife Mimi a genuine friend too.

But even they didn't know everything about her. Specifically, that she spent most evenings and weekends immersed in the *Gods of the Gates* fandom: tweeting about her OTP, writing and betaing and reading fanfic, chatting on the Lavineas server, and employing her vast enthusiasm and infinitesimal costume-construction skill to cosplay Lavinia.

One stray pic at a con, one slip of the tongue, and her reputation might suffer. She could devolve from an experienced professional into a silly fangirl in less time than it took for her to log a soil sample.

So she hadn't attended *Gods of the Gates* cons. She hadn't told work friends about her fandom. Not even friends she liked as much as Bashir.

The state regulators at her new job, though . . .

Well, the difference in culture couldn't have been clearer. The personal and the professional were inextricable there. Intertwined in the most joyful and hilarious ways.

When she arrived in less than two weeks, she'd become the fifth person on their team of geologists. The third woman. When she'd gone in to complete her I-9 last week, the other women, Heidi and Mel, had offered April a slice of the cake the team had brought to work in celebration of the women's tenth anniversary as a couple.

Mel and the two guys on the team—Pablo and Kei—were in a freakin' band together. *A band*. One that evidently performed for retirement parties and other gatherings in which their unique folk music talents couldn't successfully be avoided.

They're terrible, Heidi had whispered, her mouth half-hidden behind her water bottle, *but they all enjoy it so much, we can't say anything*.

At that moment, in that dreary state-government-bureaucrat's office suite, something taut to the point of snapping inside April had eased. Any remaining doubts had disappeared.

She'd made the right decision to change jobs, even with the pay cut. Even with the price of housing in the Bay Area. Even with the hassle of moving.

At her new workplace, she wouldn't need to shield different parts of herself for fear of others' disapproval. As of next week, billability no longer concerned her.

In fact . . .

It didn't concern her now, either. Not anymore.

"Thank you so much for the invitation, Bashir." When she hugged him, he patted her back tentatively. "I'm busy this weekend, unfortunately. I have to be at my new apartment, getting it ready for the move. But I'll be back in town late next week. Can we do dinner then instead?"

When she pulled away, he smiled down at her, looking pleased. "Of course. I'll check Mimi's schedule and text you later tonight, after we get back from dinner at her family's house. They live nearby, so I'm heading there now."

Fuck billability, she thought.

"I plan to spend the evening eating a room service burger and writing *Gods of the Gates* fanfiction," she told him. "Your night sounds much more exciting."

He blinked at her for a few seconds before flashing an impish grin. "You only say that because you haven't met my in-laws."

She laughed. "Fair enough."

"When we have dinner, I want to hear more about your writing." His head tilted; he was studying her curiously. "Mimi loves that show. Especially the pretty dude."

"Marcus Caster-Rupp?" Honestly, it could be any one of a handful of actors, but Caster-Rupp was undeniably the prettiest dude of all. Also the most boring. So boring, she sometimes wondered how one man could be so shiny, yet so incredibly *dull*.

"That's the one." He directed a pained grimace at the heavens. "He's on her freebie list. Every time we stream an episode, she's always very insistent about that."

April patted his arm. "Think about it this way: She won't ever actually meet him. None of us will, unless we move to LA and start selling vital organs to pay for our haircuts."

"Huh." His expression brightened. "That's true."

Before leaving the site, they thanked the drill crew. Then, after she exchanged one last round of goodbyes with Bashir, he climbed into his car while she boosted herself into the driver's seat of the truck. With a farewell beep, she headed toward her hotel, while he drove to his in-laws' home.

With each mile she traveled, invisible tethers surrounding her seemed to snap free, leaving her oddly, giddily buoyant. Yeah, she still had a personal drilling rig operating in her skull, but a few glasses of water would take care of the headache, no problem.

And so what if she had dirt all over her jeans? Even contaminated soil couldn't sully the essential, joyful truth.

She caught a glimpse of herself in the rearview mirror. Her smile was so wide, she might as well have been starring in a toothpaste commercial.

And no wonder. No wonder.

This was her last day in the dirt.

She was starting now.

WHEN SHE GOT back to the hotel, she dumped her jeans into a waiting plastic bag and got naked. In the shower, she scrubbed her body pink under the hot spray.

Her clean flannel pajamas felt like a cloud against her skin as she drained a glass of water and read over BAWN's latest messages. At long last, he'd decided what to write for his next fic. Monday's prompt for their upcoming Aeneas and Lavinia Week requested *a showdown between Aeneas's two lady loves*, and BAWN had been contemplating the best way to handle it for days.

Since the two women haven't met in the books or on the show, you could always come up with a fluffy alternate-universe story, which is what I'm doing, she'd written before work that morning, already knowing how he'd respond to *that* suggestion. Or—and I really think this idea might work for you—maybe Aeneas could dream about the showdown, so you can keep things canon-compliant and in his POV? What do you think?

The latter option offered plenty of opportunity for angst, so of course he'd chosen that one. BAWN was such an insightful writer, but April had to admit it: some of his fics were depressing as hell.

Less so now than when he'd started, though. Back then, even

his Aeneas/Lavinia stories had been bursting with their hero's guilt and shame when it came to Dido, all dirges and funeral pyres and lamentations. April's first real conversation with BAWN on the Lavineas server, in fact, had involved her half-joking suggestion that he use the tag *misery ahoy!* on some of his fics.

For his mental health alone, it was better for him to focus on the Lavinia-Aeneas OTP. Clearly. Writing occasional fluffy fics wouldn't do him any harm, either.

Tonight, though, she didn't have time for the Good Gospel of Fluff. By the time she finished describing her own fluffy AU fic idea—Lavinia and Dido would meet as teenage combatants in a trivia contest, their feelings for Aeneas making each round of questions and answers increasingly fraught and hilarious—she was on the verge of losing her courage. Again.

Months ago, when she'd applied for her new job, she'd decided she was done shielding different parts of herself for fear of others' disapproval. That applied to her fandom too.

On Twitter, to dodge possible professional disaster, she'd always cropped her cosplay pictures to exclude her face. But she'd failed to share her Twitter handle with fellow Lavineas stans for an entirely different reason.

Her body.

She hadn't wanted her friends on the server to see her body in those Lavinia costumes. Particularly one of those friends, whose opinion mattered more than it should.

For a ship whose essential heartbeat was all about love for goodness, sterling character, and intelligence over appearance, Lavineas fics included a surprising, disappointing amount of fat-shaming. Not BAWN's, to his credit. But some of his favorite fics, the ones he'd bookmarked and recommended to her, did.

After a lifetime of struggle, April now loved her body. All of it. Red hair to freckled, chubby toes.

She hadn't expected the same from others. Still didn't. But she was tired of fucking hiding, and she was done with more than just contaminated mud on her jeans and colleagues she only allowed so close.

This year, she was attending her fandom's biggest convention, Con of the Gates, which always took place—appropriately enough—within a sunny day's view of the Golden Gate Bridge. Countless bloggers and reporters showed up to that con, and they took pictures, some of which always ended up going viral or printed in newspaper articles or splashed across the television screen.

She wouldn't care. Not anymore. If her colleagues could openly discuss their terrible folk-music trio, she could certainly discuss her love for the most popular show on television.

And when she went to the con, she was finally going to meet her fandom friends there in person. She might even meet BAWN in person, despite his shyness. She would give all of them an opportunity to prove they'd truly understood the message of their OTP.

If they didn't, it would hurt. She couldn't lie to herself about that.

Especially if BAWN took one look at her and—

Well, no point in imagining rejection that didn't yet exist.

Worst-case scenario, though, she'd find other friends. Other fandoms more accepting of who and what she was. Another beta reader for her fics whose DMs were beams of sunshine to start her morning and the warmth of a down comforter at night.

Another man she wanted in her face-to-face life and maybe even her bed.

So she had to do this tonight, before she lost her nerve. It wasn't the final step, or even the hardest. But it was the first.

Without letting herself think too hard about it, she checked a thread on Twitter from that morning, still going strong. The *Gods of the Gates* official account had asked fans to post their best cosplay photos, and the responses now numbered in the hundreds. A few dozen featured people her size, and she very carefully didn't read replies to those tweets.

On her phone, she had a selfie from her most recent Lavinia costume. The image was uncropped, her face and body both clearly visible. Her colleagues, present and future, would recognize her. Her friends and family too. Most nerve-racking of all: if she told him her Twitter handle, Book!AeneasWouldNever would finally see her for the first time.

Deep breath.

She tweeted it. Then immediately put down her phone, shut her laptop, and ordered some damn room service, because she deserved it. After dinner, she began her one-shot fluffy, modern AU fic so BAWN could give her some feedback over the weekend.

Right before bedtime, she couldn't stand it anymore.

Block finger ready, she checked her Twitter notifications.

Holy fuck. Holy *fuck*.

She'd gone viral. At least by her modest standards. Hundreds of people had commented on her photo, with more chiming in by the second. She couldn't read her notifications fast enough, and some of them she didn't want to read at all.

She'd known how certain swaths of the *Gods of the Gates* fandom acted. She wasn't surprised to find, scattered among admiring and supportive responses, a few ugly threads.

Looks like she ate Lavinia seemed to be the most popular among those tweets.

It stung, of course. But no stranger on the internet could truly hurt her. Not the same way family and friends and coworkers could.

Still, she didn't intend to inflict that sort of harm on herself longer than necessary. It might take time, but she needed to wrestle her mentions into submission.

But . . . Jesus. Where had all these people *come* from?

Blocking all the haters in one particular thread took a while, as did muting—at least for the moment—certain key livestock- and zoo animal–related words.

By the time she finished, she had dozens more notifications. These seemed friendlier, for the most part, but she didn't plan to tackle them until the morning.

Until she noticed one at the very top, received seconds before.

The account boasted a bright blue bubble with a check inside. An official, verified account, then.

Marcus Caster-Rupp's account.

The guy playing Aeneas—fucking *Aeneas*—had tweeted to her. Followed her.

And . . . he appeared to have—

No, that couldn't be right. She was hallucinating.

She squinted. Blinked. Read it again. A third time.

For reasons yet unknown, he appeared to have—

Well, he appeared to have asked her out. On a date.

"I read a fic like this once," she whispered.

Then she clicked on the thread to find out what the fuck had just happened.

Lavineas Server DMs, Two Years Ago

Unapologetic Lavinia Stan: I saw that you wanted a beta reader for your fics? I know we don't write the same types of stories, but if you're willing to beta my fics too, I'd be interested.

Book!AeneasWouldNever: Hi, ULS. Thanks for writing.

Book!AeneasWouldNever: I figure it might be good to get a different perspective on my work, so—to me, anyway—our different styles are a bonus, not a drawback. I'd love your help with my fics, and I'm more than willing to beta your stories too.

Unapologetic Lavinia Stan: Oh, yay!

Unapologetic Lavinia Stan: My first suggestion: using the tag "misery ahoy!" so your hapless readers don't inadvertently end up running through a year's supply of tissues in one story. [clears throat] [blows nose] [stares meaningfully at you]

Book!AeneasWouldNever: Sorry about that?

Unapologetic Lavinia Stan: The good news: the tissue industry is saved!

Unapologetic Lavinia Stan: The other good news: your writing had such an emotional punch, I managed to refill several dwindling saltwater reservoirs.

Book!AeneasWouldNever: That's good?

Unapologetic Lavinia Stan: That's good.

3

Of course you chose the option that's both canon-compliant and rife with possibilities for Man Pain. Of course.

MARCUS SNORTED, THEN SAT UP IN BED.

As soon as he'd blinked awake in the early-morning dimness of a curtained hotel room, he'd reached for his phone. Before his eyes could fully focus, he'd already checked his messages from Ulsie on the Lavineas server.

Although, to be fair, that blurriness could just be a sign of advanced age. He was turning forty in a few months, and maybe he needed bifocals now. Even the special font and extra spacing didn't always help him read his screen comfortably these days.

Late last year, he'd finally asked Ulsie how old she was.

Thirty-six, she'd promptly replied.

At that bit of information, he'd heaved an embarrassingly enormous sigh of relief and hoped like hell she wasn't lying. Some of the people in their group were barely out of high school, and although he'd figured he and Ulsie were about the same age—one day, they'd discussed how they might turn to the *X-Files* fandom at some point, due to their adolescent crushes on Scully and

Mulder, respectively—the explicit confirmation that he wasn't DMing a near-teenager was . . . good.

Not that anything suggestive had ever passed between them, either in public or in private.

But still.

Ulsie's most recent message had arrived only minutes ago. He was surprised she was still awake. Glad, though. Very glad.

Shoving a pillow behind his back, he sat up against the leather headboard. Took a sip from his bedside water glass, still smiling at her snark.

Using the voice-to-text feature on his phone, he sent her a response. At least I mostly write happy endings now. Cut me some slack. We can't all be masters of fluff. After a moment, he added, Are you about to sleep? Or do you want to talk about your fic and brainstorm a bit? If you have anything written already, I'm happy to look it over.

Or, more accurately, have his computer read it aloud to him. Short messages he could handle without extra technical support, but deciphering lengthier blocks of text simply took too much time, given his recent shooting schedule.

Of course, he had plenty of time right now. Until his flight back to LA that afternoon, he planned to do nothing more strenuous than hit the hotel's breakfast buffet and visit the gym. If he wanted to, he could read her fic with his eyes. But as he'd discovered over the years, there was no need to struggle unnecessarily and no reason for frustration and shame. Not when his relatively common problem had relatively easy workarounds.

While he waited for her response, he checked his email. Overnight, he'd apparently received a confidential message in his inbox from R.J. and Ron, one addressed to all cast and crew.

In the past several days, multiple blogs and media outlets have reported rumors of cast discontent over the direction of our final season. If anyone reading this message is the source of such rumors, let us be clear: this is an unacceptable breach of both our trust and the contract all of you signed upon being hired by our show.

Your job, as always, involves discretion. If you cannot maintain that necessary discretion, there will be consequences, as per your contracts.

Well, that seemed clear enough. Talk out of turn about the show and prepare for unemployment, a lawsuit, or both. They'd received at least one similar email each and every season, all phrased almost exactly the same way.

The only difference: In recent seasons, the messages had started to make him sweat. For the sake of his coworkers. For his own sake too.

Would Carah share her deeply felt and profanity-laden hatred of Dido's final-season story arc to someone outside the cast? Had Summer confessed her disappointment about how Lavinia's romantic story line with Aeneas had ended so abruptly, in a way so inconsistent with their characters? Or maybe Alex—

Shit, Alex. He could be so reckless sometimes. So impulsive.

Had he bitched to anyone but Marcus about how the finale fucked up seasons' worth of character development for Cupid?

Despite his own discontent, Marcus hadn't said a word to anyone other than Alex, although . . .

Well, some might argue his fanfiction on AO3 and messages on the Lavineas server did plenty of talking for him.

By *some*, he meant Ron and R.J.

And if they ever found out about Book!AeneasWouldNever, there was no *might* about it. They would definitely accuse him of violating his contract terms, and he'd lose—

Shit, he'd lose everything he'd worked for more than two decades to achieve. The potential lawsuit was the least of it, really. His reputation in the industry would be destroyed in an instant. No director wanted to hire an actor who might badmouth a production behind the scenes.

His fellow cast members would likely feel betrayed too. Same with the crew.

He should give up his fanfic alter ego. He knew it. And he would, he *would*, if only the writing didn't mean so much to him, if only the Lavineas server group didn't mean so much to him, if only Ulsie—

Ulsie. God, Ulsie.

He wanted to meet her in person almost as much as he wanted a clear path forward in his career, in his public life. Under the circumstances, though, that was never, ever going to happen. So he would appreciate what they could have. What they did have.

And what they could have, what they did have, he wasn't giving up. Contract violation be damned.

After deleting R.J. and Ron's email, he ignored the rest of his inbox and checked Twitter instead.

His notifications were bristling with commentary on the photos Vika had posted of him overnight, complete with multiple references to him as a *dirty boy*. There were a few pleas for retweets and birthday wishes, as well as some impressive examples of fan art.

Nothing he either needed or intended to answer. For the most part, he used this account entirely for the sake of publicity, retweeting especially flattering pics and alerts for con appearances and upcoming episodes. Occasionally he responded to one of his *Gods of the Gates* costars' tweets, but that was about it. Keeping up the Well-Groomed Golden Retriever act was tiring enough in person; he had no intention of continuing the performance on the internet unless absolutely necessary.

His real online life happened on one site. Okay, two sites: the Lavineas server and AO3.

Ulsie hadn't responded to his DMs yet. Dammit.

He could wait a few more minutes before giving up and getting breakfast, though. With a sigh, he scrolled back further through his Twitter notifications, until he reached ones from an hour or so ago. Then he hesitated when an odd word caught his eye.

Hoifer. No, *heifer.*

Heifer?

Frowning, he paused. Read the actual tweet.

It was connected to a photo of a curvy, pretty redhead cosplaying Lavinia. She'd apparently posted the pic in response to the official *Gods of the Gates* Twitter account's request for images of fan costumes. Then some prick had attached his own commentary to the redhead's tweet, comparing her to a farm animal.

He'd tagged Marcus too, inviting his favorite actor to join in the hilarity at the very idea that a woman like—Marcus checked her Twitter handle—@Lavineas5Ever could ever imagine herself capable of portraying Aeneas's on-screen love interest.

She hadn't responded, but other fanboys had piled on afterward, and shit.

Shit, shit, shit.

He couldn't just ignore this.

He wanted to respond: *She's lovely, and I don't want to be an asshole's favorite actor. Stop watching* Gods of the Gates *and go fuck yourself.*

His agent would keel over dead. The showrunners would explode. His carefully crafted persona would fracture, maybe irreparably, in a completely uncontrolled way.

He scrubbed a hand over his face, then pinched his forehead between thumb and forefinger as he thought hard.

Minutes later, he dictated his actual response. I know beauty when I see it, probably because I see it in the mirror every day. 😏 @Lavineas5Ever is gorgeous, and Lavinia couldn't ask for a better tribute.

He tried to leave it there. He really did.

But Jesus Christ, this guy was a total dick.

Come on dude, @GodsOfMyTaints tweeted moments later. Stop the hippocritical white knight shit, like u would ever let yourself get within 15 feet of that cow.

The shitstain had left poor @Lavineas5Ever tagged in his tweet, and Marcus hoped to fuck she'd muted this particular conversation long ago. But in case she hadn't, he couldn't leave it there. He just . . . couldn't.

With a click of his mouse, he followed @Lavineas5Ever. Which made her one of only 286 people he followed, all the rest of whom were connected to the movie and television industry in one way or another. A quick glance at her profile revealed she lived in California. Convenient, that.

He couldn't DM her first, since she didn't follow him. Which was fair, since he wouldn't follow an account as uninteresting and useless as his, either.

Over two million people did follow him, however. He sincerely hoped any other assholes among those followers saw his next tweet.

I'm no white knight, just a man who likes a beautiful woman on his arm. When I get back to California from filming, @Lavineas5Ever, will you please have dinner with me?

Then he sat back against his headboard, arms folded across his chest, and waited for her response.

* * *

April blinked at her laptop screen.

Yup.

Marcus Caster-Rupp had definitely asked her to dinner.

Marcus. Caster. Hyphen. Rupp.

Not to repeat herself, but: *Holy fuuuuuuuck.*

The dude had graced countless magazine covers, biceps flexing. She saw him on her television screen every week, and had saved more than a few photos of him to her hard drive.

And he'd just . . . asked her out?

Wow. *Wow.*

If she were being picky about which of the *Gods of the Gates* actors she'd want to date, if only for a single evening, she'd definitely have chosen the guy who played Cupid, Alexander Woodroe, instead.

But Caster-Rupp was hot. No doubt about that. Not ridiculously muscular, but tall and lean and undeniably strong and fit. She'd been known to sigh over close-ups of his thick, veined forearms before, not to mention gifs of his first love scene with Dido, because *damn.* That *ass.* Round and working and . . . delicious.

He was also undeniably beautiful. That knife-edged jawline could slice heirloom tomatoes. His cheekbones were pristine, his nose just battered and forceful enough to add character to his face. All lengths of stubble suited his handsome features and emphasized his perfect lips. As did a beard. As did a clean shave. It was ludicrous and unfair, honestly.

His lush, sandy-blond hair, just starting to silver at the temples, set off his cloudy blue eyes like—

Well, like a television star's hair should set off his eyes.

He was a damn good actor too. A couple of seasons ago, his character had followed Jupiter's stern order to secretly gather his fleet and leave Dido—the woman he'd loved and lived with for a year—in the middle of the night, with no warning or even a final word. Caster-Rupp had conveyed Aeneas's naked grief and shame and reluctance with such skill, April had cried.

Then Aeneas had spotted the glow of Dido's funeral pyre in the distance, across the choppy water, and understood the implications. Because of what he'd done, she was either dying or dead, and he couldn't do anything to stop her or help. Dropping to his knees on his ship's deck, his face crumpled in agony, he'd clutched his hair and bowed his head, his breath rough pants as he grappled with horror and self-loathing at his beloved's fate.

At that, April hadn't merely cried anymore. Sobbed, more like it.

She still thought he should have won a little gold statue for that episode.

In the actor's capable hands, no one could deny Aeneas's intelligence, his huge, lonely, scarred heart—or his reluctant, growing respect for and attraction to Lavinia in the last three seasons of the show.

But there was a reason April didn't follow the dude on Twitter.

She didn't think he'd ever said an interesting word in any interview she'd seen with him. And she'd seen plenty, because the Lavineas shippers hungrily pounced on any media coverage that might discuss their favorite pairing. Unlike Summer Diaz, the woman who so ably portrayed Lavinia, though, Caster-Rupp never fed the fandom with insight or analysis or even a bare mention of the Aeneas-Lavinia relationship. Not that he mentioned the Aeneas-Dido relationship, either.

He kept things vague. Enthusiastic and one hundred percent generic.

After the first season of the show aired, most reporters simply gave up on interviews with him and just flashed a few of his biceps-flexing pics on-screen whenever they mentioned his character.

His ability to portray such intelligence on camera, such emotional depth, was a wonder. In real life, the man was all hair-flipping, cheerful vapidity, a walking, talking, gleaming, preening, Hollywood-pretty-face stereotype.

Not her kind of date, in short.

But spurning him, rejecting his kind gesture, in public would be churlish. And how could she call herself a Lavineas fan if she turned down the chance to talk with him?

Then again, maybe he was looking for a way out.

They needed to talk. Not in front of his two million followers, either.

She followed his account. Then she slid into his DMs, half expecting to find out she *had* been hallucinating, or Twitter's notifications had gone bonkers somehow and told her he'd followed her account and asked her out when he definitely hadn't.

But up the DM screen popped.

She had permission to send direct messages to Marcus Caster-Rupp. Because he'd followed her. In reality.

Weeeeeird. Exciting, but weird. Not to mention awkward. So much so that composing her initial message took several minutes.

Uh . . . hi, she eventually wrote. Nice to meet you, Mr. Caster-Rupp. First of all, and most importantly, thank you for being so kind just now. It was very sweet of you to defend me like that. That said, I want you to know: you don't have to go through with the dinner. I mean, I'm probably willing if you are, but I don't want you to feel obligated.

While she waited for a response, she quickly checked the Lavineas server.

With a groan, she flopped back against her headboard. Dammit, BAWN had responded to her earlier messages, and she didn't have time to answer him right now.

But she had a responsibility to the fandom. If he knew the situation, BAWN would understand.

Still, she wrote him a quick message. Taking care of a few last-minute tasks. Then I'll be back to chat. Sorry!

By the time she maximized her Twitter window again, Caster-Rupp had written her back.

I don't feel obligated. You're obviously very talented at making costumes, and as I said, you're also quite lovely. I would be proud to take you to dinner. P.S. Please call me Marcus.

Despite her better judgment, she beamed a little at the compliments.

Still, she called bullshit on at least one part of his message.

So this has nothing to do with wanting to spite those dicks in our mentions, Marcus? P.S. I'm April.

His response came almost immediately. I have to admit, I would also be happy to disoblige some of my more obnoxious fanboys.

She frowned.

Disoblige? What kind of vapid, pretty-boy actor used a word like *disoblige*?

Three blinking dots appeared on the DM screen. He was writing more.

> That came out wrong. Sorry. I meant to say, I think this would be good PR for me too. You know, socializing with the fans.

That was more what she'd expected of a man like him. A well-intentioned, good-natured, but ultimately surface-oriented publicity stunt.

That makes sense, she wrote.

More dots, this time blinking for several minutes.

> Fair warning, April. If we do go out, it'll probably end up in the tabloids, or at least a few online blogs. So if you're protective of your privacy, you might want to turn me down. If so, my feelings won't be hurt.

She bit her lip. I'll need a few minutes to decide. Is that okay?

Of course, he answered. Take all the time you need. It's still morning in Spain, and I'm not flying out until late this afternoon. I'll be around for a while yet.

Okay, now she was dying to ask him questions about the sixth season and the show's finale. Obviously he'd been sworn to secrecy, but surely a man that slow on the uptake might let at least one or two details slip?

A new message appeared on the Lavineas server. BAWN, reassuring as always. No worries. I'm dealing with a few unexpected issues myself. Besides, I'll be around for a while yet.

She huffed out a breath, amused by the way BAWN had

randomly, inadvertently echoed Marcus, the man whose character BAWN had written about in dozens of fics.

Should she tell him what had just happened?

No. Not yet.

She hadn't even decided for certain whether she'd accept Marcus's invitation, and she wasn't ready for her Lavineas friends to see her in the flesh. Soon, but not now. Not when she had so many other decisions to make and considerations to weigh.

Thanks. I'll be back soon, she wrote BAWN.

Climbing out of bed, she checked in the side pocket of her suitcase for a fresh notebook. She did her best thinking on paper. Always had.

Along the way, she grabbed a pen and refilled her bedside glass of water. Propped once more against the wooden headboard, she tapped the ballpoint against the first blank page and acknowledged the obvious.

If she wanted to stop hiding, she couldn't have found a more efficient means of exposure.

Assuming tonight's thread hadn't done the trick already, a date with Marcus Caster-Rupp, a world-famous television star, would make her face and body and shipping interests publicly known. At least in some circles. And she knew enough about the *Gods of the Gates* fandom that she could already see the blog post headlines. The kind ones, anyway.

**Gates Fan Accepts Date with Actor of
Her Dreams; Nerdgirls Rejoice!**

**A Fangirl Scores a Star: And on This Day,
a Million Modern AUs Were Born
@Lavineas5Ever, Stan Icon for the Ages**

Which reminded her: The Lavineas server was going to freak out, if the hysteria hadn't already begun. It probably had, since most of her friends followed Marcus on Twitter. Thank God she hadn't checked the server's main chat threads yet.

If they knew @Lavineas5Ever was also Unapologetic Lavinia Stan, and that she was tempted to turn down a goddamn *date* with half of their OTP, they would fucking annihilate her.

Well, since she'd already made her public debut as a fangirl, she might as well do it right. Might as well spell out everything she needed to do, all the parts of herself she intended to expose to sunlight.

In bold, block letters, she titled her page: ENVIRONMENTAL GEOLOGIST, REMEDIATE THYSELF.

Some of the parts of her plan she'd determined on the drive home today and over the past few months, but others she'd list now. Including the most painful bits.

1. Say yes to Marcus. Publicly.
2. Without being obnoxious about it, merge the personal and professional at work. Stop fearing exposure. (Remind self of terrible folk trio as necessary.)
3. Share Twitter handle and identity with Lavineas friends. Wear earplugs when doing so, as squealing may be heard from space.
4. Attend Con of the Gates. Meet Lavineas friends and let them see what I look like in person. ~~Even B~~
5. At Con of the Gates, enter cosplay contest.

Chewing on the inside of her cheek for a moment, she paused. No, she was going to add everything. She'd said she would, and she was no coward.

6. Address fat-shaming in the Lavineas community, even though it might alienate ~~BAWN~~ my friends.
7. Decide what to do about Mom and Dad. Once I'm sure, tell Mom in person.
8. Immediately dump any man who wants to change me and/ or doesn't seem proud to be with me in public.

There. That was it. If she wanted to dig out the poison in her personal landscape, that was how to go about it.

Leaving her notebook and remediation list within sight, she woke her laptop from hibernation mode and maximized her Twitter window. Chewed the inside of her cheek for a moment. Nodded to herself.

In the end, it took only seconds. She located Marcus's invitation amid her ballooning notifications and clicked *Retweet with comment*.

I would be delighted to have dinner with you, @MarcusCasterRupp. Thank you for your kind invitation. Feel free to slide into my DMs to work out details. 😉

Unapologetic Lavinia Stan: I mean, first the show totally ignored the books by having her actually die on that funeral pyre, but I guess you could say they were going old-school there (as in, *Virgil*-old). But having Juno bring her back from the dead? Then making Dido some sort of crazed, power-hungry, sex-starved, scorned woman basically boiling bunnies in her Aeneas obsession? As the thread title indicates: WTAF?

Mrs. Pius Aeneas: She's completely unrecognizable from the Dido in Wade's books.

Book!AeneasWouldNever: Even Virgil's Dido, before Aeneas's arrival and the intervention of Venus, was a supremely competent ruler. I hate to say it, but

Unapologetic Lavinia Stan: But what?

Book!AeneasWouldNever: The show's Dido has never been anything more than a misogynistic caricature. Carah Brown's talents are wasted in the role, although she's the only reason the character has any gravitas. Once they get past Wade's books, it'll only get worse.

Unapologetic Lavinia Stan: But why make that narrative choice? It's so much less interesting than what Wade or even Virgil did.

Book!AeneasWouldNever: I suspect it has a lot to do with how the showrunners view women.

4

HER CELL BUZZED FROM ATOP THE HOTEL ROOM DESK, and April rested her forehead against the faux-wood surface. She lifted her head, only to drop it again with a muted thud.

Without even looking, she knew who was calling and why. At some point, her mom was going to hear about the date with Marcus happening that night. It was only a matter of time, but April had appreciated every minute of it.

And now, her time was up.

One glance at the display confirmed her fears, and she heaved a sigh before tapping the screen. "Hi, Mom."

"Honey, I just saw a picture of you on *Entertainment All-Access*. I think." Her mother sounded both startled and confused. "You were wearing some sort of old-fashioned dress?"

April had wondered yesterday whether JoAnn's favorite show to watch during dinner prep would feature the story. Evidently, she had her answer. "That was me. In my Lavinia costume. You know, from *Gods of the Gates*?"

"Oh, my heavens." Her mother blew out a breath. "April, I don't even—"

A lengthy silence followed, in which JoAnn likely blinked in shock at her daughter's sudden, unexpected fame, absorbed the news, and contemplated where to begin the conversation. With curiosity? Concern? Pity? Advice?

Eventually, she'd cover all of the above. April knew that already, as well as she knew what her mother's advice would entail.

At long last, her mother chose an opening query. "How in the world did this *happen*?"

That was a question with many answers, some more existential than others, but April settled on the bare facts. Minus a bit of context, in the vain hope they could both avoid the inevitable.

"Well, I have a Twitter account where I post pictures of myself cosplaying Lavinia, and Marcus Caster-Rupp saw one of the photos Wednesday night and asked me out." She kept her voice calm, as if her world hadn't exploded in the last several days. As if her heart hadn't been skittering in her chest since the moment she'd risen that morning. "I'm staying at a hotel in Berkeley this weekend while I get my new apartment ready, and he happened to be in the area. So our dinner is happening tonight, but please don't tell anyone. I'd like to keep the whole thing as private as possible, under the circumstances."

As private as possible meant *not very private*. And that was putting it mildly.

As soon as her Twitter exchange with Marcus went viral, her mentions became . . . incomprehensible. Overwhelming. Filled with commentary both heartening and stunningly ugly. And even though she'd muted all the main threads long ago, new followers and tweets just kept coming, as did interview requests and blogger and media questions.

Her current amount of exposure was more than sufficient, so she'd refused all requests and ignored all questions. Then, just when the hubbub had begun to diminish, the official *Gods of the*

Gates Twitter account had picked up on the story and obviously seen the date, true to Marcus's prediction, as a great PR opportunity. To her dismay, they'd started promoting the shit out of the blessed event.

Which meant yet more notifications. More DMs. More threads to mute.

At that point, the story had reached her former coworkers. Because of the continued internet uproar, two of her now-ex-colleagues had seen her picture in one of the many stories available online by Friday.

They'd chatted to her about it in hushed corners of the office, and she hadn't minded their winks and nudges. But their sympathetic winces and pitying pats on the arm—*such terrible things people said, April; I can't imagine how you must have felt*—had set her teeth on edge.

When she'd walked out of her old workplace, box of belongings in her arms, she'd done so through a gauntlet of gawking and whispers.

No more hiding, she'd repeated through a suddenly tight chest. *No more hiding. Folk goddamn trio.*

Then the story had leaped from Twitter to Facebook and Insta, and from there to *Gods of the Gates* blogs and even a few entertainment news programs.

Including *Entertainment All-Access*, evidently.

She was trying not to follow the spread of her newfound fame, but how could she not? Even when each post, each televised clip, ratcheted the tension in her muscles until her shoulders ached?

"I see." JoAnn probably *had* seen the entire story only moments before, displayed for the public's viewing pleasure on television screens nationwide. "Are you okay, honey?"

Ah, concern and pity had made a simultaneous entrance into the conversation. Lovely.

"I'm good. Just figuring out what to wear for—" Shit. Rookie mistake. Normally, April never, ever introduced clothing choices into any discussion with her mother. "Just looking forward to tonight. Marcus plays Aeneas, one of my favorite characters."

Her mother ignored that gambit.

"They showed us part of that conversation on Twitter." JoAnn's voice dropped to a near-whisper. "I'm not sure posting pictures there is a great idea."

It was more or less the same advice April had received for more than thirty years: *If people are cruel, make yourself smaller and smaller, until you're so inconsequential no one can target you.*

But April was done cringing and hiding. The opinion of fatphobic randos on Twitter didn't matter, and she wouldn't make herself small just to avoid their notice. "I like showing everyone the costumes I've put together."

JoAnn responded carefully, worry and good intentions in every syllable. "That dress . . ." She hesitated. "It didn't show your figure to its best advantage. Maybe you can make one that doesn't cling to—"

It could be anything. April's arms. Her back. Her stomach. Her ass. Her thighs.

"I'm good," she repeated, her tone more curt than she'd intended.

Another long silence.

When JoAnn spoke again, her voice quavered slightly. "You said you were picking out what to wear tonight?"

April had hurt her mother's feelings, and a flush of shame crawled up her neck.

"Yes. I brought a few options, and I'm trying to decide between them." Her hands were clenched into fists, and she knew, she just knew—

"I imagine people will take pictures of you during your dinner tonight." JoAnn's faux-cheer lodged under April's skin like splinters. "A black dress is always in style, you know. And the color disguises so many sins, especially if you find a design that doesn't fit too tightly."

Black to disappear. Extra fabric to disguise.

As always, fatness was a sin, most likely mortal rather than venial.

Bowing her head, April didn't respond for fear of what she might say.

"Don't worry. I won't tell anyone about the date," JoAnn continued. "Other than your father, of course. But I'm sure he won't spread the—"

Okay, they were done. "I'd better go. I need to take a shower now so I have enough time to get ready for dinner."

"All right. Have fun tonight, honey," JoAnn said, although she didn't sound as if she expected fun to be had by anyone involved. "I love you."

Her mother meant it. April had never questioned that.

"Thanks, Mom." Her nails were biting into her palms so hard, she was surprised she hadn't broken the skin. "I love you too."

And that was the hell of it. She did.

FRESH FROM THE shower, clad in a loose nightgown, April stood in front of her tiny hotel room closet and dithered.

As she'd told her mother, she'd brought plenty of date-outfit options from her half-packed home in Sacramento. Good ones. And under normal circumstances, she wasn't prone to indecision—but these were far from normal circumstances. Whatever she chose to wear for her dinner with Marcus Caster-Rupp later that night, it had to make two simultaneous statements.

First: *I'm confident and sexy, but not trying too hard.* Because, yes, he might be vapid and vain, but he was also a famous actor and fucking *hot*, and she had her pride. Like her mother, she also anticipated more than a few candid shots of the dinner ending up online before she finished her last bite of dessert. She intended to look good in those photos, as well as in the pics she and Marcus would post on their own social media accounts.

To make that kind of statement required a formfitting dress. Not one in black, either. It required heels, loath as she was to torture her feet. It required dangling earrings.

But that was all her standard big-date garb, despite her mother's advice. Nothing too complicated.

No, it was the second statement, one directed toward Marcus alone, that was proving tricky: *You should share confidential details about the final season of your show, despite the legal and professional consequences you'd suffer upon doing so.*

And making that kind of statement—well, she wasn't entirely sure what kind of outfit would suffice. It should probably involve a hypnotist's watch. *You're getting sleepy, very sleepy, and also very prone to telling me whether you and Lavinia finally fuck, and whether it's awesome, and is there any full-frontal male nudity?*

Absent such a watch, her best bet was cleavage. Last year, the mere sight of her dress's plunging neckline had caused a date to stride confidently into a lamppost outside the Fairmont. Later, when she'd bent over to retrieve a dropped napkin during dinner, he'd stabbed himself in the cheek with his fork and yelped loudly enough to summon a nearby waiter.

Before that ill-fated evening, Blake had spent hours bragging about the intensity and thoroughness of his long-ago special forces training. Apparently, however, SEALs didn't prepare for Advanced Mammary Warfare Tactics back in the early 2000s, and neither did present-day internet security experts.

When she'd teased him about that oversight, he'd scowled petulantly at her. Right before spilling half a glass of white wine over his suit jacket when she fiddled with the pendant hanging just above her breasts.

She'd snickered then, and she snickered again at the memory. Sucker.

Okay. A wrap dress, then. Cleavage Central.

She flipped through the hangers in the closet, contemplating her two main options. That colorful medallion print or the gorgeous seafoam green?

The green dress slipped to the floor, and she could barely put it back on the padded hanger.

Shit. Her hands were shaking.

She shouldn't be nervous. She wasn't. Only—

Jesus, those Twitter notifications, blog posts, and entertainment news programs. Her mother's doubts. April's own fears.

Despite her excitement, despite her hard-won confidence, she was still human. This sudden exposure of her private life to the public eye had left her feeling . . . odd. As if she were watching herself from the outside, evaluating every nuance of what she said and how she looked.

And even apart from the public uproar and her new self-consciousness, she was meeting a man she'd seen for years on *television*, for fuck's sake. The same man whose terrible movies she'd occasionally watched with a bucket of popcorn in hand, his handsome face on the screen almost as big as the house she'd just sold.

The same man various magazines proclaimed the sexiest man alive. The same man who'd starred in countless fics she'd written, grinning and flirting and fucking his way to guaranteed happy endings, both literal and metaphorical. At least, in her imagination.

In less than two hours, she was meeting him in actual reality, and she needed not to hyperventilate. Somehow.

She should pick a dress with a soothing color.

One last glance at her closet, and she had her answer: seafoam green. No one hyperventilated while wearing seafoam green. It was the Valium of dress colors, in the prettiest possible way.

Or so she fervently hoped.

Lavineas Server DMs, Eighteen Months Ago

Unapologetic Lavinia Stan: I think I'm going to pack as many tropes into this one-shot as possible. Help me think of more, please. I already have oh-no-there's-only-one-bed, fake dating, one-bang-will-get-this-out-of-our-systems, big brother's best friend . . .

Book!AeneasWouldNever: Wow. That's quite a lineup.

Book!AeneasWouldNever: Maybe "kissing for the sake of science"?

Unapologetic Lavinia Stan: NICE. Done!

Book!AeneasWouldNever: How about some pining too?

Unapologetic Lavinia Stan: Oh, here we go.

Book!AeneasWouldNever: Unrequited love? Or he inadvertently led to his ex's death? Maybe she died in a fire he could have prevented, if only he hadn't been so caught up in duty?

Unapologetic Lavinia Stan: Jesus Christ.

Book!AeneasWouldNever: Sorry.

Unapologetic Lavinia Stan: No, don't apologize. Angst is your thing. It works for you.

Book!AeneasWouldNever: Um

Unapologetic Lavinia Stan: What

Book!AeneasWouldNever: Maybe he experiences PTSD because of his military background? Like, a bunch of his men died under his command?

Unapologetic Lavinia Stan: Holy shit, BAWN.

5

"SO . . ." MARCUS DABBED HIS PERFECT MOUTH WITH HIS starched cloth napkin, then returned it neatly to his lap. "You have a Twitter account?"

April wasn't entirely certain how to respond to that.

He hadn't seemed quite *this* dim in DMs. But maybe he had a personal assistant handle his social media accounts, and she'd never really communicated with him at all before now. Or maybe, for a man like him, she was too insignificant to remember for long?

"Yes." With her fork, she teased free a flake of the restaurant's signature house-smoked salmon and dipped it in the artistic smear of her appetizer's sour cream–dill sauce. "I do."

Their server, Olaf, came to refill her water glass, as he seemed to do after every sip. Taking advantage of the distraction, she discreetly checked her watch.

Thirty minutes since she'd met Marcus? That was all?

Dammit.

It seemed like longer since she'd entered the candlelit confines of the exclusive, expensive SoMa restaurant and found him already sitting at their window-side table. Since she'd arrived ten minutes early and expected a bit of a wait—weren't Hollywood types supposed to swan into events fashionably late?—she'd blinked at him in surprise when he'd risen smartly to his feet and greeted her with a placid smile on his handsome face.

"You look lovely." His glance at her formfitting dress had lasted maybe a half second, no more. "Thank you for joining me tonight."

He'd extended an arm toward the chair with the best view, his dark suit jacket molding attractively against his biceps, then helped seat her. Still smiling, he'd begun to make small talk. About the weather. About the traffic. About the beauty of the sunset that evening.

And that was what they'd been doing ever since, in between Olaf's visits. She was half tempted to knock over a water glass or set her napkin on fire with their table's candle, just for a little excitement. This dinner was going to be *endless*.

Heaving a small, silent sigh, she ate her bite of salmon. At least she no longer felt guilty about her preference for dinner with Alexander Woodroe over Marcus. Or—better yet—long-distance DMs with BAWN over in-person conversation with either famous actor.

Her online bestie didn't know about this date, but she intended to tell him as soon as she returned to the hotel.

First, though, she had to remain awake through three courses with Marcus. Dammit.

"I imagine your notifications this past week have been, uh . . ." His broad brow creased as he appeared to search for the right word. "A lot?"

April had to laugh at the understatement. "Definitely. I've been Googling local hermitages. Also attempting to locate nearby empty caves suitable for a life of silence and solitude."

"If you're considering life in a cave, that's probably not a good sign. I'm sorry." For the first time all evening, his genial smile died. "Are you being harassed online? Or in person?"

"Neither." Then she paused to reconsider. "Well, yes, on Twitter. Occasionally. But not in ways I can't handle with the mute and block functions, at least so far."

Yet more public exposure was coming soon. She might not be familiar with the rituals of fame, but even she knew enough to expect onlookers' photos taken of her and Marcus at a dinner table together. Even her *mother* knew that much.

Once those photos appeared online, once she and Marcus posted their own selfies, there would be more blog posts. More entertainment television updates. She might even end up a brief mention on her mother's favorite morning show.

If so, she was *not* looking forward to the subsequent phone call.

"If you do run into worse issues, please let me know." For the first time all night, Marcus's blue-gray eyes pinned her in place, their sudden alertness startling. "I mean that."

It was a sweet offer. Also pointless. "What could you even do?"

His jaw worked for a bare moment, the shadows beneath that sharp jut shifting in the candlelight. "I don't know. Something."

Instead of arguing, she merely inclined her head and allowed him to take it for agreement. Then silence reigned for several minutes as they finished their first course. Which, to be fair, was utterly delicious. He—or his PA, whoever—had chosen well when it came to the restaurant.

Also to his credit, he hadn't tried to influence her order in any way. There'd been no subtle steering toward so-called healthier options, no pointed references to the salads, none of the food-policing that stung most when it came from people who were supposed to care about her.

Instead, when the discreet server now hovering in their peripheral vision, water jug in hand, had taken her order—the three-course, fixed-price menu—Marcus had merely said it was an excellent decision and ordered the same.

Sometime while they'd been eating, his placid smile had returned. "That was tasty. What did we order for the main course again? More salmon?"

Oh, God. Compared to this meal, the half-life of radium was going to seem short.

Food, she reminded herself. *You're getting amazing food out of this.*

"Roasted chicken thighs stuffed with goat cheese and an apricot relish, alongside creamy garlic polenta and sautéed haricot verts with thyme." She paused. "Oh, and toasted pine nuts . . . somewhere. Probably as part of the relish. I can't remember for certain."

He blinked at her.

She lifted a shoulder. "I like food."

His smile broadened. Warmed his eyes.

"So it seems." There was no mockery in his voice, at least none that she could detect. Just amusement. "You also have a hell of a memory."

She waved a dismissive hand. "I checked out the restaurant last night. I'm staying in a local hotel while I deep-clean my new apartment, so I had plenty of time to study the menu online."

"I'm glad you found something you wanted to order."

He was looking down at his empty plate. When he glanced back up at her, he flicked his fingers through his hair, rumpling it attractively as he positioned his arm in a way that outlined all those muscles she'd admired from the safety of her laptop screen.

And yes, his muscles were still rather impressive in person, and he was very polite, and his hair was thick and golden in the candlelight, but Jesus, the *tedium*.

For a moment, she contemplated talking about her move, her new job, or anything she was doing over the weekend apart from this dinner, just to pass the time. If the man couldn't remember either their Twitter exchanges or the food he'd ordered minutes ago, though, that seemed like wasted effort. So instead, the two of them sat in silence once more until Olaf arrived to remove their empty dishes and refill their water glasses.

Immediately after their server's departure behind a set of swinging doors, arms piled high with plates, a sudden flash of light from the side made her flinch. Turning, she scanned that swath of the restaurant for the source of the white spots now dancing behind her eyelids.

Ah. Of course.

A man at a neighboring table had taken a photo of them with the cell phone he was now hurriedly placing in his lap, safely out of sight. That photo would probably end up on Insta or Twitter within minutes. Maybe less, if they turned their attention from his increasingly red face and he felt free to use his phone once more.

"I was wondering how long it would take," she murmured.

"Usually people are smart enough not to use their flash in a place like this." Marcus tilted his head in the direction of the maître d' station, where the suit-clad man who'd greeted her at the door was now hustling toward their photographer's table. "The management here values customer privacy and discretion, or at least the appearance thereof."

If she hadn't been so curious about the forthcoming confrontation at the other table, she'd have side-eyed Marcus for his choice of words. *The appearance thereof?*

But she couldn't spare him that amount of attention, not when the most interesting thing that had happened all night was occurring only feet away. Her elbow propped on the white-tablecloth-covered table, she rested her cheek on her fist and waited for the show to begin.

The maître d' swooped in and bent low, all sotto voce scolding, only to be met by hushed denials. Eyebrows furrowed in dismay, the man gestured at the phone in his lap, its innocent location apparently meant to serve as incontrovertible proof that he couldn't possibly have taken a flash photo inside the restaurant.

Marcus's words were barely audible. "And people call *me* an actor."

Finally, after more whispered discussion, the man at the table slid his cell into the inner pocket of his jacket, patting it as if to promise he would keep it there for the rest of the meal. With one final, narrow-eyed look, the maître d' returned to his station.

Her entertainment over, April turned regretfully back to Marcus. "I don't care about the pictures, really. I figure there's no good way to avoid them. I'd just prefer not to be blinded by a flash."

Whether she'd be able to maintain such equanimity in the face of unflattering candid shots, she didn't know. But she was certainly going to try.

"I'm sorry. Again." Mouth tight, he caught her eye from across the table. "I chose this restaurant in part because the paparazzi hadn't found me here yet. I'd hoped you could control tonight's narrative online, if at all possible."

Huh.

Her mouth opened, then closed.

"It's fine. No need to apologize," she finally said. "Marcus, I have a random question for you. Do you handle your own social media accounts, or do you have an assistant do that?"

A deep line appeared between his handsomely arched brows. "I handle them myself. Badly, for the most part. Why?"

Sitting back in her cushioned chair, she tilted her head and studied her date.

I'd hoped you could control tonight's narrative. Not something a man lacking the capacity for deep thought would generally say.

Interesting.

Disoblige could be a lucky choice of word. Even the most misguided squirrels occasionally located acorns.

The appearance thereof was pushing the bounds of belief, but he could still be parroting someone else. His agent, a scriptwriter, a director, *someone.*

Control the narrative, though . . .

That was the third time he'd said something surprisingly incisive. At this point, she either had to conclude that someone had given him a Smart-Sounding Phrase of the Day calendar, or acknowledge that he wasn't quite so dim after all. Not nearly as dim as he'd been pretending to be, anyway.

Time to dig deeper. Take more samples.

When their main course arrived moments later—yum—she smiled at him and picked up her fork and sharp-bladed knife. Her pair of chicken thighs lay in the middle of the plate, their skin crisp and browned and perfect. So perfect, in fact, a random observer might never realize there was something more than chicken beneath that surface.

With a precise cut, she halved a deboned thigh, exposing the stuffing beneath that pristine skin. Then she carved a slice and took the time to taste it thoroughly.

The dish was complex. Deeply savory, with tart and sweet notes and unexpected texture from those toasted pine nuts. Exactly what she'd wanted, although she'd had doubts about the wisdom of ordering something as unexceptional and boring as chicken thighs at such a fancy restaurant.

But she wasn't bored. Not in the slightest. Not anymore.

"I would love for you to tell me more about your work on *Gods of the Gates*." As he winced apologetically, she held up a hand. "I know you can't say anything about the final season, and I'm not asking. I'm more interested in behind-the-scenes stuff, anyway. Your daily routine and what your actual job has entailed all this time. How you train for sword fights, whether you already knew how to ride a horse when you joined the cast, things like that."

This time, when he pushed his hair back from his forehead, the motion didn't look quite so studied. Not paired with that crinkled brow.

"I'd bore you to tears, I'm afraid." His smile was still bright, still genial, but now a wee bit tighter. "Why don't we talk about my exercise routine instead? Or maybe I can tell you about working with Summer Diaz and Carah Brown?"

He'd addressed those topics numerous times, in countless articles and blog posts, and she didn't care to discuss either one. The exercise stuff would, in fact, bore her to tears, and when it came to his costars, the man was a font of good-natured platitudes.

I'm lucky to work alongside such talented colleagues, and ones nearly as pretty as I am.

They're true professionals, and as beautiful inside as outside. Like me!

The show couldn't have found more lovely, gifted actors to play Lavinia and Dido. Or Aeneas, for that matter.

No, she wanted to tackle topics that didn't allow for generic, surface-only answers.

"I won't be bored, I promise." Another neat slice of the chicken thigh, and she paused with her forkful of food just above her plate. "Did you ride horses before being cast on the show?"

"No. I didn't."

He was pushing a tiny cube of apricot around his plate with his own fork. Studying the circles it made with unusual focus as she chewed and waited for words that weren't coming.

She swallowed before digging deeper. "Do you like riding?"

"Yes." Instead of elaborating, he shoved a hasty bite of food into his mouth.

All right, no more yes or no questions. "What do you like about it?"

He pointed to his full mouth, and she nodded in understanding and waited. And waited. And waited.

His chewing had become extraordinarily thorough in the last minute or so. But if he was hoping she'd say something more or change the topic while he endlessly chewed his mouthful of polenta—*polenta*, which didn't actually require chewing—he was doomed to disappointment.

His throat bobbed as he swallowed, and she smiled encouragingly at him.

"Um . . ." His chest hitched in a tiny sigh, one so discreet she'd have missed it if she hadn't been watching him so closely. "I like being outdoors. And, uh, I'm pretty athletic, so things like riding suit me. Fit my talents, I guess."

Suddenly, he straightened in his chair. Flipped his hair back from his face with a practiced snap of his head. "To help strengthen my thighs, I had certain exercises my trainer suggested I do. I can tell you about those."

Nope.

"I imagine you had to practice a lot, even if you're naturally athletic and exercise the right way." Barreling right past his attempted conversational misdirection, she continued pressing. "Did someone from the show teach you swordplay, or did you learn how to use a sword on your own?"

At that, he met her eyes again. Finally. "You want to hear about the crew?"

"Sure." That might prove as revelatory as any other topic, she figured.

His mouth pursed, he gave a little nod.

"Okay." Putting down his cutlery, he leaned forward. "Um . . . okay. Any skill with the sword I have, I owe to them."

"How?" she asked.

Once more, she waited. And this time, the dam broke.

"From the moment I was cast, they started teaching me how to handle my sword and shield in a way that would look second nature, as if I'd been doing it my whole life." This time, she didn't need to ask him to elaborate. He just did, without prompting. "How to walk, how to sit, how to stand at attention. And if I look capable on-screen while fighting, that's due to them too."

No credit for himself. Interesting. "In what way?"

He barely hesitated. "The fight coordinators and choreographers and the stunt coordinators worked like hell to make sure each battle scene not only looked impressive, but fit each character's personality and history and the specific goals and mindset they'd have for that particular fight. Then they'd run us through the sequences again and again, until we knew exactly what to do and when to do it."

In other words: Yes, with their help and guidance, he'd practiced a lot.

He was very skilled at erasing his own efforts from the narrative, though. Especially for a man whose vanity was legendary.

"Some of those big battle sequences, they'd start preparing us months ahead," he added. "Up to a year, in a few cases. Always looking ahead, always striving to make each scene convincing and spectacular and memorable."

His blue-gray eyes were bright and intent on hers, willing her to understand the greatness of the *Gods of the Gates* crew, the extent of their hard work. He was gesturing with his broad hands now, punctuating his points with little waves and slashes.

It was like watching a ghost become corporeal once more. Life, where only a shadow once existed. Fascinating and disorienting, all at once.

She thought over what he'd told her. "So if they take each character's history into account, someone like Cyprian shouldn't fight as capably as, say, Aeneas. Because Cyprian wouldn't be as battle-hardened and wouldn't have had the opportunity to learn swordplay in the same way."

"Exactly. Sometimes they'd have to tell one of us to dial back the skill a few notches." He grinned at her, and it crinkled at the corners of those eyes in a very distracting way. "Between takes, the director would come around and ask each of us what we were fighting for in that scene. What our goal was. What had happened to us prior to that scene that would inform the moment for our character. So a battle might involve hundreds of people, but for the main actors, that scene, that fight, would also be specific. Different for everyone."

His face was mobile with passion. So much passion and intensity and . . . intelligence.

She crossed her legs under the table. Uncrossed them.

"And that's not even getting into all the work done by the weapons master, the sword master, the horse master, the VFX and SFX people . . ." He shook his head, his golden hair glowing in the candlelight, and she couldn't look away. "The show has over a thousand crew members, and they're all amazing, April. The hardest-working, most talented people I've ever met."

That didn't sound like a platitude. It sounded like a bone-deep truth.

For the first time that night, April excused herself to the restroom. Once there, she used the facilities, washed her hands, and didn't leave immediately.

Instead, she dabbed more cold water on her wrists. The back of her neck. Only two of the many places she was suddenly much too hot, even though she knew better. She *did*.

She stared at herself in the mirror. Red hair. Freckles. Brown eyes behind contact lenses. Round breasts, round belly, round thighs. All normal.

Not normal: the rosy flush on her cheeks, and the slight ache between those thighs.

Because she suddenly wanted him. Marcus. Caster. Hyphen. Rupp. The dim, vain man who was, apparently, neither vain nor dim. Or at least not as vain and dim as he pretended.

He was still gorgeous, however. Still famous.

And only having dinner with her tonight out of kindness, not desire for her company or her body or anything else specific to her.

Well, shit.

GODS OF THE GATES: SEASON 1, EPISODE 3

EXT. MOUNTAINSIDE CAVE - DUSK

JUNO waits inside the entrance, half in shadows,
expression calm and righteous. When LEDA ventures
within, Juno makes no sudden movements, aware
that the woman her husband has wronged—yet
another woman he has violated—has no reason to
trust her, and may fear the vengeance of a possessive
wife.

                         JUNO
Trust my good will, if you can. I no longer find
relief in petty jealousy, and am no longer foolish
enough to blame a mortal maiden for the rapaciousness
of an all-powerful god.

                         LEDA
I would not have betrayed you, mother Juno. Not if
resistance were in my power.
    EUROPA glides through the entrance, armed, shaking
with fear.

                        EUROPA
Whatever tortures you may choose to inflict upon
me, you can do no worse than the man you call
husband.

JUNO

I no longer call him husband. And if we make common cause, none of us need call him king of the gods for long.

GODS OF THE GATES: SEASON 6, EPISODE 2

INT. AENEAS AND LAVINIA'S HOME - NIGHT

LAVINIA waits by the fire. She's pissed. He's been fucking Anna, Dido's sister. She knows it. AENEAS enters the house.

LAVINIA

Where you have been, my husband?

AENEAS

That is not your concern.

   Whatever. He doesn't need this shit. When Lavinia cries, he walks away.

6

WHILE APRIL VISITED THE BATHROOM, MARCUS REgrouped.

Somehow, she'd gotten him talking about things he actually *wanted* to talk about. Worse, doing so in the same way he might with Alex, the one person he trusted without hesitation. Alex, who definitely wouldn't contact a blogger and say, *I think Marcus Caster-Rupp has been fucking with everyone this whole time as some kind of big joke.*

His public persona wasn't a joke. It never had been. But unless he controlled the narrative—as he'd advised her to do earlier that night—his behavior could easily be construed that way. If he chose to shed his persona, it had to be on his terms, and only on his terms. For the sake of his career, but also his own troubled conscience.

When April got back from the bathroom, Well-Groomed Golden Retriever was going to make his triumphant return to the stage, ready to perform his few hard-won tricks. Or maybe he'd simply turn the conversation to her life, her job, and let her do all the talking for the rest of the evening.

In the meantime, he got out his phone and checked his messages. Not those on the Lavineas server, since he wanted time and privacy to read any DMs from Ulsie. But by now, reactions to the showrunners' ominous message several days before should be all over the cast's private group chat. And . . . sure enough.

Carah: for the record, I'm not saying a goddamn word to anyone about this season

Carah: saving that for my fucking MEMOIRS, bitches

Ian: whoever hid my tuna, it's not funny

Carah: hahahahahaha

Ian: give it back, assholes, Jupiter needs protein for this last week of shooting

Summer: I don't know why we need a new reminder about the confidentiality clause in our contracts each season

Summer: it's a little insulting

Summer: @Carah: 👍 looking forward to reading that, hon

Alex: no one wants your pocket tuna, Ian, you probably just ate it without realizing

Maria: THIS⬆

Alex: I mean, it was like your twelfth serving of fish today, so

Peter: yeah, probably not very memorable, all things considered

Maria: do you know the symptoms of mercury poisoning, and do they involve referring to yourself in the third person as a god

At that point, the conversation derailed because of Ian's extended, defensive seafood-related rant, as per usual. The man could use a few more carbs, as well as a bit more distance between himself and his role. At least enough so that he could cease referring to himself as *Jupiter* when the cameras weren't rolling.

As Marcus slipped his phone back into his jacket pocket, he spotted another cell's camera pointed in his direction. Not the same one as earlier, though. This time, a woman from the table behind April was taking the opportunity to get an unobstructed, flash-free shot of him during his date's absence. When he looked around, at least a couple of other customers were eyeing him speculatively, leaning close to their dinner companions and whispering.

But at least they were all amateurs, rather than actual paparazzi. He'd half expected to be greeted that night by a shouting handful of people with enormous cameras clustered outside the restaurant entrance, as had happened on so many of his other dates.

Not because the paparazzi had followed him to those restaurants. Because his dates had told the media beforehand where to go.

It was unforgivably stupid. Naive. He knew it. But each time, blinking against the harsh strobe of the flashes, overwhelmed amid the roar of voices calling his name and telling him to *look over here*, the realization that his date hadn't wanted him, really, but rather the dubious perks of his odd, transient fame—

Each time, he'd floated outside himself for a moment. Disoriented. Lost.

Tonight, he'd walked into the restaurant undisturbed, illuminated only by the lingering glow of sunset and streetlights just flickering to life. Even though, if April had alerted them, countless reporters would have raced to cover the much-anticipated date.

STAR MEETS STAN, one blogger had termed the momentous occasion.

Before April had even arrived, then, he'd already considered their date more enjoyable than most he'd had since being cast on *Gods of the Gates*. Her eventual entrance into the restaurant hadn't shaken that assessment, either. This might be an evening spent together out of necessity, rather than any real attachment on either side, but he could still appreciate her company, the opportunity to admire her across the table for an hour or two, and the convenience of her location near San Francisco and his parents.

When their dinner ended, they'd take a few pics to post on Twitter and prove her haters wrong. Afterward, once they went their separate ways, all the buzz would slowly diminish. Until their meal together became simply a footnote in his Wikipedia entry, a reminder of that time he went on a date with a fan of his show, because he might be dim, but he was also kind.

That was how everyone was interpreting this dinner. As a sympathetic gesture, rather than an expression of real attraction.

They weren't wrong, obviously. But the easy assumption that *of course* he couldn't be attracted to April, *of course* he couldn't truly want to date her, pricked some raw spot within him. Made him bristle a bit. After that ugly thread the other day, he couldn't avoid knowing why everyone had made their assumptions. And if he understood, April did too.

The irony: they weren't entirely right, either.

Yes, he would have asked out anyone in her position. A troll living under a bridge. A beauty queen. Whomever.

But April was no troll. By candlelight, her hair was a gleaming sheet of copper flowing just past her shoulders, her eyes dark and sparked by fire. She hadn't covered her freckles with whatever makeup she was wearing, and he was trying very hard not to count each adorable speckle on her nose and the tops of her round cheeks. Much as he'd forced himself not to stare for longer than a heartbeat at her body, lush and faithfully outlined by that green dress she wore.

Those braying fanboys weren't just cruel. They were fools.

April Whittier was a goddess. And as the son of Lawrence Caster and Debra Rupp, as a man who played a demigod himself, he would know.

As she circled other tables on her way back to theirs, her confident stride matched her up-tilted chin. Maybe she didn't notice the stares, the way at least one cell phone camera followed her progress. Maybe she didn't care. Or maybe she was pretending not to care.

Either way, she impressed the hell out of him, just as she'd been doing all night.

She was bright. Funny. Incisive. Practical. A good listener, even when he was saying too much, too honestly. Her direct manner, her humor, the intelligent, plainspoken way she expressed herself, reminded him of Ulsie somehow.

No, looking at and listening to her throughout the remainder of their meal wouldn't prove a hardship.

Once she'd seated herself, he offered the amiable smile that had graced five straight years of photo spreads in the annual "World's Hottest Men" magazine issue. "You've heard about my job. Tell me more about what *you* do."

"I'm a geologist," she said before taking another healthy bite of her chicken.

How far did he want to take the dunce routine? Pretty far, he supposed, given his earlier slipups.

"So you make maps?" he asked.

Her lips twitched, but somehow she didn't seem to be laughing at him. More *with* him. Which was infinitely more alarming.

"That would be a geographer. Or, rather, a cartographer."

Neatly, she sliced off a manageable bite of her green beans. "I sometimes consult maps for my work, but I'm a geologist. In the simplest of terms, I study rocks."

He couldn't say he'd ever met a geologist before. To be fair, that was also true for geographers or cartographers, but he wasn't having dinner with one of those.

"Why rocks?" For once, the simplest question mirrored his honest curiosity.

She tapped the tines of her fork against her plate, pausing to think before she answered. "I guess . . ." One last *ting* of metal against porcelain, and she looked up at him again. "The Northridge earthquake happened when I was a kid, and a geologist came on TV at one point. Everything she said was so fascinating. So smart. She impressed the hell out of preteen me. After that, I was into seismology for a while."

He remembered watching news coverage of that quake himself, but the Loma Prieta quake was a much more visceral memory.

Most people had already tuned into the World Series game. He'd still been studying, though, seething with resentment all the while. And then: the ominous rumble from everywhere at once, the rattle of fragile glass and porcelain, the creak of their house moving around beneath them, the urgency in his mother's voice as she pushed him under the dining room table where they suffered together day after day. The way she tried to tuck his head beneath her body, protecting him as best she could for those few seconds on a Tuesday evening.

Why did that memory hurt so damn much?

"Then, after a geology program I did one summer in high school, I realized seismology wasn't my first love after all." April took another bite of her chicken before continuing. "That would be sedimentary rocks."

Well, his ignorance this time wasn't feigned. He wouldn't know a sedimentary rock from . . . well, any other rock. Whatever other rock types there were. His parents' desire to teach science had paled in comparison to their love of languages and history.

Her wide smile shone with just a hint of wickedness, and he shifted in his seat. "It's a love affair that continues to this day. A dirty one. Literally."

He took a hasty sip of water. Cleared his throat before speaking. "Okay. Why do you love supplementary rocks so much?"

Her smile never wavering, she dipped her chin at that, as if she were giving him credit. Acknowledging his exemplary work in the Dunce Arts. *Good one, Marcus,* he could almost hear her say in that husky, warm voice of hers.

Jesus, he was in such trouble.

Olaf came by to refill their water, but Marcus couldn't tear his gaze from April.

When she leaned forward, her cleavage—

No, he wouldn't look at her cleavage. He wouldn't.

"I love sedimentary rocks"—to her credit, she didn't emphasize the correct word—"because I love the stories they tell. If you study them closely enough, if you've trained enough, if you use the right tools, you can look at a particular spot and know whether there was once a lake there. You can know whether that area was part of a fluvial system, if a lahar came through after a volcanic event, if there was a landslide, a mudslide."

Her hands were tracing pictures in the air as she spoke, miming the movement of water and earth, a graceful visual shorthand for destruction and chaos and creation revealing itself under her scrutiny.

Shit. Even with those telling gestures, he didn't understand half of what she was saying, but he was so fucking turned on right now. Smart, accomplished, passionate women were his undoing, always, even though he knew—he *knew*—he'd never be enough for them. Not the fake him, and not the real him, either.

She waited until he met her eyes before continuing. Each word precise. Each word the echo of a siren, and he meant that in every conceivable way.

"You have to dig." She didn't look away, and he couldn't. "You have to look carefully, but there's a story waiting for you. It wants you to see the signs. It wants to be told."

Under that clear, calm gaze, he wanted to hide beneath the table once more. Cover his head and protect himself as the ground beneath him swayed and buckled.

Then she picked up her fork and speared another bite of her haricot verts, and he could breathe again. Could ignore for another moment that under his feet, the earth wasn't actually solid and still. It was moving, continually. And deep, deep below a placid, cool surface, even stone turned molten and fiery and liquid.

"Also, geology is a culmination of various sciences," she added in a casual aside. "Chemistry, physics, biology all come into play. I liked that too, because lots of different subjects interest me."

He shouldn't ask. He definitely wasn't going to ask.

And yet—

"Why do you say it's a dirty love affair?" he asked.

There it was.

Closing his eyes, he dropped his chin to his chest and exhaled hard through his nose. Shit. He didn't need yet more reason to want April, not when his gut already tightened with each glimpse of her pale, freckled skin bathed by candlelight. Not when she made a goddamn *living* spearing through surfaces and discovering what lay underneath, and he wanted to remain undiscovered. At least for the moment.

"Up until now, I've spent a good chunk of my workdays handling soil. Looking for contamination at former industrial sites and coordinating whatever cleanup is feasible under the circumstances." When he opened his eyes again, she was scraping the last bits of polenta from her plate. "The last few weeks, I've been dealing with a former pesticide facility, so the ground is contaminated with metals."

Well, that was a lot less sexy than he'd both anticipated and feared.

Despite her matter-of-fact tone, though, her work sounded . . . dangerous. Technical. Physical, in ways he hadn't anticipated.

He braced his elbows on the table, fascinated. "What will happen to that land, once the cleanup is done?"

She lifted a round shoulder. "Depending on what the owner of the site decides, it might become anything from a parking lot to a residential area."

He didn't understand. He truly didn't. How was such a transformation even possible? How could something so thoroughly poisoned became a place for a family? For a home?

"But that's not up to me, or even the consultant who'll be taking over the site starting next week." Her pale throat moved as she sipped her water, and he had to swallow hard himself. "Either the owner will devote the enormous amount of time and effort and money necessary to dig up all the contamination and dispose of it elsewhere, or they won't. Can't, in many cases."

He fiddled with the edge of his jacket cuff. "And if they won't? Or can't?"

With an arc of her hand, her forearm going from vertical to horizontal, she mimed something being dropped from above. "They'll tell the consultant to put a cap on the land. Two to five feet of clean soil over the contamination. It's cheaper. Easier."

"But?" There was a catch. He understood that, even without a single smidgen of background in geology.

"But under those circumstances, the land can never be used for any purpose that would require digging below surface level. The options for its use, its future, are limited forever." There was no judgment in her tone. It was a statement of fact, not a condemnation. "At least until that owner, or the next one, makes a different decision."

His chest hurt, and he forced himself to inhale slowly. Blow out the breath in several extended beats of his rabbiting heart.

Olaf came then to remove their plates, decrumb the tablecloth, and top off their water yet again. After he left, they sat without speaking and waited for dessert.

"You were worried you'd bore me to tears talking about your work," she finally said. "But you had it exactly backward, as it turned out."

She was watching him from across the table, her hair a silky wash of red-gold, her skin speckled with constellations, her wide mouth tilted at the corners. That wry, gorgeous smile caught at him, a hook towing him places he'd intended to avoid.

He wanted to make a different decision, though. He did.

"I'd like to go out with you again." It was a sudden rush of words, tumbling forth like the landslide she'd mentioned earlier. Mindless. Inexorable. "Dinner, if you want, or something else. An art gallery, or a museum, or . . ."

What would hold the interest of a woman like her?

How could *he* hold the interest of a woman like her?

Could he maintain control of his narrative *and* date her?

"Better yet, we can go to an indoor water park." He winked at her, forcing a confident grin. "I'm always happy to show off my hard work at the gym."

Eventually, if all went well, if he decided he could trust her, he would let her dig further beneath his surface. In the meantime, he would entertain her the best way Well-Groomed Golden Retriever Marcus knew how. It could work. It *would* work.

For the first time since he'd met her, April appeared stunned.

Her lips were parted, her eyes wide, her body motionless. She didn't make a sound, not one, before Olaf arrived in a burst of terrible timing to lay their desserts before them.

He disappeared quietly, and then it was just the two of them again.

She bit her lip, eyes downcast, and Marcus knew. Without her needing to say a word. He waited anyway, prepared to absorb the blow.

The answer was as clear to her as it was to him, evidently.

How could he hold the interest of a woman like her? He couldn't. He didn't.

"I'm sorry, Marcus," she began, her voice quiet and reluctant, "but I don't think that's a great idea."

And there it was. The kick to his chest he'd expected.

"Okay." He didn't say more. Couldn't, not through the ache beneath his ribs.

"It's just—" She hesitated. "It wouldn't work. Not under the circumstances."

Even though he hadn't asked for more of an explanation, it seemed she was giving him one anyway. He just hoped she was kind enough to cushion the blow, rather than saying it outright: *You're too shallow and stupid for me.*

And how could he blame her for thinking that, when she'd spent almost an entire meal in the company of his public persona?

"I, um, write *Gods of the Gates* fanfic," she said, her cheeks suddenly rosy. "Including some stories that are . . . kind of explicit."

Now he was the one startled into stillness and silence. She

wrote fanfiction? *Sexy* fanfiction? And given both her Twitter handle and the photo she'd posted, her OTP must be—

"I write almost exclusively about Lavinia. And Aeneas. So you can see how it would be a little weird to date you, after devoting hundreds of thousands of words to you—" She paused. "Well, not *you*, really, but an Aeneas who *looks* like you. Anyway, after devoting hundreds of thousands of words to a you-looking Aeneas falling in love and, um—"

Fucking.

The word she was looking for was definitely *fucking*.

"—*being intimate* with Lavinia," she finished.

Hundreds of thousands of words about Aeneas and Lavinia. Which meant she wasn't a short-timer or a newbie. No, she'd been posting for a while. And he'd be willing to bet her fics were as intelligent and incisive as she was, which meant she wouldn't go unnoticed on AO3 by the Lavineas community.

He'd almost definitely read her work, then.

She might even—no. He'd know if she were on the Lavineas server. Somehow, he'd know.

Still, he had to ask. Just to be certain.

"I've read fanfic on occasion," he said slowly. "Out of curiosity, what name do you post your stories under?"

Her teeth had sunk into her lower lip again, and her flush had washed away her freckles. On the tablecloth, her fingers were clasped together tightly.

She released her lip. Exhaled.

Then, with clear reluctance, she finally answered his question.

"I'm Unapologetic Lavinia Stan," she said. "Don't tell anyone, and *don't* read my fics."

Lavineas Server DMs, One Year Ago

Unapologetic Lavinia Stan: No matter what LavineasOTP might argue, I firmly believe that you can't call your fic a "slow burn" if they bang in the first chapter. That's a violation of all known slow-burn principles and subject to various penalties, including—but not limited to—major side-eyeing by yours truly.

Book!AeneasWouldNever: I was a bit surprised too. To be fair, however, it's an arranged-marriage AU. For succession purposes, they have to sleep together. The slow-burn part can refer to the emotional ties they form, maybe?

Unapologetic Lavinia Stan: They banged and enjoyed it. If it's a perfunctory boning, only mildly enjoyable for all involved, sure, I can overlook the transgression. But if multiple, mutual orgasms are had: NOPE.

Book!AeneasWouldNever: I didn't actually read the love scenes closely. Thus, I bow to your superior wisdom on this issue.

Unapologetic Lavinia Stan: THANK YOU. Now, on to more important matters.

Unapologetic Lavinia Stan: Speaking of slow burns: Are you feeling better? Fever all gone?

Book!AeneasWouldNever: Yes. Thank you for asking, Ulsie. :-)

7

THE SEXY FICS WERE AN EXCUSE, OF COURSE.

April definitely didn't want Marcus reading them or telling his two million followers about them before she'd explained herself to the Lavineas community, but they didn't constitute an insurmountable obstacle to a second date.

What did: Marcus's insistence on performing for her.

Sometimes, on certain job sites, the driller used a direct push rig to collect soil samples, instead of a hollow-stem auger rig. It was easier that way. Cleaner too.

The downside: They often couldn't get beyond a certain depth with a direct push rig.

On one job, they'd had to stop a mere three feet below the surface, because they kept getting refusal again and again. Until, in the end, they'd had to swap rigs, because they weren't accomplishing anything.

The experience was entirely too reminiscent of tonight's date with Marcus.

With their conversation about the *Gods of the Gates* crew, she'd gotten three feet down.

Then she'd hit refusal. Again and again.

If he didn't want her to see below his very attractive surface, she wouldn't. Simple as that. But since the surface didn't interest her nearly as much as what lay underneath, she wasn't courting frustration by going on a second date with him. No matter how much she suddenly wanted him.

As shocked as she remained that he evidently wanted *her*. At least enough to request a second meeting.

This was truly the oddest date ever.

She'd eaten several bites of her lemon-lavender panna cotta—delicious, not soapy-tasting at all—before she realized he hadn't spoken for quite a while. When she looked up, he was staring at her, his face . . .

It was slack. Blank.

Until, in a blink, it wasn't anymore. Instead, that aggravating, empty smile beamed out at her once more. "You really don't want me to read your stories?"

She considered the matter for a few moments.

"I mean, I guess you can. But it might be a little weird, like I said." Getting weirder by the moment, actually. "If you do, check the ratings before you start. To avoid unnecessary awkwardness, I'd skip the ones rated *E* for *explicit*."

He seemed particularly intrigued by his panna cotta now. In a slow, careful movement, he delved into the custard and emerged with a perfect spoonful. "Maybe I'll read one of your stories some-day. I can always skim key portions, as needed."

No way he'd ever actually go on AO3 and look for her fics. But still—

"*Pretty Man*, my prostitute/client modern alternate uni-verse . . ." She crinkled her nose. "Yeah, don't choose that one. You'd be skimming the whole thing."

It was one of her earliest fics, written before her partnership with BAWN, and it wasn't her best work.

Marcus looked up from another delicate spoon incursion into

his dessert. His smooth cheeks—he must have shaved right before coming to the restaurant—creased in a sudden grin.

His brow quirked. "I take it I'm the prostitute?"

"*Aeneas* is the prostitute," she emphasized.

"But he's pretty." He took his time savoring the spoonful of custard. "Thus the title."

"Well, yes." Obviously.

"And since you said Aeneas looks like me in your fics, that must mean—"

"Yes, yes." She rolled her eyes. "You're very pretty, Marcus. Which you well know."

His grin abruptly died, and she had no idea why shadows seemed to gather beneath blue-gray eyes gone solemn. Intent. So unexpectedly vulnerable that something twisted inside her chest.

Not her heart. Definitely not her heart.

"In your story . . ." He played with his spoon, looking down as he rotated it in his grip again and again. "Is he *only* pretty?"

Ah. There it was. A new layer beneath that pristine surface of his.

And dammit, yes, that was her heart aching for him. Just a little.

"He's very pretty. Gorgeous." With a seemingly idle motion, she tapped her spoon against her porcelain ramekin until he raised his stricken eyes to her again. Then she told him the rest. "Also underestimated and honorable and quite intelligent. I have no interest in writing about a man who offers nothing but good looks and easy charm. But hidden depths fascinate me."

There it was. One last chance.

And if he was as smart as she was beginning to suspect he was, he'd realize it.

Marcus blinked at her, lines scoring deep between his brows.

But he didn't say anything more, and she didn't intend to push him anywhere he didn't want to go.

She couldn't resist one final nudge, though. "Have you ever been tempted to write a fix-it fic yourself? A story where you'd put right whatever went wrong in the show? After Dido and Aeneas's relationship went off the rails, maybe?"

The throwaway remark was a bit rude, and she was sorry for that, but she wanted to hear his response. Wanted to see a bit more of the man under pressure.

He muttered something that sounded like, *You have no idea.*

"I'm—" Clearing his throat, he spoke more loudly. "I'm . . . uh, delighted with the talent and hard work of our scriptwriters, of course. And, um, that was the story we got. That was the script. It makes total sense."

From his verging-on-pained expression, his stilted words, he might have been starring in an impromptu hostage video. Ironically, it was the worst acting she'd ever seen him do, and that included his hilarious feigned ignorance of what *geology* meant earlier that evening.

She smiled at him, highly entertained.

"There's—there's no alternative script, no alternate universe, so . . ." He spread his hands. "Yes, I'm thrilled with Aeneas's story. Completely. Dido's too."

Yes. Very convincing. He was going to need to rehearse his answers a few more times before his press junket for the sixth season began.

Although . . .

Her smile widened.

Damn, he *was* smart. By playing Mr. Dim-and-Pretty all these years, he'd managed to avoid publicly discussing scripts and story lines and the way his show diverged from E. Wade's books.

Instead, he could focus on workout routines and grooming rituals, subjects that wouldn't get him into trouble with his showrunners or costars.

She leaned conspiratorially close, propped on her elbows. "There's no alternate universe, that's true." This time, she tapped her spoon against his ramekin. Winked at him. "Unless you write fanfic and come up with one. Like I do."

He didn't smile, as she'd anticipated.

Instead, head tilted, he gazed at her. Pressed his lips together. Rested his own elbows on the table and spoke haltingly, his voice barely audible despite the few inches separating them.

"Growing up, I—" His throat bobbed. "I was never much of a writer. Or a reader, for that matter."

This . . . this wasn't a tale she'd heard before. Not in any interview. Not in any blog post.

"I liked stories. Loved stories." He gave his head an impatient shake. "Of course I do. I wouldn't be an actor if I didn't. But—"

This close, she dragged his subtle scent into her lungs with every breath. Herbal. Musky.

This close, she could measure the true length of his eyelashes, trace how they fanned and turned pale gold at their tips.

This close, she couldn't miss the raw sincerity in his words, in his pained eyes.

She held very still, a steady presence as he seemed to struggle for words. "But?"

Softly. Softly. An invisible hand holding his as he faltered, not a shove in the back.

With his thumb and middle finger, he pinched his temples. Exhaled. "From the very beginning, there were issues. I took a long time to begin speaking. And once I started school, I kept, uh . . . kept reversing my letters and numbers."

Oh. *Oh.*

She knew where this was going now, but he needed to get there in his own time. In his own way. "Okay."

"My parents blamed the teachers, so they decided my mom should homeschool me. She taught at a nearby prep school, so she was more than qualified." His little huff of laughter didn't contain a single trace of actual amusement. "We all found out pretty quickly that the teachers weren't the problem. I was."

No, that couldn't stand unchallenged. "Marcus, having d—"

He didn't seem to hear her. "No matter how much she had me read, no matter how much she had me write, no matter how many vocabulary lists she made for me, I was a terrible speller. I had terrible handwriting. I couldn't write or read quickly, couldn't pronounce things correctly, couldn't always understand what I'd read."

Fuck. That early interview with Marcus, the one that had cemented his reputation as amiable but not especially bright, now seemed—

"My parents thought I was lazy. Defiant." His eyes met hers, and they *were* defiant. Daring her to judge him, to second the condemnation of his family. "I only found out there was a name for my problem after I dropped out of college and moved to LA. A name other than *stupidity*, anyway."

Chin haughty, no hint of a smile softening that famous mouth, he waited. Knowing, somehow, that he didn't need to use the word himself.

"You're dyslexic." She pitched her voice low, to protect his privacy. "Marcus, I had no idea."

That stony expression didn't flicker.

"No one does, except Alex." When her brows furrowed, he clarified. "Alex Woodroe. Cupid. My best friend. He's the one who figured it out, since one of his ex-girlfriends had dyslexia too. Diagnosed, unlike mine."

The bitterness in that last phrase painted the back of her tongue, and she pushed her panna cotta to the side. No need to get custard in her hair, and she wasn't hungry anymore, not after hearing his story.

The skin over his knuckles seemed stretched to its limits, his fists almost as white as the tablecloth beneath them. When she rested a fingertip on one of those bony knuckles, a vein in his temple throbbed.

"Marcus . . ." Since he didn't move away from her touch, she traced a gentle line across the back of his hand. "One of the smartest, most talented people I know is dyslexic. He's an amazing writer too."

Sometime after she'd beta-read and proofed a couple of his fics for the first time, BAWN had told her about his dyslexia via DM, amid a flurry of apologies for any spelling errors.

I have voice-to-text software, he wrote, but it sometimes has issues with homonyms. I'm sorry. I afraid I won't be much help proofreading your fics.

I can deal with spelling on my own, she'd written back. Where I need help is plotting and making sure I remain true to the characters, even in a modern AU. Emotional depth too. All strengths of yours. If you could help me with those bits, I'd be very grateful.

He hadn't responded for a long time.

I can do that, he'd eventually written.

"There are workarounds," she said, when Marcus remained silent and still beneath her gaze, beneath her touch. "I'm sure you've found them already."

When she withdrew her hand, he startled, then shifted restlessly in his seat.

At the heat lingering on her fingertip, the guilt churning within her gut at touching another man while thinking of BAWN, she did the same.

"Yes. Lots of workarounds." He cleared his throat. "This person you know, the one with dyslexia. The smart, talented one. Does he write fanfic too?"

She had to smile. "That's how I know what a great writer he is."

"What name does he use?" As Marcus scooped out a perfect semi-oval of custard, his attention once more seemed entirely focused on his spoon. "For his stories, I mean. In case I ever visit your fanfiction site."

Was that an offhand question? A test of her discretion?

Either way, she wasn't answering.

The linen napkin was smooth and crisp under her fingers as she plucked it from her lap, folded it, and placed it next to her half-finished ramekin of panna cotta.

It was a gesture of finality, matching her firm tone. "I'm sorry. I can't tell you that without his permission."

"Ah." After one final spoonful of the dessert, he nudged his ramekin aside too. "I understand."

Olaf appeared from nowhere to remove their dishes, refill their water, and offer coffee or after-dinner drinks. Only moments after they both refused and their server faded into the gorgeous woodwork once more, her jaw cracked in a huge, unexpected yawn.

Marcus snorted.

"Good thing we're almost done for the evening." He pointed a scolding finger at her. "Don't stay up too late on the computer, either. After cleaning all day, you need your rest."

She shook her head at him, exasperated and amused.

So he *did* remember their Twitter DMs, where she'd briefly described her plans for the weekend. Because of course he did.

His gaze held a new warmth, a fondness she wouldn't have anticipated. Not after one evening together, not given how carefully he guarded himself. At least until just a few minutes ago.

If he asked her on a second date again, after that conversation—

Well, he wouldn't. Instead, he'd asked for the check.

When it arrived, he wouldn't let her see the total, much less pay her half.

"I can get the tip, at least," she protested.

Brows high in a silent rejoinder, he pinned her with a look that said everything.

I'm starring in the most popular television show in the world. I have a multimillion-dollar home in LA. According to fashion magazines, I pay four hundred dollars per haircut and use seven different styling products every day, each of which costs more than you make per hour.

Okay, so maybe she'd filled in a few of the specifics herself, but still. Those were some damn expressive eyebrows. No wonder the man could afford that home nestled in the Hollywood hills.

Out loud, he said only, "I believe I can afford dinner."

She didn't argue further. Her exhaustion was dragging at her shoulders now, turning her legs into aching pillars, and she couldn't help a sense of . . .

Deflation, maybe.

This was over. Whatever had happened between them tonight, it was done as soon as he handled the credit card receipt and stood to go.

But after he signed his name and closed the little leather book, he didn't stand. Instead, he took a sip of water, those cloudy blue eyes—if she was judging the angle of his gaze correctly—resting on her hair. Her cheeks. Her bare arms.

Then he met her own gaze. His chest expanded in a huge inhalation, and he reached across the table. Laid his fingertips lightly on the back of her wrist and spoke as she tried not to shiver at his touch.

"If you don't want a second date with me, that's absolutely fine, and I promise not to bother you again. We can take a few selfies before leaving, post them tonight or tomorrow, and go our separate ways." That knife-sharp jaw was working again, but he managed to sound calm. Sure. "That said, I want to make certain you understand something before we leave."

With her free hand, she fumbled for her water glass. Sipped away the dryness in her throat before responding.

"Okay." Whether he knew it or not, his fingertips were moving on her flesh. Just a millimeter back and forth, in the subtlest caress she'd ever known, and it *burned*. "What should I understand?"

"Your fanfiction, whatever you've written—" His fingers stilled. "It may make things a bit awkward, a bit more complicated, but it doesn't bother me. It doesn't stop me from hoping to see you again. If that was your main reason for turning me down, I wanted you to know."

If that was your main reason.

He knew she'd been fibbing to save his feelings, and no wonder. She wasn't much of a liar. Never had been. And unlike him, she had no natural talent for acting.

As he straightened in his chair, his fingertips slid away from her wrist, and she almost snatched them back.

"If you had other reasons, though, that's fine too." His voice became oddly formal then. Solemn, as if their dinner together held more meaning for him than she'd realized. "And if this is the last time we meet, please know it was an honor to spend the evening with you, April Whittier. AKA Unapologetic Lavinia Stan."

She'd given him a final chance, and he'd taken it.

Now she had hers.

She wasn't hesitating another moment.

"Let's do a second date," she told him. "Are you free the day after tomorrow?"

That smile. Fuck, that smile.

It banished the shadows in the dim restaurant. Lit his eyes. Turned her buoyant and giddy, light as helium, as his hand reached for hers again and tethered her safely to the earth.

"Yes," he said, his fingers interlacing with her own. "Yes. For you, I'm free."

Rating: Explicit

Fandoms: Gods of the Gates – E. Wade, Gods of the Gates (TV)

Relationships: Aeneas/Lavinia, Lavinia & Turnus, Aeneas & Venus, Aeneas & Jupiter

Additional Tags: <u>Alternate Universe – Modern</u>, <u>Sex Work</u>, <u>Explicit Sexual Content</u>, <u>Dirty Talk</u>, <u>Porn with Feelings</u>, <u>Angst and Fluff and Smut</u>, <u>Hurt/Comfort</u>, <u>The Author Regrets Nothing</u>, <u>Except Maybe All Her Previous Life Choices That Led to This Fic</u>, <u>Hard to Say Really</u>, <u>But Seriously Prepare for the Smutathon</u>

Stats: Words: 12815 Chapters: 4/4 Comments: 102 Kudos: 227 Bookmarks: 34

Pretty Man
Unapologetic Lavinia Stan

Summary:

When Aeneas arrives in Latium upon the orders of his mother and grandfather, he finds himself disoriented, guilt-stricken, and without enough resources to survive. Unless, of course, he uses the one resource he values least: his astounding handsomeness.

Luckily, his first sex work client is Lavinia. He won't need another.

Notes:

This is not at all accurate when it comes to sex work, I'm certain, as I wanted to keep things fluffy. But I did intend to explore how two people defined by their appearances in totally opposite ways could find comfort and love and a sense of self-worth through the medium of sex.

———————————————

Aeneas sees the woman before she spots him. And she is definitely looking for him, or someone like him; there's no doubt about that. No woman comes to this street at this time of night for anything other than what he can offer: sex. For a price.

He hasn't decided on that price yet. This first night, he intends to play it by ear.

Once he sees her face under a streetlight, pale and crooked and homely, he knows: she'll pay plenty. This one act should make him enough for a night at a hotel, at least. And in return for shelter, he'll give her the best fuck of her life.

"No need to keep looking, sweetheart," he calls out from the shadows. "Here I am."

Only, once she sees him too, she laughs and keeps walking.

"Too pretty for me," she calls over her shoulder, and he finds himself somehow startlingly indignant.

"Excuse me," he huffs.

"Consider yourself excused," she says, not looking back, and without quite understanding why, he discovers he wants to change her mind.

8

THAT NIGHT, AFTER SHE'D SHOWERED AND CHANGED INTO her pajamas, April opened her laptop and went online. Most likely, she'd received several new DMs from BAWN, but she wasn't ready to face those quite yet, much less the Twitter reaction to whatever dinner pics had been posted already.

AO3, then, to check the reaction to her most recent story.

She'd posted her one-shot fic late last night, in response to the Lavineas server's self-declared fanfic initiative, Aeneas's Angry Boner Week.

Her contribution had received a gratifying number of kudos and comments so far. All necessary and welcome encouragement after one of her rare forays into book-canon-compliant story-telling, rather than a self-created modern AU.

In the story, Lavinia confronted one of her ex's soldiers outside the home she shared with Aeneas—a soldier who spat upon her for breaking her betrothal to Turnus, his dead leader, and threatened to do worse. Instead of calling for help from her husband, she drove away the intruder with her own sword, and when Aeneas heard about the incident, he marched toward his homely, resentful wife, inexplicably enraged by her carelessness when it came to her own safety, and—

Yeah. Their platonic marriage of convenience became decidedly less platonic, but somewhat more convenient in terms of, say, mutual sexual gratification.

April had originally intended to write a fluffy modern AU, as normal. But somehow, even before their date, picturing a hero with Marcus Caster-Rupp's face meeting, falling for, and fucking a woman—albeit a woman who looked like Lavinia, not April—in the modern world had suddenly seemed . . . *odd*. Exploitative in a way it never had before.

When she'd written the story, she'd figured returning to modern AUs might take her a month or two after their date. Until thoughts of the actor himself no longer interfered with thoughts about the character he played. Until she could separate the two more effectively in her mind once more. Until he was no longer so much of a real *person* to her, but simply the physical vessel in which her chosen hero lived and loved.

Now she was wondering whether she might have to switch her OTP permanently. To Cyprian and Cassia, maybe, forever stuck on that damn island and pining for one another. Or Cupid and Psyche, torn apart by the machinations of Venus and Jupiter.

But she wasn't ejecting herself from her favorite fandom without good reason. Contemplating her other options could wait until after a second date, at least.

Idly, she checked the other stories posted under the Aeneas's Angry Boner Week tag, and she had to laugh. Almost everyone else on their server had gone full throttle on the modern AUs, and she should have known.

Her recent online activities really *had* spawned countless fics. Aeneas's angry boners these past several days all seemed to be occurring in the presence of a Lavinia he'd met on Twitter, a Lavinia he'd saved from internet bullies, a Lavinia with whom he fell in love and lust over the course of a single, fateful dinner.

In the stories, he dispatched countless rude paparazzi, a dozen jealous Didos, and battalions of sneering fanboys, and then—his blood still hot from anger—saw Lavinia in the candlelight, eyes wide, mouth an O of shock and confusion and—

Well. Virgil's Aeneas might have ascended to the realm of the gods after death because of his dauntless piety, but in this week's fics, Little Aeneas had risen to turgid heights for decidedly different reasons.

Reading those fics was hot. Undeniably hot. Also uncomfortable in an entirely new way. At one point, she had to start skimming sex scenes, instead of lingering happily over them as she usually did, because it was Marcus in her head. Marcus on the page. Marcus making her ache.

After leaving her kudos and comments, she was eager to log out of AO3 and turn to the Lavineas server instead. And once more, she ignored BAWN's DMs, delaying what she needed to do and say.

Not much recent activity in the group threads. So far, they didn't appear to have spotted any photos of her date with Marcus on Twitter or Insta, but that was only a matter of time. And if the server's response to his public dinner invitation was any guide, she needed to prepare herself for one hell of an uproar.

Can you BELIEVE IT???!!! Mrs. Pius Aeneas had virtually screeched Wednesday night on her brand-new OMFG MC-R Asked Out a Fan chat thread, linking to the relevant tweets.

LaviniaIsMyGoddessAndSavior responded with an endless stream of heart-eyes and streaming-tears emojis, too emotional for mere words.

I TOLD YOU he was really a nice guy. I TOLD YOU! TopMeAeneas crowed. The way he defended her, I just— Her subsequent legs-spread, crotch-up gif said it all, really.

Did you see that awful thread? It really was kind of him, Lavineas-OTP wrote. That poor woman.

April had winced at LavineasOTP's post. Taken off her glasses and rubbed her eyes, wondering if she'd made a terrible mistake.

Pity. Shit, she despised pity, and the last thing she wanted to be was *that poor woman.*

Then Book!AeneasWouldNever, largely absent from the server for a few days, had interjected. Why does everyone assume he asked her out of kindness alone? I mean, look at her. She's pretty, and obviously very talented.

His comment had changed the tenor of the thread, which—after a flurry of posts agreeing with his take—had then shifted to speculation as to what the date might entail.

April had been tempted to post endless heart-eyes and streaming-tear emojis herself.

Instead, she'd simply DMed BAWN one last time before bed. Thank you. Just . . . thank you.

For what? he'd immediately responded, but she was too tired to explain.

We can talk about it this weekend. I have some things I need to tell you. For now, though, I have to get some sleep. If I don't hear from you before then, have a safe trip home, okay? xx

The blinking dots had flashed and flashed. Okay. Sweet dreams, Ulsie. I'll be back in your time zone soon.

They both lived in California. She knew that much.

She also knew he traveled a lot for work, something else they'd had in common until now. She got the sense he was a consultant of some sort, although she didn't know for sure. In recent months, they'd both mentioned evaluating their career paths and their next professional steps. Finally, she knew he was a *he*, unlike the vast majority of Lavineas fans in their group.

As soon as he'd helped set up the server, in fact, he'd explicitly informed everyone, concerned they'd feel misled or uncomfortable if they found out later.

If my presence here ever makes any of you feel unsafe in any way, please tell me, and I'll immediately bow out, he'd written. *P.S. As a cishet guy, there are certain threads that may not be as applicable to me, so please forgive me for sitting them out.*

Via DM, he'd said a bit more to April last year. *If you notice me being inadvertently creepy or offensive in any way, please, PLEASE let me know. I might not see it.*

She'd agreed, but so far, she hadn't had to intervene. Not once. Other than the prompt way he bowed out of conversations about the hotness and fuckability of various actors, his maleness didn't seem to influence his interactions on the server much.

Of course, he didn't write sex into his fics either, which had made her wonder.

Maybe sex and sexuality in general made him uncomfortable. Maybe writing sex into his fics felt somehow predatorial or boundary-crossing to him, given his status as one of the few men in their group. Or maybe he just didn't like writing explicit scenes. Some people didn't.

Not April. She loved including the Bang That Was Promised in her fics. But she'd long ago decided to either steer those particular stories toward other beta readers, rather than BAWN, or redact any explicit sections in the drafts she sent to him, because she absolutely, one hundred percent did not want to cause him any discomfort.

Her latest story, accordingly, had been betaed by TopMe-Aeneas, not BAWN, even though—for once—she'd delved a bit into canon, or at least canon-compliance.

She shoved her glasses more firmly onto the bridge of her nose.

Okay. No more delays.

She could either sit against her headboard and think about BAWN, or read the man's actual messages from that morning and respond to him. Tell him what he needed to know and gauge his reaction.

> **Book!AeneasWouldNever:** You went canon-compliant, huh? Bold choice, Ulsie.

> **Book!AeneasWouldNever:** Didn't I say you'd rock canon if you ever tried it? You really captured Lavinia's resentment at the marriage, the reluctance in her attraction, in a way most can't. Also, the description of her wielding the sword: A+. Narrating a clear action sequence informed by her character's history, her personality, and the skills she would and wouldn't have is damn hard, and you pulled it off.

She smiled at the screen. BAWN was so supportive of her work. Always.

Funny how his praise of her action sequence echoed Marcus's description of how the *Gods of the Gates* crew handled the show's battle scenes. That approach must be more common than she'd realized as a fight sequence newbie.

Later that morning, he'd sent one more message.

> **Book!AeneasWouldNever:** You said you had something to talk to me about this weekend?

Well, she supposed that was her cue. He deserved to know what was happening. In so many ways, for so many reasons.

She wanted to know more about him too. Wanted to meet

him in person at the next Con of the Gates, despite his professed shyness. Maybe tonight, once she took that first step and told him who she was on Twitter, showed him what she looked like, they could move toward a relationship that didn't exist solely online.

And if whatever was happening between her and Marcus would damage her chances with BAWN, she would happily—or at least, not overly *un*happily—DM the actor and tell him the second date was off. He could comfort himself with one of his many hair products.

Biting her lip, she winced at her own callousness.

He wasn't the shallow, uninteresting man she'd once thought him. She knew that now. He could be hurt. *Would* be hurt, if she changed her mind about their second date. But for BAWN, she'd handle the guilt and forgo the opportunity to dig deeper beneath Marcus's surface.

For BAWN, she'd expose her heart now.

Unapologetic Lavinia Stan: Thank you for the lovely comments, here and on AO3. I have a feeling I'll be writing a lot more canon in the near future. Which is related to what I need to tell you, actually.

Unapologetic Lavinia Stan: So . . . you saw that uproar the other night, when Marcus Caster-Rupp asked out a fan on Twitter?

Unapologetic Lavinia Stan: That fan was, uh, me. I use the handle @Lavineas5Ever there. Please don't tell the rest of the group yet. I will eventually, but I wanted to talk to you about it first.

Unapologetic Lavinia Stan: We had our date tonight. Dinner at a restaurant. I'm posting pics later tonight on Twitter, although other people in the restaurant probably have their own shots up already.

Unapologetic Lavinia Stan: When you're online, please let me know. Let's chat.

With that information, he could see her at long last. Face. Body. Caught talking or eating. From the side, the back, the front. In motion. Still.

Oh, God, her heartbeat was echoing in her ears. And when BAWN's response popped up within seconds, she literally jumped.

Book!AeneasWouldNever: I'm here.

Book!AeneasWouldNever: Wow. This is a surprising development.

Book!AeneasWouldNever: It's wonderful to see your face, Ulsie.

Unapologetic Lavinia Stan: Only my face?

Book!AeneasWouldNever: All of you. I just checked, and there are some very nice shots of your dinner tonight appearing online, as you said.

Wonderful, he'd said. *Very nice.*

Slowly, her heart rate was calming, the prickle of nervous sweat at her hairline diminishing.

It was okay. It was okay. He'd seen her, and hadn't turned away.

She should have known. BAWN wasn't shallow or unkind.

He hadn't even seemed especially shocked by news that she'd gone on a date with one half of their OTP, weirdly enough. Unable to resist, she did a quick internet search of her own, to discover what version of herself he'd just seen, and . . .

Yes. There she was, on Twitter and Insta and one entertainment blog post already. In some shots, those bastards had caught her midchew. In others, though, she was smiling.

In one, Marcus was leaning across the table, staring at her intently. Touching the back of her wrist in a way that made her shiver to remember, shiver to see from an outsider's perspective.

Unapologetic Lavinia Stan: You're right. I just found a few of the pics.

Book!AeneasWouldNever: I imagine it must be hard to have your private life suddenly so visible. Does it bother you?

Unapologetic Lavinia Stan: Well, it's not my FAVORITE thing in the world, but it's okay. In general, I don't give a shit what strangers think. Just the people I care about.

Book!AeneasWouldNever: Good.

Book!AeneasWouldNever: So how was the date?

Here be dragons, she thought.

Because she couldn't really tell him much about her topsy-turvy dinner with the man who played Aeneas, could she? Not without violating Marcus's privacy and contradicting his chosen public persona, which she refused to do.

Even if that hadn't been an issue, though, she wouldn't have described the date in detail. If BAWN cared about her the same way she did him, hearing those details would sting, and she wasn't about to hurt him. Not for anything.

God, if he'd gone on a date with a famous actress, she couldn't even imagine how insecure and worried she'd be. So no, she wasn't sharing specifics. And depending on how he responded to their conversation tonight, there might not be any future specifics to omit.

Unapologetic Lavinia Stan: It was pleasant. He seems like a genuinely decent man. The food was EXCELLENT too. If you make it to San Francisco for Con of the Gates, maybe we could go there? My treat.

Book!AeneasWouldNever: Any interesting tidbits? Behind-the-scenes secrets he let slip? Or personal anecdotes?

Unapologetic Lavinia Stan: Nope. None.

Unapologetic Lavinia Stan: He was very circumspect.

Book!AeneasWouldNever: Do you want to see him again?

His assumption that Marcus would be willing to see her again, that the existence or lack of a second date was entirely up to her, was flattering—but BAWN had entirely ignored her mention of meeting in person. Dammit.

And she wouldn't lie to him, so double dammit.

She hoped he wouldn't take her answer the wrong way.

Unapologetic Lavinia Stan: We agreed to meet again.

While she was still in the midst of typing the second part to her answer, the part where she'd explain her willingness to cancel that agreed-upon date with Marcus if BAWN wanted to meet in person instead, her friend's next message blinked to life on her screen.

Then—

Then, she had to swallow against the taste of bile as she read BAWN's DM. Read it again, just to be sure she'd understood it correctly. The actual information, yes, but also the possible implications.

Book!AeneasWouldNever: I'm glad we got a chance to chat tonight, because I wanted you to know I'm traveling again soon. I have a new job. Where I'm going, I don't think I'll have much internet access, if any. So this may be the last time you hear from me, at least for a while.

Book!AeneasWouldNever: I'm sorry, Ulsie.

AS SOON AS he returned to his hotel room from the restaurant, Marcus called his best friend.

"I don't know what to do." He didn't bother with formalities, not even a token apology for bothering Alex at such an ungodly hour—ha, ungodly—in Spain. "I need advice."

To Alex's credit, he only called Marcus an asshole once or twice before asking for details. Even though Alex was still filming for one last week, still suffering through that endless climactic battle sequence, and still fuming over the abrupt, surprising end to Cupid's character arc.

Thank fuck for good friends.

Gratefully, Marcus spilled the whole story, April and Ulsie and Book!AeneasWouldNever and—all of it. How he hadn't confessed his own fanfic alter ego to April, even when she'd told him about hers. How he was going on a second date with her soon. How he didn't know what to say to Ulsie as Book!AeneasWouldNever, or if he could even continue corresponding with her in that context without either explaining the truth or being a shady prick.

"Maybe I should tell her who I am." He scrubbed a hand over his face. "She probably wouldn't let it slip to anyone. When I asked her for the AO3 handle of her friend with dyslexia, she wouldn't tell me. She seemed very protective of his—my—privacy."

Which hadn't surprised him, not after more than two years of close online friendship. Still, people's online identities didn't always match their real-life selves. He was evidence enough of that.

To win a second chance with April, he'd needed to reveal something personal about himself. Something private. And after a minute or two of thought, he had. But he'd chosen the revelation of his dyslexia for a reason. If that bit of news broke, he honestly didn't care that much. Plenty of other actors were open about being dyslexic, and joining their ranks wouldn't bother him.

That particular secret wasn't as damaging as, say, the fact that he'd been aping a shallow, dim stereotype of a Hollywood actor for years. Or that he'd posted comments and written stories about his character, his show, that clearly showed just how much he hated the scripts he'd been given in recent seasons.

"I want to tell her." He sighed and slumped over his phone. "But one inadvertent word to the wrong person, and I could lose everything."

His reputation in the industry. His prospects of future gainful employment. His hard-fought pride at everything he'd accomplished over two decades and the respect he'd earned from others.

With Alex making occasional, sleepy grunts of affirmation in the background, Marcus rambled for a while longer. A *long* while longer. By the time he eventually wound down and asked point-blank whether he should tell April about Book!AeneasWouldNever, his friend was too tired to sugarcoat anything.

Alex expressed his opinion in three short words: "Dude. Your *career*."

His judgment about further DMs with April as Book!-AeneasWouldNever required four instead: "Don't be a dick."

And that was that, in the end.

So by the time April finally appeared on the Lavineas server and responded to his earlier DMs, Marcus already knew what he had to do. Had to say.

I'm sorry, Ulsie, he dictated into the microphone, and he meant it.

The prospect of a second date with April shimmered in the near distance like an oasis. Or better yet, Virgil's description of the Elysian fields in the *Aeneid*, which the *Gates* crew had faithfully tried to bring to life for the finale. Welcoming. Blissful.

Still. Cutting off communication with her as Book!-AeneasWouldNever *hurt*. Worse than Marcus had even imagined. Worse than that time Ian hadn't sufficiently pulled his kick on camera and nailed Marcus right in the kidney.

But what else could he do? Ever since he'd walked her to her car after dinner and left her with his number in her phone, a squeeze of her hand, and a kiss on her cheek—

Warm. Velvety. Rose-scented. Infinitely nuzzle-able. God, he wanted her.

—he'd been considering his options, and as Alex had helpfully confirmed, he had none. Not really. Not unless he wanted to be either a fool or an asshole.

He wasn't a fool, despite what his parents and a good chunk of the world believed. And he wasn't enough of an asshole to keep communicating with April under another name without her knowledge.

The way he'd prodded her for inside information about himself as a sort of test, the way he'd discovered her feelings about their second date and public scrutiny under false pretenses, all that was bad enough. He wasn't doing worse. Not to the woman he'd been corresponding with for years, and not to the woman he'd met tonight.

If the second date didn't work out, Book!Aeneas could return early from his business trip, and their online friendship could resume, with her none the wiser. And if the second date *did* work out . . .

Well, without all those DMs, he'd have more time to spend with April in person.

Face-to-face. Body to body. Finally.

Although he didn't honestly know what he'd do without the Lavineas community and his writing. It was going to be a hard, hard adjustment. Worth it, though. For her.

Unapologetic Lavinia Stan: You won't have internet access? Not even on your phone?

Book!AeneasWouldNever: I'm not allowed to contact anyone outside work, not on this job.

Unapologetic Lavinia Stan: Uh

Unapologetic Lavinia Stan: Are you a spy, or

Unapologetic Lavinia Stan: Dammit.

Unapologetic Lavinia Stan: Look, BAWN, I want you to be honest with me.

Oh, no. No, no, no.
He didn't want to lie to her more than he already had, but—

Unapologetic Lavinia Stan: Did you see those pictures of me, and think

Book!AeneasWouldNever: Think what?

Unapologetic Lavinia Stan: Think maybe you weren't interested in talking to me anymore, because of them?

What? What the actual, ever-loving fuck was she talking about?

Book!AeneasWouldNever: NO.

Book!AeneasWouldNever: Absolutely not. JFC, Ulsie!

Unapologetic Lavinia Stan: Okay, so if that's not it, is this about my second date with Marcus? Because if you wanted to meet in person, at Con of the Gates or wherever, whenever, if

Unapologetic Lavinia Stan: If you were interested in me
that way, I could DM him. Cancel the second date.

At the confirmation that she'd grown just as attached to him
as he was to her, that she valued the man he'd shown himself to
be online—his real self—*more* than the gleaming star he'd put on
display earlier that night, Marcus collapsed in on himself.

Chin to chest, he covered his face. Breathed deeply. Tried to
recapture the certainty that had burned so brightly mere min-
utes ago.

Dude. Your career.

He couldn't meet her in person. He couldn't.

Which meant he was going to have to hurt her now, in ways
Marcus couldn't yet soothe, and he wanted Ian to kick him again.
Harder, this time.

Book!AeneasWouldNever: I can't. I'm so sorry.

Unapologetic Lavinia Stan: Okay.

Unapologetic Lavinia Stan: Okay. I guess I'll talk to you
whenever, then.

Book!AeneasWouldNever: Ulsie, I

Book!AeneasWouldNever: Please take care of yourself.

Unapologetic Lavinia Stan: Same to you.

Book!AeneasWouldNever: I'll miss you.

Unapologetic Lavinia Stan: Sure.

Unapologetic Lavinia Stan: I'd better go now. Bye.

Before he could say anything more, she was offline and gone.

He was going to see her the day after tomorrow. Any minute now, they'd be texting about exactly when and where to meet. Somehow, in that moment, the knowledge didn't help at all.

Rating: Mature

Fandoms: Gods of the Gates – E. Wade, Gods of the Gates (TV)

Relationships: Aeneas/Lavinia

Additional Tags: <u>Alternate Universe – Modern</u>, <u>Fluff and Smut</u>, <u>Celebrity!Aeneas</u>

Collections: Aeneas's Angry Boner Week

Stats: Words: 1036 Chapters: 1/1 Comments: 23 Kudos: 87 Bookmarks: 9

Rising Fury
LaviniaIsMyGoddessAndSavior

Summary:

Aeneas's invitation was only meant to be kind. But when the paparazzi insult his Twitter date, he finds anger isn't the only thing of his on the rise.

Notes:

Yeah, so I would die for @Lavineas5Ever, and also die to be her. It's complicated, okay?

———————————————

. . . last of the paparazzi slink out the restaurant door, broken cameras cradled in their arms.

Maybe they'll sue. He can't muster any real concern, not with Lavinia candlelit across the table, her lush mouth parted in shock, her breasts heaving with the aftermath of violent confrontation.

Blood running hot with fury, he finds his cock has become a divining rod, pointing hard and true toward the only relief for such deep, deep thirst: the woman he met on Twitter only yesterday.

Dimly, he hears the shattering of glass. The gasps of other diners.

"Um . . . Aeneas?" Her voice, sweet and low, only makes matters worse.

"Yes?" He stands tall and proud and erect. In this moment, anything she wants, he'll give her.

"I think you just knocked over a water glass with your dick," she says.

And so he has.

9

"MY TRAINER SAYS I SHOULD HAVE A CHICKEN BREAST within reach at all times," Marcus told his parents the next day. "The more protein the better, especially when you're trying to bulk up."

Which he wasn't. Not now, anyway.

That didn't matter, though. For the sake of this private show, pretense took precedence over reality.

He stretched out an arm and let it rest along the top of the dining room chair next to him. With a smug smile, he cast a caressing, lingering glance over the muscle definition evident beneath and below his tee. The bulge of his biceps. The thick solidity of his forearm. The veins on the back of his hand. All evidence of endless, sweat-soaked hours at innumerable hotel gyms around the world. All evidence of how seriously he took his job and how hard he worked at it.

In his profession, in the role he'd inhabited for seven years, his body was a tool to be maintained. Kept strong and flexible both. Polished. Admired by the audience.

He appreciated the actual exercise, how it felt and what it helped him accomplish, much more than how its results looked in the mirror. But once more, this wasn't about reality.

"You're supposed to carry a chicken breast at all times?" Horizontal lines scored across his mother's high forehead, as familiar as the graying ponytail at the nape of her neck. "How would that even work? Would you bring a cooler with you everywhere?"

Under the table, he tried to find enough open space to stretch out a bit, but amid the tangle of four chairs, his parents' own long legs, and the legs of the table itself, there was nowhere to go. Fair enough. If his knees were beginning to feel a bit cramped, he supposed he could suffer through the discomfort for another hour or so.

Like the rest of this San Francisco home, the dining room was barely large enough to serve its purpose. Five years ago, flush with *Gates* money, his parents' cramped quarters in mind, he'd offered to buy them something bigger. They'd immediately, and emphatically, refused. He hadn't asked a second time.

They didn't want what he had to give. Again: fair enough.

"No cooler necessary." He lifted his shoulder in a desultory shrug. "Ian, the guy who plays Jupiter, always has a serving of fish in a pocket somewhere. A pouch of tuna, or a filet of salmon."

That much, at least, was the truth. It was only one of many reasons Marcus and most of the cast avoided Ian.

Fishy motherfucker should've played Neptune, Carah had muttered only last week.

"The practice sounds . . . dubious, at least in terms of sanitation." His mother tilted her head, eyes narrowing behind her wire-rimmed glasses. "Why would you need to bulk up? Didn't you say you were done playing . . . your previous role?"

She still couldn't bear to say *Aeneas*. Not when she believed with every ounce of conviction in her ancient-languages-devoted heart that E. Wade's books had bastardized Virgil's source material, and that the *Gods of the Gates* showrunners had only dragged the demigod's lyrical, meaningful tale further into the muck.

His father agreed, of course.

"I'm done playing Aeneas, but I need to maintain a baseline fitness and strength level, even between jobs. Otherwise, the road back is too hard. So thanks for this." With a sweep of his hand, he indicated his half-finished plate of food. "You're helping me remain a prime physical specimen. Grade-A man meat."

His father didn't look up from his own plate of poached chicken and roasted asparagus, instead dragging a forkful of the tender poultry through the green goddess dressing he and his wife had prepared in their small, sunlit kitchen earlier that morning as Marcus watched.

When his parents cooked together, it was like his sword fight with Carah. A dance rehearsed so many times that each precise movement required little thought. No effort.

His parents didn't stumble. Not ever.

Lawrence picked fragile leaves from bundles of fragrant herbs while Debra snapped the offending woody ends off her asparagus stalks. Lawrence prepared the poaching liquid while Debra trimmed the chicken breasts. Spoons flashing in the sun, they tasted the dressing in the food processor, a slight tilt of the head and a moment of eye contact enough to indicate the need for a pinch more salt.

It was beautiful, in its own fashion.

As usual, Marcus had leaned against the cabinets closest to the door, safely out of their way, and watched, arms tight across his chest or against his sides.

If he took up more space, he'd become an intrusion. Unlike most of his lessons, that one hadn't taken long to sink in.

Marcus's mother rested her fork and knife neatly on her now-empty plate. "Will you be joining us for dinner too? We planned to go shopping this afternoon, then make grilled cioppino tonight. Your father intends to char some flatbreads while I mind the seafood skewers."

On their tiny deck, the two of them would crowd around the old charcoal grill, arguing amiably as they worked within arm's reach of one another. Another version of their dance. A tango, fiery and smoky, rather than the pristine waltz of the morning.

His parents did everything together. Always had, from as far back as Marcus could remember.

They cooked together. Wore blue button-down shirts and endless khaki slacks together. Washed and dried dishes together. Went on rambling after-dinner walks together. Read academic journal articles together. Translated ancient texts together. Bickered about the clear superiority of either Greek—in her case—or Latin—in his—together. Taught until retirement at the same prestigious private prep school together, in the same foreign languages department, once Debra no longer needed to homeschool Marcus.

Long ago, they'd also conducted late-night, not-quiet-enough conversations about their son together, in mutual accord about their growing concern and frustration and determination to help him succeed. To push him harder. To make him *understand* the importance of education, of books over looks, serious thought over frivolity.

From their cowritten opinion pieces about the *Gods of the Gates* books and series, he imagined that aspect of their partnership had never entirely disappeared, even after almost forty years. Much to the glee of various tabloid reporters.

So, yes, he was going to lie to them.

He directed a casual, gleaming smile to the table at large, focused on no one and nothing in particular. "I appreciate the invitation, but I have a dinner engagement tonight. In fact, I'll need to leave in an hour so I have enough time to get ready." Tousling his hair *just so* with a practiced, easy gesture, he winked at his mother. "This kind of beauty takes effort, you know. And with the ubiquity of smartphones, cameras are everywhere these days."

Her lips compressed, and her gaze sought her husband's.

Marcus pushed his plate an inch or two farther away, leaving a knob of chicken uneaten amid the sauce. There was never enough heat or acid in their green goddess dressing. Yet another truth that had survived decades.

His father had insisted Marcus's unsophisticated palate would appreciate subtlety if they only exposed him to it often enough. But insistence alone couldn't transform reality.

That was a lesson *they* should have learned more easily.

"We'd hoped to show you the new neighborhood park after dinner tonight." Lawrence finally looked away from his wife, his familiar blue-gray eyes solemn and magnified by the glasses he wore. "We could walk together. You always liked the outdoors."

As a child—hell, even as a sulky, bratty teenager—Marcus would have leaped at the offer. Outside their home, his body in motion worked exactly as it should, and the benches by the sidewalk reliably stayed in one place, facing one direction, unlike letters on the page. His parents might finally notice the one arena where he *did* excel. Might appreciate the talents he *did* have.

He could dance at their sides, at least for the space of a single night.

Instead, he'd been tasked with finishing the day's schoolwork as his parents walked every evening. He'd been wasting everyone's time and not working up to his potential, they'd said. Translating that passage should have taken him half an hour at most, they'd said. He needed to *learn*, they'd said.

Despite his native intelligence, he was lazy and recalcitrant and required routine and fair, predictable consequences for his behavior, they'd said.

"I'm sorry," he'd told them so many times, head bowed, until he'd finally realized there was no point. There was never any fucking point. Not to his apologies, which they didn't believe. Not to his efforts, which never bore enough fruit. Not to his shame, which curdled in his stomach and left him unable to eat dinner some evenings. Not to his occasional childish tears, after they left him in the darkening house night after night and walked away hand in hand.

"I'm sorry," he told them now, and part of him was. The part that still ached watching their graceful, two-person waltz from a safe, inalterable distance.

They cared about him. In their own way, they were trying.

But he'd also cared and tried. Too hard, too long, only to receive baffled disapproval in response.

He was done now. He'd been done since the age of fifteen. Or maybe nineteen, when he'd dropped out of college after only one year.

"If you have a dinner engagement, does that mean you're dating someone in the area?" His mother's lips tipped upward in a hopeful smile.

He was bursting to talk about April, about all his excitement and longing and regret, but not with his mom. The less his parents knew about him, the less they had to criticize.

"Nope." He set his napkin beside his plate. "Sorry."

When silence descended on the table, he didn't break it.

"Have you chosen your next role?" his father finally asked.

With his thumb and middle finger, Marcus fiddled with his water glass, turning it in endless circles. "Not yet. I've had a few offers, and I'm looking over some scripts."

Lawrence had given up on the last scraps of his own lunch and was now watching his son from across the round table. In the breeze from the open window, his white hair—still reassuringly thick, which augured good things for Marcus's future ability to score silver fox roles—fluttered. Using his fingers, Lawrence carefully combed the wayward strands back into place.

Just before leaving for college, Marcus had finally noticed the pomade under the lone bathroom's sink. That old-man brand of hair product certainly hadn't belonged to *him*, and he'd held the jar in his palm, wondering at it. Confused, until he'd realized the truth.

His father *did* care about appearances. At least a little.

Back then, Marcus had exulted in the evidence that Lawrence had his own vanities, however minor compared to his son's seeming obsession with good looks and good grooming. Marcus had taunted his father about that damn pomade for months, to Lawrence's clear discomfiture, and he'd done so using his father's own pet phrase.

"*Vanitas vanitatum, omnia vanitas, pater,*" he'd singsonged whenever possible.

Vanity of vanities, all is vanity, father. Spoken in Latin for extra spite.

Each repetition of that smirking gibe had tasted sweet and bitter both, like the kumquats he ate whole from the struggling tree in their small front yard.

He wasn't a defiant, heartsick teen anymore, though. He might be tempted, but he wouldn't mention the proffered role he would never, ever take, not given the director's reputation when it came to women on set and the movie's truly terrible script.

"I'm still considering my options," he told his parents honestly.

"Hopefully you'll pick something we care to watch this time." His mother shook her head, lips pursed. "Before we retired, Madame Fourier insisted on telling us about that horrid show every week. In great detail. Even though the narrative defied history, mythology, literary tradition, and all common sense."

Lawrence sighed. "She enjoyed torturing us, once she found out you were involved. The French can be *très* passive-aggressive."

His parents looked at each other, rolled their eyes, and chuckled at the memory.

Something in that fond amusement, their easy, shared dismissal of seven years of grinding work and effort and hard-won accomplishment—

One time on set, a careless fall from Rumpelstiltskin had cracked a couple of Marcus's ribs. This felt like that, somehow. Like his chest had caved in, just a little.

Before today, his parents hadn't seen him for nearly a year. Hadn't shared a meal with him for longer than that.

For all their supposed desire for his company, had they truly missed him for a single moment? Could he even call whatever emotion they felt for him love, when they didn't either understand or respect anything he did, anything he was?

His mouth opened, and suddenly he seemed to be telling them about that one role. That one script they'd hate, if possible, even more than *Gods of the Gates*.

"I've been offered the part of Mark Antony in a modern-day remake of *Julius Caesar*." His voice was breezy. A lazy taunt. Unpleasantly familiar to all of them. "The director intends to make Cleopatra the main protagonist of the story."

In the worst, most exploitative possible way, of course. Marcus had told his agent he'd rather return to bartending than work with that director and that script.

Watching R.J. and Ron willfully misinterpret E. Wade's iterations of Juno and Dido for seven years had been painful enough. He didn't need to lend his time and talents—such as they might be—to yet another story ready to equate women's ambition with instability and evil. The violent sex scenes, numerous and full of dubious consent at best, had only been the poisonous icing atop a cake already tainted by toxic masculinity.

No, he wasn't going anywhere near that misogynistic train wreck of a movie, or that genial predator of a director.

Somehow, though, he was still talking, talking, talking. "They're all vampires, of course. Oh, and Caesar comes back from being staked somehow, intent on revenge, and starts killing senators one by one, in the grisliest possible fashion." His most vapid smile in place, he ran his fingers through his hair. "Stylistically, it's very Marc Bolan and David Bowie, so I'd be rocking guyliner, and in the 'Friends, Romans, countrymen, lend me your ears' scene, I'd only wear a strategic coating of glitter and a smile to give my big speech. I figure I'd better start putting some chicken breasts in my pockets now, right?"

A deathly silence fell over the dining room, and he squeezed his eyes shut for a moment.

Fuck. *Fuck.*

Apparently, he *was* still an asshole teenager. Striking out when hurt. Playacting the Worst Possible Son. Phrasing the truth to inflict maximum distress, then making shit up, anything he could imagine that would horrify his parents.

He was a thirty-nine-year-old man. This had to stop.

"You're . . ." His father visibly swallowed. "You're considering that role?"

He almost said it. Almost shrugged and answered, *Why not? The director says I'd look fantastic in the costumes.*

His water glass was going to break if he kept gripping it so tightly.

He put it down very gently, removing his fingers from the fragile glass shell one by one.

The truth. This time, he would tell them the unvarnished truth, with no affectations adopted for self-protection.

"No, Dad." His voice was even. Toneless, verging on bored. It was as much grace as he could muster in that moment. "No, I'm not considering the role. I had my agent turn it down immediately. Not because it violated Roman history, but because I deserve better as an actor, and I demand better in my directors and my scripts."

His parents glanced at each other again, lost for words. Stunned, perhaps, that he considered himself someone who had *standards*.

"I'm glad you're considering your choices more carefully this time," his mother finally said, offering a cautious smile. "That *Julius Caesar* remake excluded, almost anything would be an improvement over your last project."

No wonder they considered him the stupidest member of their family. He still hadn't learned.

The chair screeched beneath him when he rose to his feet.

"I'd better go," he told them. "Thank you again for lunch."

They didn't protest as he left the dining room, gathered his jacket and keys, and dispensed generic good wishes with a rictus smile. His father gave him a polite dip of the chin in the postage-stamp entry hall, which Marcus returned.

He was at the door, almost gone, when his mom reached out for . . . something. Some sort of contact. A half hug, a kiss on the cheek, he didn't know.

It didn't matter, honestly.

If she touched him right now, if either of them did, he thought he might shatter like that water glass.

He stepped back from her.

Her hand fell to her side, her green eyes stricken behind those familiar glasses.

Late one winter night, when he'd sneaked out of bed to eavesdrop at the cracked door to their tiny bedroom, he'd heard her weeping. In a tear-choked voice, she'd haltingly explained to her husband how much she missed teaching the kids in her prep school, missed working alongside him. She'd admitted that she found it nearly unbearable to sit across a table from their son day after day, trying in vain to reach him in ways his kindergarten and first-grade teachers hadn't, couldn't, while Lawrence shone in the brightness of the outside world.

She'd never make the same amount of money as her husband. Never have his seniority in their department, even if she got her position back.

"I'm feel like I'm l-losing essential p-pieces of myself hour by hour, Lawrence," she'd sobbed. "And I love Marcus, but I'm not getting through to him, and sometimes I want to shake him, but instead I just have to keep trying to get him to *learn*—"

The words had tumbled over one another, near hysterical, and Marcus couldn't doubt the truth in them. He'd carried that truth with him back to bed that night and every night.

Even as he suffered, she did too. Because of him.

So despite the bile in his throat now, he gathered her in his arms. Kissed the top of her head, and let her kiss his cheek. Offered her a wave from inside his car window.

Then he got the fuck out of there, with no idea when or if he'd ever return.

JULIUS CAESAR: REDUX

INT. CLEOPATRA'S BEDROOM - MIDNIGHT

CLEOPATRA stretches out naked on a round, velvet-covered bed, pale in the candlelight. She is everything a man wants. Beautiful and insatiable and a sultry mystery, her ample breasts perky and firm and promising all the world to any hapless man who falls under their sway. MARK ANTONY lies beside her, insensate from pleasure. She literally has him by the short hairs.

CLEOPATRA

Caesar must die. Again.

MARK ANTONY

No! Such treason would besmirch my honor!

CLEOPATRA

You must stake him!

She leans over him, her breasts speaking of sexual frenzy, and he cannot look away from their pendulous swing. No man could, in the face of Eve's temptation.

MARK ANTONY

If you insist, my treacherous flower.

CLEOPATRA

Fear not that he might rise from the dead once more.

No twice-murdered, unnatural creatures have taken
blood-soaked revenge on their enemies since the last
Ides of March, exactly a year ago today.

MARK ANTONY

Woman is the most unnatural creature of all.

10

THEY WERE DOING THE EXACT OPPOSITE OF POSING AND preening at an indoor water park. Still, Marcus hadn't objected. Hadn't asked if their plans were meant to serve as a test of some sort, although he suspected they were.

Let's meet at 11 at the Cal Academy, April had texted last night, while he stood beneath the too-hot spray of his hotel shower and let it scald him. I've been meaning to check out the natural history exhibits, and I thought you might enjoy the planetarium. (Resisted making a star joke there. Yay me.) We can grab lunch at the café. Sound good?

After emerging from the shower, he'd read her text, toweled his hair, and considered the logistics. Sounds good. Why don't we meet at the café for lots of coffee before we look at rocks and recline in a dark theater? j/k

I think I can manage to keep you awake in the dark, she'd returned. But yes, coffee first.

He'd blinked at that message for a minute, wishing he'd made his shower cold instead.

Flirtation. That was definite flirtation.

For the rest of the night, it was enough to take the edge off the slice of pain in his chest every time he thought about how he'd hurt her as Book!AeneasWouldNever, how he'd miss the

Lavineas community, and how his parents had watched him in disappointment and disapproval from across that small table.

Now here he was, standing outside a science museum café on a Monday morning, embarrassingly excited about the prospect of seeing literal stars. Even though he appeared to be the only person in sight not towing along at least one child.

"Hey!" Her voice, breathless and husky, came from behind him. "Sorry. BART and Muni were running a bit late this morning, which meant I ran late too."

When he swung around, his own breath whooshed out a bit too forcefully.

"Hey," he wheezed. "No problem. I just got here myself."

Her jeans, so skinny they were basically leggings beneath her mustard-yellow tunic, outlined the generous curves of her thighs with loving exactitude. Caught in a high ponytail, her gorgeous red-gold hair glinted in the light from the windows, and her thick-framed tortoiseshell glasses emphasized the soft brown of her eyes.

He'd dressed for discretion. Jeans. Sneakers. A basic blue henley. A baseball cap.

By all rights, no one should look twice at him today, not when April stood nearby. It was a wonder she didn't have paparazzi following *her* everywhere she went, simply to document the blazing glory of it all.

"You look beautiful." Simple fact. It had to be said.

Her mouth, soft and slightly downturned upon her arrival, twitched upward into a sweet smile. "Thank you."

When she opened her arms for a hug of greeting, he fell into them. Tugged her close, one hand spread on her back, another resting at her bare nape, where silky little hairs tickled his fingers.

Rested his cheek on her crown and breathed in roses and spring. April.

Her warm, lush body conformed to his, yielding and filling in gaps he hadn't even known existed. At his own back, her individual fingertips pressed into him, their pressure noticeable. To his pleasure, she was hugging him fully as much as he was hugging her.

She clung longer than he'd have expected, her breath hitching once. When he finally pulled back a few inches, her eyes were a little too bright behind those glasses.

"Thanks," she said. "I needed that."

Dammit.

Cupping the back of her head in his palm, he pressed a gentle kiss to the pale, freckled skin of her temple, above the arm of her glasses. "I'm sorry."

"You have nothing to be sorry for." After one last squeeze, she stepped away from him and offered a smile that looked only somewhat strained. "Let's get some coffee and look at some rocks."

He groaned in mock-torment, but took her hand and allowed her to lead him toward the coffee bar.

"Some of them will be shiiiiiiiny," she singsonged, then reached her free hand to tug a strand of his hair as they stood in line. "Just like you."

He glanced at his sneakers for a moment.

A pretty face, Ron had said. *We couldn't have found prettier.*

"Despite my years in the dirt, I have a weakness for shiny things. I'm a magpie, really." She flicked her earlobe, where looping strands of silver cascaded to her shoulders. "I'm especially fascinated by how some shiny things come to be."

It was a lure. An effective one.

His eyes returned to hers. "Tell me."

The curve of her lips had turned gentle. "Certain minerals are created under enormous pressure over vast stretches of time, making them as tough as they are beautiful."

His parents hadn't found science interesting, but he wasn't ignorant, either.

He let out a slow breath. "Diamonds."

"Diamonds," she agreed.

His laugh was a little shaky.

"'Vast stretches of time'?" He arched a brow at her. "Did you just call me old?"

She snickered. "I said what I said."

In companionable silence, they paid for their coffee and doctored it to their tastes. A splash of cream for him, milk and a generous waterfall of sugar for her.

Over the years, he'd received extravagant compliments. Often from people who wanted something from him—money, a brush with fame, sex with a star—but also from people who simply admired him for reasons flattering or uncomfortable or both.

Somehow, she'd managed to turn a discussion of minerals into praise as sweet as her coffee. Nerdy too, which somehow made it even sweeter.

No wonder she loved rocks. In her hands, on her tongue, they *did* tell stories. Ones more faceted and crystalline than any he'd managed to craft over years and years of writing fanfic.

"Diamonds shouldn't be as expensive or rare as they are, and I hate how they've been extracted from the earth and used as a justification for exploitation and subjugation. So much of the diamond industry is hateful and corrupt. That said . . ." After taking a sip of her coffee, she wrinkled her nose and added more sugar.

"The first time I saw the Hope Diamond in DC, I considered a life of crime."

When he laughed, a nearby mom with a stroller took a cell photo of him.

Discreetly, he steered April toward the windows, and they looked outside as they drank and talked about favorite museums. Or, rather, he urged April to discuss hers, since she didn't need to hear about the misery of his previous museum visits.

"Ready for rocks?" she asked, after they'd finished.

He offered his arm, and she took it. "Ready for rocks."

They spent an hour or so rambling through the museum, first peering at and handling a startlingly bright rainbow of minerals, then visiting the penguins and studying expansive dioramas rife with vegetation and animals preserved through expert taxidermy.

At the first text-intensive informational sign they encountered, she glanced at the display. Bit her lip.

Of course she remembered, cared, and wanted to know more.

"I can read it, but it'll take me longer than you. Just . . ." He sighed. "Please don't get impatient."

Her brows drew together. "Of course I won't get impatient."

And she didn't, no matter how long he took, although he still tended to favor displays that didn't require much context to appreciate them. Hands-on activities, or the enormous blue whale and T. rex skeletons, or—to April's delight—the Shake House.

"This is my first earthquake simulator." Grinning, she tugged him through the doorway. "We don't get many noticeable quakes in Sacramento, so I'm excited."

He allowed himself to be dragged toward a spot near the faux-window. "Good news, then. Now that you live in the Bay Area, you'll feel something every year or two, at least. Hopefully not a *big* something, though."

Her nose crinkled in a wince. "Well, at least we're not in Washington or Oregon. Sooner or later, those poor people are in deep, deep—"

Just then, the museum helper began talking, and he made a mental note not to move to Seattle.

As the polo-clad woman explained what would happen next, he studied his surroundings. Beside him, April was doing the same, her eyes sharp and narrowed in scrutiny as she scanned the cloth-covered ceiling, the screen disguised as a window, the blue-patterned walls and built-in shelves.

The simulator, built to resemble a Victorian drawing room inside, didn't boast many decorations on those walls and shelves. Some books, decorative plates and glasses, a mirror, a painting, a chandelier. A fishbowl too, amusingly enough. White-painted metal railings crisscrossed the room, providing handholds each small group of visitors would need in due course.

Along one wall, the screen showed a window's-eye view of the Painted Ladies near Alamo Square. The city as it existed in 1989, during the Loma Prieta quake, according to the museum employee. Eventually, she told them, the image would change to the city as it appeared in 1906, before the most infamous disaster in San Francisco history.

Compared to a *Gods of the Gates* set, the room was sparse at best. But in today's scene, he got to hold April's hand and interlace their fingers, knowing he wouldn't have to die a stupid, stupid death on camera. All in all, he'd take that trade every time. Even though more than one cell phone was now pointed toward the two of them, rather than the room or the guide explaining the gist of what would happen.

First, as the polo-clad woman explained, the room would jolt through the 1989 earthquake, then the 1906 temblor. Or at least modified versions thereof, demonstrations safe and brief enough for casual visitors. If the first, weaker, quake simulation proved too nerve-racking, they could leave before the second.

In one nonsensical scene in *Gates*'s fifth season, Aeneas rode a pegasus to visit Venus, his mother, in her lofty celestial abode. To film that sequence, Marcus had spent hours and hours perched precariously atop a giant green-painted rig assembled in a cavernous green-painted hangar and programmed to simulate the movements of an enormous winged horse in flight.

For all the precautions taken, for all his love of physical challenges and performing his own stunts whenever possible, he'd found the experience . . . disconcerting. At least at first, until he'd gotten used to the rhythm.

He figured a room that required only railings as safety measures should be just fine.

As a recording briefly explained the circumstances surrounding each earthquake, he and April leaned against their patch of railing, hip to hip. Then the re-creation of the Loma Prieta quake began, the lights flickered out, and the room rattled and shook beneath their feet.

He put his arm around her shoulders, hitching her closer as the chandelier swayed and the books hopped out of place, millimeter by millimeter.

"As a precautionary measure," he said when her gaze shot to his. She snorted. "Right."

All in all, it felt not entirely dissimilar to his memory of the actual quake, except happier. And sexier. Much, much happier and sexier. One of her breasts nudged his chest as she shifted under his arm, and he had to swallow back an embarrassing noise.

When the simulator's version of the 1906 quake began, the difference between the two temblors was immediately apparent. This quake involved not just rattling but sharp jolts and an ominous rolling sensation too, and the whole experience lasted much longer. Long enough to recall, unwillingly, that a similar catastrophe could happen again, right where they were standing, at any time.

Yet the grin on April's round, lovely face widened, moment by moment. In a burst of movement, she got up on her toes and nestled closer.

Her breast wasn't merely nudging his chest anymore. The contact had become a blindingly pleasurable press of softness, a taunt rubbing against him with each jolt of the floor beneath them.

"This is fucking awesome," she whispered in his ear as they bumped into the rail and clutched one another. "I wonder how accurate they were allowed to make it."

As she spoke, her lips brushed his earlobe, and her hot, moist breath caressed his bare neck. He inhaled sharply. Relaxed his fingers on her shoulder one by one, before their bite into her cotton-covered flesh became too possessive or painful. Slid that hand between her shoulder blades and down to the small of her back.

The two of them had an audience as they rode out their simulated earthquake, and he didn't give a fuck anymore. He gripped the rail beside him more firmly, feet spread apart for balance. Enough balance for two, as necessary.

With a single, deliberate shift of his sheltering arm, he fitted her against him front to front, heat to heat. Her lips parted in a silent gasp, and their thighs tangled. As the world shuddered around them, she braced one hand against his chest for balance, the other still reaching for the rail by his ass.

The shrieks of the children in the room disappeared, muffled by the buzz in his ears and the rocketing thump of his heart.

She didn't shift away. Instead, her warm palm skated slowly, slowly, down his chest, rubbing back and forth a bit with each jolt, stopping just above his jeans, fingers spread wide, and she wasn't watching the room anymore. Neither was he.

He bent low. Ran his nose along the pretty, pale curve of her ear, and that shiver shifting her body against his wasn't from the damn simulator.

"May I?" he breathed into her ear.

She nodded. Turned her head and looked up at him, eyes heavy-lidded, then fisted her fingers in his henley and—

The lights came on. The room stopped moving, even as his personal ground continued to shake.

They didn't move, didn't speak, didn't look away.

The recording cheerfully informed them that the real quake would have lasted three times as long, and goddamn the museum for not properly valuing historical and scientific accuracy, because he *wanted* that extra minute of stomach-pitching chaos. Wanted to taste that plump, rosy mouth and trace the bow of her upper lip. Wanted to use his teeth and tongue until she gasped and trembled again and used her hold on his shirt to bring his body closer, closer.

But some people were shuffling out of the room, chattering noisily, while others were still documenting every second of this private moment occurring in a much-too-public place.

They both deserved better than this.

He drew back, removing his left hand from—well, it had evidently moved at some point, settling just microns above the tempting swell of her ass in those tight, tight jeans. Then he let go of the rail too and offered her his right hand, which wasn't entirely steady.

She took it. "The planetarium next?"

He nodded, too overwhelmed for words. Fingers interlaced once more, they left the exhibit and walked toward the planetarium.

Would kissing her there work better than in the earthquake simulator? They'd have dim lighting, and maybe an isolated cluster of seats, and stars wheeling overhead, and if he slid his hand under her tunic, maybe—

Okay, the thought of what they could do in a dark theater wasn't helping his current situation.

"Tell me more about the Loma Prieta quake on the way there." His voice had turned raspy, and he cleared his throat before continuing. "If that's okay. I lived through it, and I should understand how and why it happened."

"Really?" She raised a skeptical brow. "Because you don't need to humor me. I'm not offended if you don't want to hear more about geology right now."

"Really." Casting aside his public persona, at least for the moment, he dug deep and let the right words—the true words— emerge. "I, uh—I'm interested in lots of things, actually. I listen to nonfiction audiobooks all the time, especially when I travel."

Stupidly, his cheeks had gone hot.

He had never, never known what to say. Who to be. How to act. How not to disappoint.

But he had to give her *something*, something real and true, since appearances alone didn't interest her. Even their undeniable sexual chemistry wouldn't be enough to keep her, not if she didn't see anything in *him* worth keeping. And maybe their years of online friendship weren't enough to entrust her with a career-destroying secret, but they were enough to entrust her with this little hidden corner of his heart.

So he forced himself to continue. "One of my favorite things about what I do"—his tongue was so damnably *thick* all of a sudden—"about—about acting, is how it pushes you to learn new skills. Like, this one terrible pilot taught me the basics of sailing."

In his peripheral vision, he could see her face turned toward him. Her absolute attention focused on him and him alone.

"The series was supposed to be called *Crime Wave.* Because I was a crime-solving dude on a boat? It wasn't the world's best concept." No network had wanted to touch that pilot. It had rightfully sunk beneath the surface of television history without a trace—except when it came to his sailing skills. "A complete flop of a rom-com helped me learn how to handle a chef's knife and chop like someone who knew his way around a professional kitchen."

"I saw that!" she exclaimed. "*Julienned by Love*, right? And your love interest was actually named—"

"Yes. Julienne. Julie. My plucky sous chef, who thought she was dying but wasn't, and who eventually became famous for her jambalaya-cheesecake fusion dish." He winced. "I apologize. I'm more than happy to refund your money personally."

Her laugh echoed in the expansive space. "Oh, I didn't pay for it. I streamed it during a free trial, just out of morbid curiosity."

That sounded about right.

"For *Gates*, I studied ancient shipbuilding and military tactics. Swordplay too, like you said the other night." He fixed his eyes on the signage ahead, awkwardly scratching the nonexistent stubble on his jaw with his free hand. "If you, um, ever wanted to hear about that. Maybe it could help with some of your fanfiction?"

When he fell silent, she slowed until he turned back toward her.

Then she eyed him up and down in frank assessment and appreciation, her teeth sinking into her lower lip, and *Jesus.* Flicking his hair and flexing hadn't bought him that kind of interest, that heat in her gaze. Not once.

"I do want to hear about your swordplay. Trust me." Her fingers tightened on his. "In the meantime, though, if you want to know more about the Loma Prieta earthquake, ask and ye shall receive."

So she told him as they walked, and she was so fucking *smart*, and made things so damn *clear* and *interesting*, without an ounce of condescension.

Shit, it was sexy. Which wasn't actually what he'd wanted from a discussion about a deadly earthquake, but there it was. There *he* was, tugging down the hem of his henley to ensure it disguised his reaction to her.

"So it was an oblique-slip rupture," she explained, reclaiming her hand so she could gesture gracefully with her arms in illustration, and he both grasped—at long last—what that actually meant *and* wanted to grasp one of those blunt fingers and slip it into his mouth. Sink his teeth into the pad of her thumb and watch those alert brown eyes turn hazy.

When her tongue wrapped around a technical term, he wanted that tongue wrapped around him too. Anywhere. Everywhere.

His desire to have his mouth on her, hers on him, wasn't oblique. It was direct. And yes, he was certain that didn't make a lick of sense in seismological terms, but he didn't care, because he wanted to lick *her*.

In the end, the planetarium was packed for their particular showing, so he behaved himself, despite the way she rested her hand proprietarily on his thigh. His *upper* thigh.

In person, everything he'd come to adore about Ulsie online seemed impossibly more intense. Her plainspoken pragmatism and calm, her kindness, her intelligence, her easy humor, her self-confidence—they all radiated from each gesture, each word, and the glow was as blinding as the lights in the planetarium when they came back up after the show.

The only time she seemed hesitant, unsure of herself, was after lunch, when they exited the museum and lingered outside the entrance in the spring breeze.

"Was this . . . okay?" A strand of her coppery hair had worked free of her ponytail, and it fluttered against her cheek. "I know it wasn't exactly a water park, but . . ."

Carefully, he took hold of that silky lock, moving it away from her face.

"I told my parents I hated museums," he told her. "I refused to go, after a while."

Her head bowed. "I'm sorry. I should have—"

"It wasn't true." He played with the end of that loose tendril. Stroked it between his thumb and forefinger, watching the way it shone in the sun. "Saying that was easier than saying I couldn't read the tiny text on all those signs as quickly as they wanted."

Easier than saying, *Your impatience makes me feel as small as those letters.*

"Marcus . . ." Her brow was pinched. "I'm sorry."

As he followed that red-gold strand of hair down to its end, he brushed his thumb along her jaw and down her neck. Lingered in the dip of pale skin between neck and shoulder, her flesh giving and soft and getting warmer by the moment.

He stroked that shadowy arc. Traced her freckles, connecting one to another to another. "Don't be sorry. I'm trying to say thank you, for showing me I could love museums."

She was gripping his hips now, head tilted to ease his thumb's path, lips parted, eyes half-closed behind her glasses. With every breath, she edged closer. Closer, until—

He couldn't stand it. He had to know.

Leaning forward, he pressed his mouth to the vulnerable curve of flesh beside his thumb, so his every word became a caress of his lips against the fragrant skin of her neck. "Thank you for a perfect afternoon. Thank you for being so patient. So smart. So gorgeous. Thank you for . . ."

Her fingers sifted through his hair, her capable hand cradled his skull and urged his mouth harder against her, and he shut up and obeyed the unspoken order.

Against his tongue, she tasted like roses and sweetness, salt and sweat. He cupped her nape to steady them both as she shuddered, then fitted his mouth more tightly to her. When he drew on her flesh and grazed her neck with his teeth, she gasped and arched against him.

That would leave a mark. Good.

And then, just as her thighs parted to let one of his in between, and he groaned in heedless want—

He heard them.

"Marcus, look this way!" one of them called out. "Is that the girl from Twitter?"

When Marcus raised his head, another man was moving closer to April, his camera lens enormous and expensive and trained entirely on her. "What's your name, sweetheart? How long have you two known one another?"

She stiffened, and Marcus didn't blame her for shifting away from him under the onslaught, but she had to know: this was just the beginning.

The paparazzi had found them at last.

JULIENNED BY LOVE

INT. RESTAURANT KITCHEN - MIDNIGHT

MIKE and JULIE are kissing passionately, Julie pressed up against the metal countertop. Unexpectedly, she sways, ill and near crumpling, and the kiss breaks. She lays her hand against her forehead and looks at him, tears swimming in her eyes. When he reaches for her, she dodges.

                         JULIE
I can't be your sous chef anymore.

                         MIKE
But . . . why? Why, Julie?

                         JULIE
What we have can never be. Trust me. It's as impossible
as perfecting my jambalaya-cheesecake fusion dish.
  *She backs away from him, step by step, supporting
herself with one hand on the counters, the walls, the
doorway to the dark dining area.*

                         MIKE
Julie! Julie, don't leave me!
  She is almost to the restaurant exit, crying.

                         MIKE (O.S.)
Don't leave me. Without you, I'll be in the
weeds . . . forever.

As he stands alone in the echoing kitchen, Mike clutches her discarded hairnet to his chest.

MIKE

Goodbye, my sweet, spicy sous chef. Goodbye.

11

SINCE ACCEPTING MARCUS'S DINNER INVITATION, APRIL had wondered how she might react to the appearance of actual, real-life paparazzi. Would she freeze? Cringe? Try to hide? Ignore them entirely and get on with things, as she'd visualized doing over the past couple of days?

In the end, none of the above.

Instead, she was entirely occupied watching Marcus put on one hell of a show. Somehow, he'd managed to draw their attention away from her in mere seconds, through sheer charisma and unabashed flirting and—

Yes. Yes, he appeared to be stripping.

Moving another step away from her, he grinned at their audience. "It's damn hot in the sun today."

Reaching down, he crossed his arms and tugged his henley upward, the friction of fabric on fabric pulling the tee underneath higher at the same time and exposing bare flesh.

It was a cool spring day. No way he couldn't feel the chill against his skin.

He knew what he was doing. Oh, he knew.

His abdomen appeared first, flat and firm and bisected by a line of silky-looking golden-brown hair, lovingly bracketed by those lickable diagonal furrows. His jeans rested lower on his hips than she'd imagined, low enough that she had to swallow hard.

Then, as he kept dragging his henley higher—slowly, so slowly—his chest came into view, muscled and lightly furred, and . . .

Nipples. Jesus, *nipples*. They all got a flash of those too, hard in the chill, before the henley was over his head and gravity dragged his tee back down a few inches.

The paparazzi were capturing everything, their cameras clicking away.

One of them finally managed to recall the reason for their presence, however. "Are you here on a date, Marcus? What's your lady friend's name?"

"Well, we all know I have no interest in museums." At his wink, one of the paparazzi actually blushed behind her camera. "But anything to impress a pretty woman, right? I suffered for the sake of beauty, as I so often do."

Yes, it was definitely an impressive show.

At least, April assumed he was putting on a show. Hoped.

Because otherwise, he'd only been acting today. Pretending to enjoy the museum, enjoy her company, in hopes of riding their obvious—if surprising—sexual compatibility into the orgasmic sunset.

Would she even know? Hadn't she been thinking only days ago that he should have won an award for his dramatic abilities? How could she assume the man she'd seen today, the man she'd briefly glimpsed at the end of dinner, was the real Marcus, and not merely another role?

He gifted their onlookers with one last gleaming smile before taking her hand again and tugging her toward a taxi just arriving at the museum's entrance. The paparazzi trailed after them, shouting more questions, taking more pictures, but he merely waved and grinned.

They were sliding into the back seat of that taxi before the elderly woman inside even managed to finish paying the driver.

To give the woman enough room, Marcus drew April down onto his lap, and she wished she could relax into the contact, melt against the heat emanating from his honed, strong body, but she couldn't. Not right now. Instead, she remained stiff against him, her back ruler-straight.

Was he thinking how heavy she was, compared to other women he'd dated?

Or—and this was somehow, illogically worse—was he thinking, *Finally, we can stop talking about fucking rocks and just get down to actual fucking?*

Marcus smiled apologetically at the wide-eyed taxi patron perched on the other side of the back seat. "Sorry to intrude. We'd be happy to pay the tip for your ride, if you'll allow it."

At that, a smile crinkled her papery cheeks, and she rapped his knee lightly with her cane. "I already put the tip on my card. Besides, I saw your performance as we drove up. That was more than sufficient compensation, young man."

He laughed, his mirth rattling through April on his lap, and he accepted the free hand the woman held out. They chatted for another minute, hands clasped the entire time, before she began to exit the taxi.

Awkwardly, attempting not to elbow him, April nudged Marcus toward the center of the back seat and maneuvered out of his lap. Sliding across, he supported the elderly woman's elbow as she slowly climbed out.

"That Lavinia girl seems nice." One more rap of her cane against his shin. "Don't screw things up." Her eyes flicked to April. "That goes for this one too."

Then she was safely on the sidewalk, and Marcus shut the door behind her, blocking out the clamor of questions and the blinding strobe of camera flashes in an instant.

His gaze immediately returned to April, now huddled against the far door. A line appeared between his brows as his smile faded to nothing.

"Where to?" the driver asked.

"I'm sorry, but we need a moment to figure that out. Feel free to start the meter." Marcus didn't look away from April. "Um . . . this taxi ride was my idea, not yours. Please let me pay for it. I'll take you back to your hotel, or wherever you want to go. We could hang out at—"

Whatever he was going to suggest, she didn't want to do it. Not until she'd had the chance to think. And their surreal duo of dates had already taken up entirely too much of her time and her thoughts, given her current circumstances.

"I need to get back to my apartment and prep a little more before my furniture starts arriving Wednesday. Sorry." She leaned forward to speak to the driver. "Please drop me off at the Civic Center station."

"Let me take you directly to your apartment instead. If that's okay with you." Marcus sounded tentative. "I'd like to save you some hassle."

It was a kind offer, and she was too tired to turn it down. "Thanks."

After she gave the driver her new address, the cab began moving, Lizzo's voice now the only noise in the vehicle.

Maybe she'd have a few minutes that night to write and get out all her tangled feelings about BAWN, about Marcus, about being on camera in ways sure to trickle into her private life. She should have plenty of time. After all, she wouldn't be spending an hour or two corresponding with her best online friend anymore.

The view outside the window blurred, for just a moment.

"Hey." Lightly, Marcus touched her elbow with a fingertip. "Are you all right?"

"I'm fine," she said, and let him interlace their fingers on his firm thigh.

That wasn't a passive-aggressive dodge, either. She *was* fine. She would be. No matter what happened with BAWN, and no matter what happened with Marcus.

And maybe—maybe—the paparazzi's intrusion had disoriented her more than she'd acknowledged. She'd already known about Marcus's media persona, after all. Its reappearance shouldn't have either surprised or bothered her.

In his inimitable fashion, he'd also protected her, drawing the paparazzi's attention away from pressing her about her name, her work, or other identifying information. Even if she knew public knowledge of her real identity was—like so much else—only a matter of time.

More importantly: Even if she couldn't trust him, not yet, she needed to trust herself and her own instincts. Those instincts were telling her the man beside her, with his grave eyes and gentle hold, was the true Marcus. Not the man who'd dismissed their day together as the necessary price he'd had to pay in exchange for physical closeness and intimacy.

Turning away from the window, she swung her knees to the side until they brushed his. "You distracted those people very capably." With one finger, she marked a line down the center of his chest. "Very nakedly too. You'll probably need a hot shower when you get back to the hotel."

His lean body shifted under her fingertip, his belly rising and falling with each quick, deep inhalation. "Not if you keep touching me like that."

Those formfitting jeans didn't quite conceal his reaction to the contact.

"Well, I don't want you to get frostbite." Through the soft fabric of his tee, she traced the top of his jeans, the band of fabric riding low against those firm, flexing abdominals. "Not when you sacrificed your body for my sake."

His voice turned low. Serious. "My body is a tool. That's all."

"Still." She scooted a little closer on the seat. "Thank you for protecting me as best you could."

His brow creased beneath that golden sweep of hair, and he captured her wandering digit in a light hold. "I only delayed the inevitable. At some point, they're going to know your name and your address. Probably your phone number too." He pressed a kiss to the pad of her finger. "I'm sorry, April."

She shrugged. "It's not your fault. When I agreed to dinner and today's date, I knew all that was a possibility. I've tried to mentally prepare myself, but if I have trouble handling it, I'll ask you for advice."

"Of course," he said, pressing her palm against his cheek. "Whatever you need."

He couldn't protect her from public scrutiny, even if he tried. Not without hiding her from the world like a dirty secret—which would hurt her so much more than even the most unflattering candid shot or intrusive phone call. Besides, protecting her wasn't his job.

Making all the inconvenient aspects of dating him worth it? Now, *that* was his job. One he could resume . . . tomorrow, maybe? If his flight didn't leave too early?

"When do you have to get back to LA?" The line of his cheekbone—it was so *distinct* under her fingertips. So sharp, like his jaw. "I need to work for the rest of the night, in preparation for the cleaning company tomorrow. But other than that, I'm free."

When his forehead crinkled this time, she smoothed the lines. "My flight leaves tomorrow morning. I wish it didn't." Then his face relaxed, his grimace lifting into a hopeful smile. "But I'd planned to work out in the hotel gym first thing in the morning, before showering and checking out. Want to join me? We could grab a quick breakfast afterward. The hotel has a decent buffet."

She dropped her hand to her lap, the nape of her neck prickling in warning.

"You want me to work out with you?" she asked.

Before this moment, she'd thought—

It didn't matter. He was treading familiar ground now, digging the same poisoned well deeper and deeper yet, and she'd abandoned that particular spot long ago.

She wasn't going back. Not for anyone, and especially not for a man whose company already came fraught with endless complications and contradictions.

"Uh, yeah." His voice was quieter now. A bit uncertain. "Early tomorrow morning. If you're interested."

Her stomach was roiling, her cheeks hot with anger and stupid, stupid embarrassment.

One more chance. Just in case she'd misunderstood.

"Tell me, Marcus." Her legs. They were touching his. She angled her knees away from him. "What do you recommend from that breakfast buffet?"

Head tilted, brow lowered, he was studying her closely.

"Um . . . I usually have the oatmeal. Hard-boiled eggs. Fruit." The words came slowly. "But there's—"

"I appreciate the invitation." To her pleasure, her smile was probably colder than the wind on his bare chest earlier, her words clear and calm. "On second thought, though, I think I'll be too busy to do anything tomorrow."

Tomorrow and for the rest of her life.

Her lips were trembling, and she pressed them tight. Breathed through her nose until the hurt stopped twisting her gut inside out.

Oh, wow, someone prodding me to work out! How novel! she wanted to cry gaily, arms spread wide in false surprise. *And how grateful I am for the suggestion of healthy food alternatives! Without your help, how would a woman of my size ever know about the importance of exercise and nutrition?*

But she didn't think she could keep her voice steady, not while saying something that revealed so much of her scarred heart. There was no point to wasting her energy on sarcasm, either. He probably wouldn't even register it as such. They never did.

My body is a tool, he'd said. Like body, like owner, apparently.

She should have known. A body like his, a face that pretty? Of course he cared about appearances more than what lay underneath. Of course.

An erection didn't mean he respected her. It didn't even mean he liked her body. Just that their pheromones were compatible, probably to his abject confusion and dismay.

She loved shiny things, always had. But he wasn't a diamond. Just fool's gold.

Marcus Caster-Rupp could fuck off to exactly the same place as all the other people—roommates, colleagues, so-called friends— who'd seemed to offer unconditional affection at first, then eventually coaxed her to visit the gym, presented her with the gift of a high-tech scale, bought her a membership to a weight-loss organization, offered her helpful nutritional tips.

Over the course of two decades, she'd occasionally dated and fucked men like him. Before that, she'd lived with people like him for eighteen years.

Enough.

She was done being fat-shamed. By him. By everyone.

Tonight, she was pouring a glass of wine and explaining exactly that to her friends on the Lavineas server. Sharing hurts she should have acknowledged long before, telling them truths she wished they'd understood without her having to say anything.

She'd try to do it gently, because they *were* her longtime friends, unlike the man sitting across from her in this cab. But she was doing it. Period. No matter how hard it was to expose herself that way, and no matter how badly they might react.

"Okay." At least Marcus was sensitive enough not to argue, not to reach for her again, even as those blue-gray eyes watched her so carefully. "That makes sense. You've got a lot going on."

"I really do."

She pulled out her phone from the inside pocket of her purse. With a few taps, she made herself a note to pick up wine along with the necessary cleaning supplies.

"Maybe—" His body still wasn't touching hers, but he'd edged a bit closer again. So close the heat radiating from him threatened to melt her resolve. Too close. "Maybe I could fly back later in the week? Help you unpack and get settled? I'm between jobs right now, so . . ."

That shyness, that incompletely masked hurt in his voice, was a ploy. An act. It had to be.

She didn't need to respond to it with softness anymore.

"Whenever someone helps me unpack, I always have trouble figuring out where everything went." Phone deposited safely back in its pocket, she zipped her purse shut. It made a satisfyingly *final* sound. Then she turned to look out the window. "I'm not sure what my schedule will look like for the rest of the week, so I shouldn't make plans. Thank you for the offer of help, though."

At that point, he seemed to understand. Enough, at least, to stop trying.

"Okay," he said again.

That was the last word exchanged between them until the cab arrived in front of her new, empty rental. They made their stilted farewells without touching a single time.

His face, the one time she dared to look, was drawn. Solemn. Resigned.

She didn't care. She *didn't*.

Once out of the cab, she walked to her entrance. Unlocked the door. Opened it. Kicked it shut. Flipped the dead bolt.

She didn't look back.

Lavineas Server DMs, Ten Months Ago

Unapologetic Lavinia Stan: You seem . . . off today. Everything okay?

Book!AeneasWouldNever: Nothing that merits complaint. But thank you, Ulsie.

Unapologetic Lavinia Stan: It doesn't need to be something of earth-shaking importance for me to listen. If you want to vent, I'm here.

Book!AeneasWouldNever: I'm just tired, I think. Sick of traveling, at least for now. Unsure where I want my career to go after this.

Unapologetic Lavinia Stan: Making a career change is hard. I only recently started applying for different positions, even though I've wanted to leave my current job for months.

Book!AeneasWouldNever: You're doing it, though, because you're brave.

Book!AeneasWouldNever: I have no right to whine. I'm very, very lucky to have my job. But

Unapologetic Lavinia Stan: But what?

Book!AeneasWouldNever: It gets lonely. I don't feel like myself around anyone, really.

Unapologetic Lavinia Stan: I'm sorry, BAWN. ::hugs::

Unapologetic Lavinia Stan: What can I do to help?

Book!AeneasWouldNever: Keep being you, Ulsie. That's more than enough. :-)

12

MARCUS LET HIMSELF BACK INTO HIS HOTEL ROOM. IT WAS dim and cold and pristine.

In the bathroom, he splashed his face with cold water, then braced his hands on the edges of the marble vanity and stood over the sink, letting himself drip.

April didn't want to see him again. That, among all the confusion of their cab ride, was clear enough.

He'd said something wrong. Done something wrong.

It shouldn't surprise him anymore, and it shouldn't hurt him anymore, either.

When he finally dried off, the towel was soft against his skin, when he wanted roughness instead. He wanted to scrub and scour his flesh until he'd uncovered a new iteration of Marcus Caster-Rupp. One whose throat wasn't thick and tight. One who hadn't lost both April's friendship and the possibility of so much more in a mere handful of days.

When he opened his laptop and checked Twitter, there they were. He and April, fingers intertwined by a colorful display of rocks. Braced against a rail, body to body, as the ground jolted beneath them. Cuddled close in their planetarium seats.

The paparazzi photos were beginning to appear too, on various entertainment sites. In those, he had his mouth open and hot on her neck, her shoulder, as she laced her fingers through his hair and held him close, chin tipped toward the sun, eyes closed behind those cute glasses.

Whatever he'd done, it was after that. In front of the paparazzi, or in the cab.

The images—

Letting out a hard breath, he scrolled down, down, down, away from them.

After checking one thread of comments at the bottom of an article, he clicked away from those as quickly as he could too, hoping April made a smarter decision than he just had. He hadn't gotten the sense she was sensitive about her body during the Fanboy Asshole Incident on Twitter, and Lord knew she was gorgeous, but anyone's confidence could be shaken by enough cruelty.

That said, someone had already created a Twitter account dedicated solely to retweeting pictures of April and adding admiring commentary. Their handle? @Lavineas5Ever5Ever. The follower count had already hit two hundred and kept rising as he watched.

If they knew her Lavineas server name, he suspected a second account might appear: @UnapologeticLaviniaStanStan.

Speaking of which . . .

He couldn't post there anymore, not without silently confirming that he'd lied to April as Book!AeneasWouldNever about his nonexistent business trip and its nonexistent ban on internet and cell phone usage, but he had to see what everyone was saying.

With one click, he was invisible. Simultaneously outside and within his longtime community. Observing. Taking comfort from his friends, even from a desolate distance.

New threads had popped up along with those new photos of

his date with April. New DM notifications too—including one from Ulsie, which couldn't be right.

He blinked at the screen. Squinted. Clicked after a few moments, his heart rate soaring to uncomfortable levels.

No, he wasn't imagining things. She'd written him in the last few minutes, even though he'd said he would be out of touch indefinitely, even though he'd hurt her with his obvious falsehood.

Unapologetic Lavinia Stan: I know you said you were going to be off on a job where you couldn't get online, but I wanted to let you know something.

Unapologetic Lavinia Stan: In case that wasn't entirely true, in case maybe your offline trip had something to do with my dating Marcus Caster-Rupp: we're not dating anymore.

Unapologetic Lavinia Stan: Which is a stupid thing to tell you, since you didn't want to meet me in person, even if I canceled my second date with him. So this was pointless.

Unapologetic Lavinia Stan: I'm sorry. My head is a mess right now, and I wasn't thinking. I won't bother you again.

We're not dating anymore. I won't bother you again.

Well, that was confirmation he'd neither wanted nor needed.

He wasn't getting a third date with April. He wasn't even certain she'd write to Book!AeneasWouldNever after he returned from his fake trip, unless he agreed to meet her in person. Which he couldn't. In theory, he could probably make up some story about why they couldn't meet, come up with some plausible explanation about agoraphobia or whatever, but he didn't want to lie to her yet again.

Yeah, he was fucked, and hurting, and he had no idea what—if anything—he could say in response to her messages. If her head was a mess, his was too. He needed time.

Accordingly, he said nothing. Even if part of him desperately wanted to ask what had gone wrong on her second date.

Shoulders slumped, he navigated back to the main list of threads.

A new topic had appeared. One started by April, entitled A BIG FAT SHAME. When he clicked, her post appeared, and it filled his entire monitor.

It was eloquent. It was heartfelt. It was direct.

It was also an answer to the question he hadn't been enough of an asshole to ask.

Unapologetic Lavinia Stan: I've wanted to talk about this issue for years now, but I wasn't sure how to begin the conversation. I've been especially nervous because the people in this community—all of you—mean so much to me, and I don't want to hurt your feelings or alienate any of you. But the simple truth is that some of you have hurt MY feelings, albeit inadvertently, just as I'm sure I've done the same to some or all of you without understanding how. (If so, please tell me. I want to know and do better.)

Unapologetic Lavinia Stan: So here's the thing: I'm fat. Very fat, in fact. Not chubby or merely curvy. FAT. A good part of the reason I was originally drawn to this particular OTP was, I think, for that reason. Lavinia's story resonated with me. Her character isn't fat in either book!canon or show!canon, but in book!canon, as you know, she's described as unattractive in terms of conventional beauty. Several of Aeneas's men even call her ugly. As we've discussed many times, the choice of Summer Diaz—who's gorgeous even without makeup and in dull, unflattering clothing—to play Lavinia undercut the resonance of that story line, but echoes of it are still there in the show, even so.

Unapologetic Lavinia Stan: I think I desperately needed to read and watch the story of how a woman most considered homely or downright hideous could earn respect, admiration, desire, and eventually love from the man she desired and loved herself. (Aeneas, of course.) I needed to witness how her character, her choices, and her words would come to mean more to him, in the end, than whether the rest of the world would call her pretty.

Unapologetic Lavinia Stan: I wanted that because of my family history. I wanted that because of my personal and romantic history too. I can't tell you how many times a date, or a boyfriend, or someone I considered a friend, has shamed me for my size. Sometimes they do so directly, but more often in ways I'm sure they consider subtle or don't consider at all. They do it by urging me to work out or take a walk with them every time I see them, or by discussing their ostensible concern for my health, or by pushing me toward what they consider more nutritionally sound food choices.

Unapologetic Lavinia Stan: But I'm not looking to be fixed. I want to be loved and liked and desired not because of my size, not despite my size, but because I'm ME. My character, my choices, my words. Each time someone I care about shows they don't care about me that same way, it hurts. It hurts more than I can easily express.

Unapologetic Lavinia Stan: So this ship, this community, is important to me. It's reassurance that better things are possible for me, and better relationships, and even real, abiding, passionate love. Not because of my size, not despite my size, but because I'm me.

Unapologetic Lavinia Stan: That's why it's painful to me when fics coming out of our community use fatness as shorthand for greed, for evil, for ugliness, or for laziness. I'm stunned by how often it occurs, given that one half of the couple we all ship is not considered conventionally attractive in book!canon. The Lavinia/Aeneas relationship, at least in the books, is fundamentally about rejecting appearances in favor of character. Yet I see fat-shaming frequently in Lavineas fanfiction, and it feels like a slap every single time.

Unapologetic Lavinia Stan: To be clear, I don't think fat-shaming is usually a conscious choice in our fics. Hatred of fatness, disdain toward fat people, is so widespread in our culture, it comes out in ways we don't intend, and I include myself in that statement. Being fat myself doesn't exempt me from having to consider my words and actions thoughtfully when it comes to fatness, because I'm part of this culture too.

Unapologetic Lavinia Stan: I'm not asking you to celebrate my fatness or make Lavinia fat in your stories or go back and change any old fics with fat-shaming in them. I AM asking, though, for you to be thoughtful any time you reference fatness in your writing. I want you to think of me and ask yourself, "Would the implications of this hurt ULS?" If the answer is yes, please do better—for me, for yourself, and for everyone else.

Unapologetic Lavinia Stan: As I wrote earlier, I don't want to hurt your feelings or alienate any of you, because you're my friends and my community. But I thought this was important, so I said it, and hopefully by discussing the issue, we can become an even better, more inclusive community than we already are.

Unapologetic Lavinia Stan: Thank you, and I'm sorry this ran so long.

Unapologetic Lavinia Stan: TL;DR: Please don't make fat people automatically awful or ugly or lazy in your fics. It makes me, an actual fat person, sad.

Unapologetic Lavinia Stan: P.S. When I say I'm fat, I'm not insulting myself. I don't use fat as a pejorative, as some do. For me, it's merely an adjective, like blond, or tall, or (TopMeAeneas's favorite) TUMESCENT. Whether it's offensive depends entirely on context, as with many descriptors.

Marcus sat back in the too-hard hotel chair and let out a slow breath.

Among all the fics he'd recommended to her over the years, at least a few included fat secondary or tertiary characters. He suspected the descriptions of those characters would now make him cringe.

Shit.

But that wasn't the worst of it. Not by far.

They do it by urging me to work out, she'd written, *or by pushing me toward what they consider more nutritionally sound food choices.*

With his goddamn life at stake, he would swear—*swear*—that his invitation to the gym, to the buffet, hadn't been a paternalistic nudge toward more exercise or so-called better nutrition. But with her background, he could see how she might interpret his words that way. He could see why she'd gone chilly, and why she'd pulled away from him, and why she hadn't wanted to look him in the eye for the rest of that endless cab ride.

Given her personal history, given the infamous, all-consuming concern for appearances he'd playacted in front of cameras for years, of course she'd believe the worst of him. She didn't yet know him well enough to do otherwise. Even with Book!AeneasWouldNever—

He pinched his forehead between his thumb and forefinger, pressing so hard, he half expected to leave fingerprints.

How had he overlooked it? How had he forgotten? She'd asked even Book!AeneasWouldNever, her longtime, faithful friend, whether her appearance had spurred him to cut off contact with her. Because she'd thought those photos of their dinner together were his first real glimpse of her, and she didn't know he'd already seen her by that point. Already admired her. Already found her unbearably sexy.

Not because of her size. Not despite her size. Because she was . . . April. Ulsie. *Her.*

And no, she hadn't seemed especially bothered by the cruel opinions of Twitter randos. But she'd been clear about that distinction in her Twitter DMs, hadn't she?

I don't give a shit what strangers think. Just the people I care about.

Either he was still a stranger to her as Marcus Caster-Rupp, and she didn't give a shit about him or his clumsy, ill-considered invitation—or she'd begun to care about him, if only a little, and he'd hurt her. Like Book!AeneasWouldNever had only last night.

Fuck.

This time, it was only a *little* after Alex's usual bedtime in Spain. And since his friend wasn't precisely an exemplar of impulse control himself, Marcus figured he'd be forgiven. Eventually. Once Alex got a good night's sleep.

"Holy shit, I've fucked up so badly," Marcus said as soon as his friend answered. "I didn't mean to, but *God*, did I fuck things up."

With admirable patience, Alex forbore calling him an asshole again. "What, specifically, did you fuck up?"

"Everything." He scrubbed his free hand over his face. "*Everything*."

"Such a freaking drama queen," Alex muttered. "Maybe you could be a bit more specific?"

If Marcus was a drama queen, then Alex was a drama . . . whatever was more powerful and dramatic than a queen. Drama dictator? Drama deity? Still, kettle-pot-blackness issues aside, Alex was listening, and Marcus planned to take advantage.

The whole story didn't take as long to relate as he'd expected. After it was done, Alex remained silent for a long, long time.

"Maybe it's for the best," he eventually said.

The phone should have splintered under the force of Marcus's glare. "*What?*"

Even across a continent and an ocean, Alex's sigh was audible.

Marcus stabbed an accusing finger at his best friend's name on the screen. "Over the course of a single weekend, I've lost a dear friend and the only woman I've truly wanted in years"—or possibly forever, but that could just be the drama queen in him swanning forth yet again—"and she's convinced I'm a fat-shaming dick as Marcus and a lying *abandoner* as Book!AeneasWouldNever. In what universe could that possibly be for the best?"

"Dude." His friend smothered a yawn. "Think about what you just said. You answered your own question."

Marcus scowled. "I did not."

"Moments ago, you just referred to yourself in the third person. Twice. As two different identities." The patience in Alex's voice sounded a bit strained. "Doesn't that seem a bit . . . overly complicated to you?"

Hmph.

"I'm a diamond of many facets." Hadn't April told him so earlier that day?

"Save the self-congratulatory shit for the camera, Marcus." A scraping noise came down the line. Alex scratching his scraggly beard, most likely. "I'm just saying you could meet a nice woman who only knows you by one name, to whom you haven't lied, and from whom you aren't keeping various secrets."

"I don't want a nice woman. I want April. Ulsie." He pinched the bridge of his nose, wincing. "Not that she isn't nice. At least, when she doesn't think I'm a dick who's trying to steer her toward exercise-induced weight loss and diet food."

Before Alex could say more, Marcus added, "I know, I know. I just referred to her as two different identities too. I don't want to hear it."

Yes, that was definitely a gusty sigh. "Then why did you call?"

"Because I . . ." He dropped his chin to his chest. "Because maybe I need to hear it, even if I don't want to hear it." Through a thick throat, he forced himself to say the words. "You think I should let her go, then? Not contact her again as Marcus, and avoid DMs with her on the Lavineas server after I get back from my theoretical, possibly-espionage-related business trip?"

"I think, based on everything you've told me, that she deserves someone who can be open and honest with her under a single name and identity." His friend's voice had gone raspy. Tired. "Can you do that? Even knowing what it might cost you?"

If he'd jeopardize his career for anyone, it would be her.

He was almost sure she wouldn't reveal his secrets. Almost.

Even though he'd only met her face-to-face twice. Dammit.

Was he willing to bet two decades of work on that near-certainty? The professional reputation he'd painstakingly accumulated over endless hours of repeating his lines and learning his craft and sailing and sword fighting and chopping and square-dancing?

Which reminded him: If *Do-Si-Danger* ever ended up on a streaming service, he was going into hiding. Much like his character, an arrogant, high-powered executive and accidental bystander to a gangland murder who assumed a new witness-protection identity and found ill-fated romance among homespun square-dancers.

That movie was fucking awful. Terrible in nearly every respect.

Still, he'd done his job. He'd treated his crew and costars and everyone else on the set like the professionals they were, and behaved like a professional himself. In the end, he'd pocketed a little money and burnished another corner of his reputation as a hard-working, easygoing actor.

But that wasn't all the movie had done for him.

He'd arrived on that set at the age of twenty-three, eager and excited and half convinced he was an irredeemable fuckup. By the time filming wrapped, he'd still kind of felt like a fuckup. But a fuckup who could be redeemed. Who *would* be redeemed, through putting in the hard work and getting better at his job in every way so he could land better parts.

Acting had brought him professional respect, yes, but also the beginnings of self-respect. It was his source of accomplishment, of community, of pride. His only source, at least until he'd found fanfiction.

Without his work, without his reputation, he'd be nothing. Have nothing. Again.

A smart, uber-competent woman like April wouldn't want him then anyway.

"Yeah. I hear what you're saying." His eyes stung, and he closed them for a moment. "Thanks."

"Look . . ." Something rustled down the line. Alex, shifting. "I'm sorry. For what it's worth, if you decided, *Fuck it, I want her more than my career,* and told her everything, I'd have your back. You know that."

Marcus huffed out a breath, unwillingly amused. "It's the sort of shit you would do."

"It's one hundred percent something I would do. Probably on live television, followed by an impromptu reading of the filthiest, most show-averse story I'd ever written." Alex's laugh was short-lived. Tinged with bitterness. "There's a reason Ron and R.J. gave me a fucking nanny. But you're not me, and I'm trying to help you make better decisions than I usually do."

After his recent arrest at a bar fight, the showrunners had saddled Alex with a paid minder to keep him out of trouble. A woman related to Ron somehow, which didn't bode well.

"Speaking of which, how's it going with"—what was her name?—"Laurel? Laura?"

With *that* sigh, Alex could have singlehandedly powered a

wind farm. "Lauren. My implacable, humorless, improbably short, annoying-as-fuck albatross."

Marcus kept his voice dry as the desert they'd shot in during the third season of *Gates*. "It's going well, then."

"It's going. She's not." Aggrievement saturated every syllable of every word. "Apparently, she'll be accompanying me to all public outings until the last season finishes airing. Even though I promised not to drink again. Or end up in another bar brawl, unless absolutely necessary."

At that addendum, Marcus massaged his temples.

"As I pointed out to Ron, she couldn't actually stop me from brawling unless she was standing on a stepstool of some sort," Alex said. "Although she's stronger than you'd think. Maybe she'd just tackle me at the knees and sit on me until I sobered up."

There was a certain grim relish in Alex's phrasing, which raised the question: Under what precise circumstances had he discovered Lauren's strength?

"She's going to hate all the premieres and awards shows," his friend crowed. "*Haaaaate*. I can't wait."

With all the evil glee in his tone, Alex might as well have been stroking a hairless Chihuahua and plotting the eruption of a henchman-created supervolcano from his secret lair.

Marcus winced. Better not to think about that ill-fated role in *Magma!: The Musical*. He could only hope April never learned of its existence, because the science behind the entire—

No. It didn't matter what April thought anymore, because they wouldn't be communicating, either in person or online. After this one last time, tonight.

He knew what he needed to do now.

"I'm glad you're getting some pleasure, however perverse, out of the arrangement. Be nice to Lauren, though. It's not her fault she got assigned to keep you sober and peaceable." A quick glance at his laptop revealed a screenful of responses to April's posts, with more appearing every few seconds. "I'd better go now, but thank you for listening. Again."

"No problem." A rustling noise. "Hold on just a second. Let me check my schedule."

While he was waiting, Marcus skimmed the first several comments. Most were supportive, but AeneasFan83—not a close friend on the server, but a longtime member nevertheless—was edging toward defensive, don't-be-so-sensitive territory in a way that made Marcus's hackles rise.

Within a minute, Alex was back. "I'll be in LA on Sunday. Want to binge-watch that British baking show late next week? I haven't heard someone say the word 'claggy' in far too long." His voice turned speculative. Almost dreamy. "I'll bet if I used the phrase 'claggy sponge' around Lauren, she'd think it meant something dirty. I'll have to try it."

Marcus didn't envy Lauren her job. Not at all.

After this disastrous week, however, Marcus figured he could use as much time as possible with his best friend. "Binge-watching claggy sponges sounds great. We'll work out the details once you're back. Take care of yourself in the meantime, and safe travels. And *be nice*."

More evil laughter, and Alex was gone.

Then it was time to think. Hard.

Marcus's response to April's thread took him embarrassingly long to compose. Finally, though, he came up with the right words. Or at least the best words he could, under the circumstances. They would have to be enough.

Book!AeneasWouldNever: Because of job requirements about internet usage, I won't be able to post here much for the foreseeable future. I shouldn't even be doing so now, but I wanted to say two things.

Book!AeneasWouldNever: First, thank you for being such a welcoming, supportive group. Over the past few years, becoming involved with this particular fandom has taught me so much about storytelling and community and—sappy as it sounds—myself.

Book!AeneasWouldNever: Second, if we ARE a community that prides itself on being welcoming and supportive, we shouldn't look away when one of our members tells us, at the cost of her own personal discomfort, that she sometimes feels alienated and hurt by things we've written. Especially since, as ULS rightly points out, the fundamental message of the Aeneas/Lavinia relationship is simple: Character over appearance, and kindness and honor above all.

Book!AeneasWouldNever: So I want to extend a heartfelt, sincere apology to ULS, for not previously considering the important issue she just raised, and for not noticing fat-shaming in fics I've recommended to her and to all of you in the past. I'll do better in the future, because of what you've written today. Thank you for that.

Book!AeneasWouldNever: Also, ULS, I'm so sorry the people in your personal life—the men you've dated—have made you feel judged or shamed. More sorry than I can say.

Book!AeneasWouldNever: Take care. I'll be back . . .
sometime. I'll miss you.

After that, Marcus set his status to invisible again. He
logged out.

And then, as he'd done so often before, he wrote until his
chest no longer ached with each breath he took.

DO-SI-DANGER

INT. THE FARNSWORTH BARN - EVENING

The barn is lofty and hay-strewn, the lighting
soft from lanterns in glass canning jars. Other
couples are still square-dancing, but CHRISTOPHER
and MILLIE have found a quiet corner. She brushes
a bit of straw off his expensive suit, and they
both laugh.

MILLIE

Only a month ago, I couldn't have imagined this.

CHRISTOPHER

Imagined what?
  He takes her hand, holding it gently. Tenderly.

MILLIE

You, allemande-ing left, easy as the breeze. Us,
together.

CHRISTOPHER

Never to be parted again, Millie. Never.
  She moves in front of him for a kiss. Suddenly,
a gunshot, then screaming. Millie collapses in slow
motion, face blank, blood blooming on her chest, as he
desperately tries to catch her, to revive her, but it's
too late. By the time he looks up, all traces of the
shooter are gone.

CHRISTOPHER

Millie! Millie, don't leave me!

But she's past answering. Face to the rafters, he howls his grief and despair and rage to the universe, knowing that he now has new motivation, new goals: to become a better man in her memory, and to avenge her. Her death will be the key to his character arc now— exactly as she would have wanted.

13

THE FIRST DAY ON APRIL'S NEW JOB, HER COWORKERS treated her to takeout sushi for lunch, with a side of light interrogation.

According to Heidi, it could have been worse. Much, much worse.

"They have this rendition of 'Blowin' in the Wind,'" she'd whispered near the printer that morning. "Mel changed the lyrics to 'Contaminants, my friend, are blowin' in the wind.'"

"Wow," April had managed. "That's . . . wow."

Her colleague nodded emphatically. "There's a verse about air-monitoring stations too. Pablo and Kei contributed that bit."

"And they considered performing that song for me at lunch? In a sort of welcoming ceremony?"

Honestly, despite Heidi's bugged-out eyes, it sounded amazing. After a week like this last one, April embraced any and all distractions from her tangled thoughts. A horrible folk concert promised much greater distraction and entertainment value than munching a sandwich at her desk alone, as she had done during her first lunch at her old office.

Creativity in any form, she appreciated. Especially when said creativity would have to cease at the end of the lunch hour, should it prove particularly ear-piercing. However, she also appreciated the kindness of not imposing that creativity upon her without an invitation.

"After some discussion, they decided it would violate the boundaries of good colleague behavior." Heidi's cerulean-blue nail polish matched her hair beautifully, and April mentally widened the scope of her wardrobe and makeup options for work. "They didn't want to force you to listen if you weren't interested. Even though they're very proud of their version of 'This Land Is Your Land.'"

Oh, the endless lyrical possibilities.

In the end, though, lunch didn't involve singing. Just a few friendly questions.

"I'm a *Gates* fan too," Mel said before selecting a piece of the spicy tuna roll with her chopsticks and transferring it to her plate. "I saw your Lavinia costume on Twitter, and it was *amazing*. How long have you been interested in cosplay?"

Of all the juicy topics Mel could have asked about, she'd chosen . . . cosplay. Not Marcus. Not the dates. Not even the publicity surrounding Marcus and those dates, or the public-yet-intimate photos splashed all over the internet and featured on several low-rated cable entertainment shows.

Despite a morning spent completing first-day paperwork and watching HR-mandated videos, April already loved her new job.

"Only this past year." Any sushi roll containing both tempura shrimp and avocado was clearly meant to be hers, so she snagged a piece. "That picture turned out well, and I'm proud of my design, but there are problematic bits. If I'd been posed any other way, you'd have seen evidence of staples and double-sided tape."

She'd intended to share her interest in cosplay and accompanying Twitter identity on the Lavineas server last week, since a few people in their community might be able to offer much-needed costume construction tips. That would have meant acknowledging she was Marcus's mysterious date, though, and after all the hub-bub surrounding her fat-shaming post, she was lying low for a few days instead.

Not that most people hadn't been kind and gracious about the topic, especially—and heartwrenchingly—BAWN. She was also locating fewer and fewer fucks to give for people who couldn't give her any in return. But a few naysayers had caused some tense moments on the server, and she had no intention of hogging the bandwidth yet again so soon thereafter.

"Do you need to borrow a sewing machine?" Pablo glanced up from his sashimi. "I have one I can lend you. It's not fancy, but it does the job."

April swallowed her sushi and sent him a grateful smile. "Thank you, but I would have no idea how to use it. Better to buy, experiment on, and possibly break my own machine."

"So you designed that amazing costume, but can't sew?" Heidi looked thoughtful. "Mel, darling, are you thinking what I'm thinking?"

"Probably not." With her chopstick, Mel was poking at the roe atop her sushi. "I was compiling a mental list of species whose eggs we consume and wondering where and why the line gets drawn."

Heidi blinked at her. "You're right. That wasn't what I was thinking."

"I know." Kei set his chopsticks neatly on his napkin. "This is about My Chemical Folkmance."

"We're still working on the band name," Pablo noted. "I voted for some take on 'She Blinded Me with Science,' but Kei and Mel told me it implied harmful things about our profession."

Her attention diverted from egg concerns, Mel regarded Heidi consideringly. "Oh. Yes. I see now. Yes, that might work, depending on what April would prefer. She just moved and started a new job, and we shouldn't pressure her to commit to anything else."

"Especially since she may have, uh, other personal priorities right now." Kei broke open his fortune cookie and scanned the slip of paper inside. "Dammit, I don't *want* to take on new adventures. I work full-time, have a family, and sing in a folk trio with an indeterminate name. Isn't that enough?"

Heidi patted his arm. "You can grab my fortune instead. It's about making wiser decisions, and I have no interest in that."

He laughed. "I'll bet you don't."

April was lost. "I'm sorry, Heidi, but I missed something. What were you thinking about? And what does it have to do with me?"

"She was thinking we could help one another, if you had the time and interest." Mel smiled at April. "We keep saying we should have costumes for our performances. You know, outfits that would work together onstage and show we're a folk group. But none of us can figure out what exactly that would look like. If you'd be willing to turn your design eye to those—"

"We could help you sew one of your costumes," Pablo finished. "If that's something that would interest you. If not, no worries."

The molded plastic chair beneath her squeaked as April lurched forward, the movement jerky in her enthusiasm.

"*Yes.*" She beamed at her new coworkers. All of them, in turn. "I would love that."

This was what she'd been missing in her work. Openness and the ability to talk about her life outside the office. Relationships built on and because of that openness.

God, the freedom was intoxicating. She was practically giddy with it.

"We'll let you get a bit more settled first, and then we can work out the details." Mel waved a ring-bedecked hand. "If you change your mind in the meantime, not a problem."

"You have a lot going on at the moment. Obviously." Heidi's nose ring glinted as she leaned back in her chair. "Look, it's really none of our business, and feel free not to answer, but—"

"Marcus Caster-Rupp is the bane of my existence as a lesbian," Mel interrupted. "If he didn't exist, I would be *all* the way at the end of the Kinsey scale, but alas."

Heidi shrugged. "I'm bi, so I embrace my status as a Caster-sexual."

"What's he like in person?" Mel asked. "Equally hot?"

While Kei rolled his eyes and stood to gather his trash, Pablo rested his elbows on the table. "Did he say anything about his skin care routine?"

"Please tell us he's actually a decent guy. He seems that way in all his interviews, but . . ." Heidi scrunched up her face in an anticipatory wince. "You just don't know."

What could April say?

"Ummm, okay." Easy stuff first. "I don't know anything about his skin care routine. I'm sorry, Pablo. You might want to check online. There might be articles about it."

He shook his head, then began consolidating his own trash. "I probably couldn't afford the products he uses anyway, but I was curious. My girlfriend says his face has 'the perfect amount of weathering.' Whatever that means."

April knew what it meant.

Those crinkles at the corners of his eyes and the faint lines across his forehead only enhanced his appeal. They were the gilt on his already gorgeous lily.

Now on to shakier ground.

"He's just as handsome in person," she told Mel. "Maybe more so."

Because in person, he was *real*. A shirt wrinkled by her fist or a loose shoelace only made him seem warmer and more solid and . . . touchable.

Face-to-face, he was still blindingly beautiful, yes, but not perfect. Not a demigod. Just a man. And since he was a real person to her now, she didn't want to talk about his sexual appeal to strangers. Like her explicit fics, the topic suddenly seemed like a violation.

His physical beauty she would gladly discuss. His fuckability? No. Not anymore.

"Whew." Mel made a show of fanning herself. "I'm not certain that's physically possible, but I trust your judgment. You're the only one who's been up close and personal with him, after all."

Finally, the most complicated response of all.

Please tell us he's actually a decent guy.

April wouldn't discuss the differences between his public persona and private demeanor. He had his reasons for maintaining that facade, whatever they were, and she wouldn't violate his privacy in that way, either. She also wouldn't violate her own by describing their final moments together or the reason for her anger.

But she could tell a circumscribed truth.

"You don't have to worry, Heidi." She did her best to smile, because she *was* telling the truth, and she wanted its sincerity believed. "He was nothing but kind to me."

Even though he'd nudged her toward the gym and a healthy breakfast, she meant that. He'd almost certainly intended the invitation as a gesture of concern, despite its inherent condescension.

And when he'd talked about the buffet, she'd cut him off before he could finish telling her the choices. Maybe he'd have kept listing weight-loss-friendly options, but maybe—

No, there was no point going over that moment yet again. She'd made her decision, and she'd live with it. No matter how many times she'd questioned her knee-jerk reaction to his words this past week.

You know, those probably are *the items he always has for breakfast, given the nutritional and fitness demands of his work.* The thought wouldn't leave her, no matter how she exhausted herself unpacking boxes and moving furniture. *You asked what he could recommend, and if that's what he eats, healthy foods were very literally all he could honestly recommend.*

Her smile faded, despite her best efforts. "I don't think we'll be going out again, so I'm afraid I won't have more insider information in the future."

Even if she changed her mind at this point, even if she texted him to propose another date—which she definitely, definitely wouldn't—he might not accept. Not after the way she'd turned cold and dismissive in the cab, and not given the hurt she'd heard underlining every word he'd said after that point.

But he hadn't forced that hurt on her, either. Hadn't transformed it into an emotional bludgeon, a way to manipulate her into changing her mind. Hadn't argued or bombarded her with texts afterward.

He'd taken his dismissal with grace.

More grace, in the end, than she'd used in issuing it.

Mel pushed back her chair and stood, sympathy soft in her gaze. "We won't ask you about him again. I promise. And if any of us gets too nosy in the future, please tell us, and we'll back off. Immediately and without hurt feelings."

"It's fine." April consolidated the leftovers on the table, carefully avoiding further eye contact. "In your position, I'd have been asking the exact same questions."

Then they all got back to work, and she spent a quiet afternoon contending with various documents.

Documents—and doubts.

So many doubts.

BAWN HAD POSTED a new fic during her workday.

Eyes prickling and hot with tears, April clicked on it that evening.

The story was confirmation, if she'd needed it. He'd lied to her. Clearly he'd had internet access long enough to get his newest work uploaded. Which would also be long enough to send a brief DM, if he'd wanted to do so. Which he didn't anymore.

As always, he'd used a phrase from E. Wade's books to title his fic. This time, he'd drawn from a passage in the third story, one containing Lavinia's thoughts about Aeneas: *Though a half god, he is no less a man. And as such, prone to blunder full as often as any of his brethren.*

Unlike all BAWN's previous fics, though, "No Less a Man" ventured into the bedroom. It didn't require an E rating, so it must not be too graphic, but it was his first story to be rated M.

That was . . . odd.

He'd used her *misery ahoy!* tag, as well as the alternative she'd once proposed, *here be angst,* and at her incidental inclusion in the story he'd written and posted without her help or input, she had to stare up at the ceiling for a minute and blink hard.

As she began to read his words from an unfamiliar remove, without having seen the story first, without having brainstormed it together or proofread it for him, she had to stop. Sinuses clogging, she got up from her half-unpacked desk and wandered into the cluttered kitchen. The darkness of the backyard through the over-sink window soothed her stinging eyes, and cool water helped her swallow past the thickness in her throat.

She tossed her shredded tissue into the trash can and sat back down at her computer. Maybe she wouldn't read his future stories, but she couldn't ignore this one.

After the first few paragraphs, she knew someone else had beta-read the story. There were more transcription errors than normal, but far fewer than would exist without outside help.

After a few more paragraphs, she was crying again, this time openly.

In the story, compliant with but not included in book!canon, Lavinia and Aeneas found themselves newly married and alone in their bedchamber, both trying their best to come to terms with a marriage neither had wanted, despite their obedience to the will of the gods and the decree of the Fates.

They kissed, pleasurably enough for both parties. They held each other. When he questioned her willingness to proceed, she gave her consent to further intimacy.

He began to stroke her arms, her hair, her back, startled but pleased by a rising swell of desire. Lavinia, though, remained stiff under his touch, and Aeneas eventually drew back in confusion.

In the context of Wade's books, using the author's character-ization of Lavinia, the reasons for her hesitation were more than clear. She barely knew her husband and had expected to marry an-other man—Turnus—instead. She needed time to come to terms with such vast and unexpected changes in her life before welcom-ing Aeneas into her bed.

But even if she'd known him longer and better, it wouldn't have mattered. Not for their first time together. Given her history, she would fear any man's response to her angular body, her beaky nose and crooked smile and jutting ears.

To relax during bedplay, she'd require gentleness. Patience. Understanding.

But BAWN's story was written from Aeneas's point of view, as ever, and he didn't have the faintest idea what his new wife was thinking and remembering, much less what she needed to relax into their lovemaking. So he blundered, exactly as Lavinia had noted he might.

Assuming Lavinia was merely shy and uncomfortable exposing her nakedness by candlelight, he snuffed out the flame of the pottery lamp by the bed.

He didn't understand how she interpreted that gesture. Of course he didn't.

He hadn't spent a lifetime being sneered at for his plainness. His own father hadn't deemed him *ugly as Medusa* and laughed uproariously at the cleverness of his own wit. No one had told Aeneas that any woman who'd deign to marry him would insist on darkness for the bedding, to better hide his homeliness.

Lavinia, however, had suffered those indignities, those wounds, and at the snuffing of the lamp, she froze and began to weep in the darkness of their bedroom. At his next touch, she ran, hiding herself away from his imagined scorn and disgust in order to rebuild her emotional walls.

When Aeneas finally located her again, sitting under an olive tree, drenched by a summer storm, he found a wife transformed. No longer wary and willing, but icy and disdainful.

He knew he'd erred somehow, but he had no idea how, and Lavinia wouldn't say.

"I'm sorry," he told her helplessly, but he couldn't explain for what.

Lavinia simply turned her back and walked away from him.

The story ended there.

April's phone rang as she was still mopping her own tears, and she didn't bother to answer. She'd changed her number several days ago, so it probably wasn't someone calling to ask about Marcus anymore, but the thought of talking to her mother—the person most likely to call—right now nauseated her.

What the gorgeously written, depressing-as-fuck story might impart about BAWN's state of mind, she didn't know. At the moment, oddly enough, she didn't care.

"No Less a Man" might have been written by her former online friend, the object of her unrequited pining, but it reminded her of another man entirely.

Marcus.

Marcus, who'd burst into her life by defending her against bullies, ones who'd targeted her for her size. No one, not a soul, would have thought any less of him for ignoring the thread, but he hadn't. Instead, he'd called her gorgeous and asked her out. Held her hand. Put his hot mouth on her neck as she shivered in pleasure and sucked until a bruise bloomed on the spot.

Marcus, who hadn't said a word about what she'd ordered and eaten during their two meals together. Even trusted friends often teased her about the amount of sugar she stirred into her coffee, but he hadn't blinked, much less chided her.

Marcus, the man she'd cut off before he could finish speaking, the man she hadn't bothered to interrogate further before declaring him canceled, the man who'd watched her with such confused hurt on his solemn face as they sat in silence in the back seat of that cab.

Early in her friendship with BAWN, when they'd worked together for the first time on one of his fics, he'd struggled with Lavinia's motivations during an emotionally fraught scene. Eventually, April had broken it down for him in the simplest possible terms.

She has trust issues, she'd told BAWN. Major trust issues. They're going to color all her reactions to Aeneas, even though she's trying her best to be fair to him.

Shit, he'd responded. I can't believe I didn't realize that before. Of course she has trust issues. THANK YOU. This really helps.

Intending no harm, people often blundered.

Sometimes they blundered because their personal histories hadn't taught them to be sensitive to certain issues. And sometimes they blundered because—

Sometimes they blundered because they had trust issues. Major trust issues.

Dammit. No wonder she was part of the Lavineas fandom.

Marcus probably didn't want to hear from her. But before she dismissed him as fool's gold, she needed to be sure, absolutely sure, she was right. She needed to try, at least one more time.

Chest tight with nerves, her breaths shallow and rapid, she opened Twitter. To her relief, he hadn't unfollowed or blocked her. Their discussion-in-progress remained on the screen, waiting for her to continue the conversation.

So she did.

Hi, Marcus. I've been thinking about your invitation to the gym. Honestly, I'm not much for working out. Is that okay with you? Also, if you're still interested in getting together again, do you have an alternate suggestion?

His response arrived within minutes, and her eyes prickled again upon reading it.

Happy tears, this time.

If you don't like working out, we won't work out together. No worries. I would love to see you again. How about I come to SF next weekend and take you to my favorite doughnut shop from when I was a kid? Or, better yet, why don't we check out various doughnut shops around your new place and rank them in order of deliciousness?

She could honestly say she'd never heard a better date idea in her fucking *life*.

Gold. She'd almost tossed aside gold and called it pyrite.

I can't wait. I'm sorry. I—

She wasn't ready to share the details of her personal history yet, but he deserved an apology and some sort of explanation, however insufficient.

I'm sorry. I had a lot on my mind the other day, she eventually typed.

No worries, he wrote again. So I'll see you on Saturday?

She touched a forefinger to the faded bruise at the base of her neck, breathless once more. Now for entirely different—entirely better—reasons.

Just try and avoid me, she told him. XOXO.

Unapologetic Lavinia Stan: After watching tonight's episode, I keep thinking: What a waste.

Unapologetic Lavinia Stan: What we saw is a waste of the raw material provided by the books. It's a waste of truly amazing actors and crew. And it's a waste of the opportunity to tell the kind of story I

Book!AeneasWouldNever: What kind of story?

Book!AeneasWouldNever: Ulsie?

Unapologetic Lavinia Stan: Summer Diaz is so talented. She's also gorgeous.

Book!AeneasWouldNever: Yes. Both of those.

Book!AeneasWouldNever: I'm sensing a "but" in there somewhere.

Unapologetic Lavinia Stan: Lavinia is supposed to be ugly. Not just plain, or dressed in unflattering clothing. UGLY.

Book!AeneasWouldNever: This is true, at least in Wade's books.

Unapologetic Lavinia Stan: That's the fundamental beauty of the Lavineas relationship, BAWN.

Unapologetic Lavinia Stan: She's a woman who's been insulted and devalued her whole life because of how she looks, even though she's smart and brave and kind. Then Aeneas comes along, and he has his own baggage, but he sees her. He SEES her. He recognizes that everyone considers her ugly, but

Unapologetic Lavinia Stan: He sees her value. He grows to love her and desire her, even as she learns to trust him. Which is hard for her, but she does it, because she loves him too.

Unapologetic Lavinia Stan: That's the crux of the Lavineas story. As much as I adore Summer Diaz in the role, I can't help but think casting her was a fucking waste of a meaningful story that people needed to see on their television screens.

Book!AeneasWouldNever: I understand what you mean. I'm not sure any other actor could embody Lavinia's intelligence and determination quite so well, but—yes. You're right. It's yet more potential wasted.

Book!AeneasWouldNever: I imagine the actors see all that too. Even Summer herself.

Book!AeneasWouldNever: Aeneas's story . . . I just

Book!AeneasWouldNever: I just have the feeling the heart of his story will be destroyed too. A man questioning his relationship to the values he's been taught by his parents and making his way in the world. Finding his own moral code. Falling in love and learning to value both himself and that love more than his past and the duties imposed on him by others.

Unapologetic Lavinia Stan: That's a lovely way to put it.

Book!AeneasWouldNever: And in the final season, the showrunners will lay all that to waste. It's going to hurt, Ulsie. The way it plays out will hurt me, and it'll hurt you too. I'm so sorry.

Book!AeneasWouldNever: I mean, that's what I guess will happen.

Book!AeneasWouldNever: But the Lavineas relationship is always there on the page, if not on the television screen. And I'm always here too, on your computer screen. Anytime you need me.

Unapologetic Lavinia Stan: I'm not sure I deserve a friend like you, BAWN.

Book!AeneasWouldNever: You don't. You deserve so much more.

14

"I'M NOT ENTIRELY CERTAIN THE WORLD NEEDED A COCROF-finut." April popped the last bite into her mouth, sugar crystals sparkling on her lips. "However, I can now feel individual electrons orbiting the nucleus of every atom in my body. If that was the creator's intent, mission accomplished."

Marcus had to laugh, despite his preoccupation with her mouth. "I love it when you talk science-y to me."

She smiled at him, freckled cheeks pink in the sun, and God, he'd never been happier to ignore Alex's advice and his own best judgment. Never.

When she'd written him Monday evening, apparently willing to let him emerge from the hole he'd inadvertently dug for himself, he hadn't hesitated or thought twice. Not given the misery of their days without contact.

The absence of April in his life had hollowed out each and every day. For an hour or two at a time, maybe, he could distract himself from that emptiness. With writing, with reading the scripts his agent sent, with binge-watching British baking shows alongside Alex. But in the end, there he was, always, alone in his echoing LA home. Lonely. Missing a dear friend and—more. Whatever else they were becoming together before he'd tripped one of her personal land mines.

So, yeah. Good judgment be damned. Despite all the complications of the situation, any chance to be with April, he'd take.

"Funny you should say that. The people at my new job have a group T-shirt, I found out this week." With a careless sweep, she brushed crumbs off her chest and onto the sidewalk, where curious birds were edging closer. "It says *Talk Dirt-y to Me.*"

Apparently science people enjoyed puns too. Good to know. "Nice."

In the sunshine, her hair resembled a flame, and Marcus couldn't resist huddling closer to the heat. He shifted until they sat hip to hip on the wooden bench. As she watched him, brown eyes intent behind her glasses, he stroked his thumb along her plush lower lip to tease free those clinging crystals.

Her neck arched, just a little.

Without breaking eye contact, he licked the sugar from his thumb, and she took a shuddering breath.

No. He wasn't going to kiss her actual mouth for the first time on a park bench in public, not where everyone could see and document the occasion. Again.

After a fraught moment, he managed to look away. Clearing his throat, he fumbled with the paper menu he'd grabbed inside the shop and took his time reading aloud the description of the item she'd just finished.

"*The coco*—" He sighed. "Shit, this one is hard. Okay, let me try it again. *The cocroffinut*—"

She clapped. "Well done."

"Save your applause until we find out whether I can do it twice." One syllable at a time. "*The cocroffinut, the world's first and most delicious coffee/croissant/muffin/doughnut hybrid, contains the caffeine equivalent of four espressos.*"

She glanced down at the empty box on her lap. "Damn. Four espressos?"

He reread the description. "Yup. Well, that would explain your newfound sensitivity to orbiting electrons."

Getting to her feet, she rolled her eyes. "Hipsters, man. Hipsters."

He grinned up at her. "You said it was delicious."

"It was," she agreed, gathering their trash. "I also thought the glazed doughnut we shared at our last place, the one the size of my head, was delicious, and it cost approximately one-tenth as much as the croco—"

"Cocro—" he corrected automatically.

"—muffinut or whatever the hell I just finished eating. It also didn't leave me in possible need of a defibrillator." Once she'd thrown their trash in the nearest recycling and waste bins, she laid a palm over her chest. "I think my heart is doing the jitterbug in there, even though I actually have no idea what the jitterbug entails."

He sat straighter. "If you need to see a doctor, I can take you."

"Nah. I'm just being overly dramatic, probably because of all the caffeine." She waved a dismissive hand. "Don't mind me."

Whew. He'd really prefer their third date not necessitate medical intervention, if at all possible. Especially since he had hopes for the evening.

High hopes. *Turgid* hopes, to use one of TopMeAeneas's favorite adjectives.

"Being a drama queen is my job, lady. Hands off." Leaning back again, he rested his arms along the top of the bench. "Speaking of my job, I actually learned how to jitterbug for a historical miniseries. I could show you."

Lindy Hope, the inspirational—if entirely fictional—story of how swing dancing turned the tide of one World War II battle, hadn't exactly broken viewing-audience records, but at least he'd gotten some decent moves and a decent paycheck out of it.

"Why don't we walk while you tell me more?" She held out a hand. "I'm too caffeinated to sit still."

He accepted her hand and got to his feet, interlacing their fingers as they headed toward the water. "Um . . . what do you want to know?"

Normally, he'd steer the topic toward hair care or workouts, or mention only the most superficial things he'd learned over the years. Before showing up at their first doughnut shack a couple of hours ago, though, he'd already disposed of that particular shield.

She was meeting him as he really was today, like it or not.

The possibility that she might *not* like it had his own heart skittering a bit. As did the possibility that he was tossing his reputation into the garbage alongside their cocroffinut detritus, because if she ever revealed him as a faker to the world before he was ready, before he could explain—

She wouldn't. She wouldn't. He trusted her that far, and he trusted his own ability to do sufficient damage control if she proved him naive.

His fanfic alter ego, though . . . no amount of PR and damage control could stop the knowledge of that from destroying his career.

Eventually, maybe he could tell her he was Book!Aeneas-WouldNever.

Not now. Not yet.

"Okay, fun stuff first." She was swinging their hands in a huge, swift, jerky arc, and yes, he could definitely tell she'd had more than her usual share of caffeine. It was fucking *adorable*. "What's the most memorable movie you've ever been part of?"

He snorted. "That's a tougher question than you might think.

I've been acting for over twenty years now. There are lots of possibilities to consider."

For some reason, the bad roles were so much easier to remember than the movies whose premieres he'd attended with sincere pride. Probably more entertaining to hear about too.

Her stride was becoming an uncharacteristic sort of half jog, half skip, her hair swinging around her shoulders with each hyperactive, bouncing step. "Then tell me all of them."

"Since that could take weeks, I'll choose a representative sampling." Damn, he needed to hustle faster to keep up with her. "My worst film overall was probably, um . . . *Hounded*, I guess."

Her brow crinkled as she thought. "You were a perfumer in that one, right? Wrongly accused of a terrible crime?"

"Yes. A master perfumer, nicknamed the Hound for my extraordinary sense of smell." After an exaggerated inhalation through his nose, he continued, "Which I then employed to hide from the authorities while locating my wife's real killer."

"As one does." Her voice was as dry as the California hills in October. "And of course his wife's murder served as his motivation. Of course."

"Fridging at its most banal. Eventually, I discovered that my business rivals had formed a secret cabal, hired an assassin, and framed me in hopes of removing me from the perfume industry permanently."

"Spoiler alert," she chided him, lips quirked.

He huffed out a laugh. "My scenes mostly involved *sniffing*. Turns out, it's hard to make sniffing attractive or interesting to an audience. Which is some explanation as to why the movie flopped." God, the reviews. Those *reviews*. Not to mention the phone call from his parents after they'd seen one of the sparse local showings. "It did inspire an X-rated parody, though, from what my costars told me. One with a particularly clever name."

As they walked, he waited, confident she could come up with it. She bit her lip for a few moments, then brightened. "*Pounded!*"

"Brava, April." Lifting their joined hands above their heads in triumph, he grinned at her. "That movie apparently involved a lot of sniffing as well. Among other activities. It also made more money than its inspiration. Probably featured better acting too."

He'd wanted her to giggle, but she didn't. Instead, for no reason he could fathom, her eyes had turned solemn, and he shifted his shoulders under the weight of her regard.

"You're joking about it, but you must have learned a lot about perfumery for the role," she finally said. "I may not know you well, but I can already tell you're a professional. You care about your craft."

Why that twisted his heart until it ached, he couldn't have said.

"Uh, yeah, actually." He squinted into the distance, where the water awaited them, blue and cool and comforting. "I visited a perfumery school in France. A world-class perfumer can identify over a thousand different scents, mostly by associating smells with specific memories. I worked on that a little. Learned about the history of perfume. Watched one woman grind ambergris with a mortar and pestle too, just for kicks."

"What *is* ambergris?" she asked. "I've always wondered."

He smirked at her. "Hardened whale feces that washes onshore."

"You set me up for that." Her eyes narrowed, but her mouth was twitching. "Shame on you. Now I have to go through my perfumes and find out just how much whale poop I've been spraying on myself for dates."

Her perfume today smelled primarily of roses. His nose wasn't particularly sensitive, as he'd discovered during that idyllic week in France, but he could also detect a trace of musk. And . . . other stuff, which real perfumers could no doubt pinpoint in a flash.

Where exactly she'd sprayed that perfume, he shouldn't consider in public.

"Anyway, so that was one memorable role. The absolute worst script I ever had was probably for *1 Wheel, 2 Real*." At her confused glance, he clarified. "The uplifting coming-of-age story of a troubled unicyclist. I think it got released directly to the DVR of one guy in Tulsa."

When she laughed, she slowed down a fraction. "Holy shit. You can unicycle?"

"Of course," he informed her loftily, nose in the air. "Like any serious thespian."

Well-Groomed Golden Retriever Marcus would never use that term, of course. Even as himself, it sat oddly on his tongue. Too grand. Too lofty. A thespian, as opposed to an actor, demanded respect from the world at large, not simply others within the entertainment industry. A thespian possessed talent, not merely the capacity for hard work and a pretty face.

Pulling him to the edge of the sidewalk, she came to a dead halt. "But you *are* a serious thespian, Marcus."

All that caffeine had clearly gone to her head. She sounded . . . angry, almost.

He lifted a shoulder, offering her a placating smile. "I've tried to be. I don't know how successful I've been."

"You've been up for a bunch of awards. You star in the most popular television program in the world. When you left Dido behind and spotted that damn funeral pyre from your ship, I nearly required medical intervention for my weeping-related dehydration issues."

She spoke slowly, as if to a blockheaded child, and he bristled instinctively at that familiar tone. At least until the actual meaning of her words sank in. Then he flushed hot with embarrassment and kicked at a crack in the sidewalk.

"And all those nominations weren't just for *Gods of the Gates*," she added. "There was that Stoppard play too, and the astronaut role."

Starshine. He'd played the only survivor of a catastrophic incident aboard the International Space Station. Maybe the indie film hadn't done as well as he'd hoped in theaters, but yeah, for that red carpet, he'd probably strutted a bit, truth be told.

She stepped in closer, until they could communicate in near-whispers. Until she could study him up close, her attention sharp as the hero sword he'd never actually swung in his *Gates* battle scenes.

"But in all honesty, probably the most demanding and impressive role you've played isn't any of those." Her chin was firm, her tone still determined and confrontational for reasons he couldn't fathom. "Is it?"

He frowned at her, lost.

Maybe that time he'd played Posthumus in an adaptation of *Cymbeline*, given the language issues, but—

"I'm not sure which role you mean," he told her.

When she arched a fiery brow, he knew he was in trouble.

"It's you. Marcus Caster-Rupp. The performance of a lifetime." She laid her palm on his chest, over his heart, as if she were taking its measure. Maybe she was. "The vainest, dimmest actor on the planet, who's actually neither. Seemingly shallow and shiny as a puddle, but deep as the Mariana Trench."

Deep? *Him?*

What the actual fuck?

"Explain it to me, please." She spoke politely, but it wasn't a request. It was a demand. "Sooner or later, the paparazzi are going to find us again. Before I watch your next performance, I need to understand."

That flaming hair should have warned him. Somehow, she was his crucible, burning away everything but the truth. Forcing him to speak it aloud and purify himself before her.

He opened his mouth. Closed it, unsure what to say or how to begin.

Her hand gave his sternum a gentle but firm pat. A warning. "Don't bother pretending you don't know what the Mariana Trench is, either. I streamed *Sharkphoon*, and those chompy bastards came rocketing up from that trench into the cyclone. You told the president about the danger in your white lab coat and safety glasses, to no avail."

Stupidly, he couldn't help wondering whether she'd watched the movie in 3-D, because the scene where the mother shark ate that cruise ship in three giant bites was really enhanced by—

Nope. Not the point right now.

He let out a slow breath. Closed his eyes.

Why had he ever imagined she might simply accept his change in demeanor without remarking on it? Without asking what it meant?

The woman standing before him was Ulsie, the beta reader who challenged any inconsistencies in his stories.

The woman standing before him was April, who made a living out of comparing surfaces to what lay underneath.

The woman standing before him was the woman he wanted. That simple.

So at long last, he opened his mouth again and gave her what *she* wanted.

The truth.

Enough truth for now, at least.

<u>1 WHEEL, 2 REAL</u>

EXT. THE MEAN STREETS OF PORTLAND - MIDDAY

*EWAN looks at the beautiful, quirky girl with the bright
pink hair sitting beside him, his unicycle propped against
the back slats of their bench. Suddenly, he realizes she
knows everything about him, but he knows nothing about her.*

                         EWAN
What's your name?

                         PIXIE
It doesn't matter.

                         EWAN
Of course it matters.
  *She crinkles her nose adorably and laughs, idly
juggling as she speaks.*

                         PIXIE
It really doesn't. Right now, what I want, what I
need, what I think, my goals, and even my name are so
much less important than you, Ewan. Your story. Your
life. Your redemption.
  *Near tears, he tries to smile and presses a quick
kiss on her mouth.*

                         EWAN
I've never felt so understood before now. If someone
like you had been in my life earlier, I think—

                         PIXIE
What?

                         EWAN
Maybe I wouldn't have gotten mixed up in that
unicycling gang to begin with. And now, I'm starting
to think maybe—maybe—
   (he takes a shuddering breath)
I could switch from one wheel . . . to two.
   *Pixie beams at him. This is the happiest moment of
her life.*

15

THE FOGGINESS OF THE MORNING HAD BURNED AWAY BE-
neath the sun, and Marcus glowed golden in its rays. In that light,
given the right cinematography, he could have been the demigod
he'd played so ably for years. He could have been a figure of myth,
or the stalwart, knightly hero of young April's fevered imagina-
tion and current April's most fevered fics.

But no camera was filming him, and this wasn't a story, and he
was no invincible half god. Not if she looked more closely.

His mouth had pressed into a tight grimace, and he directed
that famous blue-eyed gaze anywhere but at her. At the sidewalk
beneath their feet, at the businesses they'd already passed, at the
sparkling water they'd begun to approach. If he suddenly sprinted
from her and dove into the Bay to escape this conversation—
perhaps sprouting a tail like the one he'd sported in *Manmaid*,
his tragic film about a half-human sea creature cursed to love a
woman allergic to kelp—she wouldn't be shocked.

He didn't run, though. Instead, he just looked . . . lost.

Then that knife-edged jaw firmed, and his eyes speared her.
She stilled her caffeine-induced fidgeting, even as her pulse still
pounded in her ears and his heartbeat thudded under her palm.

"When I was fifteen, I gave up." That rich, low voice was flat.
Devoid of all the emotion he'd poured into the words of countless

screenwriters. For these, his own words, he allowed no jagged edges, no half-crumbled handholds for her to grasp and pull herself closer to him. "I was going to disappoint everyone. Disgust them. It didn't matter how hard I tried, or how often I apologized."

Careful. Careful. No inflection or sympathy or anything he could misinterpret. "Everyone?"

"I told you my mom homeschooled me. Until I finished my schoolwork, I didn't go outside, and my parents weren't big fans of organized sports. I didn't see other kids a lot. When I did, I didn't know what to say." One shoulder twitched upward, a casual movement turned convulsive. "My parents were my world. They were everyone."

"You gave up." She repeated his own words, breath held against the possibilities contained in that phrase.

"I'd always been a good mimic. I'd practice to myself in my room. I had my parents down cold by then. That pompous guy from all the historical documentaries my parents loved too. The actors from the Royal Shakespeare Company, whenever their performances came on public television and my parents made me watch." His smile was thin and brittle. "Without even having to think about it much, I knew him. What he'd say. How he'd say it. His posture. What gestures he'd make."

Her frown of confusion must have caught his attention.

"My first and longest-running role. The Worst Possible Son. Vain and lazy and stupid and careless and everything else they hate." With a casual sweep of his hand, he flicked back a lock of sun-streaked hair. A demonstration. A reminder. "It was easy. So much easier than before."

She closed her eyes.

Behind her lids, he shrank into a lanky, lonely boy. Angry. Hurt.

Not hard, not the diamond she'd once named him. Already golden, she guessed, even as a teenager. Like gold, so soft he could be gouged and warp under too much pressure—unless he shielded himself somehow. Unless he wedged something flinty and immovable between himself and the relentless, grinding weight of his parents' displeasure.

The Worst Possible Son, he'd said. Vain and lazy and stupid and careless.

If they despised him then, they didn't despise the real him. They couldn't hurt the real him. They couldn't even *see* the real him, if they ever had at all.

It was defiance, a middle finger held up to the heavens. It was armor. It was . . .

Jesus, it was enough to make her throat burn, her hand on his chest curl into a fist.

Once all threat of tears had disappeared, if not her lingering helpless rage, she opened her eyes again. Met his.

She got it. She really did. The origins of his act, the catalyst for his longest-running role. But he was a man grown now, so why? Why was he still playacting?

He was watching her carefully, his tone so remote it frightened her. "I didn't intend to keep up the act once I left for college, or after I dropped out and moved to LA. I had no idea what to say or do unless I was in character, but I tried. And eventually, I got a bit more practice talking to everyone, especially once Alex moved in with me. He helped me feel more comfortable around other people."

Shy. Dammit, he was *shy*.

How had she not realized that before?

Also, note to self: *Don't tell Marcus you originally wanted to have dinner with his best friend instead of him.*

"Before *Gates*, I didn't have to deal with many interviews. Then I got the role of Aeneas, and . . ." His throat worked. "Suddenly, there were so many questions, and so much more of an audience for whatever I said, and I wasn't prepared. Alex and I had run through likely questions, but we never thought anyone would hand me a fucking book and ask me to read a page about Aeneas aloud."

Fuck. Fuck, she knew which interview he meant. That infamous two-part segment on a morning news and entertainment show, her mother's favorite.

Her mom had even mentioned it during a phone call later that day, so many years ago. "Didn't you used to read those books? You can watch the interview on mute, though. That boy is handsome, but not exactly a sparkling conversationalist."

April had streamed it on YouTube that afternoon, complete with sound, despite her mother's warning. She'd played it again less than two weeks ago, before her dinner with Marcus, as mental preparation for their planned date.

Both times, she'd studied Marcus as the host handed him a book with small text and asked him to read a steamy bit aloud. On live television. Without warning. With—as she now knew—dyslexia, which he'd been taught to consider a defining weakness and source of shame.

Still, he'd tried, stumbling over the words until the host and audience had laughed uncomfortably and the show broke for commercials.

A few comments beneath that video had speculated he was drunk, but the group consensus had coalesced quickly: stupid, not hammered.

Why is their IQ always the inverse of their fuckability?

With a face that pretty, I guess he didn't have to learn to read, right?

"You saw the interview, I take it," he said, and she tried to compose her expression. "At that point, I knew I was dyslexic. I wasn't ashamed of it, not by the time I got cast in *Gates*."

She wasn't sure whether to believe that, but she nodded anyway.

Beneath her hand, his heartbeat hastened as he told the story. "But in that moment, I just . . . blanked. Panicked. I was sweating under the lights, and people in the studio were still whispering to themselves and laughing, and when we came back after the commercials, I heard myself answering questions as *him*."

"The Worst Possible Son," she said. The role he'd played more often than any other, the role that had offered him protection from scorn so often in the past.

God, now that she knew, she could see it so clearly. The transition between the man who'd occasionally looked down and fumbled for words even before E. Wade's doorstop tome landed in his lap, and the man who'd preened for the cameras during the rest of the two-part interview.

"Well, not entirely." His smirk didn't crinkle the corners of his eyes. "Somehow I had enough sense to make sure I came across as an especially friendly dunce, so as not to alienate our potential audience. So it was a variation on my original role. More the Well-Groomed Golden Retriever, less the Worst Possible Son."

The biting edge to his words was meant to hurt *someone*. Himself? Anyone who'd scorn him? Both?

"I get it." At least, the essentials of the situation. "But why not act differently for your next interview?"

His jaw shifted. "The showrunners were amused. They said it was less boring than my usual interviews, and since we weren't allowed to say much about the script or the show anyway, I might as well entertain the audience a different way. After a while, I think they kind of forgot it was an act at all."

To them, his humiliation was amusing. *Entertainment*. Goddammit, no *wonder* the show went off the rails once those motherfuckers couldn't follow Wade's books anymore.

"I also realized pretty quickly how easy I had it, compared to the other cast members." Marcus's voice had turned raspy and tired, and her hand rose and fell on his sigh. "They were always getting asked for character insights or opinions about the books versus the show, but once the media decided I was dumb, they didn't bother giving me hard questions. I didn't have to deflect or lie. I could just flex and primp and talk about my exercise routine. Eventually, most outlets stopped asking for individual interviews entirely, which was a relief."

"Because you didn't know what to say," she said. "Not as yourself."

He inclined his head, a mute agreement.

Now they'd reached the heart of the issue. His heart, beating steadily under her palm. His heart, evident in every bit of truth he'd offered her.

She stroked him with her thumb, a gentle arc of a caress. "Because you weren't comfortable in your own skin."

"No. Not like I am now." For the first time since the conversation began, he touched her in return. His hand covered hers, pressed it close to the soft, nubby fabric of his sweater. "But once I had that version of myself established, April, I was kind of stuck."

An elderly couple was walking arm-in-arm on the sidewalk nearby, chatting amiably as they drew closer. Close enough to hear things Marcus didn't yet want revealed to the world.

Even though the two wizened men weren't listening, she still lowered her voice to a thready whisper. "What do you mean?"

He edged closer. Ducked his head to speak directly into her

ear, that golden hair cool and silky against her cheek. Softened his voice to match hers.

"After a year or two, I thought about changing my public persona, but I didn't want *Gates* fans to think I was just fucking with them this whole time as some sort of weird, mean joke. I'd have to explain *why* I'd been pretending, and I didn't know how to do it in a way that would satisfy them but not humiliate me." He blew out a breath, and it tickled her earlobe enough to make her shiver. "To be frank, I've also been happy not to answer questions about scripts the last three seasons."

That was as close to criticism of the show as she'd ever heard him venture. And as part of the Lavineas server, whose denizens linked to and analyzed every interview he gave, no matter how vapid, she would know.

Another gesture of trust, offered this time without prompting.

The couple had passed by them and shuffled farther down the street, but she didn't back away. The intimacy of their position warmed her against the spring breeze, and he smelled—

A perfumer would know, could tease apart each delicious, herbal note. He'd said so.

She couldn't. All she could do was inhale and sway closer and—wonder.

"Did you explain all this to your ex-girlfriends? Why you were different in private than in public?" she asked. "Because if I hadn't pushed just now, I got the sense you'd have avoided the subject as long as possible."

The material of his jeans teased against her knit leggings, thigh against thigh, and her lips parted.

"I haven't had many relationships, April." He wasn't speaking into her ear anymore, but facing her from inches away, gaze as steady as that rhythmic heartbeat. "Just to be clear."

Oh, he was very, very clear. From the heat radiating off him, his blown pupils, she suspected a glance downward would make his current state even more undeniable.

His hand tightened over hers. "And for the most part, I *wasn't* different in private. Not until I knew them and trusted their discretion. Once I did trust them . . ." He leaned back a tad and ran his free hand through his hair. "I tried to transition slowly. At that point, things fell apart, for obvious reasons."

With those bare centimeters of distance, she could breathe a little more easily. But her thinking remained muddled by pheromones and the lightning strike of lust, and she had no idea what he meant.

At her frown, he elaborated. "They began dating me based on my public persona, and then found themselves with someone entirely different. Someone inexplicable and kind of boring. When I'm not filming or working out, I like to stay home and listen to audiobooks, or go online, or wr—" He paused. "Or ride horses. Or watch baking shows with Alex. I was, um—"

When he took a half step away, the morning chill sneaked between them. "I was a disappointment, I guess."

To his exes, the change must have seemed inexplicable. And to Marcus . . . dammit. He must have felt rejected for who he really was. Again.

"On top of that, dating someone in the public eye is hard on a relationship, even without other issues," he said. "You've already experienced a few of the downsides. Did the paparazzi find you last week?"

"Yeah." If she sounded like she didn't care, that was almost entirely the truth. Especially at this moment, with this man only inches away.

Now that the fog had lifted, sunshine highlighted the starbursts of fine lines at the corners of his solemn eyes, the brackets surrounding his perfect mouth, the creases running across that noble forehead. Somehow the lines didn't look like flaws, even in the unfiltered, unforgiving glare. Instead, they only transformed his unmistakable prettiness into something earthier, something she could grasp in her fist and take between her teeth and *consume*.

Honestly, if she hadn't begun to *like* him so much, she would find his excessive handsomeness extremely aggravating. And despite all her affection, she still wanted to rumple all that beauty, wanted to sink her fingers into that shiny, silky hair and *pull*, even as she traced the jut of his jaw, sharp as flint, with her tongue.

What sound would he make if she bit him there?

When he swallowed, his throat bobbed. "Is that why you changed your number?"

He was breathing faster now, and fuck, she wanted him gasping in need. For her. Only her.

She shrugged. "Once they figured out my name, I had a few calls and some pictures taken. But changing my number helped, and they seemed to lose interest after a couple of days." *Once they concluded we weren't dating anymore.* "I figure the reprieve will end soon, and that's okay. It's a price I'm willing to pay."

What strangers said didn't concern her.

Her mother's phone calls, however, she'd dodged since that first date.

"Are you sure?" With a gentle fingertip, he urged her face toward his again. "Because you're right. They'll find us again. Find you. If you decided to protect your privacy and stop seeing me, I'd understand."

He'd bared himself metaphorically for her today. It was enough. More than enough, despite the dangers of their involvement.

So she had every intention of baring him literally. Tonight, if possible.

"Maybe you'd understand. I wouldn't." Boldly, she stepped into him again. "If I want you, I'm not letting a few strangers with cameras stop me from having you."

Dropping her hand from his chest, she slid it around to his back. Slipped a fingertip below the hem of his sweater and teased the hot, bare skin just above his jeans.

As he bit off a rough sound, she walked him back, back, back, their thighs tangling with each step, until he was pressed against a sturdy-looking wrought-iron fence, and she was pressed tight to him.

Her heart was thumping hard enough to shake her, and it wasn't due to all that caffeine.

Once she got on tiptoe, she laid her mouth on his jaw. The merest hint of stubble abraded her lips, a welcome friction. The tight-stretched flesh there tasted like salt on her tongue, and vibrated with his low moan.

She took that skin between her teeth and licked.

His hips bucked, and she gloried in the way he ground against her so fiercely, just for one mindless moment.

"What do you say, Marcus?" Back against that fence, where passersby couldn't see, she slid both hands beneath his sweater and stroked up the satiny line of his spine, then dragged her nails lightly going back down. "Should I have you?"

He didn't answer in words. He didn't need to.

It seemed she'd burned all the gentleness out of him, and good riddance. He fisted her hair in one hand and splayed the other wide on the swell of her ass, hauling her tighter against him. Her own sweater had ridden up, and those knit leggings didn't blunt the sensation of his thigh nudging between hers, the jut of his cock against her belly.

She might have backed him into that fence, but she wasn't in control. Not anymore.

"Turnabout," he murmured against her neck, open mouth hot on her skin, and licked the spot. Nipped it. "You still have a mark here. Good."

Her back hit the fence as he flipped their position, and he settled hard between her thighs. She huffed out a labored breath, dizzied and so fucking turned on she wanted to scratch and claw until he made the ache go away.

His teeth and tongue scored a path of fire up her neck, under her own jaw, and then—

Oh, his mouth claimed hers like a battle prize, hard and desperate, and she opened to the claim without hesitation.

Later they could try tender and sweet, but right now she wanted his tongue in her mouth, his teeth on her lower lip, and his groan swallowed by her panting breath. She wanted that possessive hold on her ass to squeeze her closer, closer, as the tug of her hair turned her nerve endings incandescent.

Here, he tasted like sugar instead of salt. Like mint. Like darkness and heat.

"So sweet," he rasped, then slanted his fierce, reddened lips across hers once more, and she moaned into his mouth as he rubbed against her *just right*. His jeans were loose enough that she could slide both hands beneath the denim if she kept them flat, slide them beneath his ultra-soft underwear too, and then she was sinking her short, blunt nails into the satiny, clenching, round cheeks of his ass and staking her own claim.

At the sting, he ground against her again with a low, rough

noise and twined their tongues greedily. His herbal scent was turning muskier, deeper by the moment, and her own overheated skin prickled with growing dampness.

He couldn't wrap her legs around his waist and fuck her against this fence. Not in daylight. Not in public. Not given her size. But the next time she fished her technicolor vibrator from her nightstand, she had a new fantasy to ride to a bed-shaking orgasm.

When his mouth eventually lifted a hairsbreadth from hers, she chased it.

Then she heard the sound too.

"Hey, you two! Get off my property!" It was a disgusted shout, originating from the doorway of the house beyond the fence. "That's way too much tongue for a Saturday morning!"

Marcus gave a quiet snort, and he whispered in her ear, "Apparently we can come back later this afternoon to dry-hump against his fence again."

"During normal business hours." Regretfully, she slid her hands out of his jeans. "Although there are also public indecency charges to consider."

He rested his forehead against her shoulder for a moment, still breathless. "Fair point."

Then, with an odd sort of groaning whine, he levered himself away from her and turned to offer the man in the doorway his usual charming smile. "Our apologies, sir. We'll be on our way now."

The man emitted an unappeased grunt and disappeared back inside his house.

As they returned to the sidewalk, Marcus cupped her hips and maneuvered her in front of him. Almost close enough to touch, but not quite. "Stay here for just a minute, please."

If she arched her back just a tad . . . yes. There.

As her ass pressed against the ridge of his erection, his fingers tightened to a pleasurable bite through her leggings. "April . . ." He sounded as if he was speaking through clenched teeth. "You're not helping matters."

Okay, then. No more below-the-waist contact, at least for now.

Instead, she tipped back her head, laid it against his shoulder, and smiled as they waited for his body to calm. "Really? Because it felt like I was helping."

"Helping me get arrested, maybe."

"To echo a wise man: fair point." Luckily, her current state of swollen arousal wasn't quite so obvious, but *God*, she needed to squeeze her thighs together. "Want to hold my purse?"

"What does that have to do with—" He paused. "Oh. Yeah. That'll probably work."

Still, neither of them started walking. Instead, he hitched her a bit closer, and they just . . . cuddled for a minute, her head on his shoulder, his strong, broad hands lightly stroking her sides and hips and arms. When he eventually folded her into his embrace, she rested her arms on top of his.

After a moment, he kissed her temple, then laid his cheek there.

It was the gentleness she'd told herself she didn't want.

Turned out she was a liar, because she wanted it all. His teeth and his tenderness. His pretty face and his laugh lines. The respected thespian and the hammy star of *Sharkphoon*.

The gold and the pyrite.

Turning her neck, she pressed a soft kiss to the underside of his jaw. "Come home with me. Please."

He didn't hesitate, not even for a breath.

"Yes," he said. "Yes."

MANMAID

EXT. SHORELINE AT THE BASE OF THE CLIFFS - DAWN

*CARMEN has waded chest-deep into the surf, fully
clothed, and TRITUS flicks his tail idly to stay upright
before her, gazing adoringly into her seafoam-green eyes.*

CARMEN

When will you return?

TRITUS

Whenever you need me.
  She casts him a shy glance through her lashes.

CARMEN

What if . . . What if what I need from you, you can't
give?
  *He frowns, confused. Then realization dawns, and so
does desire. He swims closer.*

TRITUS

Trust me. I may only be half human, but I'm all man.

CARMEN

You mean . . . ?

TRITUS

Let me show you.
  *But as they touch for the first time, hands
entwined, her legs against his tail, her eyes widen,*

and not in desire. Suddenly, she is struggling to
breathe, gasping and staggering away from him.

CARMEN

My—my allergy! To kelp! I'd—
(gasps)
forgotten!

TRITUS

No! My curse! It has finally come to pass!
The tragedy of their love overwhelms him, and he
swims away, disappearing beneath the waves.

16

"SO THIS IS WHERE I LIVE." APRIL WAVED HIM INSIDE. "IT'S an in-law apartment, so I have my own entrance, and it's relatively private."

Marcus glanced around. "Looks like a great find, especially in this area."

An open floor plan, excluding the bedrooms and bathroom. Not overly spacious, but cozy. Well maintained too, with gleaming hardwood floors and stainless appliances and marble-looking countertops. Once she had the chance to settle in, he suspected it would become much more welcoming than his own LA home with its aggressively modern interior design. Served him right for not overseeing the process himself, of course, but he'd been overseas at the time and eager to come back to a finished house.

"Sorry about the boxes." April shifted from foot to foot. "I haven't had time to put everything away or get art on the walls."

The white marble console table in the entryway—she'd chosen stone rather than wood, no surprise there—didn't wobble when he rested a hand on it, its surface cool and smooth and solid under his fingertips. "I'm impressed by everything you've managed to unpack in such a short amount of time."

She pursed her lips, but her little hum sounded like doubt.

By the time he'd followed her to the apartment, some of her confidence and her unabashed, intoxicating sexual aggression had faded. Right now, her gaze was darting around the room, seemingly cataloging all the space's flaws. This was as nervous as he'd ever seen her, and that included their first dinner together and their first encounter with paparazzi.

Which was unfortunate, because the change allowed his blood to cool and his head to clear too. Enough that he remembered his resolution to discuss one last sensitive topic with her before they bared themselves to one another.

Not that he'd assumed they would, and she could change her mind now or whenever she wanted. But he'd hoped. Fantasized.

"I know it's not what you're probably accustomed to—" she began.

"April." He shook his head at her, an eyebrow raised in gentle reproof. "My parents are prep school teachers, remember? I grew up in a house not much larger than your apartment."

Her face brightened slightly at the reminder, but the stiff set of her shoulders didn't entirely ease. "That's right. I'd forgotten."

She was anxious about his judgment. That was obvious enough. What wasn't: whether all her nervousness really stemmed from her half-settled home.

They'd come to her apartment for a purpose, one she'd made clear. But now that the prospect of so much intimacy, so much literal and figurative nakedness, loomed before them, did she worry he might judge her and find her lacking in an entirely different way?

"Umm . . ." She wandered toward the kitchen area. "Are you hungry? We could eat lunch, if you'd like. I have some leftover pizza. Some leftover fried rice too." Her shoulder lifted, and she opened the refrigerator and scanned the shelves. "Sorry. I haven't done much cooking since the move. Not that I cooked much before then, either."

He wasn't going to get a better opening than that.

She didn't move from the refrigerator as he walked up behind her. Not even when he wrapped his arms around her from behind, looping them just above her waist. Her body was still within his embrace. Stiff, although she didn't move away.

After a few seconds, she relaxed, melting into him the way she had earlier.

Ducking his head, he rested his chin on her round shoulder. "I like to cook. Which is good, because my job means I have to be careful about what I eat. How I exercise too."

And there it was. He might as well have been holding a piece of her stone countertop. No surprise there.

"April . . ." He pressed a quick kiss to the newest bruise on the side of her neck. "After those doughnuts this morning, I'll probably eat nothing but protein and vegetables for the rest of the day. I can't have leftover pizza or fried rice. I'm not especially hungry anyway. But—"

She was closing the refrigerator door and twisting out of his arms and moving away from him, and he didn't try to stop her. He just kept talking and hoped she was still listening.

"—I don't expect anyone else to eat or exercise the way I do. It's a part of my job. That's all." He gestured to the shiny refrigerator. "So if you're hungry and want pizza, have pizza. If you want fried rice, have fried rice. If you want to eat more doughnuts the size of your head, or another of those croco—"

"Cocroffinuts," she muttered, finally meeting his eyes again.

"—whatever the fuck those things are, you should do it. Despite the very real risk that more caffeine might actually make you levitate." He tried to infuse each word with every bit of sincerity he could muster, every bit of reassurance. "What I eat or don't eat is irrelevant."

He shouldn't know why she'd turned cold in the cab after their day at the museum. But he *did* know, and before they fell into bed together, she needed to hear the truth.

His body was a tool for his job. He intended to keep it strong and durable and flexible. If the attention he had to pay to food and working out would trigger anxiety for her or make her uncomfortable in ways she couldn't get past, then they both needed to know that now.

She'd paused several feet away from him, leaning a hip against the countertop. Behind those adorable glasses, her brown eyes were narrowed. Assessing.

It wasn't enough that he was telling the truth. She had to believe it too. He intended to project earnestness and credibility using every trick in his actor's playbook.

He kept his stance open under her scrutiny, his hands relaxed, his gaze steady in return. Before her, he stood calm and stalwart, the very exemplar of trustworthiness.

Another long pause, and then she inclined her head and took a small step toward him. "Fair enough."

The sudden release of tension weakened his legs, and he propped his butt against the countertop for extra support as he cast her a sidelong glance. "You mentioned lunch. Do you want to eat something?"

For the first time since they'd arrived at her apartment, a wicked edge turned her smile sharp. Predatory. Jesus, he'd run past SFX fireballs on set that weren't as hot as April with that particular expression on her face.

Best of all, her expression meant he'd done it. He'd navigated a verbal minefield without a script or character guiding his words—*him*, of all people—and that gorgeous incendiary device of a smile was his reward.

"Not food." Another step closer. Another. "In other matters, I could be persuaded."

His breath whooshed from his lungs.

April, her red-gold hair spread over his thighs as he arched into her hot mouth and trembled.

That particular image had brought him to orgasm numerous times over the past week, almost as often as when he imagined the sounds she'd make as he licked her, how she'd buck in his hold and toss her head as he held her in place, how she'd tighten around his fingers when he sucked her clit, how she'd pulse and moan as she fell to pieces under his mouth.

Just an hour ago, though, his cock had strained against the zipper of his jeans at the genesis of an entirely different fantasy. That one he could make happen, if she was willing. Right now, in her kitchen, with daylight pouring through her windows.

He held out a hand. "Come here."

No hesitation. Her fingers intertwined with his, and she didn't pause or protest when he turned her and tugged until her back pressed against his chest. The counter behind him was hard and cold, but he barely felt it anymore. Not given the heat and softness in his arms.

The pressure of her generous ass against his growing erection turned his eyelids heavy. Especially when she did exactly what she'd done on that sidewalk earlier. Tipping her hips, she rubbed up and down slowly, a caressing taunt.

He ran his nose along her neck. Sank his teeth a millimeter into her earlobe, glorying in her gasp and the clutch of her hands on his arms.

His fingers flirted with the hem of her sweater. "Can I touch you?"

"Anywhere."

He licked the rim of her ear. "Anywhere? Really?"

"Really." Twisting her neck, she pulled his mouth to hers for a brief, wet kiss, sucking his tongue until his vision turned white around the edges.

When she faced front again, her head against his shoulder, he let his hands roam under her sweater. His palms stroked over her rounded belly, up her sides.

Soft. She was so soft everywhere. Full of curves and secret valleys.

Her satiny skin was heating under his touch, even before he brushed a thumb along the swell of her breast, right above her bra. Her supportive, thick-cupped underwire bra. Too thick for him to feel even a hint of her nipple, and too supportive and stiff to allow him to tug it down in a comfortable way for her.

Fine. That could come off later. Her breasts weren't his primary goal right now, anyway.

He stroked downward again. Trailed his fingers just above the waist of her leggings.

Thank fuck for stretchy fabric.

Her breathing hitched, the movement slight but definite under his lips on her neck. He mouthed and sucked and licked, one hand spread on her belly as the other slid beneath her leggings, slid beneath her smooth underwear, only to encounter slickness and heat between those trembling thighs.

She let out a choked sound, and he paused. "Okay?"

"*Yes*." Her hips tipped, pressing her tighter against his hand. "Please."

Even with forgiving fabric, there wasn't much room to maneuver, but her warm, wet sex nestled perfectly into his hand. So perfectly.

Carefully, he teased apart her hair and lightly stroked his fingertips along her folds, learning the intricacies of her by feel alone. She quivered beneath his touch, delicate and soft, and when he teased her entrance with his forefinger, she parted her legs wider, leaning more of her weight against him as her hands reached back to clutch his hips.

But he slipped up, up, up again, exploring until he found it.

Slow. Slow. He circled her clit gently, and her nails were gouging into his thighs now as she huffed out soft little noises. When he dipped lower again, she was even wetter. Even hotter. This time, he slipped a fingertip just inside, playing. Rubbing.

She arched against his hand and whimpered, and he smiled.

"Do you like something inside you when you come? Something to clench around?" Her cheek was feverish under his lips. Unable to stop himself, he ground his stiff dick against her ass, and it made him burn even hotter. "Or is the clit alone better?"

Her voice was a strangled whisper. "Both. I want both."

This time, he didn't stop with a tease, but pressed a finger inside her. Two. Jesus, she was swollen and slick and so fucking hot. So fucking tight too, even though her body offered no resistance whatsoever to the penetration. He hooked his fingers. Rubbed.

She exhaled shakily, then turned her face into his neck when his thumb found her clit again.

By now, he was supporting both of them with the help of the

countertop, grinding his jeans-covered cock against her in rhythm with her own rocking hips as she bit off moans with each circle of his thumb, each twist of his fingers.

She began to stiffen against him, her flesh twitching under his thumb, around his fingers, and he tangled his free hand in her hair and urged her lips against his.

She was too far gone for kissing, and he didn't give a fuck. As she panted into his mouth, he greedily swallowed every breath, every sound.

Another circle around her swollen clit. Another.

Then she gasped and arched and broke, sagging back against him as she squeezed his fingers and pulsed against his thumb and made low keening noises.

Gently, he stroked her through every twitch, every hitched breath.

When she was done coming, he removed his hand from her leggings, turned her in his arms, and let her watch, eyes heavy-lidded, as he licked his fingers clean.

A bit tart. Earthy, which seemed appropriate for her. Perfect.

The sunshine through the over-sink window gilded her. She was flushed and dewy and languid, leaning heavily against him, and he wished he had enough talent to capture that look on film. Not that he wanted anything to puncture this private, idyllic bubble of a moment.

With his thumb, he stroked a strand of hair away from her still-damp temple. "That was even better than I'd imagined."

Her voice was husky. Amused. "You . . . you imagined this? Making me come in my kitchen?"

"The kitchen part was improvised." He chased the flush on her round cheeks with his lips, letting it warm him. "But when you rubbed that amazing ass against me on the sidewalk, I wanted to get my hand into your pants and grind against you as you came around my fingers."

She let out a breathy sound, and he drew back to grin at her.

"So smug," she said, and he was almost certain that was meant to sound like a complaint. But there was too much affection in her tone for that, too much satisfaction.

"Where's your bed?" He ducked down to trace the plump peninsula of her earlobe with his nose, then with his tongue. "I want to see you spread out for me."

She made that sound again, and yes, he would admit it.

As she led him by the hand to her bedroom, his smile was definitely smug.

Lavineas Server DMs, Eight Months Ago

Book!AeneasWouldNever: Hey, Ulsie. You didn't reply to my messages yesterday?

Book!AeneasWouldNever: Which is fine, but I wanted to make sure everything was okay. It was the first day I hadn't heard from you in

Book!AeneasWouldNever: Well, months, I guess. Anyway, if you haven't had time, I completely understand, but I just wanted to check on you.

Unapologetic Lavinia Stan: oh god i'm sorry broke a glass and cut my leg last night, ended up in the emergency room

Unapologetic Lavinia Stan: before the stitches they gave me the good pain meds so i've been kinda out of it sorry, still am i guess

Book!AeneasWouldNever: I'm so sorry you got hurt, Ulsie. Are you okay?

Book!AeneasWouldNever: Please, PLEASE tell me you had someone else drive you home, and have someone taking care of you now.

Unapologetic Lavinia Stan: taxi time, bitches

Unapologetic Lavinia Stan: not bothering friends so late, and no way i'd call my parents

Unapologetic Lavinia Stan: no worries i'm fine now aeneas's confused boner week is taking care of me, fanfic ftw

Unapologetic Lavinia Stan: turgid tumescent throbbing confused boners ftw really

Book!AeneasWouldNever: Ulsie—

Book!AeneasWouldNever: Shit. I wish I

Book!AeneasWouldNever: Please be careful, and call someone if you need help.

Book!AeneasWouldNever: I'll be checking on you whenever I can.

Unapologetic Lavinia Stan: velvet over steel mofos velvet over fucking steel

17

MEN LIED, TO THEMSELVES AND TO HER.

Cocks didn't.

Confronted with so much truth—veined, thick, glorious proof—even she couldn't doubt it anymore. He wanted her. As she was.

April lifted her head and stole a glance at Marcus, currently kneeling between her thighs as she lay sprawled naked on her bed. For privacy, they'd drawn semi-sheer curtains across the windows, but some sunlight was still peeking through. Her room was aglow with it, every inch of her lit and exposed, and his erection had gone from impressive to painful-looking when she'd spread her legs for him.

Which was only fair, because the sight of him had her squirming restlessly.

He was golden in the filtered sunshine, strong and lithe and honed, leashed energy vibrating in every movement. When he hunkered down lower and slid his hands slowly up her thighs, over every dimple and swell, his longer strands of hair in front swung down, shielding his eyes from her.

They couldn't have made eye contact anyway, though. He was watching the path of his splayed fingers, or rather her flesh as it prickled and burned beneath his deliberate caress. To her disappointment, he didn't veer inward, toward the juncture of her thighs, but kept moving up, up, up. Past her hips. Over the mound of her belly and the silvery-pink stretch marks there, up her ribs, until he nudged the sides of her heavy breasts. But he didn't linger there either, instead finding and following the lines of her collarbones with his thumbs, and trailing his knuckles lightly down the lengths of her arms.

She left her palms turned upward and exposed to him. It was probably an unnecessary statement, given the openness of the rest of her body, but she'd wanted them both to know: she was choosing to trust him.

He wasn't a stranger anymore, and she didn't intend for this to be a one-night stand. If he walked away now, if he turned a critical eye on her body, he would hurt her.

Still, she lay there, the vulnerable, sensitive cups of her hands pale beneath the stroke of those golden fingers. His body a cage around hers, on hands and knees, he leaned forward and nuzzled into her right palm. Pressed a soft kiss there.

Then he trailed that sharp-edged jaw, ever so slightly rough at this point in the day, back up her arm, and rubbed into her neck until she actually giggled.

She could feel him smile against her skin, and she was done lying still. His shoulders and triceps passed beneath her hands, his skin warm and smooth, every muscle obvious and delineated in a way hers were not and had never been. The light dusting of hair across his upper chest, dark golden and springy, she petted. His nipples she lightly thumbed to peaks, smiling herself as he arched over her and breathed out hard.

Then she was stroking down his belly, solid and flat and bisected by more crisp hair, and suddenly, he wasn't quite so leisurely anymore.

He sat back on his heels, between her legs. Her exploring hands he nudged aside with a murmur of apology, something about how long it had been, and how little restraint he had left. His own hands swept upward, until he was cupping her breasts for the first time. They spilled out of his gentle hold, too big for containment, and he gave a little pleased-sounding hum.

"So soft." It was a murmur, as if to himself.

With his thumbs, he was circling her areolae, watching the smooth skin furl in response. Then the pads of those thumbs were feathery on her nipples, brushing back and forth as her legs involuntarily parted further.

Hunkering down again, he rubbed the near-stubble on his jaw over the upper swells of her breasts. She gasped, and then his mouth was hot on her nipple, sucking, teasing, flicking, playing with the faintest hint of a tooth's edge, as his fingers plucked the other. He switched, and she shifted again. Arched up against his mouth, greedy for more pressure.

Breast play had never much interested her, to be honest, but the sensation was electric now, her lower belly turning heavy and liquid. He didn't linger, though, maybe because his breath was growing as short as hers.

After a minute, he was dragging that jaw down again, down more, and then his breath teased through her coarse hair. When he parted her with his fingers, she squirmed, the cool air and anticipation both unbearable. He made a low, amused noise, and she wanted to smack him, but she wanted his mouth on her more, so she waited tensely.

The bastard blew on her clit, a stream of cool air, and he was going to pay at some point in the future for that. She was trembling by then with the need to raise her hips to that teasing mouth, to fist her fingers in his hair and shove his face exactly where she wanted it.

Then he licked her, unhurried and thorough, and she moaned instead. Loudly.

His arms were heavy on her thighs and hips, holding her in place as he settled down and got to work. His tongue was as strong and sensitive and agile as the rest of him, and God, his unrelenting patience as he flicked and sucked and nosed through her slickness—

"Fuck," she whispered, delving her fingers through his hair, clutching his shoulders. "Marcus—"

At the sound of his name, he sucked on her clit a little harder, and she couldn't stay still. When her hips lifted, he held her down, held her in place, forced her to accept his pace with the unrelenting strength of his arms. None of it hurt, nothing, but she wasn't going *anywhere*, not unless he wanted her to, even though she was so much bigger than him.

The force of that knowledge whited out her brain for a moment, and she whimpered.

He lifted his head for a moment, raising himself up on his arms enough to make eye contact, and she groaned at the sudden absence of that incredibly talented tongue.

"Everything okay?" His mouth was wet with her, his pupils wide and dark. "If I do something you don't like, just tell me. Or if you want me to stop—"

Okay, enough talking. Back to licking.

"I'll let you know if I have any complaints." She lightly pushed at his shoulders and raised her hips again, because God, *please*. "In the meantime, for the love of—"

Even as a demigod, he'd never looked quite so self-satisfied. "Say no more."

Tangling her fingers in his hair, she let out a breathy, appreciative gasp at the darting flick of his tongue. Jesus, if he'd learned that swirling motion for a role, as he had so many of his other impressive skills, she was applauding his choice of parts and possibly nominating him for a retroactive porn award of some sort.

He was sucking on her clit again, flicking it with his tongue, and his thumb was circling her entrance, pressing just inside and rubbing around and around, and she was rocking and arching against him, grinding against his mouth as her chin tipped back and her world became brightness behind her eyelids. Fuck. *Fuck.*

And then—

His mouth was gone. He was scrambling off the bed, reaching for his jeans, and she lay there and trembled in near-orgasm and scowled at him with the full force of her displeasure.

His hands were unsteady too as he smoothed the condom over his cock, and he winced apologetically as he caught her eye. "Wasn't sure I could last long enough inside you for a third orgasm, and I want to feel you come around my dick."

"Hmph." That was reasonable enough, she supposed, and she stopped glaring. "Do you want on top, or . . ."

He flopped down on the mattress, his face flushed and eager and oddly young. "I'd love to have you ride me, if that's good for you. So I can watch you above me."

Her own face warmed at that, and the pleasure wasn't entirely sexual.

She straddled his lean hips. And because she was apparently a vindictive bitch when sexually frustrated, she took her time about positioning him and sinking down on his cock. She lowered herself slowly, swallowing him inch by inch, eyes locked to his, hands braced on his thighs behind her as he stretched her wide.

"*April,*" he protested, but he had no right to complain, and he knew it.

She was so slick and ready, the penetration was nothing but

pleasure for her, and she clenched around his thickness within her and smiled with her own brand of smugness as she slid down, down, down on him.

By the time she was done, by the time she had his cock hot and hard and wholly within her, he was panting and hitching his hips against her weight, his blue-gray eyes dazed and frantic. But in that position, with her size, she had the power now.

Leaning forward, she tucked her hair behind her ears and petted his dampening chest.

"Everything okay?" Shit, she had to grind against him. Just a little, because she was still so very close, and her eyes went half-lidded with the jolt of sensation. "If I do something you don't like—"

"Yes, yes." His smile was tight and pained but genuine. "I'll let you know."

She forced herself to still. "I'm taunting you, obviously."

He huffed out a little laugh. "Obviously."

"But I mean it too," she told him.

"I know. I appreciate that." Each of his hard breaths lifted that flat belly, shifting her like an ocean's wave. "Now let me—"

His thumb found her clit and rubbed slowly, and she closed her eyes entirely.

Oh. *Oh*. Yes.

Leaning back again, she braced herself and began to rock on him. Not up and down, because she was too far gone for that. Back and forth, against that agile, teasing thumb, as his cock filled her and spread her wide.

"April." His other hand was squeezing her hip in a possessive hold. "*April*."

When he shifted beneath her, she cried out, the bolt of pleasure between her thighs unexpected. Despite her weight, he was lifting his hips beneath her in shallow, short thrusts, fucking her from below as she clutched his thighs, his lifted knees, anything she could take hold of. Fuck, he was so strong, so hard within her, swelling and somehow pressing deeper, rubbing her inside and out, and his thumb—

The pressure burst, and she was making loud, harsh sounds, clenching around him again and again, heedless of anything but how fucking good he felt moving inside her, still circling her clit, levering himself up to kiss her hard before he fell back again and bucked his hips and shouted and shook.

He kept his hand on her until the end, coaxing every last twitch from her sated flesh. When she slid to the side, reluctantly parting from him to collapse boneless onto the mattress, he cupped her cheek and kissed her softly and sweetly. He tasted like her. His fingers were still slick with her.

That touch, that unhurried kiss were a statement, she knew, made silently and immediately, before she had even a moment to wonder and worry.

He repeated that statement after they both made quick trips to her bathroom, with the way he immediately climbed back into bed and cuddled close, encasing her with all four limbs in a way she would soon find smothering but welcomed for now. He was stroking her back in long sweeps, murmuring in her ear about how fucking hot it was to watch her riding him, how the sounds she made when she came pushed him into his own orgasm just as much as the feel of her squeezing him, how next time he was going to make her fall apart with his mouth alone.

They were all welcome words, but not his actual message.

He didn't need to say it aloud. She heard anyway.

This wasn't just a fuck.

I love your body.

I'm not going anywhere.

SHARKPHOON

INT. OVAL OFFICE – NOON

*DR. BRADEN FIN stands with GIRL IN BIKINI #3
before the president, his tight swim briefs covered
only by his white lab coat, both still splattered
with the blood of his fallen, chomped-upon colleague.
He's also wearing safety glasses and a look of
grief and determination. The president is staring
up at him, steely-eyed, elbows on her desk, fingers
steepled.*

> **PRESIDENT FOOLWORTH**
> You're wasting my time. This is no emergency.

> **BRADEN**
> Madam President, it is. You don't understand. The
> typhoon is so powerful, the sharks so enormous,
> nowhere is safe. Not our aircraft carriers. Not our
> nuclear facilities. Not even here, with the Reflecting
> Pool so close to the White—

> **PRESIDENT FOOLWORTH**
> (smiling coldly)
> The Mariana Trench is a continent away. You're
> dismissed.

*A gust of wind and the sound of breaking glass.
A shark crashes through the Oval Office windows and
bites the president in half, then gulps down the other*

*half too and disappears out the same window in pursuit
of other victims.*

Girl in Bikini #3 lays a consoling hand on his arm.

GIRL IN BIKINI #3

You tried to tell her.

*Shaking his head sadly, he puts his arm around her
and goes back to work.*

18

IN THE END, APRIL ORDERED YET MORE TAKEOUT FOR
dinner—steamed chicken and vegetables for Marcus, red curry
with shrimp and rice for herself—and he accepted her invitation
to stay the night. Cuddled together on the couch, they binge-
watched an old season of his favorite British baking show until it
was much too late, before finally stumbling back to her bedroom.

There, they rested on their sides in her bed, naked, legs en-
twined, face-to-face in the blackout-curtained dimness of her
room, only the distant glow of a bathroom nightlight illuminat-
ing their expressions.

With one hand he held hers. With the other he played with
a strand of her hair. For a first-time sleepover as a couple, the
silence between them was surprisingly comfortable. Not strained,
or full of unspoken tension and awkwardness.

Still, she was going to break that silence and possibly *make*
things awkward.

The question might seem less fraught in the darkness, though.
At least, she hoped so. "Marcus?"

"Yes?" He sounded remarkably awake, given his efforts that day.

Against her kitchen counter, of course. In bed. Then, just an
hour or so ago, with him kneeling on the floor of her living room,
her legs draped over his shoulders as she reclined on the blanket-

covered couch and clutched a throw pillow and moaned and came so hard against his eager, inventive mouth, she wanted to bronze his tongue. But only after she was finished with it, naturally.

"Do you ever worry . . ." she began.

She paused. Brushed an exploratory fingertip along that elegant cheekbone, down that slightly battered nose, along that famously sharp jaw.

"Do I ever worry about what?" The prompt was encouraging, rather than impatient.

The whorl of his ear was warm under her fingertip, the skin of his earlobe soft. She tried her best to memorize the feel of both, even as he turned his head to kiss her palm.

Millions of people could recognize him under the blinding lights of a red carpet. But if she touched him like this long enough, maybe she'd be able to recognize him even in the darkness, by feel alone, in a way that made him uniquely hers.

The possessiveness in that thought should alarm her. It was uncharacteristic, especially when it came to a man she'd known for only a limited time, and a man staggering under so much baggage, both openly stated and unacknowledged.

For some reason, though, it seemed as if they'd known each other for years. As if he *understood* her, instinctively, a feeling she found both impossible and irresistible. Their teasing back-and-forth that night had come so easily, their discussions about underproved dough and the relative harshness of the judges' critiques as comfortable as if they were longtime friends.

Still, his work and his fame complicated his relationships in ways she'd never before had reason to consider. And now that she did have cause to think about those complications, she couldn't dismiss them without a discussion.

She started again, this time determined to say what needed to be said. "Do you ever worry that I'm attracted to the character you play on television, or the person you pretend to be in public, rather than the real you?"

He was quiet for a minute, the crease between his brows deep despite the stroke of her fingertip over the spot.

Shifting to his back, he stared up at the ceiling instead of meeting her eyes, although his hand didn't relinquish hers. "I, uh . . ." He let out a long breath. "I told you about how my relationships have ended in recent years."

She squeezed his fingers in silent response.

His head turned, and he caught her eye again. "Normally I would be nervous about that happening again. But you've been pretty clear from the beginning that the guy I pretend to be in public doesn't appeal to you. At all."

Well, no. She couldn't really argue with that.

"You don't seem interested in surfaces, really. More what lies beneath. Maybe because of your work, or maybe that's why you chose your profession to begin with. I don't know." He rubbed a thumb over her knuckles. "But it's one of the things I like most about you."

Stupidly, her face heated at his admission of affection, even in the darkness.

She knew why she liked digging down deep, searching for stories, searching for contamination, rather than focusing entirely on surface beauty. Discussion of her childhood could wait for another day, though, when they'd been dating longer.

She deflected with a bit of playfulness.

"You're not wrong." After tiptoeing her fingers up his chest, she reached up to tug a silky lock of his hair. "That said, your surface is really nice."

His smile gleamed in the dim glow filtering in from her bathroom nightlight. "Yours is spectacular." He turned on his side again, his knuckles trailing over the curve of her breast. "You know, maybe—"

That much temptation was difficult to resist, but she managed to gently move his hand away. "I appreciate the compliment. But you didn't answer the rest of my question, Marcus."

He flopped onto his back again with a sigh. "Dammit. I'm no good at words, April."

Nope. She wasn't accepting that as an excuse.

Instead, she merely waited and let the silence do the urging for her.

"Just . . ." His fingers tightened on hers. "Just . . . hear me out until the end, and if I say something wrong, please let me explain myself."

Well, that seemed ominous.

"I'm not worried you're attracted to the guy I play in public, like I said." He shifted his weight on the bed restlessly, lips pursed as he resumed staring at the ceiling. "As to whether I'm worried you might be attracted to the character I play on *Gates*, rather than the real me . . ."

His chest rose and fell. Once. Twice.

"Maybe," he finally, reluctantly said.

He'd asked her to hear him out until the end, and that didn't seem like an end to her. So she kept waiting, even as her brain whirred with arguments and justifications and doubts. But she tried to push aside those thoughts, because formulating her response while he still spoke wouldn't actually let her listen to him. Really, actively *listen*. And when a man as reticent as Marcus—the real Marcus—shared uncomfortable truths, only a fool wouldn't give him every bit of her attention.

"You, uh, told me you write fanfic about Aeneas and Lavinia."

He licked his lips, a flash of tongue that sparked a response between her legs totally inappropriate for the moment. "I—I might have looked up some of your stories, and they're . . ."

"Sexual," she supplied, after he paused for a few beats.

His little nod mussed his hair against her pillow. "A few of them."

"Most of them." She wouldn't lie, and she wasn't embarrassed. Not about having written explicit content, anyway. "Or at least on-page sex occurs in most of them, even if sex isn't the main"— she couldn't resist—"thrust of the story. So to speak."

He half groaned, half laughed at that. "Don't distract me, Whittier. This conversation is hard—*difficult* enough as it is."

Dammit, he was right. Back to listening, instead of dirty punnery.

Finally, he raked the hair back from his forehead and kept talking. "Okay, so here's my point: In your fics, there's sex involving the character I play. And when you describe Aeneas in your stories, he doesn't look like the Aeneas of Wade's books. He's not dark-haired or barrel-chested. He doesn't have brown eyes. Instead, he's . . . leaner. Golden. Blue-eyed."

He really had read her stories, evidently. Which was both flattering and alarming.

And she couldn't deny it. "He's you. Or at least, he looks like you."

"Yeah." Letting go of her hand, he pinched his forehead between thumb and forefinger, eyes squeezed shut. "Now that we're dating, I think that could maybe be a bit, uh . . . confusing for you? At least sometimes?"

When he didn't add anything for a few moments, she shifted onto her own back and forced herself to think about what he'd said and offer him the most truthful response she could, untainted by her instinctive desire not to alienate him in any way.

"It can be disorienting." It was a low-voiced, hard-fought admission. "I'm part of a private Lavineas server, and sometimes they post GIFs of your—Aeneas's—sex scenes, and—"

He'd gone very still beside her.

"—when we were naked, when your hands were down my pants and when you were inside me or licking me, I swear to God I didn't picture those scenes. But sometimes, when we're not actively in the moment, I get these . . . flashes." She swallowed over a dry throat. "Like, *I've seen that before*. Your ass. Your chest. Your expression. Things like that."

Before he could respond, she rushed on. "I'm not embarrassed that I've written fanfic, and I'm not embarrassed to have written about sex in those fics. But now that I know you, I don't think I can include any more explicit scenes in my Lavineas stories, because it'll seem too . . ."

He didn't try to help, maybe because she wasn't sure he was still breathing. She had to find the words on her own, and she bit her lip as she searched for the right ones.

Copper on her tongue, she chose carefully. "It'll seem too intimate, now that I know you. Invasive. And the last thing I want to do is inadvertently picture you—Marcus, the man I'm dating—having sex with another woman. Even if I'm writing about Aeneas, a fictional hero. I may love Lavinia, but I have no desire to share you with her, even in my imagination."

Shit. She was assuming a lot. Way too much for this point in their relationship.

She cleared that dry-as-sand throat. "Not that we're exclusive—"

"I want to be exclusive," he interrupted. "Just so you know."

She paused, blinking up at the ceiling in shock. "You do?"

"Yeah. I do." For the first time during their conversation, he sounded entirely sure of himself. "Do *you* want to be exclusive?"

Her bitten lip hurt as she began to smile. "Definitely."

"Good." There was that smugness again. Irritating but flattering too.

In one short syllable, he'd declared her someone important in his life, someone he wanted to himself with a possessiveness equal to her own. And yes, that was definitely *good*.

"Okay, then. I guess we're exclusive now." She turned her head on the pillow to look at him, her grin now wide enough to make her cheeks ache. "That was fast."

He was looking at her too, his mouth soft and curved. "I'm almost forty. That's at least two hundred in Hollywood years. I don't have time to waste."

"That only applies to women, unfortunately. Not men." Her wrinkled nose expressed her disgust for that particular double standard. "Your industry is sexist as fuck."

"No kidding. You would not *believe*—" He stopped himself. "Hold on. We weren't done talking about, uh . . ."

Her smile faded. "Whether I want Aeneas, not you?"

He was breathing again, and meeting her eyes, but he still hadn't reached out. Which meant she needed to keep talking, because they were just beginning as a couple. An issue of trust could break them before they really began, so she had to be absolutely clear with him.

"You're an amazing actor." When he looked away from her, shoulders hunched in embarrassment, she touched his forearm. "No, don't shrug that off, Marcus. Listen to me."

Expression pained, he met her eyes again, and that was her cue to continue. "I love Wade's version of Lavinia, above any other character in the series. I was so disappointed when Summer Diaz was chosen for the role." When his lips tightened, she clarified. "Not because she's a bad actor. Because her casting negated a lot of what I found important and appealing about Lavinia and her romantic and personal arcs in the books."

At that, he nodded in understanding.

"The fact that I didn't transfer to another fandom once the show began airing is mostly due to you, I think. Not your appearance, although you're obviously gorgeous, but your performance. You're *that* good, Marcus. I can't believe you haven't won a bunch of awards."

She scowled at the injustice, then got back to her point.

This was the part she needed to get right, because she was telling him the absolute truth. She might find their situation confusing at times, but she had no doubts as to which man was lying in bed beside her. She had no doubts as to the identity of her brand-new boyfriend. She had no doubts as to who and what she actually wanted.

"Millions of people have read Wade's books. Even more have seen you play Aeneas. They know him, and they know his story. I know him. I know his story. I've *written* stories about him for years, and so have hundreds of others. And don't get me wrong. I still think he's great. I still think *you're* great, in your portrayal of him." As she'd done earlier that day, she laid a palm over his heart, its beat unshielded by clothing this time. "But I want to know *you*. Marcus Caster-Rupp, not Aeneas. I want to know *your* story. I'm attracted to *you*. Because what's hidden, what's real, is always more interesting and important to me than appearances or performances."

He was watching her so carefully, that line between his brows not completely gone.

When he spoke, his voice was barely louder than a whisper. "I'm no brave hero, April."

Why he seemed to consider that such a damning confession, why he was staring at her with such pleading and anxiety, she had no idea. But she intended to remove that worried expression from his face, the sooner the better.

"I don't . . ." His jaw worked, and each word seemed dragged from his throat unwillingly. "I don't always do the right thing, or the courageous thing."

At her snort, he actually jumped a little.

"So you're human, rather than a fictional character or an actual demigod." She waved off that particular concern. "How terrible and disappointing. Also, to be fair, Aeneas did some shitty stuff too. Like, for example, abandoning the woman he'd been sleeping with for a year without bothering to tell her goodbye."

His brow unpinched a tad, even as he sprang to his character's defense. "The gods instructed him—"

"Blah, blah, blah." She rolled her eyes. "His moral responsibilities didn't begin and end with the residents of Mount Olympus. He could have left a damn note, at least."

His nostrils flared as he exhaled. "Okay, okay. You're right. That was shitty. But it was one of the bits included in both the *Aeneid* and Wade's books, so there was no way to play it differently."

BAWN had made the same argument to her before, and he'd been equally wrong then. "Of course. Because your showrunners were always so very faithful to the source material they were given."

He didn't bother arguing, probably because there really *was* no good counterargument. Instead, he only grinned at her and took her hand again, interlacing their fingers. "No comment."

"Oh, I think that's comment enough." She scooted closer to him. Closer again, until she was pressed along the length of his side, softness against taut strength. Heat against heat. "If you're still worried I don't know who you are, *show* me who you are. I'll prove I can differentiate the man from the performance."

"I'll—" His voice choked to silence as her open mouth roamed along his shoulder. Over the ridges of his ribs. Down to that blessed divot at his hip, then in and down again. "I'll try my best."

"Thank you. Now I intend to try my best too."

After that, her mouth was too occupied for further discussion, and once she was through with him, that worried expression was gone, gone, gone, replaced by dazed pleasure and appreciation and a sort of panting beam in her direction.

"April . . ." He reached for her afterward, dragging her up into his sweaty, trembling arms. "Jesus. California should declare your mouth a national treasure of some sort. A landmark? *Something*."

Smiling as smugly as he ever had, she basked in every well-earned bit of praise. Lord knew she wasn't going to argue with him.

He might have mastered unicycling and chopping and emotive sniffing and swordplay, but she had her own particular set of skills when it came to swords. They deserved appreciation too.

Rating: Teen And Up Audiences
Fandoms: Gods of the Gates – E. Wade, Gods of the Gates (TV)
Relationships: Aeneas/Lavinia, Aeneas/Dido, Lavinia & Dido
Additional Tags: Alternate Universe – Modern, Alternate Universe
– High School, Competition, Fluff, Emotional Sublimation through
Trivia Domination, Jealousy, The Author Doesn't Actually Know a
Lot of Trivia, She Probably Should Have Chosen Another Premise,
Whatever, Too Late Now
Collections: Aeneas and Lavinia Week
Stats: Words: 1754 Chapters: 1/1 Comments: 34 Kudos: 115
    Bookmarks: 8

Trivial Concerns
Unapologetic Lavinia Stan

Summary:

Dido and Lavinia don't like one another. More specifically, Dido hates
Lavinia for dating Dido's ex, and Lavinia does her best to avoid Dido.
But when trivia competitions call, a woman must answer.

Notes:

A response to the prompt: *a showdown between Aeneas's two lady
loves.* Thank you to Book!AeneasWouldNever, as always, for your in-
sightful, patient, supportive beta services.

. . . next round, their score now tied.

A new question appeared on the screen. *This movie won James
Cameron a golden statuette for Best Director in 1998.*

Well, that was obvious enough. Lavinia managed to ring in first. *"Titanic."*

"Ah, yes." Dido straightened into her Class President stance, eyes narrowed. "The story of how true love never dies, even after a lengthy separation."

Lavinia rolled her eyes. "Rose eventually had kids with another dude, Dido. She got over it."

The unspoken message: *Maybe you should too.*

"She waited eighty-four years to say goodbye to Jack. *Eighty. Four. Years,*" Dido retorted, hands on her hips.

Lavinia threw her own hands in the air. "Instead of waiting eighty-four years, maybe she should have moved her butt a bit to the side and shared the damn board with him in the first place!"

"Ladies—" the teacher in charge began.

"If he'd let her, she would have!" Dido yelled. "But he just turned into a Popsicle without warning her!"

They weren't talking about Rose and Jack anymore, if they ever had been, and Lavinia took a deep breath.

Aeneas was her boyfriend. She loved him. But the way he'd ghosted Dido right before junior prom, at his parents' demand, was cruel, and she wouldn't make excuses for him. She and Dido might never be close, but she knew the other girl had hurt then, and was still hurting now. Truly.

"You're right." She met Dido's tear-bright eyes. "But then he was gone, and he wasn't coming back, and she deserved to be happy again without him. I know he would want that, because he truly cared about her."

Dido nodded, a jerk of her trembling chin.

"Maybe we can move on?" the teacher prodded.

Lavinia eyed Dido questioningly. The other girl nodded again, and even tried to smile at Lavinia. It was shaky, but genuine.

"I think we can," Dido said.

The next day, when Aeneas saw the two girls huddled around the same cafeteria table at lunch, laughing together and sharing secrets, he turned on his heel and ran.

19

AFTER APRIL RETREATED TO HER TINY OFFICE-SLASH-guest-room with her coworker Mel, the women chatting about seam allowances and detachable panels and other topics that totally baffled Marcus, Alex turned toward him on the overstuffed couch.

"So you just followed your girlfriend home like a stray kitten and refused to leave her lap afterward?" Alex raised one dark brow, clearly amused. "Good move. Pathetic, of course, but effective."

Well, he wasn't *wrong*, necessarily. Irritating, yes. Incorrect, no.

As Alex knew all too well, after that first night with April, Marcus just . . . never left San Francisco. Not for longer than a weekend, anyway. Not for the past month.

He'd kept a nearby hotel room reserved in his name, paid for with his credit card, but he hadn't spent much time in the suite. If at all possible, he never intended to. Its availability was more a statement to April. A declaration that he wouldn't assume his welcome in her apartment, even though they were together now. Reassurance that if she tired of him, she could send him packing, and he'd have someplace to stay, even in the dark of night.

So far, though, she hadn't seemed to mind his near-constant presence in her life and home. So far, he hadn't experienced a single moment of regret for the choice to stay there.

Nothing was keeping him in Los Angeles, not until he picked

another role, and he hadn't done that yet, despite the ever-more-anxious emails sent by his faithful agent. April's apartment was more comfortable than his house, if significantly smaller and less expensively furnished, and his filming schedule had kept him away from LA for months at a time before. The extended absence didn't bother him. The Bay Area, despite its painful associations for him, had always felt more like home than Southern California anyway.

His current location also offered a certain amount of extra protection from paparazzi, who would travel north from LA for exclusive pics of a television star with his new girlfriend, but only grudgingly and for short periods of time.

Most importantly, staying in the area meant he now knew April hit snooze two times every morning. He'd memorized how her hazy brown eyes finally, reluctantly, blinked open in the warm glow of dawn as she stretched in bed, her hair tousled and her soft body shifting against his. He understood how the scent of her changed after one of her infrequent days on a job site, from roses in the morning to sweat and earth in the evening. He'd tasted her skin after one of those site visits, and after a lazy, shared weekend shower, and after she'd cried while reading a particularly bitter-sweet fic and he'd erased her tears with his mouth.

Staying meant he could spend his weekday mornings reading scripts and writing fics to post under a new name, before shopping for food and working out at the hotel gym in the afternoon. Staying meant making her dinner in the evenings. Making her laugh. Making her come.

Any mockery he might receive he considered well worth the reward.

"Can't say I blame you for settling in," Alex added. "Looks like a very comfortable lap."

At that, Marcus narrowed his eyes at his friend. He hadn't

missed the swift but appreciative glance Alex had given April upon meeting her earlier that afternoon, or the way she'd blushed and almost *giggled* upon shaking Alex's hand.

She hadn't blushed and giggled when she'd met Marcus, he knew that for a fact.

Clearly he needed to find a less handsome best friend. That was the only sensible solution. Especially since said best friend was staying overnight in April's apartment as their first joint guest, which now seemed an unwise decision.

Alex's grin had only grown more obnoxious, and he held up his hands in feigned surrender. "No need to scowl at me like that, dude. I was stating an objective fact, not indicating any desire to climb into your lap of choice." He snorted. "Besides, when it comes to female company, there's no room at the inn. I'm full up."

Excellent. "Lauren?"

As if Marcus didn't know. Alex had been bitching nonstop about his assigned minder for weeks via text and email and occasional phone calls. At some point, Marcus expected a carrier pigeon to arrive at April's apartment with a note strapped to its ankle reading GODDAMMIT LAUREN IS SUCH A FUCKING DOUR MILLSTONE. Or maybe a telegram instead: LAUREN SAYS TWO DRINKS MAX STOP WHICH IS UNFAIR BECAUSE SHE'S SO SHORT I COULD JUST REST MY BEER ON HER HEAD STOP.

"Who else? I'm surprised she let me visit you this weekend without requiring hourly reports as to my good behavior." Alex flopped back against the sofa and glared in the direction of the front door. "R.J. and Ron directed her to keep watch over me anytime I'm outside my home, and the stupid woman is too stubborn to acknowledge she's being exploited."

That was a new line of argument. "How so?"

"Today is her first day off in weeks. And you know I don't sleep well, so I tend to leave the house at odd hours, and I'm required to let her know when I do, which means *she* doesn't sleep well, and . . ." Alex had crossed one ankle over his opposite knee, and his foot was jiggling, jiggling, jiggling. Not surprising, given his ADHD and accompanying tendency to fidget, but the movement seemed especially agitated today. "She looks tired."

Marcus raised his eyebrows. "Does she?"

"She considers you a good influence, apparently. At least in the company of your girlfriend. That's why she finally took time off." More glaring into space. "She'd better be sleeping today."

How to say this? "Um, Alex, have you considered that, uh, maybe your feeli—"

"Enough about the stubby but persistent thorn in my side," his friend interrupted, willfully ignoring Marcus's interjection. "Did you see the email and group chat earlier today?"

Yes. Unfortunately, yes, Marcus *had* seen both the email from their showrunners and the messages flying back and forth among their *Gates* colleagues.

> **Carah:** yet ANOTHER fucking email about our goddamn nondisclosure agreements and warnings not to share or malign the scripts or face GRAVE REPERCUSSIONS

> **Carah:** is it one of you bitches leaking scripts and blabbing about how this season sucks like a Hoover that gets off on dust, or

> **Ian:** I think the finale's great

> **Alex:** of course you do, your character arc didn't get brutally slaughtered

Alex: unlike the tuna population in your vicinity

Carah: hahahahaha

Summer: Con of the Gates is coming up, and the thought of answering questions about this season and what happens to Lavinia and Aeneas just

Summer: gaaaaaaaah

Peter: I heard Ron and R.J. intend to back out of their panels at the last minute, citing "prior commitments"

Carah: prior commitment to not getting their asses reamed by fans who saw those leaked scripts, maybe

Maria: but no one realizes the leaked bits are real yet

Maria: all TOO real

Peter: I know it wasn't me or Maria showing people those scripts

Peter: was it one of the rest of you, or the crew, or . . . ?

Marcus: for the sake of our careers, hopefully the latter

Ian: how do you know it wasn't Maria, Peter

Ian: oh, that's right, your mouth is surgically affixed to her ass, so if she told anyone you'd know

Maria: did you watch The Human Centipede AGAIN, Ian

Peter: mercury poisoning, Maria, remember

Peter: hallucinations from all the tuna

Maria: oh, yes, very sad really

Ian: I mean you KISS her ass all the time, dipshits

Ian: there are hour-long YouTube compilations of all your interviews together, where you're making puppy dog eyes at her and it's EMBARRASSING

Maria: more embarrassing than watching YouTube compilations of your colleagues in your free time?

Carah: hahahahaHAHAHA

After Ian stopping replying, the rest of the discussion had largely involved the press junket for the final season's premiere, and everyone's upcoming con appearances. But it had left him wondering—

"Please tell me you didn't leak those scripts," Marcus told Alex.

It wasn't a far-fetched notion. Alex tended to make decisions in a heartbeat. Then he'd leap with both feet, shaky ground be damned, only to find himself bruised and bloodied and unable to explain afterward why he'd made the jump at all.

He wasn't self-destructive, exactly. Just . . . impulsive.

Executive function issues, he'd drawled to Marcus after that last, fateful bar fight, aping nonchalance over FaceTime despite his swollen-shut eye and scraped cheek and shaking hands. *You're not the only one whose brain works a little differently than most.*

"I didn't leak those scripts." Alex's smile was a little too wide and pleased for Marcus's comfort, despite the firm statement. "That said, I was so intrigued by the stories I've been beta-reading for y—"

"Shhhh," Marcus hissed, waving a frantic hand. "Not here."

The women were talking in the other room, and it sounded as if they were running the sewing machine Mel had brought over, but they could easily overhear a conversation in the living room if they wanted to. Which would be disastrous. Utterly disastrous.

Alex's smile vanished, but he obligingly lowered his voice to a whisper. "You still haven't told her?"

Marcus shook his head.

"You don't trust her?" his friend mouthed.

In the month he'd spent in her home and her bed, there had been no revealing blind items in blogs, no new intimate details about him or his life in the tabloids, no tell-all interviews on entertainment television shows. Her coworker Mel, for all the woman's enthusiasm about *Gates*, didn't seem to know a thing about him other than the basics: his name, a few of his roles, his status as a onetime local. All April had told her, according to Mel, was that he was *kind*.

Given the circumstances, given the way he'd doubted April and concealed crucial information from her, he'd had to fight a wince at that description.

No, Marcus hadn't spotted a single sign that she would ever betray him to anyone. Which he should have known from the moment he found out she was Ulsie, but he hadn't had sufficient faith in his own instincts *or* her, and now he was paying for it.

Leaning closer to Alex, he spoke in a bare whisper. "I do trust April."

"Then why haven't you told her?" His friend's brow furrowed. "If you're serious about her—"

"Of course I'm serious about her," he snapped, as quietly as he could. "But if she found out I kept something so important from her this whole time . . ." *She has trust issues*, April had written about Lavinia. *Major trust issues.* "I don't know if she'd forgive me. I'm not willing to risk it."

A lie of omission wasn't quite as heinous as an outright falsehood, he'd repeatedly informed himself. Plus, he'd basically stopped corresponding with her as Book!AeneasWouldNever as soon as they'd begun dating, so it wasn't *much* of a lie, and surely no one would blame him for—

"Dude." Mouth pinched, Alex shot him a chiding look. "*Dude.* I don't blame you for tossing aside my advice last time, but— *dude*."

"I know. Just . . ." Shoulders slumped, he sighed. "Just tell me what you were going to say, but leave out the beta-reading, okay?"

After one last tight-lipped stare of disapproval, the other man obliged.

"I was reading *Gates* fanfiction the other night, since you told me about *April's* online alter ego on AO3," he said with a hint too much sarcasm, "and I was intrigued. So I read a few Cupid/Psyche fics too. They were *amazing*. A vast improvement over the actual scripts, honestly, especially this last season."

Oh, God. Marcus thrust a forefinger in the direction of April's guest room, where her coworker—whom neither of them knew well—could probably hear every damning word his friend had just uttered.

Rolling his eyes, Alex waved off the silent rebuke. "They're playing some sort of horrible folk music now as they sew. They can't hear anything."

When Marcus listened closely, he heard the acoustic guitar and off-key wailing too. It was awful, in an objective sense. But also good, in that the music drowned out Alex.

"What kind of stories did you read?" Marcus asked. "Out of morbid curiosity."

His friend winked. "Only ones rated E, for *explicit*."

Of course. Of course.

Alex's head tilted, and his brow creased. "I'm not entirely certain why so many fans seem convinced I'm a bottom and in desperate need of getting pegged by Psyche, but . . ." He lifted a shoulder. "Maybe they're right. So I wrote my own Cupid-getting-pegged fic, only with an original character as my pegger-in-chief, because I thought it would be creepy to involve our coworkers, even tangentially. My pen name is CupidUnleashed."

Marcus pinched his forehead and groaned.

"I chose only the best tags. *Porn without Plot. Smuttity Smut Smut. Half-Human Disaster Cupid. Bottoms Up. The Peg That Was Promised.*" Elbows akimbo, Alex leaned back and rested his head on his linked hands. "So far, I've received over a hundred comments and four hundred kudos. Someone named SoftestBoiCupid dubbed me 'the Bottom Whisperer,' and I think it was a compliment."

Okay, now Marcus was jealous as well as worried. None of *his* fics had reached anywhere close to a hundred comments. Probably due to a critical lack of pegging.

"In between all the lube and mutual orgasms, I included lots of pointed commentary about how Cupid had changed too much over the years to ever abandon anyone he truly loved, no matter what Venus and Jupiter told him to do." Alex grinned. "It was very satisfying, on a variety of levels. I think my next fic will be a modern AU where Cupid is starring in a popular television show, one which the incompetent, overprivileged showrunners irretrievably fuck up in the final seasons, and he meets a woman who helps him get over his resulting depression by—"

Marcus sighed. "Pegging him."

"—pegging him." Somehow, his friend's smile gleamed even more brightly. "How did you guess?"

Marcus rolled his eyes. "I'm glad you enjoyed writing your story, but Alex, you need to be careful. If anyone found out—"

"Lauren knows."

Marcus's groan was so heartfelt, it actually hurt his throat.

"She caught me working on it one day, and I told her if she wouldn't let me have fun in real life, I could at least have a good time in fiction. She must have read the story once it posted, because she said she hoped Cupid's partner used less lube next time." Alex pursed his lips in thought. "For such a humorless harpy, it was quite a good comeback. I was impressed."

"*Alex.*" Jesus fucking Christ, his friend's career was *done*.

"Don't worry." Alex waved a dismissive hand. "She won't say anything to anyone."

Gulping air, Marcus forced himself to speak slowly. Precisely. "You told me part of her job was to report to Ron and R.J. about what you do off set, especially anything objectionable. Writing fanfiction critical of your character arc is more than objectionable. It's grounds for firing you, and potentially actionable in a legal sense. Believe me, *I know.*"

When it came to his own fanfic transgressions, the email earlier that day had only strung his nerves that much tighter. The prospect of imminent doom didn't appear to inspire so much as a single fidgety twitch in his best friend, however.

"Well, she caught me a week ago, and I haven't heard a peep from Ron and R.J." Still sprawled back against the couch cushions, Alex shrugged. "I didn't think that was the sort of thing she'd report. Guess I was right."

The drone of terrible folk music and the buzz of the sewing machine stopped, and both men looked toward the guest room. Moments later, Mel and April emerged, smiling.

"I think we almost have it done. Just a few more pieces to attach, and one more fitting. We're leaving the sewing machine here, but it shouldn't get in your way, Alex." Mel bumped shoulders with April. "Then it's time for My Chemical Folkmance's new costumes, exclusively designed by April Whittier."

April snorted. "Tim Gunn taught me well."

"I'd be happy to talk to one of the show's costume designers, if you two wanted some insider tips or tricks for cosplaying Lavinia." Arms crossed, Alex drummed his fingers against his biceps as he glanced toward Marcus. "Who do you think is the best bet? Marilyn? Geeta?"

April smiled at her guest. "Thanks, Alex, but Marcus already offered to talk to someone for me. I told him I didn't want to cheat."

So far, she'd refused to show Marcus her sketches or her costume-in-progress, saying she wanted to surprise him when it was done. Secretly, he hoped the outfit was tight. Very tight. But he hadn't said so, because she would look gorgeous either way, and he wasn't a *complete* jackass.

He turned to Mel. "We're going to grab dinner soon. Do you want to join us?"

By now, she and Pablo had visited the apartment several times for sewing purposes, and Marcus had met the rest of April's closest colleagues at least once, after joining them for lunch at a restaurant near their office. To their credit, they'd treated him pretty much as he'd have expected them to treat any boyfriend of April's, despite the occasional cell photos taken of them by other customers as they ate.

He liked her coworkers, and he liked the way April seemed comfortable in their presence, still herself in every essential way. Plainspoken. Practical. Confident. A couple of weeks ago, she'd even stopped looking surprised every time they texted her about socializing outside of the office.

In her colleagues' company, he hadn't said much, to be honest. Mostly, he'd eaten his lettuce wraps and listened. But every word he *had* uttered had been his and his alone, rather than lines from a character he'd scripted long ago.

It was a self-administered, low-stakes test of sorts. One measuring his nerve, his willingness to grow and change.

He wanted to be a man she could respect, not just privately but in public too.

More importantly, he wanted to be himself whenever cameras weren't rolling.

It would take time. Effort. But so had everything else he'd achieved over almost four decades, and no matter what he'd been told as a child, he wasn't and had never been *lazy*. Just unsure, or not quite brave enough to do what was necessary.

"Thanks for the invitation. I wish I could say yes." Mel wrapped one of her many, many scarves more securely around her neck. "Saturdays are my date nights with Heidi, though. Another time?"

The assumption: he wasn't going anywhere, so they would have plenty of occasions to eat dinner together in the future.

He smiled at her, pleased. "Of course."

Once they'd all said their goodbyes to Mel and she'd disappeared into the dusk, April headed toward the master bedroom to gather her purse and a sweater while Marcus finger-combed his hair in the entryway mirror above the console.

"Should have played Narcissus instead of Aeneas," Alex muttered.

Marcus raised a middle finger in his direction.

When April reappeared in the living room, Alex beamed at her and proffered his elbow with a courtly flourish. "To your chariot, my lady?"

"Uh . . ." Her cheeks turned rosy, and she made a weird choking noise as she accepted his arm. "Okay. Thanks."

Marcus glared at his best friend, who merely raised a cocky brow in return.

"Tell me, April," Alex was saying as they exited her apartment. "Would you say that Cupid is a bottom? Because I'm very intrigued by the fanfic community's interpretation of the character, especially his proclivity for being pegged."

And there it was. She was giggling again, even as she blushed harder. *Giggling*, and the back of Alex's stupid head should have caught fire from the force of Marcus's scowl.

"Oh, he's definitely a bottom. A bratty one, I'd say." She sounded breathless but thoughtful. "Or maybe a switch?"

Then, after a squeeze of Alex's arm, she let go of him and held out her hand for Marcus instead. He interlaced their fingers immediately and swept past his friend, allowing a surge of triumph to puff his chest just a tad as he stared meaningfully at Alex.

"Bratty is about right, April," he said, and pretended not to see his friend's own raised middle finger in response. "You have him pegged. So to speak."

Rating: Explicit

Fandoms: Gods of the Gates – E. Wade, Gods of the Gates (TV)

Relationships: Cupid/Original Character

Additional Tags: Alternate Universe – Modern, Porn without Plot, Smuttity Smut Smut, Half-Human Disaster Cupid, Bottoms Up, The Peg That Was Promised, Actor!Cupid

Stats: Words: 3027 Chapters: 1/1 Comments: 137 Kudos: 429 Bookmarks: 40

Taking Him Down a Peg
CupidUnleashed

Summary:

Cupid has a hard day on set. Off set, things get equally hard. By "things," I mean his penis.

Notes:

Thanks to AeneasLovesLavinia for the beta. You're the best, dude. Also, any resemblance to current worldwide television hits is entirely unintentional.

No, wait. The opposite of that last one.

Robin's hands on his bare chest were small but hot and so very soft. "What happened today? You seem . . . tense."

She was straddling him now, her solid, welcome weight keeping him in place. Maybe he could move if he tried, but he didn't. No, he wanted that sense of helplessness right now, that sense of safety. More than that. He wanted to forget, to drown in pleasure until he couldn't think.

"The usual," he sighed. "As I've said before, the showrunners were incompetent from the very beginning. The only things that saved them were the talented crew, my fellow actors, and the books. But now that we're past the books, everything's gone wrong."

She was frowning down at him, concentrating. Concerned. "How can I help?"

"Take me," he said, and she got up on her knees and began to move over him, only to halt at his next words. "No. *Take me.*"

She bit her lip, even as her cheeks bloomed with heat. "Are you sure?"

"You bet your ass I'm sure." He grinned up at her. "Or, more accurately, my ass."

When they laughed together, he was certain of two things.

First: she was going to peg his brains out that night.

Second: by the time she was done, he would no longer care that his character's entire arc had been torpedoed in the final season for no damn reason.

20

"WHAT DO YOU THINK?" APRIL GAZED UP AT MARCUS FROM her couch the next evening, nose crinkled in concern. "Is it terrible? I've only begun tackling book canon recently, and I'm not sure my writing voice is particularly suited to it."

After Alex had left for the airport and April had disappeared into the bathroom for a shower, Marcus had retreated to her little office. He'd sat at her desk for a good half hour, listening as his text-to-speech app read the draft of her most recent fic aloud to him, once and then a second time. For those few minutes, he'd allowed himself to become Book!AeneasWouldNever again, beta-reading his friend Ulsie's writing to check for character consistency and plot holes and any other tarnished spots he could help her buff to a gleam. As always, he'd jotted a few nearly indecipherable notes to himself as he listened.

The familiar routine had settled around him like the fur-lined cloak he'd worn in *Gates*'s wintry first season. Warm. Comforting. So heavy his shoulders hurt.

In one sense, her request was helping them reclaim parts of their relationship she'd never know they'd lost. But even in that welcome moment of reclamation, he couldn't entirely be honest with her. If he gave her exactly the same feedback as his fanfic alter ego would have, in exactly the same way, she might grow suspicious. She might recognize him as her longtime friend and writing partner.

Besides, the version of him she knew now hadn't spent years helping with her fics and writing his own. He wouldn't be as familiar and comfortable with the revision process as Book!AeneasWouldNever, both in general and with her. Which meant he couldn't be as helpful to her for that reason too.

If they kept doing this for months or years to come, if she kept asking him to read and respond to her stories, maybe he could slowly transform into the writing companion he'd once been in a credible way, a way that wouldn't set red flags flapping. But not now.

It was a bitter note on his tongue, noticeable even amid so much sweetness.

Because this moment *was* sweet. And so was her story.

"I think you underestimate yourself," he told her. "There are a few words that are a bit too modern"—dammit, he needed to make this plausible—"or at least, the scriptwriters never had us say them, and we should probably look up when they came into common usage. 'Okay,' for instance. But otherwise, I think you managed to capture the feeling of the books."

Her expression smoothed. "Oh, good. I wanted to figure out a way I could keep writing in this fandom without it getting, uh, weird. Especially if I included explicit content."

Which she had. Very ably and descriptively. That particular content had necessitated some explicit readjustment of his jeans in her office, because *damn*.

In the past, when she'd written about an Aeneas who looked like him, he'd avoided beta-reading sex scenes, a stipulation Ulsie had accepted without demanding an explanation. By mutual agreement, she'd excised those bits before sending him her drafts, noting any major developments he'd missed in a dry author's note of a sentence or two.

But at the beginning of this fic, she'd described a dark-haired, stocky Aeneas, thick with muscle, eyes as richly brown as fertile soil. Book!Aeneas, not Show!Aeneas. Not Marcus, in any recognizable way.

So, yes, he could and would read those bits now, and do so without discomfort.

Well, without the old, familiar type of discomfort, anyway. Which reminded him: "Also, during one of Aeneas's love scenes with Dido, Carah and I were told that the word you used for, uh . . ."

Eyes bright behind her glasses, she raised her brows in amused inquiry as he squirmed.

"You shouldn't use the word 'pussy,'" he finally forced out. "It's anachronistic."

In all her modern AU fics, that term was more than acceptable. But not in canon-compliant stories, given the time period involved. Wade had used a different word instead. One Marcus was even more reluctant to utter, in case April found it offensive.

She pushed her frames up onto the bridge of her nose. "So I may need to cross the C-word Rubicon, is what you're telling me."

"If you want a canon-compliant term that's less euphemistic than, um, 'wetness.' Or 'heat.' Or . . . things like that."

Shit. He was getting hard again, his gaze involuntarily drifting down to the flirty hem of her soft, swinging nightgown, which only reached midthigh when she stood and rucked up even higher when she sat. When she shifted her legs like that—

Oh, that was deliberate. Her saucy wink only confirmed it.

The rest of his feedback could wait.

He tackled her on the sofa, maneuvering them both as she

giggled—finally, a giggle *he'd* elicited, so Alex could just fuck right off—until she was flat on her back and his hips had fallen between her open, round thighs and his hand was sliding between those thighs, beneath her nightgown.

"Use that word again," she whispered in his ear minutes later, as he pressed his open mouth against her neck and moved above her, inside her. "The first one. Say it."

She was tight around him, trembling, so wet now he could hear every thrust. When he raised himself a bit higher above her and ground against her sex, she gasped and closed her eyes.

He told her the absolute truth, then, hot into her ear, his teeth on her earlobe. "I love your pussy. *Love* it. When you're at work"—he managed to slip a hand between them, down low, because he wasn't lasting much longer, and shit, the *sound* she made when he rubbed her clit—"When you're at work, I fist my dick and think about filling your pussy with my fingers, my cock, my tongue . . ."

She arched beneath him and rocked, pushing against his fingers, fucking herself on his cock. Then she broke with a sob, shuddering, her sex convulsing around him as he bucked into her and gripped her hip and groaned.

Afterward, they lay panting on the couch, and she ran a hand down his damp spine. "That was an inspired performance, worthy of the academy's recognition. The award for best initial foray into dirty talk goes to . . . Marcus Caster-Rupp! Hooray!"

With a huff of amusement, he angled his head so he could press a row of soft kisses down her sweaty neck. "If I was inspired, you deserve all the credit."

Yes, he was definitely fine reading her sex scenes now.

In fact, he was going to encourage her to write more of them. The sooner, the better.

LATER THAT NIGHT, over a belated dinner, they talked more about her story.

"My only other concern, at least upon first reading, is whether Aeneas is a bit too . . ." Marcus waved his forkful of spaghetti squash, searching for the right phrase. "He may be a bit too *emotionally aware* for a man of his background and time period."

She nodded thoughtfully, twirling strands of pasta around her own fork. "I can see that."

There was no offended snap in her voice, no hurried defense of her writing choices and characterization of Aeneas. As she chewed, though, she was blinking down at the table, no longer smiling.

"I'm sorry." Reaching across the table, he covered her free hand with his. "April, I'm sorry. I should have said that more gently. Besides, what do I know? Nothing."

At his touch, she looked up. "You *did* say it gently, and you're completely right. I just . . ." Her mouth trembled, but she pressed her lips tight. "What you said, it reminded me of things my former Lavineas server friend used to say. The guy I told you about."

"The one who has dyslexia too," he said slowly.

Her obvious grief twisted his heart. Her unwitting insight into his lie twisted his gut.

"Yeah." Her shoulders, now slumped, hitched upward a millimeter. "He kind of acted like a dick at the end. But we were friends for a couple of years before that, so it's hard to just . . . get past it. I miss him."

"I'm sorry." The words emerged ragged, and God willing, she would never know how much he meant them. "I'm so sorry, April."

She stared down at her plate for another few moments before raising her head, eyes glossy, and offering him a faltering smile. "Thank you, but it's okay. I'm okay. And none of what happened with him is your fault."

As small as he'd once felt in front of the disappointed, disapproving gaze of his parents, as guilty and *wrong*, this was somehow worse. Even as a child, he'd been able to cling to a thin thread of conviction: *I'm trying my best. There is nothing more I can do.*

That fact—that he was offering everything he had, everything he was, to them, and it *still* wasn't enough, would never be enough—had rended something inside him. It had shadowed him for so many years. Too many years.

Now he had to acknowledge a worse feeling: a guilt that wasn't helpless, but fully earned.

I could do something more, but I won't. Because I'm scared I might lose everything.

His palm was getting sweaty. After one last squeeze of her hand, he let it go and disguised his distress by busily straightening the napkin in his lap. "How did you start writing fanfic? What drew you to it?"

She considered the topic for a minute, the pinched sadness leaving her face as his distraction served its purpose. "Please don't take what I say next the wrong way, but I mostly started writing fanfiction out of sheer spite. Your showrunners fucked up Lavinia from the beginning, and I was so *pissed*. I wanted to fix what they'd done and put back everything I loved about her and her relationship with Aeneas."

Well, he couldn't blame her for that.

"So I took what was best about the books—Lavinia, the contours of her relationship with Aeneas—and what was best about the show—that would be you, Marcus—and mashed it all up into gloriously fluffy, smutty fics, and it was pure pleasure. Especially once I found a community on the Lavineas server, and . . ." She trailed off. "A good friend and writing partner."

Another wrench in his chest.

If he could, he'd meet her tale with his own, as a sort of apology. He'd tell her how a young woman in full, impressive Aeneas regalia had mentioned *Gates* fanfiction at a convention, and he'd been curious and bored enough that night in his hotel room to find some and start reading. Only to discover that some of the stories, the best ones, echoed and expressed insights about his character and the show that he hadn't shared with anyone but Alex. Only to find he could use modern technology to make reading so, so much easier than he remembered.

That night, for the first time, he read something other than scripts of his own volition. Without pressure. Without stakes. For sheer enjoyment, about something he valued. About something where *he* was the expert, for once.

It was life-altering. Triumphant, in ways he couldn't fully express, to discover that he *could* read and love it, entirely for himself and no one else.

But even in the best fics, there were aspects of his character other authors missed. It was his compulsion to share his own insights that eventually drove him to write his first one-shot as Book!AeneasWouldNever. No one knew who the fuck he was or cared whether he misspelled the occasional word or dictated instead of typed. He did it for himself alone.

He'd expected crickets or criticism, not kudos. Not support, despite his shoddy editing.

And then, somehow, he was part of a community. Somehow, he *enjoyed* writing, and it was yet another proud reclamation of himself, for himself.

Somehow, he'd found Ulsie. April.

Somehow, through fandom, he'd discovered who he was. His own interests. His own talents and possibilities, after decades of pretending to be someone he wasn't, *believing* he was someone he wasn't.

But he couldn't share any of that with April. If they stayed together, such a crucial part of his history would remain forever sealed, and she'd never hear that particular story.

Across the table, she was finishing their late dinner as they sat in comfortable silence. When she looked up and saw him studying her, her lips curved. She stretched out her leg to tease his bare ankle with her big toe. It tickled a bit, as she very well knew, and he snorted and shook his head at her.

Unapologetic grin wide, she shrugged and turned back to her remaining garlic bread.

If you're still worried I don't know who you are, show *me who you are,* she'd told him, and he couldn't. He couldn't. Although, last night, he'd lain awake in her bed long after she'd fallen asleep, his arm possessive around her waist, and wondered.

Whatever lay between them, he was holding it in his hand and squeezing as hard as he could, keeping it close and safe and tight in his grasp, hoping all that effort and pressure would transform them. Into a diamond, as she'd once explained to him. Brilliant. Hard to damage.

Maybe what they had wasn't rock, though. Maybe it was water.

Maybe the harder he squeezed, the less he actually held.

But he didn't know how to open his fist. Not when it came to April. Not when it came to his career and his public persona. Not when he knew precisely, *precisely,* how it felt for that outstretched hand to remain empty. Always empty.

"Marcus?" April's gaze was gentle. Concerned. "Are you—"

Then, as if he'd summoned her with his earlier thoughts—a horrifying possibility—his cell rang, and DEBRA RUPP appeared on the screen.

"It's my mother. I can call her back later," he told April.

Much later. Possibly never.

She waved her fork dismissively. "It's your choice. I certainly won't be offended if you want to talk to your parents."

He didn't, so he let the phone ring itself to silence while they both watched. A few seconds later, there was another chime. A voicemail. His mother had left a voicemail.

With a simple tap of his forefinger, he could delete it without listening. Instead, he lifted the cell to his ear and listened, consciously straightening his shoulders and letting the back of the chair brace him against whatever he might hear.

"Marcus, Madame Fourier saw your picture in one of those trashy magazines at the grocery store. She told us you've apparently been in San Francisco for weeks. Visiting your new girlfriend from Twitter, according to the article. She was obnoxiously pleased to know more than we did concerning your whereabouts and activities. We had assumed you were back in Los Angeles or on set somewhere."

He couldn't quite decipher his mother's tone. Was she hurt he hadn't informed them of his proximity or visited in the past month? Aggrieved that her former colleague had been gifted an opportunity for gloating? Or was she merely stating facts?

"Call us at your earliest convenience, should you find yourself so able."

Well, *that* was definitely sarcasm.

After he'd heard it all, he deleted the message, as he probably should have done when his instincts first urged him that way, and pushed the phone away a few inches. Then another few inches, more, more, until he couldn't reach farther across the table, and April laid a light, warm hand on his forearm.

"Marcus?" So low. So sweet.

Would she still be so sweet if she knew everything?

He shook his head, shook the thought away.

Their hidden history on the Lavineas server didn't matter, not right now. *This* part of himself he could show her. This story he could tell, even though it gathered and thickened in his throat in a way that made speaking difficult.

Really, the outlines of the situation were so simple. It was stupid to struggle so hard for words. "I, uh, I hadn't told my parents I was in the area, but one of the teachers at the school where they used to work saw an article about us and informed my mom. She wants me to call her back."

She'd want him to visit, because he always had to come to them.

From the doorway to their kitchen, he'd make himself small and watch them dance.

"Do you want to call her back?" April's voice was absolutely neutral.

She'd taken off her glasses at some point, scooted her chair closer, and those brown eyes were soft and patient. Full of affection and trust he didn't deserve.

"They—" He cleared his throat. "They hate the show. Did I tell you that?"

Silently, she shook her head.

"They've hated all my roles, I think. But especially Aeneas, because they both taught classical languages, and they feel like the show slaughtered Virgil's story." His hand wasn't entirely steady when he reached for another sip of water. "Which it did, of course, but I still didn't—"

Her knees were abutting his now, nudging softly. A reminder of her closeness.

His voice cracked. "I d-didn't expect them to write op-ed articles about the 'pernicious influence' of the show, and how it 'promotes a disastrous misunderstanding of foundational mythology.'"

That particular piece had run in the nation's most popular newspaper, and after his computer had read the text aloud to him, he'd regretted his choice. If he'd read it himself, in print, maybe he could have pretended he'd gotten it wrong somehow. Mixed up the letters. Misunderstood, as he so often did.

In his parents' articles, they never mentioned their son or his role on the show. Not once. But of course, the names made the connection obvious, and he could have predicted the public reaction, the tittering about how such learned parents had birthed a son like *him*.

"I thought it would be different. As an adult, I mean. I thought being around them would feel different someday. Once I had a career and friends and something outside them. But it never does, and April—" He turned to her, and her eyes were glassy again, for him, and he couldn't bear it but couldn't stop himself, either. "April, I'm so fucking angry every time I see them."

When she took his hand, the desperate force of his grip must have hurt.

She didn't complain. Didn't move away.

"I hate it. *Hate* it," he spat. "How they despise all my roles, and how they wrote those articles and will probably write more, and how they looked at me like I was dumb and lazy and—and *worthless*, even though I swear to God, I tried. I tried and tried, as hard as I could, and I was just a fucking *kid*, and they were *teachers*. How could they not have *known*?"

Later, he'd wondered whether their prep school discouraged kids with special needs, or whether his parents were just too stubborn to admit that their child, the product of their genes and guidance, could prove flawed in such a fundamental way. Whether the shame of it had blindfolded them, plunging them all into darkness.

It didn't matter, though. Not really.

Either way, they'd never seen him for what he was, what he

could become, what he *had* become, and what he would never, ever be.

They still didn't.

His cheeks were wet, and she was blotting them with a napkin, and he was too lost to feel embarrassed. "I know they love me, and I love them, but I don't know how to forgive them."

A lifetime's worth of hurt spilled over them both, and she waited patiently and held his hand securely in hers and dried his tears, and if he were a warrior like the man he'd portrayed for so long, he'd have pledged his fealty, his life, to her right then. Laid his sword at her feet, relieved.

She was easing him upward, guiding him to the couch, and tucking him into her body once they were seated. His head on her shoulder, his arms as tight around her as he could make them without hurting her, his face buried in her rose-scented neck.

"I don't know how to forgive them," he repeated, whispering into that soft, secret hollow.

Her fingers were combing through his hair, stroking him. He closed his eyes.

When he didn't speak for a while, she laid her cheek on his head. "We can talk about that, if you want, or I can simply listen. Or we can stay like this, if silence would help."

There was no judgment in her voice. No impatience. No disdain, at his weakness or his ingratitude or his tendency to *feel* more than was comfortable sometimes.

He hadn't known. How could he have? Nothing in his past, amid all his successes and ill-fated relationships, could have predicted the dizzying *relief* of laying his heart before her, unshielded, only to discover—

Only to discover that she'd protect it for him.

So he could talk. Finally, he wanted to talk about it. Wanted to listen.

He took a shuddering breath against her throat. "Tell me what you're thinking."

"I think . . ." Still tunneling her fingers gently through his hair, she paused before continuing. "I don't think forgiveness is something that can be owed."

Against his face, he could hear her labored swallow. He could feel it.

"Especially if that forgiveness hasn't been earned. Even if the person who hurt you is also someone who—who loves you." Her fingers stilled, her warm palm cradling his skull. "You can choose to offer it. But you don't owe it to anyone. Not even your parents."

She was cupping his face, lifting it from her shoulder. Meeting his eyes, her own suddenly fierce. She spoke faster now, with more certainty.

"If you don't want to see them, don't see them. If you don't want to talk to them, don't talk to them. If you can't forgive them or don't want to, then don't fucking forgive them." She nodded, either in emphasis or to herself, he wasn't sure which. "If you do want to forgive them, that's okay too. If you want to talk to them or visit them, I'll support you however I can. There's no right or wrong answer here, Marcus. Just whatever answer would make you happiest."

That had never been the point, not with his parents.

For decades, the three of them had been bound by expectations and obligations, rather than any particular regard for something as inconsequential as his happiness, or even theirs. But if he shed those strangling tethers, if their bond became something he could choose or not choose, as he desired . . .

He didn't know what that would feel like. Whether his anger

and hurt would fade into insignificance, finally. Whether forgiveness would come more easily, or whether he'd find himself confident in his decision not to offer it.

"I've never—" He pinched his mouth shut and thought back. Scrolled through decades, searching, but his instinctive claim was correct. "I've never talked to them about how they made me feel back then. How they make me feel now. Instead, I just pretended to be someone else. It seems . . . wrong not to forgive them for things I never said hurt me."

She was back to picking her words with care. "Do you want to talk to them about it?"

"I . . . I don't know," he finally said.

Shit, so much unguarded emotion was exhausting. Head muddled by fatigue and uncertainty, he was resting on her shoulder again, curled against her side, her body a bulwark in a gale. Her fingers were playing with the hair at the nape of his neck now, her other arm warm around his back.

When it came to his parents, he truly had no idea how to proceed.

All he knew: None of his characters, none of his artifice had ever offered him this kind of shelter, this kind of comfort. Only April.

Despite the dread and shame curling in his gut, then, he wasn't telling her about Book!AeneasWouldNever. He wasn't confessing his lie of omission.

This circumscribed openness might not be everything he wanted. She might never know all of his story. But what lay between them was more than he'd ever had before, more than he'd ever dreamed he could grasp, and he wasn't risking it.

No, he wasn't risking it.

He was squeezing tighter.

Lavineas Server DMs, Seven Months Ago

Unapologetic Lavinia Stan: Are you going to next year's Con of the Gates?

Book!AeneasWouldNever: Attending events as a fan isn't really my thing.

Unapologetic Lavinia Stan: Because you don't like crowds, or . . . ?

Book!AeneasWouldNever: Something like that.

Unapologetic Lavinia Stan: Okay

Book!AeneasWouldNever: It's just

Book!AeneasWouldNever: Meeting my online friends in person doesn't seem like a great idea to me.

Unapologetic Lavinia Stan: You're shy?

Book!AeneasWouldNever: Sometimes?

Unapologetic Lavinia Stan: Because please know: you don't have to be nervous around me. I don't care what you look like, or whether you're awkward face-to-face, or—whatever. We've been friends for a long time now, and I'd love to meet you in person.

Unapologetic Lavinia Stan: for coffee

Unapologetic Lavinia Stan: or dinner? Just the two of us?

Book!AeneasWouldNever: I wish I could. Please, please believe that.

21

AFTER A DAY FULL OF DOCUMENTS, APRIL CAME HOME TO
yet *more* documents.

Not lab results from soil samples this time, or reports from
consultants in which they misinterpreted data or used the wrong
screening levels to draw their conclusions, but television and
movie scripts. Actual Hollywood scripts, each containing a role
Marcus's agent thought he might like, or a role already offered to
him before he even caught his first glimpse of the story.

Some he'd have to audition for, others he wouldn't. Some
would offer a substantial paycheck, others not much above scale.
Some boasted big names as costars or producers or directors, and
others counted on the story itself as the main draw.

His agent, Francine, had her preferences, of course, but she
mostly just wanted him to choose *something* and have it hit the
public before his post–*Gods of the Gates* recognizability began to
wane. Or so he'd informed April over their dinner of mustard-
roasted salmon and garlicky mashed cauliflower. During the
afternoon, he'd baked some sort of savory flatbread too, for her
sole, enthusiastic consumption.

That salmon was fucking incredible. So was the rest of their
meal.

He'd shopped for the food. Paid for the food. Washed the dishes, changed the sheets, and even run a load of her laundry. Hung some pictures where she'd indicated she wanted them.

If he never chose another role, she was planning to keep him as a househusband.

Maybe that should be a joke, but it wasn't.

And as her mother kept hinting, maybe April should be alarmed by how quickly he'd moved into her home and become a familiar, essential presence in her daily existence. Instead, it seemed . . . natural. As if he'd been in her life for years, although she'd met him only weeks ago.

She trusted him. Somehow, even after such a short time, she trusted him.

As his scripts proved, they wouldn't always have this sort of time together, either. Soon he'd return to LA or report to some international location for filming, and they might not see one another for weeks or months at a time.

So if he wanted to stay, she wasn't showing him the door. This alignment of their lives, their schedules, wouldn't last forever, and she intended to appreciate every minute of it.

"I hoped you wouldn't mind if we talked through my choices." Using his phone, he forwarded one of the relevant emails to her from his postdinner spot on the couch. "Normally I would have had something lined up months ago, but I couldn't seem to decide, and I figured I could use a break once we finished filming *Gates*. Francine's right, though. I need to pick a project soon. I could use a sounding board."

"You hoped I wouldn't mind?" She opened up her laptop on the cleared kitchen table and eyed him over the top of her glasses. "Marcus, we've been over this before. I'm an incurably nosy bitch. Of *course* I want to see your scripts."

He snorted and kept scrolling through his messages for more scripts to send. "I tried talking to Alex about it, but he's no help. He just keeps telling me to launch a line of hair care products and be done with it."

To be honest, for a man whose vanity was much less all-encompassing than he pretended in public, Marcus *did* spend a lot of time on his hair. Even on days when he wasn't doing anything important.

Better to withhold comment.

As her laptop booted up, she hummed happily, eager to get started, and even more eager to spend time together.

This past week, she'd devoted two evenings to writing and revising her one-shot for Aeneas's Sad Boner Week, another to working on her Lavinia costume, and yet another to sketching possible performance outfits for the Folk Trio Formerly Known As My Chemical Folkmance. Which was now, due to Mel's successful lobbying efforts, the Indium Girls instead—despite Pablo's initial protest that two of the three band members were not, in fact, female.

"No worries." Kei had waved off that concern. "The contradiction will only add to our mystique."

"It'll change again next month," Heidi had whispered near the staff refrigerator later that day. "Whatever you do, Whittier, don't design the costumes around the band name."

The nights April told Marcus she wanted to work on her various hobbies, he didn't quibble. Other than giving her an occasional lingering kiss and offering tentative but useful advice on her fic, he'd mostly left her to her own devices. Instead of pouting, as some of her exes would have done, he'd amused himself listening to audiobooks or simul-bingeing yet more baking shows with Alex via FaceTime.

"Claggy sponge!" Alex kept gleefully shouting, his voice loud and all too clear through the cell phone's speaker. "*Claggy god-damn sponge!*"

After the evenings they'd spent apart, she'd rewarded Marcus's patience at bedtime. He'd seemed more than satisfied with the tradeoff. So satisfied, in fact, that he insisted on returning the favor, and by the time *she* was satisfied, he was hard and hot and ready to climb aboard the Good Ship April for another naked, mutually enjoyable voyage.

Despite all the sex, though, she'd still felt guilty. It was past time they had an evening together, especially doing something that mattered to him.

"Okay," Marcus said after a few more minutes. "I've sent you the three main contenders."

Yes, he had. There were three new messages in her inbox, complete with attachments. But before she could open them and satisfy her curiosity, she needed to know more.

For the moment, she moved her laptop aside so it didn't block her view of her boyfriend. "Now that *Gods of the Gates* is almost done, what's your next step? Where do you want your career to go? What sorts of roles are you looking for? And why are these your three main contenders?"

For most of a decade, he'd been fitting movies and television roles in between seasons of filming *Gods of the Gates*, choosing his projects from the limited selection that both interested him and would work timing-wise. The absolute freedom he now had, to pick whatever role he wanted, no matter when and where filming would occur, was a recent development.

Sometimes she got the sense that all that freedom disoriented him a bit.

"I don't think so." He lounged back against the sofa cushions, his smile suddenly sharp-edged with challenge. "You like figuring things out, so do the work, Whittier. You tell *me* why these are the three roles I'm considering."

It felt like avoidance to her, as well as a genuine dare, but he knew her all too well. She *loved* shit like this. A mystery. A test of her insight. An invitation to discover stories within stories. Not to mention the carnal promise contained within that lazy, inciting smile.

She raised her brows, meeting his insolence with her own. "If I get it right, what's my reward, Caster-Hyphen-Rupp?"

At that, the tension broke, and he snickered.

Once he'd recovered himself, though, he looked her dead in the eye. Then he slowly scanned her, all the way from her haphazard ponytail to her curling toes, pausing at a few key spots in between. Her heavy, unbound breasts, nipples pebbling against thin, soft cotton. The lavish swell of her hips and belly. Her dimpled thighs, caressed by the brush of her lounge pants when she shifted under his stare. The juncture of those thighs, where he'd settled and teased and explored so many nights now.

A flush burnishing his cheekbones, he stretched magnificently on the couch.

He knew exactly what he was doing. He knew exactly how he looked. All his training for various roles and all his acting experience had taught him body awareness the likes of which she'd never witnessed before.

As he stretched, his thin tee rode up his flat belly, his biceps straining the sleeves. He arched his spine, his head thrown back in a way she recognized from their more intimate moments.

Not that this moment lacked intimacy.

He relaxed back into the sofa with a satisfied purr. Her labored swallow caught his attention, and that knife-sharp smile returned.

"Your reward?" Now displayed full-length along the couch, he folded his hands beneath his head and blinked heavy-lidded blue-gray eyes at her. "For each role you analyze correctly, I'll take off a piece of clothing. And if you get all three right, you can have whatever you want. Anything."

Twirling a loose strand of hair around her finger, she eyed him consideringly. She knew for a fact he was currently wearing three—and only three—items of clothing. The perfect number for her purposes.

It would take so little effort to get him naked. Even less to ride that handsome face of his once he was hot and needy and stretched out beneath her.

"Game on," she said.

SHE HAD TO skim, of course, and she didn't read the scripts all the way to the end.

Later, if he wanted her to read every word, she would. For tonight, though, for this particular challenge and discussion, that kind of intense scrutiny wasn't necessary.

He watched her as she read, his steady attention on her a caress rather than an irritant. Whenever she took a break and glanced around her screen, she met his eyes and had to fight her own flush at the heat in that stare.

She kept waiting for him to grow bored, to produce his fancy headphones and listen to his latest audiobook, but he didn't. He just lay outstretched and waited for her judgment.

The scripts varied so widely, she didn't think she risked confusing them. Still, she typed a few notes to remind herself of what she'd read and concluded.

By Hook/By Crook: TV series set in Victorian NYC. Dramatic mystery/suspense. Slow-burn romance.

Central characters: semireformed thief (female)
and former prostitute (Marcus), who combine
street smarts to find murderer targeting victims
too marginalized to garner sufficient police
attention. Audition required. $$-$$$.

Exes and O: Indie film. Dramedy. Ophelia (O),
for REASONS, ends up living with various ex-
boyfriends as roommates. Jack (Marcus), whom
she left and has missed ever since, is romantic
endgame. No audition required. $.

In theory, there was a second movie script competing for Marcus's attention, but that was blatant misdirection on his part and not worth her notetaking efforts.

She pushed aside her laptop. "You lied to me, Marcus."

He jerked on the couch. Paled.

"April . . ." Sitting up in a rush of movement, he pressed his lips together. "I'm so sorry. I didn't . . . I shouldn't have . . ."

His words faltered as he stared at her, stricken.

That seemed like an overreaction to a harmless bit of deception, but she already knew Marcus was, well . . . sensitive. To his own emotions, but also hers. Alex might—in an epic example of pot/kettle fuckery—call him a drama queen, but she didn't consider her boyfriend's vulnerability a weakness.

If he ever decided to shed the masks he used to protect himself, she would be more than willing to serve as a different sort of shield for him. She'd happily guard his tender spots from the unkind scrutiny of outsiders. For his own sake, but also because—selfishly—she wanted him to need her.

More than that.

She wanted him to love her. She could admit it, at least to herself.

"It's okay." Moving over to the couch, she settled beside him and pressed a comforting kiss to his cheek. "Luckily for you, I don't mind trick questions."

"Trick . . . questions." He let out a shuddering breath. "Yes."

Once he'd relaxed against her, she poked his arm. "Despite what you said, you gave me two main contenders. Not three, you cheater."

His face brightened at her declaration, a sun unshadowed by clouds once more, and that expression alone was enough to tell her she was right.

Still, he lifted an arrogant brow, his composure now restored in its entirety. "Maybe, maybe not. Let's hear your reasoning."

Turning to face him, she tucked one leg beneath her and let loose.

"No way you're choosing *Julius Caesar: Redux*. You love ancient Rome, but not enough to work with that director. Even I've heard the rumors about him, which is saying something." Her lip curled. "Besides, that script is shitty, and you don't need to take roles simply to get a paycheck anymore. You can pick a project befitting your talent and intelligence."

"Befitting my—" His mouth worked. "My talent and intelligence."

He seemed stuck on that phrase, but she had a challenge to win, so she wasn't lingering.

"It wasn't a very convincing trick, honestly. If you want to fool me, you'll have to do better than that." She shook her head at him. "You're too good for that movie, in every possible way. It's not a contender. Your agent shouldn't even have sent it to you."

He stared at her then, blue-gray eyes wide and unexpectedly solemn.

When he eventually spoke, his voice was quiet. "I told her not to send me any more projects from that director, no matter how much his films make at the box office. Nothing else from that screenwriter, either, because the script was a misogynistic piece of shit. Just like you said."

"Score one for Team Whittier." Licking her forefinger, she traced an invisible tally mark in the air.

When he didn't move, she indicated his clothing with a jerk of her chin.

"Make like a dancing firefighter on a Vegas stage," she said, "and strip."

His grin was slow as he straightened on the couch, and so was the peekaboo tease of his tee rising, then rising more, until that hard chest came into view. Finally, his bared muscles shifting with impressive fluidity under that hair-dusted flesh, he yanked the shirt over his head and flung it in her lap.

When she gathered it in her fist, it was still warm from his body heat.

She licked her lips with deliberate care, knowing his eyes would follow the movement. "One down. Two to go."

Sitting back, he rested a hand on her knee. Traced the oval of her kneecap. "I can't wait."

There was a smile in his voice, even though his face was down-turned, his eyes on his fingertip circling, circling, circling.

"The indie movie . . ." When she pressed her thighs together, he glanced up and slanted her a wicked grin. "It's a limited com-mitment, more so than the TV series. That probably appeals to you. It's cleverly written. It's a chance to show your emotional range. It'd also be one of the few comedic roles you've taken, and your first since you became as famous as you are."

His finger had strayed to the inside of her knee now, teasing the thin skin there through the flimsy barrier of her lounge pants. "Why haven't I accepted, then?"

"It's not much money, but I'd guess that isn't your main concern."

"No?" It was another near-purr, languid and sultry.

Those strong hands urged her to her feet and stood her between his legs, where he still sat on the couch. Without warning, he tugged down her wide-legged pants, his palms hot as they skimmed down the sides of her thighs, her calves.

She was still wearing panties, but she suspected that state of affairs might not last much longer, given the way he slipped a thumb under her waistband and stroked along her belly.

"No—*oh*." When he settled her on his lap, positioning her so she straddled his hips, that bulge in his jeans pressed *right there*, where she was aching and growing hotter. "Th-the cast is such a large ensemble, you might not get enough chance to shine. I also wasn't sure Ophelia had much of an identity outside her exes."

He hummed in agreement and palmed her ass. Rocked her against him. "Two points for Team Whittier."

Her patience was nearly exhausted. She wanted his mouth, then she wanted his dick, and she didn't want to wait longer than necessary for either.

"Then take off your fucking jeans," she told him.

His eyes flared, and he didn't hesitate further. Shifting her off his lap for a moment, he tugged down his jeans in a single, swift movement before kicking them aside. Then he was touching her again, dragging her closer, his possessive hands on her ass urging her back astride him.

With only two thin, soft layers separating his cock from her sex, each upward hitch of his hips lit sparks behind her half-closed eyelids.

"One more to go." His voice was a rumble now, a deep vibration against her shoulder.

Her chin tipped back, and he mouthed her neck. "The television show—"

Shit. His hands were sliding under her shirt, stroking up her back and circling forward, and if she didn't finish her analysis *right now*, she clearly never would, and if she didn't finish, she wouldn't win, and if she didn't win, she couldn't watch him strip naked before she rode that smug, sexy face of his.

Well, she probably could. But it would feel even better knowing she'd *won*.

"More tricks, Caster-Hyphen-Rupp?" She took one last moment to appreciate his hot tongue teasing that spot beneath her jaw, the pressure against her swelling clit. "So be it."

When she rose to her knees on the couch, he groaned at the loss of friction. Then groaned harder when she reached down and pushed him back against the cushions, sliding her fingers beneath the top edge of his boxer-briefs.

"Raise your hips," she told him, and he obeyed long enough for her to yank the fabric just below his firm, gloriously round ass.

His cock bobbed against his ridged belly, hard and thick and wet at the tip.

She didn't touch it yet, even though she could. Even though she wanted to.

He shook his head at her chidingly, but his voice was hoarse. "That's cheating, Whittier. You didn't earn that yet."

"I didn't cheat." She stared down her nose at him, cheeks aflame with lust. "Unless I'm mistaken, you're still wearing your boxer-briefs."

That cocky smirk should be illegal. "So I am. Not, however, in the intended manner."

"And not for much longer," she told him. "Lie down."

At the flick of her finger, he stretched out full-length on the couch once more. This time, when she straddled his thighs, she did so with her fist tight around his burgeoning cock, and apart from a few semifrantic rolls of his hips, he didn't offer any more distractions or interruptions.

She gave him a firm stroke before speaking again, and he jerked beneath her and grew even harder in her hand. "I saw Francine's note about where the television series's showrunners hope to sell it." The same cable channel as *Gods of the Gates*. "If they succeed, that should ensure a decent budget, and I'm sure your involvement in the show would help them make their case. The role has action sequences, but a strong emotional core too. I suspect you like the way they gender-flipped the characters, compared to the norm."

She licked her palm. Stroked him again as he bit off a loud moan.

"I spent the longest with that script, because I was looking for telltale signs the show intended to shame sex workers. I couldn't find any." With her free hand, she stroked up that flat belly and over his chest as he squirmed between her thighs. "My guess? You were drawn to the role because everyone, even the female lead, dismisses your character as just a pretty face and fuckable body at first, but there's much more to him. It's a smart script, Marcus. The best of the lot. Good money too."

"So why—" He was arching beneath her and gasping now, to her infinite satisfaction. "Why haven't I auditioned already?"

Her hands stilled. Dammit. She'd hoped he wouldn't ask that.

"I don't know," she said slowly. "I couldn't quite figure it out."

After blowing out a hard breath, he managed a wry tone. "If

you do figure it out, let me know. Because I have no idea, and I was hoping you could tell me."

"Okay." This deserved her full attention, and his too, so she removed her hands from his body and placed them on her own thighs. "Do you have any theories?"

He subsided down into the couch again. "I don't want to leave you, of course. But the audition would only keep us apart for a day or two, so that's not it. Not all of it, anyway. And I don't want to stop acting entirely, so that's not the issue either."

Reaching up, he tucked a swath of her hair behind her ear. "I haven't been able to make myself audition for months now, and I don't know why. Even though it feels *ungrateful* to waste these opportunities. Foolish too."

"It's not foolish." She laid her palm over his heart, as she'd done before. "There's no right or wrong answer here. Just—"

"—whatever makes me happiest," he finished, a slight smile lightening his expression. "I hope that's true."

She rolled her eyes. "Of course it's true. I wouldn't lie to you."

He winced then, his flinch sudden and violent, and she hurriedly scrambled off his lap.

"Did you get a cramp?" She scanned him, but couldn't see an obvious issue other than his flagging erection. "Where are you hurting?"

He squeezed his eyes shut. "No, I—"

Her cell rang, cutting him off, but she ignored it. "What can I do to help?"

"Please, answer your phone." When she didn't move, he shooed her away. "I'm fine. I just need a minute."

Preoccupied with his mostly naked, possibly hurting state, she didn't check the screen display before answering her cell. It was a mistake.

"Hi, sweetheart! So glad I caught you at home tonight."

Her mother's voice rang through the connection, bright and cheery. Too bright and cheery, which meant Mom was anxious. Probably because her daughter hadn't been answering her calls regularly.

"Hi, Mom." Dammit. Dammit, dammit, dammit. "Yes. For once, we decided to stay in and relax, instead of going out."

Marcus was shooting her a quizzical look as he tugged his boxer-briefs back around his hips, no doubt wondering why she was lying to her mother. She and Marcus hadn't spent an evening out since Alex's visit, partly to avoid paparazzi and partly because they both seemed to be natural homebodies.

Apparently he hadn't noticed her rejecting JoAnn's calls.

"You're—" Her mom cleared her throat. "You're still seeing your young man?"

April bit back her instinctive, petty response. *Do you need a fainting couch or smelling salts? I know you must be shocked.*

"Yes." It was polite, and the best she could manage.

Her mother didn't ask for more details, thankfully. "In that case, I'm issuing an invitation for two. Your father and I would love to have you both here for my birthday lunch, if you can make it. The first Saturday in July, just the four of us."

The air in the apartment had turned damp and chilly against her exposed legs. April wrapped her free arm around herself, curling inward as she dropped her chin to her chest.

There was no good way to refuse. If April said the exact date didn't work, another would be proposed, then another, until it became clear the date wasn't the real problem, and she'd have to address issues she wasn't ready to raise yet. Make declarations she'd wanted to consider further before meeting her parents again.

When April was a child, her mother had worked so hard to

make birthdays special. She'd arranged dizzying spreads of gifts. Parties that included everyone in April's class. Streamers and balloons and, one year, a petting zoo in their backyard.

Even cake, whatever type April requested.

"One cheat day per year, sweetheart," JoAnn always said. "Make the most of it."

April should be willing to attend her mother's celebration, despite everything. In recognition of all those other birthday parties, if nothing else, because Mom really did care. Mom really did work hard and want what was best for her daughter and hope for her daughter's happiness with each phone call, each visit, each reminder of what health and beauty and love required.

Marcus's arms wrapped around her from behind, warm and hard and supportive, and she swallowed past the obstruction in her throat.

"Hold on just one second, Mom." Muting the phone, she stared blankly into the kitchen and asked him. "My mom wants to know if you can come to her birthday lunch the first Saturday in July. They live in Sacramento, so it'll be a half-day trip."

No hesitation. "Of course. I'll put it in my calendar later."

Before he could say more, she unmuted the phone. "We'll be there. Just email me the details and let me know if we can bring anything."

"Perfect." There was an awkward pause, which her mother eventually filled with yet more cheery chatter. "Nothing too exciting is happening here, although your father and I are considering spending a weekend in Napa next month. He got some new clients, and they recommended this vineyard—"

No. No, April was done talking about her father. That much she knew.

"Listen, Mom, I need to get to bed early, so I should let you go." Marcus's hands, stroking up and down her chilled arms, paused. "Talk to you soon."

How her mother managed to fill absolute silence with hurt, April would never understand. Even from two hours away, the guilt of it dragged her head lower.

"All right. Love you, sweetheart," JoAnn finally said.

After another swallow, April stated the truth. "I love you too."

She couldn't disconnect fast enough. When she turned in Marcus's arms, he was staring down at her, forehead creased, and she didn't want questions from him. Not now.

Her hands were unsteady, and she fisted them. "I won, right? With the final script?"

He slowly nodded.

"Then get naked," she told him. "After that, I'm claiming my reward."

As he removed his boxer-briefs, she stalked toward the bedroom, flipped the light switch, and waited for him to follow. Once he did, she greeted him by stripping off her shirt and tossing it in a corner, then tugging down and kicking away her panties.

He inhaled sharply and bit his lip, but his brow didn't smooth.

"I don't want to talk about the call right now," she told him. "I will later, I promise."

He nodded again, this time with more certainty. "Okay."

In mute defiance, she planted her fists on her hips and stood there absolutely naked, the overhead light at full brightness, so he couldn't possibly fail to see her for who and what she was. Every curve. Every roll. Every freckle. Every stretch mark. Every inch of her bared and his to take or leave.

He took his time studying her, then stepped closer. Closer

again, until their legs tangled and the crisp hair on his thighs rasped against her sensitive skin.

The stroke of his knuckles down her neck was careful. Tender. "What do you need, April?"

All this evening, they'd been discussing wants, not needs. But at this moment, for her, maybe the two were the same.

"As my reward, I want you to fuck me with all the lights in this room blazing." She tipped her chin higher, refusing to break eye contact. "I want you to look at me the whole time. Can you do that?"

Against her belly, his renewed desire began to make itself known, and the hardening of his cock felt like triumph. Absolute victory, over a foe she'd been battling and battling for decades now.

He laughed, even as his hands rose to cup her breasts. "Of course I can do that. I've done it before, and it would literally be my pleasure to do it again." Then he hesitated. "Only . . ."

Victory slipped from her grasp, and she had to stiffen her legs to keep upright.

"Yes?" she managed to say, her sinuses burning with tears she would not, *would not* shed in front of him.

His hands left her breasts, and she bit back her sob.

Then he was cradling her face, his thumbs caressing her cheeks in gentle arcs as he pressed his lips to her forehead, her temple, her nose. Her damned traitorous mouth, which was trembling.

Neck bowed, forehead to forehead, he made his own request. "After I fuck you, can we make love? With the lights still on?"

When she surged up on her toes to kiss him, he took that— correctly—as a yes.

As it turned out, what she wanted and what she needed weren't precisely the same thing.

That night, fortunately, he gave her both.

Rating: Explicit

Fandoms: Gods of the Gates – E. Wade, Gods of the Gates (TV)

Relationships: Aeneas/Lavinia

Additional Tags: <u>Alternate Universe – Modern</u>, <u>Angst and Fluff and Smut</u>, <u>The Saddest Erection Ever</u>, <u>Ghost!Lavinia</u>, <u>Eventual Happy Ending</u>, <u>Even Though They're Both Dead at the End</u>, <u>But Together</u>, <u>Which Is What Really Counts Right</u>, <u>Aw Man You're All Going to Hate This Aren't You</u>

Collections: Aeneas's Sad Boner Week

Stats: Words: 2267 Chapters: 1/1 Comments: 39 Kudos: 187 Bookmarks: 19

Love Lifts Him Up Where He Belongs
Unapologetic Lavinia Stan

Summary:

Aeneas has spent twenty years getting hard to a ghost. The love of his life, long dead. Lavinia, who vanishes whenever he attempts to touch her.

Then, one day, she doesn't.

Notes:

Special thanks to my new beta. :-)

At night, she appeared before him once more. A bit more *translucent* than she'd been in life, but otherwise entirely, heartbreakingly herself. All sharp angles and features, lopsided smile and lank brown hair dusting her shoulders. The sweetest sight imaginable.

For twenty years now, he'd watched her float around their bedroom, clad in the same thin, short nightgown she'd worn to sleep one night, curled in his arms, never to wake again. Until she did, as a ghost. *His* ghost. His wife. His beloved.

As always, it felt both perverse and completely natural, how his body responded to the sight. If he could, all of him would rise to meet her, on whatever plane she still inhabited, but for now, only one part of him could. She smiled shyly at his condition, so shyly no one would suspect how she talked him through stroking himself some nights, her eyes bright and hot on him as he gasped and heaved and spurted against his belly.

They couldn't touch. At the attempt, she'd vanish immediately, and sometimes she took days to return. When she did, she looked shaken. Ragged. Eyes bleak.

He didn't know where she went, and she wouldn't talk about it. But after the third time, after he spent a week despairing that she might not be able to return at all, he no longer reached out to her.

Tonight, though, something was different. As he lay in bed—awash in want, in grief, in love—his breath stuttered. She reached out for *him*, as she hadn't done for two decades.

Her long, gentle fingers caressed his cheek.

They were warm.

22

"I'M STILL THINKING ABOUT HOW I WANT TO TACKLE Aeneas's Inconvenient Boner Week." April readjusted her rearview mirror for the thousandth time. "Yesterday, it occurred to me that maybe I could go back to modern AUs without things getting weird, as long as I kept using Wade's version of Aeneas, rather than yours. Which, admittedly, makes him a million times less hot, but sacrifices sometimes have to be made for the greater good. And by 'the greater good,' I mean 'explicit fucking in my fics.'"

Marcus snorted, but she kept rolling before he could formulate a better reply.

"Speaking of explicit fucking, I should show you my friend TopMeAeneas's latest magnum opus, "One Top to Rule Them All," which is sort of a sexy mashup of *Gods of the Gates* and *Lord of the Rings*. She took the *mount* part of Mount Doom very literally."

The closer they got to Sacramento, the chattier April became.

And yes, she was funny, and yes, he wanted to hear whatever she had to say.

But this wasn't a happy type of chatty, or even the overly caffeinated cocroffinut type of chatty. Instead, it was the type of chatty where she seemed to want to fill any possible silence, leaving no space for extended thought.

As she talked, she was paying sufficient attention to the highway, but she was also fiddling with the climate settings, the music selection, and the angles of the air vents, restless as she drove in a way Marcus had never witnessed before.

This was anxiety. Plain and simple.

In passing, sometime during their first month together, she'd told him her father was a corporate lawyer, her mother a homemaker. At the time, he should have wondered why she'd failed to add more detail, but he hadn't. Which was a mark against him, obviously, but also a testament to how deftly April could turn a subject away from anything too uncomfortable. Also an indication that maybe, just maybe, she handled other people's messy emotions and history better than her own.

Still, if she wanted to chat, he'd chat. If she needed distraction, he'd provide it.

He'd give her anything she wanted or needed, something he'd been trying to prove to her in earnest for the past month, ever since she'd stood naked and shaking in front of him beneath the stark light of her bedroom and asked him to fuck her as a reward. *Her* reward.

She didn't understand yet, but she would.

He loved her, *loved* her, and she was his reward. Touching her was a gift to *him*.

That night, he'd finally understood just how effectively she'd managed to shield her own vulnerabilities, despite all her seeming openness and the wattage illuminating them both.

The next morning, he'd been determined to learn more. To understand her better.

When he'd woken in darkness, an hour before her alarm was due to sound, she was already awake. At his movement, her head had turned toward him, and her eyes weren't heavy-lidded with sleep, as they should have been following such a late night.

She was fully alert. Thinking so hard, he was surprised he couldn't hear the friction.

"Tell me," he'd said, and gathered her into the crook of his body, an arm under her neck, the other stroking her arm, her hip, her flank as he eased her into the unfamiliar role of little spoon. "Tell me about the call."

The sheets smelled like them. Like sex and roses, and everything he'd dreamed of.

"My parents . . ." Unexpectedly, she laughed, the sound jarring in the predawn stillness. "The irony, Marcus. The fucking *irony*."

"I don't understand." He nosed the crown of her head. Pressed a kiss there.

"They're going to love you. *Love* you. They'll approve of you more than they ever approved of me." She paused. "But not just the real you. The fake you too, the public you. Even if they saw the difference, I don't think they'd count it as important. Maybe my mom would. Not my dad, though."

The thought hadn't occurred to him before, but—"My parents would have killed to have you as their child, instead of me."

Maybe that should have hurt, but somehow it didn't. The knife's edge of his grief had blunted since he'd shared it with April. Since he'd realized he had a choice in how his relationship with his parents would proceed in the future, if it proceeded at all. Since she'd told him he didn't owe them forgiveness or anything he didn't want to give.

Besides, how could he begrudge some alternate-universe version of his parents for adoring and admiring April, when he did the same?

"Thus the irony." She wiggled closer. "All your best qualities, everything that makes you remarkable—that's not what my father cares about. He's all about appearances. Surfaces and selling himself to clients. We're estranged, but my mother is absolutely loyal to him, and she has her own—" As she hesitated, her breathing became a bit ragged. "She has her own concerns. So things can get complicated."

When she'd fallen silent after her predawn confession, he hadn't pushed her.

Instead, he'd asked her what she needed from him, and she'd whispered into the darkness.

They'd made love slowly, and not just because she was already tender and slightly sore from their night together. Without urgency, in the dim coolness of her bedroom, in the shared warmth of her bed, he covered her, moved over her, took her beloved face between his hands and made certain—absolutely certain—she saw him seeing *her*.

Because that was what she'd needed.

Yes, he was beginning to understand her now. It had taken him longer than it should have, but he would make up for lost time today.

She hadn't asked for his help, because that wasn't her way. He was helping anyway.

If she needed space from her father, Marcus could give her that space, and she'd already told him how to do it. Her father cared about appearances. That being the case, there was literally no one better suited to occupy his attention and keep him away from April than the Well-Groomed Golden Retriever.

He had his character. He had his script and plenty of motivation.

As soon as they arrived at her parents' house, he'd be ready for action.

It shouldn't be much longer, either. The traffic was moving steadily, so they had maybe twenty more minutes to go. April kept glancing in her rearview mirror, as if longing to turn back, but she also kept driving.

After chatting about several more of the latest Lavineas fics—most of which he'd already, secretly, read—April fell silent.

Not for long, though.

"I saw you looking over the scripts again yesterday," she said, adjusting the fan speed up another notch, then back down again a moment later. "Did you make any decisions?"

Discussing his career might help distract her a bit longer, but there honestly wasn't much to report. "Nope."

Some of his options no longer existed, not after such a long wait. Others he still couldn't make himself commit to, despite all logic and common sense.

When she made a sort of encouraging hum, he willingly elaborated. "I fully understand how lucky I am to have access to those kinds of scripts, and I'm grateful. I really am. I don't take my ability to make a living from acting for granted, and I appreciate the opportunities and experiences I've had more than I can easily express."

"I know you do." She flashed him a quick smile before turning back to the road. "When you talk about your work, your gratitude shines through every word. It's endearing as hell."

Her regard, her affection, settled softly within his chest, as it always did.

With her, he was always warm. Always full.

"I think there are some great scripts in that stack, but I'm just . . ." When he paused, she didn't try to fill in the words for him. Finally, he made himself say it. "I'm not sure I want any of those roles."

None of them felt quite right. Worse, he didn't know which Marcus should show up for an audition. The real him? Some iteration of the man he'd played in public for almost a decade?

If he wanted to change his narrative, this was his best chance.

He shook his head. No, it wasn't a matter of *if*. He *did* want to change his narrative. It was more a matter of *how*. It was also a matter of courage. And as he'd told April before, he was no Aeneas when it came to bravery.

"So those roles aren't what you want. That's okay." April reached out to squeeze his knee. "You have time, and you'll get other offers. Once the last season of *Gods of the Gates* starts airing and you're back in the international spotlight, Francine's inbox will probably be flooded."

Maybe so. But by then, he'd have ensured a long, long gap between projects.

Unwilling to pursue the topic further, he turned toward April as much as the seat belt would allow. "Speaking of fame, how are you feeling about Con of the Gates? Are you ready for all the attention you're going to get?"

The convention was coming up next weekend, and they'd decided to make their semi-official debut there as an acknowledged couple. No more avoiding the paparazzi, at least for that weekend. Instead, they would enter the premises proudly and together.

He couldn't wait. He wanted to show her off, and she seemed both amused and pleased by his eagerness to do so.

When not occupied by the cast's group panel, an individual Q&A session, and various photo op stints, he intended to have her by his side whenever possible. Although, of course, she had her own commitments, some more recent than others.

"I think I'm ready." The rapid drumming of her fingers slowed. "I've already set aside what I want to pack, and my Lavinia costume is totally done, other than a bit of hem work."

His mouth opened.

"And *no*, you still can't see it." Her grin was just a tad evil.

"You'll have to wait until the cosplay contest, just like everyone else, Caster-Hyphen-Rupp."

Oh, he loved when she called him that. It meant she was feeling *saucy*, and saucy was a million times better than anxious.

Since talking about the con seemed to relax her, he would ask as many questions as necessary. "What about the session with Summer? How do you feel about that?"

Only days ago, the moderator for Summer's Q&A session had unexpectedly dropped out. The con's organizers, obviously aware of both April's love for Lavinia and her current online notoriety as his girlfriend, had promptly invited her to moderate the session instead. After some thought, she'd agreed.

Marcus had already introduced the two women via a quick FaceTime chat to smooth over any potential awkwardness. Afterward, Summer had sent him a text. Not that you needed my approval, but I like her. She seems confident, too, which will help. But take care of her during that con, Marcus. It's hard on all of us, but I don't think you can understand what it's like to be a woman in the spotlight. Especially a woman who's not used to it, and *especially* a woman who might not be the sort of girlfriend the press and public expect you to have.

It was kind and thoughtful and totally, one hundred percent Summer. Which was why, when Ron and R.J. had fucked over Lavinia and Aeneas in the final season, Marcus had grieved not just for his own character's arc but also for his devastated colleague and friend.

Because of how closely they'd worked together over the years, she and Carah were probably the two cast members who saw him most clearly, but neither woman had ever betrayed that knowledge to the press. Not a single time.

Maybe he and all three of his favorite women could have dinner together during the convention. Maybe, in their company, with their guidance, his path forward in his career would be clearer.

Their advice couldn't be worse than Alex's suggested hair care products and slogans, after all. *Try Caster for hairstyles that last-er!* Or, for extra-hold hair spray: *Hairstyle had a Rupp night? Let Marcus hold you!*

"I'll be fine moderating. I don't mind public speaking." April raised a shoulder. "I should be receiving Summer's bio and the questions sometime this week, so I can familiarize myself with what I'll need to say ahead of time."

He forced himself to ask the next obvious question. "When are you seeing your online friends? Have you set a time?"

Last week, while April was at work, he'd logged on to the Lavineas server in invisible mode and spotted her announcement from the night before. At long last, Unapologetic Lavinia Stan had told everyone she was also the Lavinia fan dating Marcus, and he was honestly surprised the entire internet contained enough bandwidth for all the squeeing that had occurred.

This means you're going to the con, right? RIGHT??? TopMe-Aeneas had asked, once the furor had somewhat subsided. WE NEED TO GET TOGETHER! OMG, WE HAVE TO! LAVINEAS POWERS, ACTIVATE!

Millions of crying-face and heart-eyes emojis later, arrangements had been made.

But he wasn't supposed to know about those plans, at least not in detail. Even though he did, and even though he would have given last year's paycheck from *Gates* to join them as Book!AeneasWouldNever.

He was still writing, and Alex was still beta-reading the stories, and Marcus was still posting them under his new pen name, AeneasLovesLavinia. So far, though, they hadn't received much traction, which was understandable but disheartening. And it was inexpressibly lonely to loiter outside the community he'd helped found, looking in.

April was worth it, though. A million times over.

"Sunday morning, we're all meeting for breakfast. I may visit the vendors with TopMeAeneas afterward, unless one of the panels looks particularly enticing." Flipping on her turn signal, April exited the highway and decelerated down the ramp. "We're almost there now. Five more minutes."

Her fingers weren't drumming against the steering wheel anymore. Instead, they were gripping the leather so tightly, her knuckles had turned white and knobby.

Somehow, the sudden silence was even worse than that anxious chatter. Her lips were a thin, pinched line, her cheeks pale, her chin truculent and upturned.

Unexpected rage licked a trail of fire up his spine.

He wasn't going to make April talk about a subject that obviously upset her, but he could act on her distress anyway.

Her father wasn't getting anywhere near her. Marcus would make fucking sure of that.

He hoped Brent Whittier had a stick or a chew toy available, because the Well-Groomed Golden Retriever had come to *play*.

Unapologetic Lavinia Stan: And by that, I mean: On Twitter, I use the handle @Lavineas5Ever. Which, as you may recall, is also the handle used by the fan Marcus Caster-Rupp asked out on a date. Which makes sense, since I'm that fan.

Unapologetic Lavinia Stan: Yes, he's wonderful and makes me very happy, and no, I can't tell you much more than that. But I wanted you to know. So now you do! ❤

TopMeAeneas: OH MY SWEET JESUS!!!

LavineasOTP: Holy shit

LavineasOTP: Hoooooooly shiiiiiiiiiiiiiiiiiiiiiiiiiiiiiiiiit

Mrs. Pius Aeneas: This is the day foretold by our elders. The day a Lavineas fan got to touch MCR's jawline and find out if it will, in fact, cut your fingers with its sharpness!

Unapologetic Lavinia Stan: No stitches yet. No promises for the future, however.

TopMeAeneas: THIS IS WHY AENEAS IN YOUR FICS IS WADE'S AENEAS NOW

Unapologetic Lavinia Stan: Yeah. I didn't want to write a man with my boyfriend's face and body getting it on with another woman. Even Lavinia. I'm selfish like that. :-)

LaviniaIsMyGoddessAndSavior: YOU HAVE TO TELL US

LaviniaIsMyGoddessAndSavior: DOES HE REALLY SMELL LIKE MUSK AND CLEAN SWEAT AND MAN

Unapologetic Lavinia Stan: Kind of? Especially after he works out?

TopMeAeneas: [legs-spread, crotch-up gif]

23

THE NIGHT BEFORE SHE VISITED HER PARENTS FOR THE first time in a year, April had lain sprawled and wakeful next to Marcus, determined to reach some sort of verdict.

Sometime after two in the morning, clarity had arrived.

When it came to her mother, the land beneath her feet was contaminated. She could either continue living with a soil cap, a thin veneer of pleasantness over profound damage, or dig out the problem.

The process wouldn't be easy. It would cost her, maybe more than she realized.

Then again, she'd never been much interested in surfaces.

It was time to dig and dispose.

Luckily, she'd thought before finally, gratefully falling asleep, *I'll have Marcus by my side. Holding my hand. Reminding me, when I forget, that I'm not the contaminant. Even if my parents wouldn't agree.*

Only she'd been wrong. Completely, humiliatingly, gut-churningly wrong.

Marcus wasn't by her side, not even for a minute. He wasn't holding her hand.

Instead, he was chatting with her father at the opposite side of the open-plan first floor. Laughing. Sharing workout and nutrition tips, some of which Brent repeated to the house at large, his tone genial enough that outsiders wouldn't understand just how pointed his commentary was, and whose flesh those verbal arrows were intended to pierce.

Marcus's support and affection had never faltered before, and she'd counted on both as a bolster today. More than that, she'd relied on them as proof, to her parents and herself, that everything they believed, everything she'd been told for eighteen years, was wrong.

Marcus's fingers intertwined with hers, the way he beamed at her, would announce her triumph more clearly and loudly than words.

I'm fat, and he wants me.

I'm fat, and he doesn't need me to change.

I'm fat, and he's proud of me.

Now she was just another big girl the hot dude didn't want near him, at least not in public. Which was precisely what her parents expected, and what her mother had warned her to expect too, in all those concerned phone calls April had stopped answering.

Honestly, she didn't give much of a fuck about what her father thought or believed, not anymore. But when she'd pictured this conversation with her mother, she'd imagined Marcus nearby, his proximity a silent reminder that she was desired and appreciated, that her happiness was worth painful conversations and setting hard boundaries.

Instead, she was doing it alone, because of course she was.

Of course.

As the two women had set the table, her mother had already whispered of her unease, brows puckered over warm brown eyes. "Are you certain this isn't a publicity stunt, sweetheart? It just seems so . . . unlikely."

That anxiety was real. So was the love in that familiar gaze.

They only made her words sting more. When April had de-
fended the genuineness of her relationship with Marcus, her
mother's unstated but clear disbelief stung too.

Now, as they put the final touches on their *celebratory gourmet
spa lunch*, as her mother called it, the two of them were treading
yet more of that same contaminated ground.

"I saw a few pictures in the tabloids." JoAnn checked the done-
ness of the pan-roasted salmon, then transferred the fillets to a
platter. "I'll send you some links for foundation garments. They'll
smooth things out a bit, so you'll feel more comfortable when
the paparazzi take candid shots."

"Foundation garments have literally never made me feel more
comfortable," April replied, trying to keep her tone wry rather
than bitter. "Quite the opposite, as a matter of fact."

Her mother laughed. "You know what I mean."

Oh, April did know. Physical comfort meant nothing, if dis-
comfort would help deter the censure of loved ones and strangers
alike. JoAnn had learned that the hard way.

During her first year of marriage, she'd gained fifty pounds.
Then promptly lost it again, once she realized that above a certain
weight, her husband wouldn't invite her to socialize with his col-
leagues, wouldn't dance with her in public, wouldn't touch her
in private.

It was a one-time mistake, never repeated. Brent still bragged
about how his wife lost all her baby weight within a month of giv-
ing birth. And since JoAnn hadn't wanted to risk failure a second
time, April had remained an only child.

She'd been born small and remained slim—until puberty. Then
the number on the scale started creeping upward, week by week.
Until, finally, her mother pulled her aside to share the story of
that first wedded year and the lessons to be drawn from it.

"Boys care about these things more than we girls think, and I don't want you to be blindsided like I was." JoAnn's hand was soft and cool and tender against April's flushed, wet cheek. "Sweetheart, I'm only saying this because I love you, and I don't want you to get hurt."

That was the common refrain, always.

I love you, and I don't want you to get hurt.

It was far, far too late to avoid hurt. But at least that story had confirmed what April already suspected. Already feared.

Her father had stopped bringing her to the firm's family events. The only photos of her around the house dated from before puberty. At her older cousin's wedding, when her maternal grandmother urged him to dance with his daughter, he'd simply pretended not to hear.

He was ashamed to be seen with her.

Yes, it hurt. Badly. Yes, she'd eventually seen a therapist about it.

But honestly, the man was a dick in so many ways, it was relatively easy to cut ties with him. They didn't talk. They barely saw one another outside afternoons like this, and even then, her mother remained a constant buffer and mediator. Spending time in his disapproving presence still made her nervous, but it didn't devastate her.

Her mom, though, was sweetness inextricably swirled with a toxin JoAnn didn't and would never recognize as harmful.

In ridding herself of the taint, April would most likely lose the sweetness too.

Still, she'd told Marcus he had the right to set parental boundaries for the sake of his happiness, and she needed to follow her own advice. JoAnn's love for April didn't justify the harm she'd done, and April's love for JoAnn couldn't save their relationship.

Not unless things changed. Not unless April spoke and her mother actually listened.

Today, she was speaking. The rest was up to her mother.

Spoonful by spoonful, JoAnn was dolloping low-fat yogurt-dill sauce onto the plates. Still talking. Still worried and loving and hurtful.

"Have you considered surgery, for your . . . problem?" Her mother always stumbled over the word, as if fatness were an obscenity. "It might make things easier, especially with a man like Marcus. And you know how concerned I am for your health."

April could hardly forget, given the frequency of her mother's reminders.

"I could come and help you recover afterward, if you wanted." When her daughter didn't respond, JoAnn tried a different tack. "But I know that's a big step. If you're not ready, maybe you could try his diet and exercise routine instead. It could be something you have in common, like it is for your father and me."

Growing up, April had wondered what kept her parents together. JoAnn, fluttery and well-intentioned and cheerful. Brent, confident and self-absorbed and dickish. Married almost forty years now, yet still strangers in a very real way. A couple that never seemed more distant than when they stood beside one another.

Well, now she knew: burpees and lean protein had saved their marriage.

It would be kind of hilarious, if only her mother didn't always look so afraid every morning when she stepped on the scale, and every evening when she stepped on the scale, and all those other times during the day she stepped on the scale too.

After leaving for college, it had taken April three years to stop weighing herself after every meal. Another decade to throw away the scale entirely.

Her mother was twisting lemon slices to garnish each plate, which meant lunch was almost ready. They were running out of time, and April was running out of courage.

She couldn't wait until after the meal, as she'd planned.

They were doing this now.

"Mom." She placed a hand over her mother's, stilling those skilled, perfect movements. "I need to talk to you for a minute. In private."

JoAnn's forehead crinkled. "We're about to eat, sweetheart. Can't this wait?"

"I don't think so," April said, and nudged her mother toward the privacy of the guest room.

JoAnn's birthday lunch wasn't the right place for this, but it was a conversation that needed to occur face-to-face, and April wasn't sure when she'd return to her childhood home. She wasn't sure *if* she'd return. It all depended on what happened next.

After living with a man like Brent for decades, her mother was exquisitely sensitive to the potential displeasure of loved ones. She was already twisting her hands anxiously, already half-ready to cry, which was part of the reason they'd never had this conversation before. Reducing Mom to this state made April feel like a monster. It made her feel like her father.

"What . . ." Her mother started at the click of the door, even though April had closed it behind them as quietly as possible. "What's wrong, sweetheart?"

Okay. She didn't need Marcus.

In the end, she was always going to have to do it on her own, anyway.

"After today, I don't want to see Dad again. Ever." Any minute,

Brent would wonder why his wife wasn't serving him with sufficient speed, and this conversation would end. April didn't have time to prevaricate. "Being around him brings me nothing but anxiety, and I'm not subjecting myself to that anymore."

Her mother gulped at that first, firm statement, eyes going glassy and terrified.

For years, she'd lamented the estrangement between father and daughter, coaxing April in phone calls to visit for his birthday and send him Christmas gifts before whispering, her tone meaningful, that he'd asked how she was doing.

April didn't believe it. And even if he had, was that—a passing thought as to her general welfare—really enough to indicate his grief at her distance and his desire for greater closeness?

Was that really enough to make him an actual father?

No. No, it wasn't.

Now April was declaring her independence, cutting him out of her life entirely, and all her mother's worst fears were coming true, and it was horrible, *horrible*, to be the person to inflict that necessary blow.

"Sweetheart—" Her lips trembling, JoAnn reached toward April. When her daughter continued speaking, though, she dropped her hand and fell silent.

"From now on, our relationship won't include him." Her mother would exploit any seeming uncertainty, so April didn't offer any. "If you can't visit me without him, I'll understand. But I won't see you either, then."

Late last night, April had formulated different versions of this conversation.

He doesn't love me, she'd tell her mother. *Maybe I still love him a little, only because it's hard* not *to love your father. I definitely don't like him, though. I'm done.*

But that would have invited her mother to insist *of course* Dad loved her, men just showed it differently, and April simply needed to understand. Accept. Deny her anxiety, deny what she needed, even though her chest felt wrung dry, emptied, at the prospect of seeing a man who was supposed to love her no matter what, but didn't.

He didn't.

Her mother did. Which only made the rest of this conversation worse.

"How our relationship will look after today is up to you." Acid was climbing April's throat. Bile. "Not just because I won't see you when he's present, but because things need to change between us. Even without his involvement."

JoAnn was openly crying now, her knees collapsing beneath her as she sank onto the edge of the bed, her spine bent as she huddled in on herself, and at one time, April would have cut out her own heart to prevent her mother from looking like this.

In some ways, she had.

That ended now, even if she felt monstrous and unclean.

"I don't want to talk about my body with you ever again." No matter how her voice shook, she had to make her boundaries clear. Absolute and unmistakable, so their violation couldn't be mistaken for confusion. "I won't discuss what I eat or don't eat. I won't discuss how I exercise or don't exercise. I won't discuss how I look or don't look. I won't discuss test results or medications. My weight, my health, and my clothing are all off-limits."

JoAnn's eyes were red-rimmed now, her lips parted, her head shaking in mute befuddlement or denial or some other emotion April couldn't parse through her own grief.

"I know you worry about me, I know you want to help, but

that doesn't change what I'm telling you." Salt was stinging her eyes, blurring her vision, and she slapped away the tears and kept standing, kept talking. "Please believe me: The next time you bring up my body, I will end our conversation. I'll walk out the door or hang up the phone. The next time you send me links to articles about weight loss or exercise, I'll block your messages."

For once, she was glad of her mother's timidity before the assurance of others. It meant April could get out this next part before the weight of her own love dragged her under and drowned the words that needed, at long last, to be said.

"If that's not enough, if you can't stop, I'll cut off all contact with you." Despite her mother's gasp, despite her own crying, April maintained eye contact as best she could. "B-because you hurt me, Mom. You're hurting me."

Her mother sobbed out loud then, hands fisted at her sides. "I *love* you."

At that, April had to bow her head. After swallowing back more acid, though, she raised her chin once more.

Maybe her words cracked, but they were certain. They were honest. "You l-love me, but you still hurt me. When I talk to you, when I see you, I end up half-convinced that who I am, what I am, is wrong and abhorrent and needs to be *fixed*."

"You're not abhorrent," JoAnn whispered, face crumpled and lined. "I never, ever thought that."

The raw truth in that declaration drove April to reach for her mother's hand. JoAnn's fingers were slender and cold and unsteady. So fragile, April couldn't squeeze too hard for fear of breaking them.

Still, her mother needed to realize. "But that's how you make me feel."

Everything she'd scripted in her head last night, she'd said. All but the last bit. And the voices of the two men were getting louder, closer, so she needed to say it now.

"Dad will never, ever understand how he's hurt us. Even if he did understand, he'd never acknowledge it." April gave her mother's hand a gentle shake. "But you're not him. Please, Mom. Please think about whether you want to keep hurting me, now that you know you are."

Her mother's tears were silent now, their trails glinting in the sunlight through the window, her pain etched in lines around her pale mouth.

"I only wanted to help," she whispered.

April pressed a kiss to the back of her mother's hand, the skin there more papery and thin than she'd recalled. Lightly freckled, despite sunscreen and spot-reducing hand creams.

In her mind, her mother was still young and glamorous. Sheathed in slender, formfitting dresses, makeup perfect as she left on her husband's arm for his firm's holiday parties, calling out last instructions for the babysitter until Brent got impatient and yanked her out the door.

But she wasn't young anymore. Neither was April, really.

They were running out of time to fix this. To fix them.

The only way forward was honesty. "It doesn't help, Mom. It only hurts."

Then the guest room door was opening, and the amiable, man-to-man chuckles of Marcus and her father stopped abruptly.

Brent frowned but didn't move closer to his wife. "JoAnn? What—"

"I think we'd better go," April said. Somehow, Marcus was right there beside her, his hand resting warm and strong on her shoulder. She instinctively stepped away from the contact. "I'm sorry to miss lunch, Mom. I left your present in the den."

In her peripheral vision, she could see Marcus staring down at her, brows drawn, hand frozen in midair, but he didn't matter now. Her mother was still sitting on that bed. Still hunched, narrow shoulders shaking as she wept silently, so as not to embarrass anyone with her heartbreak.

Bending down, April kissed the top of her mom's head. Inhaled the powdery scent of flowers, maybe for the last time.

"When you've had a chance to think, call me." She was wetting her mother's hair, so she lifted her face after one last inhalation. "I love you, Mom."

With her father blustering protests and demands, her mother crying, and Marcus trailing silently behind her, April gathered her purse and left her parents' house.

Her eyes might be blurry, but her back was straight.

Good thing too. This hellacious day wasn't over yet. Once they were five minutes down the road, she was having Marcus pull over.

Her mother wasn't the only person who'd hurt her today.

She didn't intend to let it happen again.

Rating: Mature

Fandoms: Gods of the Gates – E. Wade, Gods of the Gates (TV)

Relationships: Aeneas/Lavinia

Additional Tags: <u>Alternate Universe – Modern</u>, <u>Angst and Fluff and Smut</u>, <u>Arranged Marriage</u>, <u>Lavinia Has Body Image Issues</u>, <u>For Obvious Reasons</u>

Stats: Words: 1893 Chapters: 1/1 Comments: 47 Kudos: 276 Bookmarks: 19

Untouchable
Unapologetic Lavinia Stan

Summary:

Lavinia knows exactly why her husband doesn't touch her, doesn't kiss her, doesn't bed her. Possibly, however, she may have made a few assumptions along the way. Ones Aeneas intends to correct.

Notes:

Thank you to my fabulous beta, Book!AeneasWouldNever! He's been helping me work on emotional heft in my fics, so whatever such heft this story has belongs rightfully to him.

———————————————

At night, the irony choked her. Somehow, having a beautiful husband, having a husband she'd grown to love, had made her married existence so much worse, so much more painful, than if she'd simply married Turnus instead. Turnus, her fiancé before fate—and parental interference—had broken the engagement. Turnus, all brown curls and bluster and righteous anger and wiry strength.

Turnus, who would have bedded her in darkness, fucked her from behind whenever possible, and avoided looking at her face the same way he'd avoided looking at her face since meeting her.

But at least he'd have taken her to bed. Unlike her actual husband.

Her husband, golden in the sunlight. Her husband, smooth muscles and features polished to perfection. Her husband, polite and attentive and distant as the moon overhead.

For Aeneas, evidently, no amount of darkness was sufficient to disguise whom he'd married, whom he'd have to fuck. For him, she was more than simply homely and awkward and everything else her father had ever told her. She was untouchable. So ugly he couldn't abide a fingertip's worth of contact.

Or so she might have gone on believing forever, until she got drunk one night. Very, very drunk. For the first time ever. At Dido's bachelorette party, drowning her stupid envy over how Aeneas's ex—now Lavinia's faithful friend—had managed to get over the man and move on in a way Lavinia never could as his wife.

When she came home in a cab, he met her at the end of their driveway, forewarned of her arrival by Dido's text. When she staggered, he tugged her against his side and supported her with a strong arm around her shoulders.

When she looked blearily up at him and slurred, "Don't have to touch me. Know you don't want to. Made *that* clear enough," he stopped dead on their front sidewalk, still holding her, brow furrowed in confusion.

Then, when she repeated the horrible, humiliating truth, he glared at her with eyes blazing like the stars above and spat out his own truth.

"I have wanted to touch you every minute of every day for months now," he said. "What the actual, ever-loving fuck are you *talking* about?"

24

APRIL HAD SHRUGGED AWAY HIS ATTEMPTED COMFORT IN her parents' guest room, so Marcus didn't try to reach out to her again. Instead, he silently accepted her keys, passed her the tissue box and a bottle of water, set the GPS to her apartment's address, and began driving them home.

She didn't want him to touch her. That was her right, and no doubt she had good reason to distance herself from him. He simply didn't understand what that reason was. And he might not be allowed physical contact, but he could still steal glances at her as he drove. At stop signs and red lights, and when he needed to wait behind someone making a left turn.

In fleeting glimpses, he scanned her tear-stained countenance for some hint of what he'd done wrong, and found . . . nothing. Nothing.

Her face was speckled stone. Impervious.

His confusion and anxiety ballooned by the moment, filling his skull until he wondered how his ears hadn't popped from the pressure.

Without warning, she pointed to the right. "Pull off here." They'd reached a little park not too far from the freeway, and he obediently turned into its lot. "Pick a space without anyone else nearby, please."

The farthest corner of the lot offered spots with the most privacy, and he chose the last space on the end. Within moments, the car was parked, and the hum of the engine went quiet, but he kept his hands clutched tight on the steering wheel. Because he was nervous, and because he needed to keep them away from her until she was ready to be touched.

He studied her blotchy face and the balled-up tissues in her lap, his jaw aching with tension, his need to offer comfort overwhelming but stymied.

She didn't speak. Not one word.

"April . . ." he finally said, her name a gravelly plea. "I don't know what happened with your mom, and I don't know how I fucked up, but I obviously did. I'm sorry."

He'd thought he understood. Her father was an asshole, and being in his company upset her. If Marcus offered himself as a human barrier, then she could spend time with her mother and escape the visit home unscathed. Simple as that.

Only she'd emerged metaphorically bloodied instead, and Jesus. Jesus. Evidently he hadn't helped at all. Best he could tell, he'd hung her out to dry instead.

His skin fucking *crawled* with shame at having inadvertently abandoned her in need. It was the absolute worst feeling. The *worst*.

Had he simply not listened hard enough? Or had she told him less than he'd realized, less than he needed to support and protect her? And if so, how could he have failed to notice such a glaring omission?

After another torturous silence, she finally responded to his apology, her words blunt and abrupt and startlingly loud in the hushed confines of the car.

"My father despises fat people. Including me. My mother wants to save me from the judgment of people like him, so she constantly advises me about my body." She pressed her trembling lips together. "I told her today I would no longer visit her if the two of them came as a package deal, because I have no desire to see him ever again. Then I said I would cut off contact with her entirely if she didn't stop discussing my body."

Metal in his mouth. He'd drawn blood somewhere, lip or cheek or tongue, and it felt right. Blood *should* be spilled in response to what she'd just told him.

That motherfucker.

There were assholes, and then there were—

He didn't even know what the right term for her father was.

Even then—even ravaged by tears, her cheeks blotched with distress—April glowed in the sunlight through the window. How her father couldn't see her beauty or value, how he'd turned away from the daughter who should have been his greatest pride, Marcus had no idea.

And her mom. Her *mom*.

In some ways, that was almost worse, wasn't it? In the end, a dismissal by her malignant asshole of a father might be easier to shake off than the inadvertent slights of her mother.

Brent wasn't worth a moment of April's time or a single one of her tears. But JoAnn . . .

JoAnn wanted to protect her daughter. JoAnn had the best of intentions. JoAnn loved her daughter, loved her sincerely, but hurt her anyway. Again and again.

The thought of April growing up like that gutted him.

Fuck, he wanted to hold her. *Needed* to hold her. Instead, as he tried to find the right words, he fisted the steering wheel so hard he was surprised he didn't pry the leather free.

But when his mouth opened, she held up a hand. "Let me get this out, please."

More copper spilled over his tongue, but he nodded.

"I wanted you by my side today, holding my hand. To show them I don't need to change how I look to have a good relationship, and to support me as I had a hard conversation with my mom." She rubbed her bloodshot eyes and sighed. "I really needed my boyfriend, not the public version of you. But I didn't tell you any of that, so you don't have to apologize. It's fine."

Amid the upheaval of the afternoon, her near-instant forgiveness was graciousness he hadn't expected and wasn't certain he even deserved. Maybe she hadn't told him enough before the visit, but he should have asked what she needed from him, not assumed.

His failure roiled his stomach, but this wasn't about him. Not at its heart. He had to remember that.

He didn't speak until she met his eyes again.

His hand was an inch from hers, but he didn't close the distance. "May I?"

When she nodded, he let out a slow breath and interwove their fingers, placing their joined hands on his thigh. With his free hand, he reached over and swept away a stray tear from her jaw, keeping the pad of his thumb gentle and light on her salt-stained skin.

She didn't flinch or edge away. Thank fuck.

His incipient nausea eased as the dread—his fear that this afternoon would end their relationship, that she'd never forgive him—drained away with each arc of his thumb.

"April . . ." Bowing his head, he lifted their tangle of fingers to his cheek and rubbed. Kissed her knuckles. "You'd said you and your father were estranged, and you seemed anxious about the visit. So my goal today was to keep him as far away from you as possible. Since you said he was all about appearances, I figured the best way to do that was to be—"

"Not yourself." Shit, she looked tired. He hoped she'd let him drive them the rest of the way to Berkeley. "I get it. Well, now I do, anyway."

He'd make it up to her. When she saw her mother again—*if* she saw her mother again—he'd do whatever she needed. Be whatever she needed.

And in the meantime, he'd give her all the love he could.

He'd give her love because she deserved it, and because he couldn't help it. He was so fucking smitten with her, his adoration spilled from him like water from a fountain or blood from a wound. He exhaled love with every breath. It floated behind him with each step, bright as fireflies in the dark of night.

Most of all: he'd give her love because he wanted to earn her love in return.

And to do that, he needed to make absolutely certain she understood why he'd disappointed her, and just how sorry he was for doing so.

"Within two sentences, I could tell your dad was a dick. Which I'd already guessed, since you're estranged, but it wasn't hard to see why." He sighed. "Your mom seemed genuinely affectionate with you, though, so I thought it was safe to leave you two alone, while I kept him away. I'm so sorry."

Her hands were icy, and he chafed them, trying to lend his warmth.

She watched, her exhaustion visible in her boneless slump and painted in dark circles beneath her eyes. "She is genuinely affectionate. That's not the problem."

"I know that now. I'm sorry," he repeated, his voice raw. "If I'd had any idea she was badgering you like that, I never would have abandoned you."

"No need to apologize." Her jaw cracked with her yawn. "You didn't know. I didn't tell you."

As she sagged against her seat, she began shivering, even though it wasn't actually cold in the car. Emissions be damned, he promptly turned on the engine and set the thermostat as high as possible, flicking her seat warmer onto its hottest setting too.

She didn't protest.

He cradled her face in his hands. "April, I swear I'm nothing like your father. In general, because he's an asshole, but also . . ."

When he trailed off, shifting in discomfort, she filled in the rest.

"You don't care that I'm fat." Nuzzling her cheek against his palm, she closed her eyes again. "Which I should have known from the beginning, given the way we met."

On the Lavineas server? What did that have to do with her size?

"Given the—?" He paused. "On Twitter. Yes, given the way we met."

Shit, he'd almost forgotten. Almost revealed exactly how long they *had* known one another. Jesus. As if the afternoon somehow required even more drama and conflict.

He brushed his lips over her forehead, then her nose, before giving her a brief, gentle kiss on the mouth. "I love your body exactly the way it is, April."

"I believe you." Her faint smile lightened his heavy heart. "Even an actor of your talent couldn't fake how you look at me. Especially when we make love."

Lustful and lovestruck and speechless. That was how he felt when they made love, and how he probably looked too.

April's body was perfect exactly as it was. Brent Whittier could go fuck himself.

"I had no idea that was the crux of your estrangement with your father." After one last tender stroke of her hair back from her forehead, he shifted fully back into his own seat and put the car in drive. "I knew it was an issue with some of your dates, but not with him. I really am sorry."

At first, she didn't respond. Tipping back her head, she closed her eyes. His guess: worn out by all the upheaval, she'd be asleep within thirty seconds.

Then, when they were almost out of the parking lot, she seemed to register his words.

Her eyes blinked open, and she put a hand on his arm, stopping him from pulling out onto the road. He braked, then turned to her again.

"What's wrong?"

Was she still too cold? Did she want to get out of the car and sit on one of the park's sunlit benches together?

"Marcus . . ." Her brow was pinched. "How did you know I'd been fat-shamed by dates before?"

His hard swallow seemed to echo in his ears.

Fuck. *Fuck.*

Some of her exes had been assholes to her because of her body, but she'd never told him that. At least, she'd never told *Marcus* that.

In fact, she'd only ever broached the topic of dickish dates once in his presence. Namely, when she'd posted about fat-shaming on the Lavineas server, and he'd read the post and responded. As BAWN.

He opened his mouth. Pinched it shut again.

The choice lay before him. He could lie. He could say he'd deduced the existence of horrible exes, based entirely on that whole gym-and-buffet misunderstanding from months ago.

Or he could come clean. At long last, he could stop hiding the truth from her.

He knew which choice a good man, a good partner for her, would make. But he also knew something else with a certainty that sickened him.

If he'd told her the truth entirely of his own volition, he might have had a chance to salvage things. Only admitting his lie of omission now, after he'd been caught—that was the part she wouldn't be able to forgive.

April, who cared only about the truth beneath all the pretty lies, was never going to trust him again, and he couldn't blame her. He didn't.

But he still needed to explain, to try, because he loved her, and she deserved the truth. No matter whether she still loved him after he told her. No matter whether she'd ever loved him to begin with.

"Marcus?" She didn't sound sleepy anymore. Not in the slightest.

Dropping his chin to his chest, he tried to ignore the acid climbing his throat and breathed shallowly through his mouth. If his sudden nausea got any worse, though, he'd have to open the car door to spare her upholstery.

Without a word, he backed up, up, up, until they'd reached the far, empty corner of the lot once more.

With every inch he reversed, April straightened in her seat. Grew more alert, her gaze sharp as a blade against his throat.

Then they were parked, and he was almost out of time.

One last look, while she still trusted him. One last stroke of her cheek. One last moment hoping that maybe—maybe, despite everything he knew about her—she would accept his heartfelt apologies and they could still have a relationship.

Her skin was icy. And now, so was his.

"I'm Book!AeneasWouldNever," he said.

Lavineas Server DMs, Six Months Ago

Unapologetic Lavinia Stan: I feel bad. Well, kind of. Kind of not.

Book!AeneasWouldNever: ???

Unapologetic Lavinia Stan: I was a bit snippy with AeneasFan83 just now, in her thread about the "historical inaccuracy" of non-white people in the show. But honestly, BAWN, does she think POC were a Victorian invention?

Book!AeneasWouldNever: I'll look at the thread in a minute, but I have faith that if you were snippy, she deserved it. Especially since her take is total bullshit.

Unapologetic Lavinia Stan: THANK YOU

Book!AeneasWouldNever: I'm here to defend your snippy honor whenever needed.

Unapologetic Lavinia Stan: To be fair, I was already upset before the whole POC-wouldn't-have-been-in-Europe-even-though-there-is-a-shitload-of-contemporaneous-proof-they-totally-fucking-were conversation, and I probably took that out on her.

Unapologetic Lavinia Stan: And just to be clear, even if there weren't people of color back then in Europe (AND THERE WERE), our show featured a fucking PEGASUS, so sit down with your hot, racist take on historical accuracy, lady.

Book!AeneasWouldNever: Another excellent point.

Book!AeneasWouldNever: So what was already upsetting you before you saw the thread?

Unapologetic Lavinia Stan: It's kind of a long story.

Book!AeneasWouldNever: You don't have to tell me. Ignore the question.

Unapologetic Lavinia Stan: No, it's okay.

Unapologetic Lavinia Stan: Without going into too much detail, I met a friend for dinner, and she disappointed me.

Unapologetic Lavinia Stan: I thought she accepted me the way I am, but

Unapologetic Lavinia Stan: She wants to fix me. Improve me.

Book!AeneasWouldNever: WTF?

Unapologetic Lavinia Stan: She had to speak up, BAWN. Out of CONCERN.

Book!AeneasWouldNever: I'm certain you already know this, but: You don't need to be fixed or improved. You're perfect just the way you are.

Book!AeneasWouldNever: I'm so sorry. That must have hurt.

Book!AeneasWouldNever: I don't have a ton of friends—maybe three? And they're all coworkers. But they would never do that to me. You deserve better.

Unapologetic Lavinia Stan: Given how kind and funny you are, I'm shocked you don't have an enormous circle of close, loyal friends. But quality over quantity, right?

Book!AeneasWouldNever: Honestly, I'm still surprised sometimes to have ANY friends. I didn't growing up.

Unapologetic Lavinia Stan: Being a kid is so awkward.

Book!AeneasWouldNever: Yes. Anyway, I'm forever grateful for the friends I do have. Definitely including you, Ulsie.

Unapologetic Lavinia Stan: I feel the same.

Unapologetic Lavinia Stan: Thanks for listening, as always.

Book!AeneasWouldNever: Any time.

Unapologetic Lavinia Stan: I don't let everyone in, and it hurts to do it and be disappointed.

Book!AeneasWouldNever: I'm an expert at disappointing others, sadly.

Unapologetic Lavinia Stan: Well, you've never disappointed me.

25

APRIL WAS CRYING AGAIN. WITH HURT, YES, BUT ALSO RAGE.

So much goddamn rage.

Marcus was Book!AeneasWouldNever. At one time, that would have been her most fervent wish, to have the two most important men in her life somehow merge into one. To not have to choose between them. But now—but now—

All this time. All this time, he'd pretended they'd met as strangers at a restaurant. All this time, he'd fucking *lied* to her.

"April, I'm so sorry. Please forgive me." When Marcus tentatively reached out to dry her tears again, she slapped his hand away.

"Why?" That single syllable was so choked with betrayal, she could barely understand herself. "Why didn't you say something?"

He raked a hand through his hair. Gripped it in his fist so hard he must have ripped some out. "I wanted to, April. Fuck, I would have done anything to let you know."

Jesus, what bullshit. Exactly how gullible did he think she was?

"Anything." She laughed, a horrible, scraping sound. "Anything except *tell me*."

Such a small slip-up he'd made. So easy to dismiss, to explain away, if his stumble hadn't involved something she couldn't second-guess or doubt.

She'd decided months ago not to mention being fat-shamed on dates to Marcus. It was a very deliberate, very conscious omission, one intended to spare her pride. She'd told herself that part of her past didn't matter, really, not when he *did* love her body exactly the way it was.

If she hadn't caught that damning little slip, would he ever have told her? And how long, precisely, had he known the truth?

"Did you know who I was when you asked me out on Twitter?" Her tone had hardened now. Turned colder, as her tears dried.

He frantically shook his head. "I had no clue who you were. I swear. Not until you told me at dinner."

That blank look of shock when she'd shared her fanfic name. Those initial, probing questions about Marcus—about *himself*, and how she felt about him—on the Lavineas server. All those conversations where he pretended to know almost nothing about fanfic.

"You've been keeping this a secret from our very first date," she whispered. "From our first fucking date."

He grabbed the back of his neck, squeezing hard. "April, you have to understand—"

"Oh, how wonderful." She'd never used that voice, rich with sarcasm and disdain, on him before. Not even once. It made him flinch, and she was savagely *glad*. "Yes, *please* tell me what I have to understand. I can't wait to find out."

"If anyone knew I was writing fix-it fics in response to the show, if anyone knew the things I said about the scripts on the Lavineas server . . ." He sounded so sincere, each word a heart-wrenching plea. A hell of a good actor, as always. "I could have lost the role of Aeneas. I could be sued, potentially. And no one would want to cast the guy who—"

Enough. She didn't need a lecture on how grave the consequences could have been, or how grave they could still be. Of course his showrunners would be unhappy. Maybe even his colleagues. But he'd lied to her, and she wasn't letting herself be dragged off-topic.

She held up a steady hand. "I get it, Marcus."

"I don't think you do." His lips tightened, just for a moment. A flash of anger, when Marcus was never, ever angry at her—at least, not until he was caught in a lie. "Not really."

Ignoring that attempted feint, she cut to the most crucial, most hurtful part of this absolute shitshow. "I also get the real issue here."

"The *real* issue?" It was almost a growl.

"You don't trust me." She sat back in her car seat and laughed again, and the sound was just as horrible, just as sharp, as before. "We were friends for over two years online, and you've been living with me for months, and you *don't trust me.*"

She'd been so sure of him. Of them.

And from the very beginning, she'd been building a relationship on quicksand.

The anger had faded from his expression, and the desperate shake of his head must have hurt his neck. "No, April. *No.* That's not—"

She bit her lip, her cold, calm facade cracking. "I w-would never have told anyone. Not a soul. Not my coworkers. Not our friends on the Lavineas server. Not my mother. *No one.*"

The honest fucking truth, and she hoped he recognized it.

"I know that!" He flung his hands in the air, his own voice breaking. "Do you honestly think I don't *know* that?"

The air seemed simultaneously too thin and too thick to breathe, and she wanted to fling open the car door and run. Instead, she stayed and faced him dead-on.

"Right. Of course." Her lip, now bitten red and raw, stung as she gave him a mean little smile. "Except for one problem: if you *knew that*, if you *trusted me*, you would have *said something*."

He clawed at the seat belt as if it were strangling him, finally stabbing at the release to fling it free. The violence of the motion didn't seem to satisfy him, though, and his chest heaved with labored breaths.

"I was scared." It was a blunt, rough statement, unvarnished enough that her desolate sneer faded despite her best efforts. "When we met in person, I was cautious about sharing something so damaging, and I think that's understandable, even though you may not agree. Then I knew I could trust you, but I didn't—"

Jaw clenched with frustration, he seemed to search for words.

"I didn't trust that I'd say the right thing when I explained. I didn't trust that I'd be enough to make you stay, once you knew I'd been hiding something so important all this time. From that first date." His brows had drawn together, a mute plea for understanding. "I love you, and I was terrified you'd leave me."

Her sudden inhalation removed all the remaining oxygen from the car. Dizzy and sick, she stared at him.

I was scared.

I love you, and I was terrified you'd leave me.

Even desolate and enraged, she couldn't dismiss the naked honesty in the admission. Couldn't pretend to herself that he was playing her, misleading her, wheedling for her forgiveness through strategic, manipulative vulnerability.

At long last, he was letting her see him without any barriers, any artifice, any deception between them.

And it was too late. Too goddamn late.

Outside the car, children shrieked in a game of keep-away from across the park's expansive grassy field. The sound was distant, almost inaudible over the ringing in her ears, the subtle creak of her seat as she sagged into it all at once.

Her voice wasn't angry or disdainful anymore, but still thick. Still despairing. "For months, you've known much more about me than I realized, and you kept that information from me. It's a horrible violation of trust. You realize that, right?"

It was disorienting. Sickening.

Every conversation they'd had, every moment of their relationship, she'd now have to revisit and question. When had he lied? When had he simply not told her the truth? When had he used his knowledge as BAWN to further his own purposes as Marcus?

He'd definitely pumped her for information about Marcus as BAWN, she knew that for certain. And then—and then he'd cut off contact on the Lavineas server. Just like that.

"When BAWN s-stopped"—she inhaled through her nose, exhaled a hitching breath through her mouth—"when *you* stopped writing me on the server, I told myself I'd done something wrong, or you'd finally seen me and realized I wasn't anyone you c-could want. You were m-my—"

Her sob shook her shoulders, and he bowed his head.

She sniffed back more tears. "Y-you were my best friend, and you just . . . left. With no good explanation, only some dumb excuse that was obviously untrue. You lied to me as Marcus, but you lied to me as BAWN too. You *a-abandoned* me."

Tipping her head back, she stared at the gray fabric of her car's ceiling and waited until she could speak intelligibly again. "You hurt me, lied, and violated my trust because you were scared."

"I'm so sorry." He sounded agonized. Helpless in the face of her despair.

"Your public persona." Fretfully, she rubbed her forehead. "You said you've wanted to drop it for years, but you haven't. For the same reason, I assume. Because it's too hard, and you could lose everything, and you're scared. Too scared to pick your next role, because you'd have to decide which version of you would show up on set."

The statement didn't require an answer, and he didn't give her one.

Instead, after a deep breath, he squared his shoulders. "Can you forgive me?"

The question was gruff, his eyes glassy as he met hers.

She opened her mouth, then pinched it shut. Once. Twice.

When she continued staring at the ceiling, silent, he spoke again. "You don't owe it to me. I know that. My love doesn't buy me absolution, and I didn't say it to sway you. I said it because you should know. No matter what happens between us now, you should know that you're loved. Even if you don't forgive me."

Her cheeks were already tight with salt, and she was crying again. Still.

He loved her. She believed that. And in some ways—in many ways—he really was such a good man. So good, she'd almost believed they could make it work, against all odds.

But she knew the answer to his question, because she knew herself.

She didn't want to say it, but she would. She had to.

"No," she finally said. "I can't forgive you."

He made a raw, wounded sound, and that only made the tears come faster.

Rolling her head to the side, she finally looked at him again. He was a blur through her flooded eyes, his expression indistinct, and maybe that was for the best.

She knuckled away the wetness from her chin. "I want to go home."

His love for her didn't buy him forgiveness, and hers didn't mean she'd offer it. Which meant this would be their last time alone together. Ever.

When he reached for her hand, though, she didn't pull away.

Her fingers were trembling and cold, and so were his. He pressed a tender kiss into her palm, then carefully placed her hand back into her lap.

He clicked his seat belt and put the car in drive. "When we get back to Berkeley, I'll pack my things."

Her breath hitched again, hard.

But she didn't argue.

Gods of the Gates: A Howl from Below (Book 2)
E. Wade

"Build a pyre," Dido told her sister, Anna, as the wind snapped the sails of Aeneas's fleet and speeded him away and away and away. "Upon it, place all the possessions of our life together. Our bridal bed. The clothing he once wore. All the weapons he abandoned."

As he abandoned me.

Once, she too was a weapon. A sword, shiny and sharp and lethal. The Berber king Iarbas had found her so, when she'd arrived in North Africa and begged from him a small plot of land, a place of refuge before she resumed her travels.

"Only such land as can be encompassed by an ox hide," she'd pled sweetly.

His agreement had come after the amused, tolerant laughter of his men. His wise advisers.

Silly woman. Silly request.

First, she honed her blade until a fingertip's pressure could quarter a man where he stood. Then she took that smelly hide and cut it into such fine, thin strips that she could encircle a substantial fertile hill.

There she'd settled, she and her subjects, before expanding her rule outward and outward again.

A ruler. A queen. Respected and beloved by her people, by Aeneas.

Amidst her fevered passion, her people had grown restless. So had he.

When the pyre was built, she climbed atop and lifted the sword he'd once presented to her while kneeling, the blade laid flat on both his palms. The flat no longer interested her. Only the point.

Her lips, mouthing final words no one would hear, stilled at the sight of him.

Another demigod, equally a trickster. Cupid.

His wings folding gracefully behind him, he glided to a halt atop her mountain of grief. Watched her, sorrow in his expression.

"Have you come to increase my devotion?" Her laugh was the screech of metal, cold and terrible. "It has already driven me to destruction. What more do you intend?"

"No, betrayed queen." His voice was low, resonant with determination. "I come to free you."

She tried to laugh again, but it emerged as a helpless sob instead. "I was poised to free myself."

"Not like this," he told her. "Not like this."

The arrow he loosed into her breast then wasn't sharp or hot. It was blunt and cold. Lead.

And for the first time since she'd caught sight of Aeneas aboard his ship, brown curls caressed by the breeze as he neared her shores, she was once more a blade. So much of one, she had no need of the sword still pointed toward her heart. Not anymore.

The thought of Aeneas brought only disgust, not lust. Not frenzied longing.

Cupid inclined his golden head. "Thus, we are both freed. You from a doomed love. I from the selfish dictates of my treacherous mother."

With a flick of his wings, he gathered her up and deposited her at the base of the pyre.

"I must return to Psyche." His hand reached to steady her, but she needed no assistance. "You know what you must do."

She did. She did.

She would don the mantle of her reign once more, guarding her people from threats without and underneath. Human transgressors, and those who'd crawl from the depths of Tartarus through the gate that gaped within her city walls.

As Cupid become a gilded smudge on the horizon, Dido took a torch and set fire to her life with Aeneas.

26

MARCUS'S HOUSE KEY STILL WORKED. EVEN THOUGH IT felt like it shouldn't.

Somehow, over the past months, April's small in-law apartment had become his home instead. A place that was theirs, not just hers. A place he wouldn't have to leave, not ever.

He'd let himself wallow in that fiction, until he almost forgot it *was* fiction.

When his front door opened, the frigid air-conditioning within hit him like a slap, and he shivered. Inside, the chill tightened his lungs, but he hadn't taken a deep breath in almost twenty-four hours anyway.

April had shunted him aside—rightfully; of course rightfully—nearly a day ago, and he was still short of air. Still claustrophobic in a trap of his own making.

Nevertheless, he forced himself to walk inside and shut the door behind him. Lock it. Set the alarm, because his home was filled with valuables, even if he currently felt worthless.

His keys and wallet went on the console by the door, in a hammered bronze bowl. His shoes belonged in the entryway closet. His broken heart . . . well, he couldn't organize that away.

He shoved his shaking hands in his pockets and contemplated the airy expanse of the first floor, all open floor plan and high ceilings and sunlit windows and impeccable furnishings. White walls and metallic accents and minimalist, low-slung furniture.

He'd never really felt at home anywhere before meeting April. Not even here.

His throat ached. He headed to the kitchen for a glassful of chilled sparkling water from the dispenser in the refrigerator door, his footsteps faintly echoing in the spartan space.

The cheap water bottle he'd bought at a gas station had warmed during the trip from Berkeley to Los Angeles, and he'd left it in the car. He didn't need any unnecessary reminders of today, however inconsequential.

Every time he let his mind wander, April was crying again.

In another age, he'd have knelt before her then. Prostrated himself. Anything, anything that would serve to appease at least a small corner of his endless, ever-unfurling self-loathing.

He'd wept too, of course—but not until he'd left her home, because damned if he'd cry in front of her. Not like that. It would be inadvertent manipulation, because she cared about him. He knew it, even if he also knew he didn't deserve it.

If she ever forgave him, if she ever took him back—and she'd do neither—he didn't want her to do so out of pity. Never seeing her again would hurt less.

Probably. Maybe.

He sipped his water, the carbonation an irritant to his already-raw throat.

Beneath his palm, the polished concrete countertop was smooth and cold. Laying his phone on top of it, he idly scrolled through recent messages on his cell.

Texts from Alex about the optimal thickness of hot-water crusts for savory pies, as well as complaints about Lauren's dampening disregard for both British baking shows and pegging. An obscenity-laden screed from Carah via DM, something to do with the upcoming awards season. An email from his father, which Marcus deleted without reading. A half dozen more emails from his agent, which he kept but didn't open. A missed phone call from Summer.

The cast chat had been active the last few hours too. Active and on edge, probably because of the upcoming convention.

Carah: SURPRISE, SURPRISE, MOTHERFUCKERS

Carah: Ron and R.J. officially backed out of Con of the Gates, citing a too-heavy workload

Carah: Too-heavy workload, my sweet ass

Alex: I'm assuming they mean the workload for their Star Fighters project, since they were nowhere to be found on OUR set this last season

Alex: Except in front of the cameras, naturally, for special features and interviews highlighting their genius and dedication

Maria: Well, they certainly weren't working on our scripts

Ian: They were around plenty, whiners

Peter: More tuna hallucinations, poor Ian

Peter: It's a shame everyone will miss Ron and R.J.'s session,

The Art and Science of Failing Upwards As Cishet White Guys

Ian: Fuck you, Peter

Ian: You're a has-been

Ian: and since you've never been on a successful show before, you have no idea how things work, especially off on your stupid little island

Alex: Is Tuna Rage a thing? Like 'Roid Rage, only smellier and less articulate?

Maria: "Fuck you, Peter"?

Maria: Oh, Ian, I'm so sorry

Maria: I'm afraid Peter requires a certain level of

Maria: how should I put this

Maria: personal hygiene? yes, personal hygiene

Maria: when it comes to his lovers

Maria: I'm pretty sure anyone who smells like the Catch of the Day is disqualified, sadly

Carah: ooooooooooooh

Carah: the rare and elusive piscine BURN!

Carah: FIGHT FIGHT FIGHT FIGHT

Ian: That's right, Maria

Ian: I suppose you WOULD know all about Peter's requirements for sex

Summer: Stop right there, Ian

Maria: No, go on, I'd like to hear this

Alex: Ian, Peter might not have an IV tuna drip and muscles upon muscles, like some sort of steroid-induced pecs Inception, but he will fuck you up, my dude

Alex: and so will I, to be clear

Peter: Thank you for the kind offer, Alex, but there would be nothing left of him by the time I was through

Peter: and that's only if Maria doesn't get to him first, because she would transform him singlehandedly into a fine pink mist

Peter: So please, Ian, finish what you were saying

Carah: IT'S MY FUCKING BIRTHDAY UP IN THIS BITCH

Carah: NO TUNA IS SAFE TONIGHT

> **Peter:** Ian?

> **Alex:** Yo, Ian

> **Carah:** IAN, COME BACK

> **Maria:** He swam away, like his beloved fish

> **Maria:** which are vertebrates, unlike him

> **Summer:** Oh, wow. ::high-fives::

> **Carah:** ICHTHYOLOGY SHADE, I LOVE MY GODDAMN LIFE

If Marcus could have smiled, he would have.

Instead, he drained the rest of his water, set the glass in his deep, wide sink, and prepared to remove his suitcases from the car and literally unpack his relationship with April.

After several trips outside, he set the luggage on his California king bed and unzipped everything, determined to empty every compartment, every pocket, every dark hiding place.

Dirty clothing goes in the hamper. Clean clothing goes in drawers or on hangers. Toiletries go in the bathroom. Tech goes in either my nightstand table or my office.

If he kept repeating the next steps to himself, he couldn't think beyond the moment. Couldn't remember.

It was all so easy. Mindless. Mindless was good.

One armful at a time, minute by minute, everything settled back into place. Clothing, toiletries, tech, emotions. His life, restored to its state pre-April. If he didn't know better, he'd think he'd never left at all.

Then he saw it, carefully tucked inside a pocket, cushioned from damage with newspaper.

"I changed my mind," she'd told him one Saturday, as they'd stood on the cliffs above the Sutro Baths and watched the tide roll in. "I thought you were a diamond, and then I thought you were gold. But none of that was quite right. Not once I knew you better."

After squeezing his hand, she'd let go of him and gone digging in her oversize purse.

"I'll be glad to hand it over." The setting sun sparked in her hair as she shook her head ruefully. "It's heavy as fuck. You'd think it would be easy to find for exactly that reason, but . . ."

He'd help her, only he had no idea what the hell she was talking about. "I'm sorry?"

"I got you a gift," she told him cheerfully, and kept digging.

He stared down at her, speechless. The last time anyone had given him a present with no ulterior motive, no special occasion or achievement to celebrate—

Well, that had never happened before. Not once in his memory.

"There it is." Lifting her head, she smiled with satisfaction and put something extremely heavy in his palm. It was wrapped in newspaper, but vaguely round. "Open it."

The sheets of newspaper crinkled as he carefully unfolded them, revealing . . . stone. The most beautiful stone he'd ever seen. It was a rich, intense blue, speckled with white, veined in what appeared to be gold. A polished sphere, cool in his cupped hand.

"It's lapis lazuli." With a fingertip, she tapped the stone. "When we went to that gem and mineral warehouse the other weekend, I picked it up. While you were in the bathroom."

He'd have appreciated anything she gave him. Movie tickets. One of those fossilized pieces of feces—coprolites?—they'd seen in the warehouse. A soda. Whatever.

But this . . . this was gorgeous, as lovely as the woman who'd gifted it to him.

Then she kept talking, and his heart swelled to fill his entire chest and push up into his throat.

"Lapis is a metamorphic rock. The original rock is subjected to intense heat and pressure, and then . . . this." She laid her palm on his chest, over his expanding heart, her touch reverent. "Beauty."

He'd bitten his lip, unable to respond directly to the implied praise without weeping. "Those veins in the rock aren't actually gold, are they?"

"Nope." She lifted a shoulder, the movement a bit jerky. "Pyrite. Fool's gold. Sorry."

Shit, she thought he was criticizing the gift, and nothing could be further from the truth.

"Gold couldn't make this any more beautiful than it is." Tipping up her chin, he kissed her with all the adoration one man's overfull heart could contain. "Thank you. I love it."

Maybe she hadn't said the words, but he'd recognized the gravity of her offering. It wasn't just a sphere of stone, but—

Her heart. It had felt like her laying her heart in his palm, despite all her fears.

When it came to bravery, April possessed more than her fair share.

When it was much too late, he'd been brave too. He'd told the truth, all of it. He'd exposed his heart to her without artifice or omission and told her, *This part of me is pyrite, not gold.*

And once she knew, she didn't want him. He was a liar, valuable only to a fool who mistook him for something more.

And now that she was gone, he was no longer *more* to anyone. He was no longer a sphere of rich, speckled blue, polished and beautiful but substantial too. Weighty in his palm, then and now.

Now he was a speck of a man. One of the sunlit dust motes that sparkled and floated inside her car, glinting and aimless and adrift.

Yes, he was angry that she'd dismissed his concerns about his career with such blithe disregard. But he was angrier at himself. Still. Always.

He never learned. He never, ever learned.

His phone buzzed from the top of the dresser. Another text from Alex, who'd apparently received Marcus's own message at long last.

Dude. I'm so sorry, read the bubble on the screen. I'm coming over.

Marcus exhaled. Thank fuck. He needed his best friend, and he needed something to both puncture the silence of his house and quiet the cacophony in his head.

Alex could do all of that easily, with a single rant about unrealistic judging expectations in televised baking competitions. Especially if he brought—

Another incoming message. I know it's not your usual thing, but wanna get drunk? I can pick up booze on my way there.

Yes, Marcus wrote back. Please.

He didn't unwrap the lapis sphere. Instead, he placed it, still swathed in newsprint, in the back corner of his closet, behind the shoe box containing a pair of hiking boots he'd never managed to break in.

There, it couldn't taunt him with what he'd lost, and it couldn't remind him of what he'd never truly had.

APRIL WAS DONE hiding. Which meant, unfortunately, that she was going to Con of the Gates tomorrow, less than a week after her breakup with Marcus. Public scrutiny and potential humiliation and her own misery be damned.

She didn't fool herself. It wasn't going to be comfortable. After all those tweets and blog posts and articles, too many people knew her face now. They knew her body. There would be no hiding in a crowd, and no hiding the fact that she and Marcus hadn't attended the con together.

Cynics would roll their eyes and say they'd recognized a publicity stunt from the start. The unkind would laugh instead. *So much for his white-knight ambitions*, they'd crow. *Even such a gifted actor couldn't pretend to want a woman like* that *for long*.

Whatever. If they judged her, fuck them.

And even if she'd *wanted* to hide, like hell she'd let her Lavinia costume—the product of hours of dedicated effort by Mel and Pablo—languish in a closet out of cowardice. And there was no way she'd ever, ever skip her long-awaited gathering with her closest Lavineas friends.

They'd notice her distance from Marcus and wonder, of course. Hopefully, they'd be kind enough not to ask. Or, failing that, smart enough to ask with a fresh tissue box nearby.

After tucking the last of her clothing and travel toiletries into her suitcase, she zipped it shut and rolled it just inside the apartment door. Afterward, she sat on her couch beneath a blanket and listened to a podcast.

She tried to pay attention, but she kept thinking Marcus would find the topic interesting. Not so much because he paid special attention to unsolved serial killings, but because he was as hungry for knowledge as anyone she'd ever met, his innate curiosity matching her own.

Fuck, she missed him.

When she realized she hadn't registered the last ten minutes of the podcast, she turned it off. In the gathering darkness of her living room, throw pillow held to her chest, she sat and stopped trying not to think about it. About them. About her life without him.

So quickly—or maybe *not* that quickly, now that she knew he was BAWN—Marcus had made ample space for himself in her daily life and thoughts. But he wasn't everything, and he wasn't all that mattered to her. Her work and her costume and her upcoming meeting with her Lavineas friends were proof enough of her non-Marcus interests. So were her dinner plans with Bashir and Mimi next week.

She wasn't lost. She *wasn't*.

Even if his absence from her home, her bed, her arms, left her hollow-eyed and aching down to her joints some days. Even if she watched British baking shows while she ate takeout for dinner, because claggy sponges and underproofed dough reminded her of him.

Even if she loved him, and he loved her in return.

When she shut off her bedside lamp way too late at night, she still saw him behind her eyelids, face crumpled and stricken and adoring as she railed against him in her car. Eyes wet, but too honorable to use his tears or his love as tools to force her forgiveness.

Sometimes, as she turned onto her side and flipped her pillow yet again, she wondered if the conversation would have gone differently under other circumstances. If she hadn't still been raw and chilled and exhausted from that long-overdue confrontation with her mother, still on edge from the proximity of her father and Marcus's abandonment of her at her parents' house.

He'd blasted the heater for her. Warmed her seat. Cupped her face. Apologized earnestly.

But her rage and hurt had still been lingering just beneath the surface, much too easy to access. The slightest scratch to her composure would have unearthed all that volatile emotion, and he'd provided much more than a mere scrape.

With his deception, he'd gutted her.

With her sharp words, by withholding her forgiveness, she'd

gutted him right back. That was clear enough. If the devastation in those expressive eyes hadn't told her so, his body language would have. On the way out her door, he'd moved like a man broken, cradled into himself and guarding against further jolts.

Five days had passed since then. Out of respect for her stated wishes, he hadn't called or emailed or DMed. That first night, he'd only texted her once. Two simple words he'd already told her, ones she knew he meant sincerely.

I'm sorry.

Scared. He'd been scared, so he'd hurt and misled her.

She couldn't blame him for that, but she couldn't seem to forgive him, either. Not when she remembered the wrenching pain of BAWN's sudden, now-explicable estrangement. Not when she considered all those months he'd pretended ignorance when it came to reading and writing fanfiction; all those months he'd failed to acknowledge the intimate knowledge he held of her, born out of years of friendship; all those months he'd secreted that same advantage, the understanding of who and what he really was, out of her reach.

No wonder she'd felt as if she'd known him for years. She had. But not all of him. Not enough of him.

She didn't hate him. She wasn't angry anymore. She was just . . . tired.

The warm, bright spotlight of his love was gone, and the shadows left behind were fine. She was fine.

Absolutely fine.

Or she would be, if she could convince herself she'd made the right choice.

Lavineas Server DMs, Five Months Ago

Unapologetic Lavinia Stan: What do you do when you feel down for no good reason?

Book!AeneasWouldNever: What's wrong? Are you okay?

Unapologetic Lavinia Stan: I'm getting my period soon. Nothing is wrong, but everything is wrong.

Unapologetic Lavinia Stan: I hope you're not squeamish about things like that, because if so: TOO LATE, SUCKER.

Book!AeneasWouldNever: Since approximately half the humans on this planet either have gotten or will get periods, I've always found that particular brand of squeamishness ridiculous.

Unapologetic Lavinia Stan: So you're the type of guy who would buy his girlfriend tampons at the grocery store?

Book!AeneasWouldNever: This is not a hypothetical. In past relationships, tampons have been procured. Back rubs have been dispensed. Bloodstains have been removed from sheets and clothing.

Book!AeneasWouldNever: And in case you were worried, my manhood has nevertheless remained intact. Despite what some men seem to believe.

Unapologetic Lavinia Stan: Well, I'm certainly glad you reassured me about your intact manhood, BAWN.

Book!AeneasWouldNever: I'm so sorry you're not feeling well, Ulsie.

Unapologetic Lavinia Stan: Thank you.♥

Unapologetic Lavinia Stan: Also, thank you for distracting me from my woes via our discussion of tampons. I had not anticipated that particular conversational tangent.

Book!AeneasWouldNever: I try to maintain a certain air of mystery.

Unapologetic Lavinia Stan: You're a constant surprise, my friend. A riddle, wrapped in a mystery, inside a grocery store with Playtex in your cart.

Unapologetic Lavinia Stan: You never answered my question, though. What do you do when you feel down?

Unapologetic Lavinia Stan: Do you drink tea? Take a bath? Watch a terrible movie? Read? Eat a pint of ice cream? Have a glass of wine?

Book!AeneasWouldNever: At various times in the past, all of the above. But these days, I mostly

Unapologetic Lavinia Stan: Yes?

Unapologetic Lavinia Stan: BAWN?

Book!AeneasWouldNever: I mostly talk to you.

27

AFTER APPROXIMATELY TEN SECONDS OF SHARING A HO-
tel suite with Alex, Marcus remembered exactly why they were no longer roommates.

His best friend was many things. Ridiculously loyal. Sharp as a sword's edge. Sympathetic in the face of his friend's abject, self-inflicted misery. A good distraction from said misery, which was why Marcus had suggested sharing a suite in the first place.

What Alex wasn't: restful.

Marcus had been hoping for a nap before the evening's events began. His first photos with fans were scheduled that night, fol-lowing Alex's Q&A session, and the participants paid plenty for the privilege. He wanted to look fresh for them. He wanted to *feel* fresh for them.

Since Alex had talked nonstop during the lengthy car ride from the airport, all through their check-in process, and down every single hallway leading to their suite, though, all hopes of a nap were likely to die a much-lamented death in the near future.

"—don't know why Lauren's so worried." After flopping face-first onto his queen bed, Alex propped himself on his elbows and began tapping on his phone. "I didn't do anything particularly objectionable to the fan. I only suggested that if she didn't have anything better to do with her time than insult total strangers, she should occupy said time by going and fucking herself. It's not my fault she went straight to the tabloids, and it's certainly not Lauren's either. Ron and R.J. aren't going to fire her over something as minor as *that*."

Marcus frowned. "What did the fan say to you?"

"Not to me." Alex's finger stabbed at the screen with unwonted force. "To Lauren."

Ah. That explained things, at least somewhat.

Lauren's appearance could best be termed *unconventional*. She was short and round. Very short and *very* round, with comparatively skinny legs and bright eyes and sharp features and a near-constant frown.

She reminded Marcus of a small, plump bird, honestly. A cute one. But he could see how strangers with ugliness inside might look at her and see only ugliness outside.

"Don't ask me what that *fan*"—it sounded like an epithet, spat that way in Alex's most cutting tone—"said to her. It was vile and hurtful, no matter what Lauren claims. I don't *care* if she's used to hearing things like that. It's not happening in my presence. Not if I can help it."

Alex shoved a rough hand through his hair, his scowl thunderous.

Nope. No nap occurring anytime soon.

"I'll go get us some ice," Marcus offered. "Do you need anything while I'm out?"

"Nope. I'm going to plot out a fic where Cupid's arrow makes a horrible, insulting woman so eager to fuck herself that she can't eat or drink, just masturbate, and then she dies of masturbatory malnutrition." He paused, thoughtful. "Or maybe she'll just pass out and learn her lesson. I don't usually kill people in my stories."

That was Marcus's cue. "Okay, I'll be back soon. Try not to get fired while I'm gone, please."

"No promises," Alex muttered, and bent over his phone again.

The conference hotel was built around an atrium that rose to skylights far above, the hallways on each floor open to that central square and looking down on the madness below. According to the hotel map on the inside of the door, the ice machine was located on the exact opposite side of his floor's square, as far away as possible.

Fine. He could use a few minutes of quiet.

The door shut behind him with a bang. Bucket tucked under his arm, Marcus wandered to the other side of the hallway and glanced idly down at reception. Most of the *Gates* cast and crew in attendance at the con should be arriving shortly, so he checked for familiar faces.

The chances were infinitesimal, with thousands of people crowding the hotel.

Still, there she was. Tiny but recognizable down below. Almost at the front of the check-in line, suitcase by her side, waiting patiently as the discreet lobby lighting set her hair ablaze.

He'd desperately hoped she'd come. Prayed she wouldn't.

But he'd known what she'd decide to do, in the end. April wasn't a woman to abandon her responsibilities, and she'd agreed to moderate Summer's Q&A session and meet their—her— friends from the Lavineas server at the conference. She wouldn't skip the event, even if she wanted to.

And maybe she wouldn't mind being near him again. Maybe her gut hadn't been seething with almost-constant nausea since their confrontation. Maybe she didn't find herself sleepless and replaying their last conversation in her head, searching for what she could have said differently, regretting the choices she'd made weeks and months before.

She might be fine. On his less selfish days, he even *hoped* she was fine.

He was not.

After that horrible car ride, he no longer visited the Lavineas server, even invisibly. Seeing her name, her avatar, turned his lingering nausea acute. Even writing fanfic evoked too many memories now—of Ulsie's careful, cheerful beta-reading comments, of April's glee at particularly smutty stories, of the community he'd helped create and then lost.

April hadn't posted a story on AO3 since he'd left. He didn't know if he'd have the heart to read it if she did.

The sources of joy and meaning in his life seemed to be extinguishing one by one, and he had only himself to blame. No wonder his stomach was roiling, his head throbbing daily.

From his spot far above, he watched her take her turn at checkin. He watched her wait as they ran her credit card and checked her ID. He watched her accept her room keycard and head for the elevators, where she passed out of his sight.

Then he trudged down the halls to the ice machine, filled the bucket, and tried not to remember why his life had become as cold and hard as the ice rattling with each step he took.

Moments after he returned to the room, though, his own wretched, unceasing heartbreak dulled in the face of fresh disaster. This time, in the form of a single, terrible email.

"How long does it take to get ice?" Alex asked as the door swung shut. "Did you personally trek to the Arctic tundra and cut the cubes yourself?"

He was still on the bed, still hunched over his phone. Still, evidently, determined to fill every spare moment with conversation.

"The machine is on the other side of the—" Marcus sighed. "Never mind. I'm sorry I took so long."

A quick check of the bedside clock dashed all remaining hope of a nap. The two of them had, at best, ten minutes to rest before heading downstairs for their first scheduled appearances.

"*Fuck*," Alex groaned. "I have a new message from Ron. The subject line is 'Inappropriate behavior and possible consequences.' As if I don't know what horrible things they could—"

Abruptly, his mouth slammed shut, and his brows drew together.

As Marcus watched, concerned, Alex scrolled down. Then back up again, apparently rereading the message, and down a second time.

His breathing changed, becoming rough and fast, until he was blowing out air like that maddened bull Ron and R.J. had incorporated into the fourth season for no good reason.

Red flags of color stained his cheeks, which was never, ever a good sign.

"Those motherfuckers," he whispered. "Those cruel motherfuckers."

Alex was going to tell him all about it anyway, probably at an uncomfortable volume, so Marcus took his friend's phone and slowly, painstakingly, read the message for himself.

Unacceptable rudeness to a fan, in violation of behavioral expectations, blah blah blah. *Contractual obligations*, blah blah blah. Nothing too surprising or untoward, and nothing that would elicit the sort of reaction Alex—

Oh.

Oh.

At the bottom of the message, Ron had added a less legalistic addendum.

> *P.S. I suppose this is our fault, for saddling you with such an ugly minder. Tell Lauren to put a bag over it, if she has to, but stop letting her face get you in trouble. Although that doesn't fix the rest of her, right?*

Ron had added a crying-laughter emoji to the end.

They'd also cc'ed Lauren. *Those cruel motherfuckers*, indeed.

Shit. Marcus needed to fix this, or at least buy them some time. Without giving his friend's phone back, if at all possible.

They didn't have many minutes left before Alex's first scheduled event, but he couldn't go onstage in this state, and he certainly couldn't be trusted to send a professional, non-career-ending reply to such a casually cruel message. Not until he'd had time to calm himself.

What were their reasonable options? "Listen, Alex, why don't we take a walk before—"

"No time." Color still high, his friend got to his feet, put on his shoes with two quick shoves, and prowled toward the suite's door. "Let's get going. I have a Q&A session to attend. You can keep the phone for now."

Marcus slipped the cell into his jeans pocket, as close as possible to his crotch, where retrieving it would require the sort of intimacy he and Alex didn't share.

Which was . . . good?

So why did Alex's relinquishment of the phone only make Marcus more nervous?

Down the endless hallways they marched, Marcus offering

smiles to fans and blaming Alex's upcoming session for their unwillingness to pause for selfies.

Alex, uncharacteristically, didn't say a word. He just looked straight ahead and strode down the corridors, every movement efficient and forceful.

Mere minutes ago, on his way back from the ice machine, Marcus had contemplated watching the first few minutes of Alex's Q&A session from the wings of the stage, then escaping back to their room for a long-awaited, well-deserved, unconscious respite from both his misery and Alex's endless talking.

Now he wasn't going anywhere. Not when they reached Alex's assigned hall. Not when the moderator and conference organizers greeted them with effusive courtesy. Not when they were both ushered backstage and shown seats neither of them used.

After another minute of silence, Marcus tried again. "I know you're angry, but—"

"Don't worry." His friend's voice was cool, in contrast to those livid stripes of color on his cheekbones. "I'll be fine."

Which was somehow both more and less reassurance than Marcus had hoped to receive.

When the moderator announced Alex, he nodded once at Marcus and strode onto that stage as if he were entering a boxing ring.

This was—

Marcus moved closer to the edge of the curtains, until he could see his best friend pacing with a microphone in hand, rather than sitting next to the moderator. That smile, gleaming through his shaggy beard, was wild and sharp and familiar.

It usually preceded something apocalyptic.

This was very, very bad.

Lauren had been given a special seat at the end of the front row, and she was watching Alex carefully, her brow furrowed even more than usual. Perched on the edge of her folding chair, she appeared poised to do . . . something. Throw herself in front of him, maybe, or yank him from the stage.

Despite her evident worry and Marcus's own concerns, however, the session proceeded normally. Maybe Alex's answers were a bit crisper than normal, and maybe his high color never faded completely, but he was charming and intelligent and everything the showrunners wanted him to be in public.

At least, until the final question of the session.

The woman in the third row was nearly shaking with nervousness, but she stood and stammered out her query anyway. "Wh-what can you tell us about the final season?"

"Your question is about the final season, correct? You're asking what I can share about it?" Alex's grin burned even brighter under the stage lights, and Marcus knew. Somehow, he just *knew*. "Thank you for such a fantastic closing question. I'd be delighted to answer."

Marcus was already moving toward the center of the stage, already attempting to formulate some excuse, any excuse, to pull his friend away, but it was too late. He was too late. So was Lauren, who shot to her feet at the first sign of trouble.

All they could do was stop and watch and listen, horrified, as Alex endangered his entire goddamn career in a towering rage.

"As you know, cast members aren't allowed to say much about episodes that haven't aired yet." His anarchic, fury-filled beam in place, he stopped pacing and spoke clearly and distinctly to the cameras capturing his every word for live streams worldwide. "However, if you're interested in my thoughts about our final season, you may want to consult my fanfiction. I write under the name CupidUnleashed. All one word, capital *C*, capital *U*."

Other than a few scattered gasps at the announcement, there wasn't a sound from the audience. Not one. Arms wrapped around her torso, face screwed up in horror, Lauren dropped back into her seat and hunched in on herself.

With a courtly flourish, Alex set down his microphone on the seat he'd been provided but failed to use. Then he raised a forefinger and picked up the mic again.

"Oh," he added breezily, "those stories will also give you some insight into my feelings about the show in general."

Lauren had covered her face with both hands, her head bowed.

A long pause as his smile improbably broadened. "Also, fair warning: Cupid gets pegged in my fics. Delightedly and often. It's not great literature, but it's still better than some of this season's—" He winked at the audience then, allowing them to fill in the word for him: *scripts*. "Well, never mind about that."

Because of the live streams, because of the cell phones recording his session, there could be no denying his words later, no way to spin them except as he'd intended them. Provocation, deliberate and pointed.

There was a faint whimpering sound then, and if Marcus had to guess, he'd say it originated from Lauren.

Alex waited another moment, head tilted in thought. Then he smiled one last time.

"No, that's everything." Another little bow. "I'm done."

He strode offstage to the sound of shocked murmuring and stopped next to Marcus, his body exuding unbelievable heat. Eyes clenched shut, he was once again heaving out breaths like that bull, ready to scrape the ground and charge.

"Alex." When his friend didn't respond, Marcus tried again. "Alex."

This time, Alex managed to focus on him.

"You really are done, unless you find a way to do damage control immediately." He laid a careful hand on his friend's shoulder. "I'll be back in the room as soon as the photo sessions are finished, but you need to call your agent and your lawyer and anyone else in your camp who can help. Right now."

Alex's eyes closed again, and his shoulders finally dropped. He nodded.

"I know," he said, his voice resigned but not apologetic. "I know."

<u>Lavineas Server</u>
<u>Thread: WTAF Is Up with This Season's Scripts?</u>

Unapologetic Lavinia Stan: There are so many issues. So many.

Unapologetic Lavinia Stan: I still don't understand why the showrunners moved the story from ancient Rome to quasi-medieval Europe. (Yes, I know what BAWN will say.)

Mrs. Pius Aeneas: "Trying to ride the coattails of Game of Thrones."

Unapologetic Lavinia Stan: Exactly. But even a thousand years later, people weren't saying "stressed out." Even *I*, a woman who does NOT dabble in canon, know THAT.

Book!AeneasWouldNever: Thank you for saying it so I didn't have to, MPA.

TopMeAeneas: Even apart from all the anachronisms, the dialogue just seems so much more . . . rudimentary? . . . than in the first three seasons.

Book!AeneasWouldNever: That's not a coincidence. One book per season. Three books.

Book!AeneasWouldNever: The showrunners never understood the characters. They relied on the books and the actors. Now the books are gone, and the actors will do their best to sell what they're given, but they can't simply make up plots and dialogue.

Book!AeneasWouldNever: At least, that's the rumor. I don't know for sure.

28

APRIL SKIPPED ALEX'S Q&A SESSION, SCARED SHE MIGHT see Marcus there. Afterward, though, she couldn't avoid hearing about it.

"He just . . . *announced* it," a guy with stylized wings on his tee said to a circle of his friends, looking shocked but titillated. *Cupid Gets Shit Done, No Diaper Needed*, the shirt read. "Without any prompting. And apparently his fics all include pegging?"

Edging behind a large potted plant, April listened to the fourth iteration of this conversation she'd encountered in the last ten minutes, hoping to glean some piece of information—*anything*—that might mitigate her worries for Alex.

A young woman with Psyche's trademark circlet on her head crinkled her brow. "Pegging?"

Another fan, her T-shirt emblazoned with a map of the under-world, beckoned the first woman closer and whispered in her ear for a minute.

"Oh." The Psyche fan blinked. "*Oh.*"

At her expression and pinkening face, they all laughed.

"Filming for the final season's done, right?" Another of their friends, a fortysomething man with a plastic sword strapped to his hip, sounded highly entertained. "At this point, can they still fire him?"

Cupid Tee snorted. "Maybe not, but they can sue him. I'd be shocked if they didn't."

When the group began moving toward one of the halls for their photo sessions, April didn't follow, and she didn't attempt to eavesdrop on any more conversations. They all contained the same basic information, and they all offered her one inevitable conclusion.

Alex was fucked.

She was now glad she'd missed his session, and she did *not* intend to watch any of the countless YouTube clips uploaded within minutes of the incident. If Alex was sometimes an asshole, he was also loyal and funny and entertaining. She liked him. And she had no desire to watch him throw away his life's work in a fit of what—according to onlookers—seemed to be total, mysterious, grinning rage.

Which didn't mean she wasn't looking up his fanfiction. Immediately. If anyone in the *Gates* universe needed a good pegging, Cupid was *definitely* that character.

As she began edging toward the elevators, she drew more than a few stares and whispers, as she had from the moment of her arrival earlier that afternoon.

Even after a couple of hours at the hotel, and despite her mental preparation, all the attention still disoriented her. Some of her fellow con attendees merely looked, or took pics and videos from afar, and she could live with that. But the people who approached her with comments and queries and entirely too much familiarity for her comfort . . .

She wanted to hide from them. Not because she was shy, or ashamed of herself or her appearance or her former relationship with Marcus.

Because she was grieving. Because speaking Marcus's name

hurt. Because the winks, the innuendo, the excited questions were streams of salt poured into wounds that hadn't even begun healing.

"Is that . . ." a woman in a *Dido's Vengeance Tour: 1000 BCE* tee hissed, elbowing her friend. "That's the fan Marcus Caster-Rupp was dating. We should ask her—"

April walked faster.

Suffice it to say, some time alone wouldn't come amiss, even though this was only the first night of the con. Thank fuck she hadn't accepted room-sharing invitations from the Lavineas crew, even TopMeAeneas.

After retreating gratefully to her quiet, peaceful hotel room, she took off her shoes and propped herself comfortably against the headboard. Finishing all of Alex's fics would only take a couple of hours, if she was judging his word count correctly, and she was more than willing to devote that much time to them. She didn't particularly want to answer more questions about Marcus in the near future.

In the end, she was reading at her laptop for longer than two hours. Much, much longer. Until she'd missed all the remaining scheduled events for the evening, and giggling groups of *Gates* fans were no longer stumbling down the hall and shushing each other at top volume.

Alex's stories were fascinating. More than that. *Revelatory*, in so many ways.

Before each of his fics, he thanked his faithful beta reader and fellow writer, AeneasLovesLavinia. The laws of probability informed her who *that* author had to be. BAWN, unwilling to use his former pen name, lest he draw her attention to his continuing presence online and hurt her further. Marcus, either unable or unwilling to stop writing.

Now that she knew BAWN and Marcus were one and the same, she had to wonder what drew him to fanfic in the first place. What he got out of writing, and writing stories about Aeneas in particular, especially given the risk to his employment if anyone found out. What the Lavineas community, the community he'd left behind—for her sake, of course for her sake—meant to him. How it felt to remove himself from that circle of friends and start over again, his stories now without a guaranteed audience.

It had to hurt. How much she couldn't say. Probably more than she realized.

Maybe it was foolishly sentimental, but once she realized who AeneasLovesLavinia must be, she read his stories, the ones written during their time together in Berkeley, before Alex's.

They were recognizably Marcus's work. More than that, they were—

April lowered her head. Bit her lip until she tasted blood.

AeneasLovesLavinia's stories were *swoony*.

His trademark angst was never completely gone. There was always a jittery undercurrent of nervousness on Aeneas's part, a fear Lavinia would find out about his fraught past with Dido and judge him harshly for it.

For the most part, though, his new fanfiction centered around love, not pain.

Story by story, Marcus's Aeneas lost more and more of his heart to his wife. Determined to win hers in return, he did his best to woo her, to make her *see* his devotion, to battle past her insecurities and defenses, until they reached a hard-fought happy ending.

No one else would recognize the real-life parallels.

April could hardly miss them.

Once she'd blown her nose and applied cold, wet washcloths to her eyes and questioned all of her recent life choices, she switched back to Alex's stories, and *holy fuck*.

The pegging. Oh, God, the pegging was glorious.

That wasn't the aspect of his writing leaving her agape and concerned.

His fic depicting Cupid as an actor on a popular *Gods of the Gates*-esque show was beyond pointed. Beyond damning. It was searingly blunt about what he considered the strengths of the show—the crew, the cast, the source material—and what he deemed its key weakness.

Namely, incompetent and unpleasant showrunners.

Everything he wrote confirmed what she and most other Lavineas denizens already believed, as well as a few things Marcus had hinted at in private. But neither she nor her fellow fans had ever, ever thought a cast member would say those things so clearly and publicly.

Turned out there was a reason they'd never expected that kind of honesty from a *Gods of the Gates* actor. Because it damaged careers. Specifically, Alex's.

As soon as she finished reading his fanfic, she searched for recent tweets about him, as well as new posts on entertainment blogs and websites, because there was absolutely no way knowledge of his online alter ego wouldn't cause an uproar. Not given the content of his stories.

The search lasted seconds. Less than that.

Alex's name was everywhere. He was trending on Twitter. He was the subject of breathless articles on the internet and smirking tidbits on television. On her laptop screen, he was looking out at her from a generic hotel dais, his face ruddy, his smile feral, his reputation in his chosen industry damaged. Maybe irreparably.

According to the most reliable blogs, *Gods of the Gates*'s furious showrunners were considering legal action or eye-popping monetary retaliation. One of Alex's costars, the guy who played Jupiter, had denounced him on camera as an ungrateful turncoat. Worst of all, everyone seemed to agree: future directors and producers would avoid working with Alex, for fear he might turn on them in public as well.

Unhireable, one article called him.

CASTING POISON, an entertainment show's chyron read. ACTOR'S WRITING PROMPTS BACKLASH.

His agent and lawyer were apparently working feverishly behind the scenes. Marcus too, of course. The articles didn't say as much, but she knew him. He would be in the midst of the chaos, trying to support his friend and help however he could.

Before she quite knew what she was doing, her phone was in her hands, and she was tapping out a quick text to him.

When you get a chance, please tell Alex I'm thinking of him and wishing him luck. I hope he's okay. After a moment, she added, No need to respond. I know you're both busy.

Delivered, her phone told her. Good. He hadn't blocked her number.

Within a minute, he'd written back, and just that simple fact made her eyes blur yet again. It didn't even matter that his response was brief.

Lauren's fired. Too late to fire him, since filming's done. He might be able to avoid fines and a lawsuit, but IDK.

He'd responded. Not only that, he'd told her private information he wouldn't want disclosed to the public—even though they weren't officially together anymore, and she had reason to feel vengeful.

He trusted her. He *did*.

Okay, she wrote. Thank you for telling me.

Marcus didn't respond a second time. Not then, not later that night.

As she waited for a text that never came, she kept scrolling through Twitter, kept reading more articles about Alex and the ruins of his hard-won Hollywood reputation, kept questioning herself and how she'd excoriated Marcus less than a week ago.

He should have *known*, she'd told him so self-righteously. He should have trusted her with his online identity. He should have laid his career in her hands once he found out she was Unapologetic Lavinia Stan, heedless of the danger to his livelihood and the reputation he'd built over two decades of endless, dedicated work.

And he should have done all that, according to her, even though public knowledge of what he'd said, what he'd written, would have damned him to Alex's same fate.

The words had rolled so easily off her tongue, as if she knew what the fuck she was talking about, as if she understood the consequences he would invite. But as he'd tried to tell her, she *hadn't* understood. She really hadn't, as the aftermath of Alex's revelation made clear.

Maybe Marcus still should have trusted her. After a month together. After two. But for a man who'd found his first, hard-won taste of self-worth and pride through his career, she could see how he would hesitate, even then.

Of course, he'd said trust wasn't the main issue. Not in the end. *I was scared. I was terrified you'd leave me.*

And she had.

On her laptop, she found herself searching for his parents' articles about *Gods of the Gates*. They weren't hard to find, given how extensively tabloids and entertainment reporters alike had publicized the obvious rift between Marcus and his mother and father.

Even years before meeting Marcus in person, she'd found the media's fascination with that rift ghoulish, and she'd refused to read any articles on the topic. But now—now she needed to understand.

Stomach churning, she sat on her bed and studied his parents' op-ed essays, inspecting them for some connection to Marcus, some telltale indication that these were the people who'd birthed and shaped him.

It was like seeing Marcus through a funhouse mirror, his image distorted and unsettling.

His intelligence was transformed into disdain. His facility with writing turned dry and unemotional. His life's work warped into a source of shame rather than pride. His place in their lives rendered so small they didn't have to acknowledge it.

But she could see him, still. On her couch. In her arms. Unsteady and wet-eyed and whispering in a cracked voice about what he owed them. What they deserved from him.

If he could forgive them, good for him.

She couldn't. She wouldn't.

He didn't owe them anything. She, on the other hand, owed him an apology.

For all her talk about trust, she hadn't prepared him for her own parents or her volatility after time spent in their presence. She hadn't described the disgust on her father's face when she needed new clothes, in a larger size, yet again. She hadn't told him how her mother would stand naked in front of a mirror and pinch folds of her own flesh, near tears as she evaluated whether she was still thin enough to be loved by her husband.

She hadn't explained the abject humiliation of realizing a man who'd just seen her naked, who'd just been *inside* her, wanted her to have a different body instead, and she hadn't shared her heartbroken rage when that same man would expect her to get naked, spread her legs, and offer her deficient body to him again, regardless.

Those pieces of her past were crucial to understanding her, as crucial as his online identity was to understanding him. But neither of them had said a word.

I was scared. I was terrified you'd leave me.

Even if she wanted to fix things between them, though, even if she *could* fix things between them, now wasn't the time, and this hotel wasn't the place. They both had responsibilities and meetings and friends to attend to.

As if on cue, her phone buzzed with a text from a number she'd entered into her contacts only yesterday. Cherise's—AKA TopMeAeneas's—number, shared through a DM on the Lavineas server in preparation for the con.

Sorry to text so late. Hope I didn't wake you up. Didn't see you on the server tonight, so I wanted to give you a heads-up: we're all still meeting for breakfast on Sunday, but you'll see us tomorrow morning too. Like hell we're missing your cosplay contest debut, woman.

Well, fuck. Time to wet yet another washcloth and claim even more tissues.

These were different tears, though. Happy tears.

She had a community now—communities, actually; plural—and she didn't need to hide anything from any of them. Not at work, not online, not anywhere. They knew her and accepted her, exactly as she was. They wanted to *support* her.

Thank you, she finally wrote back, vision blurry from fatigue and the aftermath of tears. But you don't have to come. I know there are other sessions happening at the same time.

Cherise sent three rolled-eyes emojis, then one more short, decisive note. Expect a cheering section, ULS. You deserve it.

At this point, April was beyond words. A row of heart-eyes emojis would have to express her emotions sufficiently, at least for the night. Then she set aside her phone and got ready for bed, because she needed her sleep and strength for the day to come.

In the morning, she had a remediation plan to finish enacting.

No more hiding, she'd vowed in that other hotel room months ago. *No more hiding*.

The cosplay contest was tomorrow morning, and she intended to wear her Lavinia costume with pride, despite all the cameras and all the whispers. Her friends, apparently, would be there to cheer her on. Then she'd moderate the session with Summer Diaz. Afterward, she'd email Mel and Heidi about how it went, as they'd demanded last week.

No doubt about it. She'd definitely stopped hiding her body and her fandom.

Maybe, once the weekend was over, she could stop hiding her heart too.

EARLY THE NEXT morning, Marcus visited the vendors and bought an Aeneas mask, much to the amusement and bemusement of bystanders. After signing a few autographs and taking more selfies, he returned to his room.

It was half-empty now. Alex had left the night before, either in obedience to Ron and R.J.'s demands, upon the advice of his lawyer and agent and PR team, or in pursuit of Lauren. Marcus was pretty certain he knew which one.

So far, his friend had responded once to Marcus's texts: Going to fix this. Don't worry.

As if that were possible. But there was nothing more he could do for Alex from the con, and he had responsibilities and obligations all day. Also one other event he refused to miss, no matter how fraught and painful the circumstances.

In jeans and a basic long-sleeved tee and his mask, his appearance didn't merit a second glance. The scheduled hall was crowded despite the relatively early hour, but finding standing room off to the side didn't prove a challenge either.

April wouldn't see him, but he still intended to see her.

The cosplay contest entrants stood clustered at the foot of the stage. Even amid so many bright and wild and impressive costumes, spotting her took him only a glance. Maybe because of her hair, or maybe because—to him—she'd always shone as brightly as a woman under a spotlight. A star, in the truest sense of the word.

Her cloak still concealed her costume, and she was looking down at her phone. As he watched, though, she jerked her head up, her mouth fell open in startlement, and then she was beaming and holding out her arms and getting embraced by two very familiar figures. Scarf-bedecked Mel and blue-haired Heidi, her coworkers and partners in costumery, had evidently arrived to watch the contest.

As of last week, April hadn't expected them to come, and the touched surprise in her smile as she basked in the support of her colleagues, of her friends, made his throat prickle.

Other people were surrounding her as well, people she didn't seem to recognize. After a brief conversation, though, she was hugging them too, laughing, and he had to know.

He moved closer, still unnoticed. Closer. Close enough to read one of the lanyards.

Cherise Douglas, it read. Then, in parentheses below: *TopMe-Aeneas on AO3.*

His chin dipped to his chest, and he gathered himself before moving away once more. All those people calling out to one another and grinning and hugging were no longer his community, just as April was no longer either his best online friend or his girlfriend.

He wouldn't intrude. Couldn't intrude, not without inviting Alex's same punishment.

Then the contest was starting, and April shed her cloak, handed it to Mel with a flourish, and got in line. From what he could tell, her costume didn't appear all that different from the Lavinia garb she'd modeled on Twitter, if somewhat brighter and better-fitting.

When she mounted the side steps and took her turn walking across the stage, though, he saw the difference. They all did. Halfway across, she turned to the audience, paused, and undid some hidden fastenings. Moments later, she'd somehow—somehow—turned Lavinia's skirts into a cape and done something with her bodice that revealed a second, entirely different costume created from her first.

Breeches. A doublet. A sword hidden beneath her transformed dress.

Aeneas. She was dressed like Aeneas now, through some clever trickery.

She stood there ablaze under the bright lights, before all the cameras trained on her, laughing. Gorgeous. Simultaneously warrior and maiden. Lavineas, her OTP, made flesh. Proud, *proud* as she swept a courtly bow in response to audience applause and a few wolf whistles.

Marcus knew that set of her chin. Defiance.

Despite the vulnerabilities he only now understood, she was revealing herself to the world and daring it to judge her body, her passions, her accomplishments, her life. And she was doing so with a community of people supporting her, surrounding her, because she'd allowed them to know her, truly *know* her.

It was triumph. More than that, it was bravery. Sheer courage.

Aeneas couldn't match it, demigod or no. Marcus couldn't, either.

But maybe, like all the other skills he'd struggled to master over the years, it simply required practice.

Once April had been presented with her runner-up ribbon and trophy—which he considered a grievous miscarriage of justice—he returned to his room and gathered his own courage.

Email would have to suffice, because he didn't think he could muster the right words out loud.

In the end, he kept the letter straightforward. Which didn't mean they'd understand what he was trying to tell them. But it needed to be said, regardless, because he owed the declaration to himself as well as them.

The closing paragraph summed everything up, as his mother had said it should when they'd spent endless hours crafting essays that were never, ever good enough.

I love you both. Nevertheless, if you can't respect me or my work, I don't want to visit you anymore. I've been successful because I've been lucky, yes, but also because I've worked hard and because I'm good at my job. I'm proud of what I do and what I've accomplished. I'm especially proud to have achieved so much despite the complication of my dyslexia. If you can't feel the same, I'll understand, but I won't subject myself to your disapproval any longer. If you truly love me in return, accept me as I am. If you can't accept me as I am, maybe you need to rethink your definition of love.

He signed off as their loving son, possibly for the last time.

He proofread the dictated message as best he could.

With a shaking finger, he pressed *send*.

Then, his phone in his sweaty palm, he tapped the number he'd stored in his contacts weeks ago, just in case he ever found enough courage.

Maybe he still hadn't. But at least he'd found sufficient inspiration and motivation. Enough to do what he should have done years before.

Vika Andrich answered on the second ring, ambient conversation almost drowning out her greeting. She was down in one of the hallways below, no doubt, surrounded by crowds of *Gates* fans and gathering information for her next blog posts.

"Vika speaking." She sounded distracted. "How may I help you?"

"This is Marcus Caster-Rupp," he told her, his voice hoarse. "I have a few misconceptions I'd like to correct. How would you feel about an exclusive interview this evening?"

There was a long, long pause.

"Hold on a moment." When she spoke again, her surroundings were quieter. "May I be frank?"

He swallowed hard. "Certainly."

"I'd feel like it was about time," she said.

Rating: Mature

Fandoms: Gods of the Gates – E. Wade, Gods of the Gates (TV)

Relationships: Aeneas/Lavinia

Additional Tags: <u>Canon Compliant</u>, <u>Angst and Fluff</u>, <u>Guilt</u>

Stats: Words: 5,937 Chapters: 3/3 Comments: 9 Kudos: 83
    Bookmarks: 4

Sparring

AeneasLovesLavinia

Summary:

Aeneas teaches his wife swordplay—and waits for the day she draws blood.

Notes:

Thanks to my beta. He knows who he is.

Lavinia was growing more comfortable with a sword in her hand.

That was true in bed, of course, and he was a selfish enough man to appreciate her increased skill there. But the bed wasn't where she was growing to trust him, thrust by thrust.

At night, she permitted his caresses and ventured her own, willing but awkward still. That wide-eyed look of shock each time she shuddered and came apart in his arms hadn't yet disappeared. Her lingering hesitance charmed him, even as her pleasure prompted his.

Under the blazing sun, in the dust, she was a different woman.

Clothed and confident, she swung back at him. She parried. She *engaged*.

You must learn, lest I and the other guards of the Latium gate fail, he'd told her.

It was true enough. It was also an excuse, one he refused to relinquish after sparring with her the first time.

Her endearing, lopsided smile bright, she moved her elegant, angular body without hesitation, certain he wouldn't wound her. Some swords, it seemed, she considered more dangerous than others.

One day, she wounded him instead.

"Tell me about Carthage, husband," she said as she knocked aside his blade and made an advance. "How did you spend your time there?"

His concentration slipped, with predictable results. The gash on his thigh welled with blood, and she gasped and found a clean corner of her stola to press to the injury.

She choked out apologies, and he consoled her, and he wondered.

If she knew—if she *knew*—how he'd left behind the last woman he'd loved, abandoning her without a word; if she'd stood on the deck of his ship, at his side, and watched a queen light herself afire in desolation at his cruelty; if she understood him for what he was and what he'd been and what he'd done—

Maybe she wouldn't accept his sword in bed, and maybe she wouldn't laugh and use one to parry his thrusts in the dusty yard they shared.

Maybe she'd turn it on him instead.

29

"—SO CYPRIAN AND CASSIA WILL NEED TO MAKE SOME hard decisions about what they mean to each other, and what they're willing to sacrifice for one another and for humanity," Maria said in response to the moderator's question, before turning to Peter. "Anything you want to add?"

As she'd spoken, he'd been gazing at her the entire time, rapt, mouth quirked slightly in a smile. "Another question that will become paramount is whether the island where they've been shipwrecked for years is still their prison, or whether it's become their home. Otherwise, I think you've covered everything I'd planned to say. As always."

Her expression impish, Maria wrinkled her nose at him. "If that's a hint that I talk too much—"

"Never," he swore dramatically, one hand clapped over his heart as the audience laughed. "I hang on your every utterance, my lady."

"There's a word in Swedish that applies here." Maria propped her elbows on the table in front of her and gazed conspiratorially out at the session's attendees. "*Snicksnack.* Nonsense. Total bullshit."

Carah snickered at that. "I thought I'd be the first person bleeped today."

"Swedes are a foulmouthed lot, I've found," Peter said very clearly into his microphone, while Maria grinned at him. "I can only conclude that long winters encourage vulgarity."

Marcus shook his head at them both. By the time he got on Twitter later, that particular exchange would have already gone viral, one of many such exchanges that had become memes and gifs over the last several years. He knew it already.

The closeness and seeming devotion of his two castmates fascinated even people who'd never watched *Gods of the Gates*. Maria and Peter had never, ever dated each other, as far as anyone—including Marcus—knew, but that only seemed to encourage the speculation, rather than dampen it.

The moderator turned to him then, the last cast member who hadn't answered a question specifically about his character. "Marcus, can you talk a little bit about Aeneas's arc over the course of the show? I know you can't share any spoilers for the final season, but can you tell us more about the state of your character as everyone prepares for the big showdown between Juno and Jupiter?"

Usually, Marcus didn't get such probing questions.

Here it was. Another moment of decision. Another chance to be brave, or not.

April wasn't in the audience. He'd looked, hard. Maybe she'd needed to prepare for her session with Summer, which was occurring in less than half an hour, or maybe she hadn't wanted to share a room with her ex-boyfriend in public.

It didn't matter. Her bravery might have inspired him, but this wasn't for her.

It was for himself.

He'd seen the question ahead of time. He knew what he needed to say.

"I think . . ." A sip from his water bottle helped relieve his throat's dryness. "I think, when we meet Aeneas in the first season, he's a man who's lost his home, but not his identity. He may have been sailing for months, sometimes far from land and at the mercy of Neptune, but he has a very clear sense of purpose and self. *Pius Aeneas*. A warrior and leader dedicated to the will of the gods, whatever that might entail."

His castmates were staring at him now, all wide eyes and furrowed brows, and no wonder. He didn't dare look out into the audience, which had gone very quiet.

"But—" More water, and he kept speaking. "But after being ordered to leave Dido, the woman he loves, in such a cruel and damaging way, after standing on the deck of his ship and helplessly watching her burn on a funeral pyre comprised of their life together, he finds himself unable to reconcile his personal sense of honor with his obedience to Venus and Jupiter."

Another gulp of water. Another deep breath, before he continued to defy his public image so completely, there could be no mistaking his previous artifice.

"By the time he meets Lavinia, he's wrestled with the contradiction between duty and conscience, and is trying to determine what piety actually means to him. He's not the same man. Especially after he begins to build a life with his wife, one not defined by battle and bloodshed." Marcus offered a feeble, thin smile to the room without actually making eye contact with anyone. "How that'll play out in the final season, I'm afraid I can't tell you."

The moderator, a reporter from a well-known entertainment magazine, was blinking at him. "Oh—okay. Um, thank you, Marcus, for that—" The older man paused. "Thank you for that very thoughtful answer."

In the front row, Vika was watching Marcus. When he inadvertently met her gaze, she inclined her head with a faint smile. An acknowledgment. Encouragement, perhaps.

"Well, uh . . ." The moderator still seemed a bit shell-shocked, but he eventually glanced at the papers in front of him and pulled himself together. "I believe we have time for audience questions."

Several moments of general upheaval ensued before a woman near the back of the room stood, accepted a microphone, and addressed the panel. "This question is for Marcus."

"No fucking duh," Carah muttered, and patted his arm comfortingly.

To his surprise, though, the woman didn't address the obvious dichotomy between his previous public persona and the version of him who'd spoken moments before.

No, what she asked was infinitely worse.

"My boyfriend and I have an ongoing argument," she said, gesturing toward a guy in a *Gates* tee who sat slouched and smirking in the seat beside her. "He's convinced you only dated that fan as a publicity thing, or as some kind of political statement. I told him you're a great actor, but there's no way you were faking that expression whenever you looked at her. So who's right?"

Dimly, Marcus wondered what expression he wore whenever he looked at April. Thunderstruck, probably. Lovesick.

The moderator heaved a sigh and glared at the woman. "Please make sure all future questions involve the show, rather than matters of an entirely personal nature. Let's go to the next—"

"No," Marcus found himself saying. "No, it's okay. I'll answer."

Before April, he wouldn't have realized the real implications of this question, the stance the woman's boyfriend was actually taking. But now he knew, and he wouldn't let it go unchallenged.

April might not want him anymore, but he wasn't going to

stand by while that smirking asshole or anyone else dismissed their relationship as a PR stunt or political statement.

"My relationship with Ms. Whittier is real." He spoke directly into the mic, each word deliberate and chilly. "She's an incredibly intelligent and talented woman, as well as gorgeous."

The boyfriend snorted at that, and Marcus stared at him. Kept staring, stony and expressionless, until that hateful little smile evaporated.

"I consider myself fortunate to have dated her, and I would be proud to have her by my side at any and all red carpets, if she were willing to accompany me." One brow raised challengingly, he turned back to the woman. "Does that answer your question?"

"Um . . ." She dropped back into her seat with a distinct thump, eyes wide. "Yes. Thank you."

It wasn't enough to make up for how he'd hurt April, but at least he'd proven one thing.

Whatever else he was, he wasn't her goddamn father.

Right now, for the first time in years, he was only himself. No more, and definitely no less. Whether that would be enough—for her, for *Gates* fans, for his parents—he couldn't say.

But at long last, after almost four decades, it was enough for him.

TWO MINUTES BEFORE their session was due to begin, Summer Diaz rushed into the backstage area and offered April a quick, slightly sweaty hug.

"I'm so sorry," she gasped. "The group panel ran long. There were a *lot* of audience questions. Awkward ones."

"Oh?" April tucked her hair behind her ear, doing her best not to appear as starved for information as she actually was, especially if said information included Marcus. "What were people asking?"

One of the conference organizers was waving at them, trying

to catch their attention. April deliberately shifted until Summer blocked any view of him.

The other woman was watching April carefully, her breathing slowly returning to normal. "Among other things, why Marcus suddenly sounded like a PhD candidate, instead of the most handsome village idiot on earth. Whether his relationship with you was real, or just a publicity stunt."

April's mouth was gaping. She knew it, but the air in the hotel suddenly seemed unusually thin, so much so that she needed to gulp for breath.

"What—" Another shallow breath. Another. "What did he say?"

"Quite a bit. Let me see." Summer tilted her head. "The highlights: he's shy and dyslexic and happy to explain more in an interview that should be posted either late tonight or tomorrow."

Holy fuck. *Holy fuck.*

He'd done it. He'd disposed of his old persona in the most public way possible, short of interrupting a royal wedding to announce his dyslexia via interpretive dance before setting fire to a series of hair products.

Not that he would ever set fire to his hair products. He was very, very attached to them. Especially his soft-hold mousse, which smelled like rosemary and fluffy clouds and money.

"How did the audience react?" The central, terrifying question.

Summer lifted a shoulder. "They were sympathetic, albeit confused. I think the interview will help smooth over any ill feelings, once it's posted."

April gripped the back of a nearby chair, knees literally weak with relief.

"And . . . what did he say about me?" It was nearly a whisper, because the con organizer was coming closer, but she wasn't sure she could have spoken louder under any circumstances.

"You're intelligent, talented, and gorgeous." One by one, Summer ticked off the adjectives on her fingers. "Your relationship is real, and he's proud to be with you."

April closed her eyes then, willing the tears back into her sinuses.

"We're already a minute late." The organizer sounded harried. "Are you two ready?"

Eyes still closed, April nodded.

"Sure," Summer said. "April?"

Then they were moving out onto the stage, squinting under the lights, and April was looking down at her notes and trying to concentrate on the job at hand. More people kept shuffling into the room, standing at the back as she introduced Summer to the audience, and she couldn't help but wonder whether they too were coming straight from the full-cast panel, whether they'd heard what Marcus had said. About himself, about her. About them.

Can't think about that now.

"Summer," she said, angling herself in her chair to face the other woman more directly, "to start us off, can you explain what drew you to the character of Lavinia?"

The rest of the session was a blur, punctuated in places by Summer's keen empathy for her character and the intelligence with which she answered questions about her work, the books that had inspired the series, and the experience of acting on a show with such a broad global reach. Through it all, April tried her best to remain clear and present and prepared for whatever might occur, but it all went smoothly, more smoothly than she'd even hoped.

Then, as planned, they had ten minutes left for questions and answers.

One of the con volunteers picked an audience member, someone April vaguely remembered joining the session moments after she'd introduced Summer.

The tall, generously rounded girl, who couldn't have been much older than twenty, smiled shyly as she looked at April. "Hi. I'm Leila, and I was hoping to ask a question."

April smiled back, as encouragingly as she could. "Hi, Leila. Go ahead. Summer would be delighted to answer any question you might have."

The girl's brow crinkled. "No, I mean I was hoping to ask *you* a question."

Oh.

Oh, shit.

In her peripheral vision, she could see Summer taking out a cell phone and feverishly thumbing away, which seemed odd and sort of rude under the circumstances, but April supposed no one in the audience was paying attention to the actor right now anyway.

No, they were all looking at her, and they all knew what this young woman wanted to ask about. Marcus. Of course, Marcus.

The con organizer was waving at her from the side of the stage, mouthing something. *It's up to you*, if she was interpreting the man's exaggerated lip movements correctly.

Her privacy was at stake here, but so was her pride.

So was her heart.

Marcus would eventually see this, she knew. At the very least, he'd hear about it, from Summer or someone else. And maybe she hadn't thought the convention was the right place to have this conversation, and maybe she hadn't intended to expose her heart to a hall full of strangers before speaking to him directly, but she wasn't going to evade the question, whatever it was.

He loved her. He *loved* her, and Marcus had already loved too many people who'd failed him. Who'd ignored his needs. Who'd refused to acknowledge him publicly.

She was proud of him and for him, and whatever happened between them next, he needed to know that.

After a shuddering breath, she mentally hiked up her big-girl panties and answered the young woman. "Sure. What's your question?"

"At the cast panel—" Leila gestured vaguely toward the door. "You know, the one that happened right before this session?"

April tipped her head in acknowledgment.

The girl continued, "Anyway, at that panel, Marcus Caster-Rupp said he wasn't with you as a publicity stunt."

"Our relationship has nothing to do with publicity." The words were firm. Definitive. "The first time we met, the attraction was immediate and mutual."

And that remained true whether she meant their first online meeting or their first date.

"Oh. Good." Leila's brief smile was beautiful, wide enough to plump her cheeks adorably. "Are you two still dating? Because it . . ." The microphone picked up the little catch in her throat. "It meant a lot to me to see you two t-together."

When April met the girl's eyes, she saw pain and need there. The same pain and need that had clawed at her for decades, and the same pain and need that had drawn her inexorably into the Lavineas fandom.

Please tell me people who look like us can be loved.

Please tell me people who look like us can be desired.

Please tell me people who look like us can have happy endings.

She bit her lip. Dropped her chin to her chest. Considered what to tell the girl. Dammit, she hadn't intended to say any of this, but—

"Not to sound like a social media status update, but it's complicated." The audience chuckled, and she huffed out a small sound of amusement too. "Let me make one thing absolutely clear, though: If we do break up, it won't be because our relationship was fake, or because he doesn't like how I look. He wants me exactly as I am. Believe me"—she slanted the audience a smile dripping with smug confidence—"*I know.*"

Leila giggled at that, and April laughed with her and reached for a well-deserved sip of water. Only to see, when she turned away from the audience, someone standing at the far edge of the stage, blocked from the sight of session attendees by a curtain.

Not the con organizer. Not a volunteer.

Marcus.

His chest was heaving, as if he'd run through the hotel to reach her. He was clutching his cell, and April suddenly knew exactly whom Summer had been texting earlier and why.

He was staring at her, face pinched into a concerned frown. It was easy enough to read his lips, to interpret the sweep of his arm toward the unseen audience. *I'm sorry.*

When she smiled at him, his gaze turned soft. Still worried, but gentle and affectionate.

"Leila, you didn't ask me this, but I want to make something else clear." She spoke into her microphone, but she was looking at him. Always, always at him. "If Marcus and I break up, it won't be because I want to, and it won't be because I don't love him."

He'd gone very, very still, his face grave.

"I do love him. Of course I love him. How could I *not* love him?" It was an impossibility, really. An inevitability, from that first direct message on the Lavineas server. "He's such a talented man. Incredibly knowledgeable and smart and so curious about everything."

At his sides, his hands twitched and curled in on themselves, but he didn't glance away. Not once.

"There's so much more to him than what he's shown the world, and all of it is even more impressive than the person you see on your television and movie screens." A vast understatement. She hoped he understood that someday. "He isn't perfect, just like I'm not perfect. He makes mistakes, because of course he makes mistakes. He isn't an actual demigod."

His lips were parted, his eyes bright with more than the overhead lights. Which was fair, because she was suddenly near tears herself.

"He's just a man. A good, good man who deserves all the love and happiness he can handle." She tipped her chin to him then, a quick gesture of affirmation before turning back to the audience. "Doesn't hurt that he's the prettiest man I've ever met, either."

Then they were all laughing again, and the familiar sound of his amusement rumbled from the side of the stage. Which came as a relief, because she didn't want him to think she was dismissing him as *only* a pretty face, undeniably pretty as that face might be.

"Okay, let's focus on questions for Summer now." She peered into the audience, searching for the appropriate con volunteer. "Who's n—"

Suddenly, the microphone was plucked out of her hand.

"Excuse me. Sorry to interrupt. Just a quick note before we move on." Marcus was looming over her chair, his hand resting on its high back, his thumb caressing her nape in a spot that always made her shiver. "That is, if Summer doesn't mind."

His colleague was sitting back in her chair, hands laced in her lap, a satisfied grin splitting her elfin face. "Take as long as you need, Marcus. I'm in no hurry."

"Great." He turned to the audience. "Leila, I have something I want to make clear as well. Just as an addendum to April's answer."

The young woman got to her feet again. "Uh, okay?"

"Ms. Whittier seemed uncertain on the matter, so let me clarify for you." His voice was clear and sure, and warmth crinkled the corners of those famous blue-gray eyes. "We're not breaking up. Not if I have anything to say about it."

It was April's turn to stare at him, shocked into stillness. He lowered his microphone and faced her, free hand lifted and waiting for her permission.

She nodded.

His palm gentle on her cheek, he studied her features with care. "Do I have something to say about it?"

"You do." She barely recognized her own voice, hoarse with relief and love.

"Well, then." Ducking his head, he pressed a soft kiss on her trembling lips. Another. Then he raised his microphone again. "It's official. We're still dating. That's the answer to your question, Leila."

April appreciated having such an unambiguous statement on the record.

Honestly, though, Leila would have figured it out anyway, along with everyone else who streamed the video or read the session transcript later. Especially once April surged to her feet and yanked Marcus close and used her hands in that soft, soft hair to pull him down to her.

The kiss was long. It was loving. It was fervent. It involved more tongue than was appropriate for an event advertised as family-friendly.

And for *Gods of the Gates* fans, it was a kiss that launched a thousand new fics.

Rating: Mature

Fandoms: Gods of the Gates – E. Wade, Gods of the Gates (TV)

Relationships: Cupid/Psyche, Cupid & Venus, Psyche & Venus

Additional Tags: <u>Alternate Universe – Modern</u>, <u>Celebrity!Cupid</u>, <u>Fan!Psyche</u>, <u>Come On You Know It Had to Happen</u>, <u>April Whittier Is Living the Dream</u>, <u>The Peg That Was Promised</u>

Stats: Words: 925 Chapters: 1/1 Comments: 22 Kudos: 104 Bookmarks: 7

One Kiss to Legendary
SoftestBoiCupid

Summary:

Psyche still doesn't believe Cupid will put her first, now and always. But when his mother attempts to come between the couple at a fan convention, he'll show Psyche the true depths of his devotion—and his passion. In public, and in private.

Notes:

If you weren't at Con of the Gates, you should have been. The YouTube video doesn't do the kiss justice. Like, AT ALL. All hail April Whittier, rightful queen of the *Gates* stans!

———————————————

As the session moderator, Psyche wasn't meant to be answering questions herself. The possibility hadn't even occurred to her. Who would want to talk with her, a boring geologist, when Cupid, the single hottest man on the planet, was sitting beside her?

And yet.

When she looked up, she spotted the next audience member with a question, and to her abject horror, it was Venus. Gorgeous and perfect and vengeful—and Cupid's mother, her strangling love enough to have prodded him into his most heinous acts.

"Look at you," the goddess made flesh sneered. "No son of mine would desire such a woman. He's a star. You're a mere fan. Your so-called *relationship* is a publicity stunt. Admit it now, Psyche. Before the world, so everyone can know you for the liar you are."

Tears pricked her eyes. But before they could fall, warm, gentle thumbs had brushed them aside.

"Let them know you for the woman you are," he corrected, and the microphone carried his words to the entire hall, loud and clear. "Let them know you for the woman I love."

Then he gathered Psyche into his sheltering arms, heedless of his mother's screech of dismay, and kissed her and kissed her until she could have sworn he'd grown wings and carried them both to the heavens.

That night, for the first time, she pegged him.

EPILOGUE

"I CAN'T BELIEVE IT WAS IAN ALL ALONG." APRIL FROWNED at Marcus from above the screen of her laptop. "Was he sharing scripts with his wife, or . . . ?"

Marcus stretched out on her couch, hands behind his head, and reveled in the moment. Her, working happily on her latest one-shot fic at the kitchen table. Him, between projects and luxuriating in the time to read and write his own stories, catch up with their Lavineas friends as BAWN, and generally drag April to bed whenever possible.

They'd been together almost two years now. Engaged for almost a year.

Last month, they'd put his LA house up for sale and begun looking to buy a home in the San Francisco area instead, something large enough and within easy commuting distance of April's work. The real estate agent had been instructed to avoid anything too close to his parents, although he and April dutifully visited his childhood home every few months and spent awkward afternoons with his mom and dad.

Awkward, but no longer especially painful. Not after the letter he'd sent, and not after his parents found themselves the focus of April's cool, narrow-eyed scrutiny and pointed defense of him at every conceivable opportunity.

Frankly, he got the sense they were terrified of his fiancée. Which, given her opinion of them, wasn't necessarily inappropriate.

"Nope. Not Ian's wife." Oh, this was the best part. He couldn't wait to see her face. "He was sharing scripts with his personal tuna purveyor in exchange for a discount."

Slowly, she closed her laptop screen, staring at him.

"He . . ." Her head tilted, her coppery hair falling over her shoulder. "You're telling me Ian violated his contract in exchange for lower seafood prices? Did I understand that correctly?"

"Yup." He popped the closing consonant for emphasis.

"Wow. Wooooow." Sliding her glasses off her nose, she blinked at him. "The show's been over for months. Why is this coming out now?"

"Ian's playing someone less fit in his new show, so he stopped training as hard. Less need for training, less need for protein. Less need for protein, less—"

"—need for tuna." She tapped the arm of her glasses against the table. "Huh. Ian got ratted out by a newly impoverished, vengeful tuna salesman. I have to admit, I didn't see that coming."

He grinned. "I don't think Carah has stopped cackling since we found out this morning."

Fishy motherfucker, she'd written in the cast chat. *Literally and figuratively. HahahahaHAHAHA.*

He and his *Gates* colleagues had remained friends, some closer than others. All of them, however, closer to him than he'd have expected two years ago, possibly because now they actually *knew* him. Every few days, someone would post an update, and they'd talk about their new movies and shows, or their families, or possible group get-togethers.

They had, however, kicked Ian out of the group chat that morning, because *really*? A tuna purveyor?

"Oh, and Summer says hi, by the way." Idly, he scratched his chest hair. "She wants to have dinner with you the next time we're in LA."

Since that first convention together, his former on-screen wife and his real-life fiancée had become good friends, in part because they'd had so many opportunities to spend time in each other's company. At awards shows and cons. During visits to LA. Also for a few weeks last spring, as he and Summer filmed in San Francisco.

Much to his parents' bewilderment and April's amusement, his initial post-*Gates* project had involved playing a very familiar character: Aeneas. Specifically, Aeneas from Virgil's *Aeneid*, rather than Wade's version or—he suppressed a shudder—Ron and R.J.'s iteration.

For the first time, he'd helped produce his own film. A two-hour movie for a big-budget streaming service willing to invest in somewhat quirky projects, as long as big-name stars were attached. Stars such as, for instance, Marcus and Carah and Summer.

His fans had stuck with him after he'd discarded his public persona, so he'd had his choice of other quality roles. But moving behind the camera was his way of ensuring greater say in the script and his characters and coworkers. It was also a challenge and a set of new skills to master. And much to his satisfaction, he'd been able to coordinate shooting a few key scenes in San Francisco, as close as possible to the woman he loved.

Not that April couldn't do without him when he was filming elsewhere. He'd been lonely so many years before meeting her, though. Too many to easily accept months spent apart, especially if alternatives were available.

When he'd first tentatively broached the idea of coproducing and starring in a new version of the *Aeneid* alongside Carah as Dido and Summer as Lavinia, April had laughed and laughed until she'd literally collapsed onto their bed and cried with yet more laughter.

"You—" After wiping her face, she'd tried again. "You realize this is basically one big fix-it fic in response to *Gods of the Gates*, right?"

Well, he hadn't thought about it that way, but . . .

"Kind of?" He'd winced. "I guess?"

"God, you are the *cutest*," April had informed him, and then she'd pulled him down onto the bed on top of her, and the conversation had abruptly ended.

The memory of that evening was more than pleasant. It was downright *motivational*.

Accordingly, he rearranged his body slightly on the couch, angling himself toward April. She was still watching him, rather than ducking behind her laptop screen and tapping on her keyboard, and he took full advantage of his opportunity.

One hand still behind his head, he trailed the other down the center of his bare chest, stopping just above the waist of his low-slung jeans.

Her breath audibly caught, and he grinned at her, slow and hot.

Then a phone dinged.

"Yours or mine?" he asked.

She glanced across the table. "Mine. My mom."

It went to voicemail, as her mother's calls often did.

Only now, after two years, was JoAnn able to conduct occasional conversations without a single reference to weight loss or exercise. As soon as those subjects arose, April promptly hung up, but the older woman never seemed to learn.

Nevertheless, April continued giving her mother chance after chance to change.

"In the end, it's not really about me," she'd explained after yet another truncated conversation. "It's about her own fears. I'm not sure she even realizes she's doing it."

But April didn't always have the energy or inclination to discover whether JoAnn could abide by her boundaries for the length of a phone call, and on those days she'd let her cell ring itself into silence.

Marcus wished she'd just block JoAnn once and for all, but it wasn't his decision.

At least they didn't visit in person anymore. Not after that first disastrous lunch, where JoAnn had kept nervously pointing out low-calorie menu options to her daughter.

Under the table, he'd taken April's hand in his. She'd clenched it tight enough to hurt.

Then she'd let go, stood, slung her purse over her shoulder, and walked out of the restaurant without another word.

The older woman had started crying at the table, small and curled in on herself, and he'd wanted to feel sorrier for her than he did. But he'd witnessed April's brittle rage and grief after that disastrous birthday visit, seen her naked and shaking and suddenly, uncharacteristically unsure he'd still want her under bright lights, and no.

No, he wasn't any more forgiving toward JoAnn than April was toward his own parents.

"JoAnn," he'd said before following April out the door. "Please do better than this. If you don't, you'll find yourself without a daughter, no matter how much she loves you."

That night, April had huddled in his arms under an enormous mound of blankets, cold in a way he'd experienced only once before.

"I'm not doing that again," she'd whispered against his neck, eventually.

He'd laid his cheek on the top of her head. "You don't have to."

Fortunately, despite the interruption of her mother's phone call, she didn't appear cold now. Not in any sense. Everywhere her eyes lingered on his seductively posed body, heat flushed along his skin and burned a path straight to his hardening cock.

"My goodness, Grandmother." Her voice a low purr, she pushed back her chair and eyed the growing bulge in his jeans. "What a big—"

A phone dinged. Again.

Closing his eyes, he pinched his forehead. "Yours or mine?"

"Yours. Let me see who it is." There was a moment of silence. "Shit. Marcus, I think—" Footsteps, and then his phone landed on his belly. "I think you should look at the message."

Reluctantly, he opened his eyes and checked his screen, stroking her hip with his free hand and hoping she wouldn't cool off during the interruption. Other than their Innocent Driller and Lustful Geologist role play, the Little Red Riding Hood game was his favorite, bar none.

Once he saw who'd sent the message, he sat up so fast, April jumped.

"E. Wade wrote me." Agape, he stared at his phone. "Why did E. Wade write me?"

She rolled her eyes. "There's at least one obvious way to find out, Caster-Hyphen-Rupp."

Activating the text-to-speech function on his cell, he set the phone on the coffee table and turned up the speaker's volume.

Hello, Marcus, the author had written. *Please forgive the intrusion, but I heard your adaptation of Virgil's* Aeneid *is coming out soon, and I wanted to congratulate you. Your portrayal of Aeneas was one of the few highlights of that damnable show, and I'm eager to see what you can do with the character given minimally competent scripts.*

April was beaming down at him, pride shining in her soft brown eyes, and he took her hand and pulled her onto his lap. Cuddled close, she listened to the rest of the message in his arms, softness against muscle, heat to heat.

If you ever decide to write your own scripts, a bit of advice to keep in mind: As we're both aware—all too aware—some scriptwriters believe death and misery and stagnation are more clever, more meaningful, and more authentic to reality than love and happiness and change. But life isn't all misery, and finding a path through hard, hard lives to joy is tough, clever, meaningful work. Yours sincerely, E. Wade.

He opened his mouth, but didn't have time to say anything before the message continued.

P.S. I like your fics, but they need more sex. Just FYI.

P.P.S. If you want tips on those scenes, both your fiancée and Alex Woodroe possess quite a talent for them.

Aghast, he met April's wide-eyed gaze. "E. Wade knows I write *Gates* fanfic."

"E. Wade thinks I have a talent for explicit fucking," April countered. "Please put that on my gravestone."

Ah. A timely reminder of the game-in-progress Wade's message had almost derailed.

Ducking his head, he trailed his mouth up the curve of her neck. "You *do* have a talent for explicit fucking. I can say that for a fact."

She laughed. Then, when he nipped her earlobe and licked the sting away, she shivered.

Urging her down onto the sofa, he tugged off her lounge pants and panties and spread her pale, round thighs. He stroked down those thighs, then slowly back up, watching every inch of flesh pass beneath his hands.

Her voice was choked. "My goodness, Grandma, what big"—as

he knelt close, gaze hot on his fingers toying between her legs, her breath caught in a whimper—"eyes you have."

He looked up and met her own eyes. This time, as always, he gave the phrase all the emphasis it deserved, meaning every word. "All the better to see you with, my dear."

Her answering smile was soft, like her gasp when his teeth sank into a dimpled, delicious spot on her inner thigh. Like her sprawled, tempting body. Like her gaze on him in the dawning light of her bedroom each morning.

Like her heart. Like his.

Together, they were forging a joyful path through lives that were sometimes hard. But they were both clever, both tough for all their softness, both willing to work. For each other, and for their own happiness.

That was all the meaning he needed. Enough to last a lifetime.

"My goodness, Grandma." Fist in his hair, she was urging his mouth where she needed it, confident and playful and gorgeous. Exactly how he wanted her, now and forever. "What big teeth you have."

His favorite bit had arrived, and none too soon. "All the better to eat you with, my dear."

Then he settled down and got to work, as determined as ever to give Little Red Riding Hood—April, Ulsie, his fiancée, the woman he would always, always love—her very own happy ending.

Just like the ones in their fics.

Just like the one she'd given him.

ACKNOWLEDGMENTS

THE EXISTENCE OF THIS BOOK IS ITS OWN HAPPY ENDING for me, joyful and hard-won and achieved through love. My love for the story, of course—but also the love of my friends and family, and the love of my agent and publisher for their books and authors. I want to thank everyone who's supported me in the creation of this novel, but that would double its length, so I'll focus on a few key people instead:

Sarah Younger, my agent, pushes so hard for me and my work. She's uber-professional, always, but has also made her personal commitment to my stories clear, and I'm so grateful. Her advocacy and ambition on my behalf, her hard work and kindness, mean the world to me.

Elle Keck, my amazing editor, believed in me and this book and pushed me to keep polishing it until it shone. Thank you for shepherding me through this process so skillfully and with such patient good humor, and thank you for wanting me as one of your authors. I'm beyond grateful.

I owe a huge debt of gratitude to everyone else at Avon who worked on this book too, especially Kayleigh Webb, Angela Craft, Laura Cherkas, and Rachel Weinick. Also, I am so grateful Avon snagged my favorite illustrator, Leni Kauffman, for the gorgeous cover! Leni: This image made me (and many others) cry, because we saw ourselves in it in a way we rarely experience. I can't thank you enough.

Margrethe Martin spent endless hours discussing geology with me over FaceTime—to the point where my phone repeatedly died on us—and she later read my draft to make sure I got everything right. Which I didn't, but she helped me fix that. It was so generous and kind of her, and the act of a true friend. Thank you. And thank you for taking me to both the Shake House and the rock warehouse, despite your doubts as to my sanity! I was so tickled to be able to include both in the story!

Emma Barry read this story and improved it immeasurably, as she always does, and I'm so appreciative. But I'm even more appreciative of her: her kindness, her thoughtfulness, her infectious laugh, and the way she believes in me way more than I've ever believed in myself. Lucy Parker's insight into the book also meant the world to me, as does her friendship.

To all my other Romancelandia friends on Twitter, who support me always and helped me power through my edits as the world burned: Thank you. *Thank you.* Special gratitude to my dear friends Therese Beharrie, Mia Sosa, Kate Clayborn, and Ainslie Paton.

My husband loves me without conditions, just as I am. With him at my back, anything is possible. Anything. My daughter is sunshine in my life, so dazzling and warm I have to blink sometimes. Every time I see her in my personal sky, my day turns bright. My mother has had one of the hardest stretches of her life recently, but she is still moving forward, still determined, and still so caring to the people she loves. Thank you for being my family, all of you, and thank you for loving me.

And, finally, to all the fanfic writers out there: I love *you*. For over a year, my anxiety meant I couldn't seem to read published books, but I could still lose myself in your work. Hilarious stories, gut-punching stories with unparalleled angst, stories of such un-bounded creativity and talent I could only read in awe—you offer them all to the world for free, and you saved my sanity (or at least its remaining shreds). A special shout-out to the Braime fandom, among whom I lurked for that year. You, uh, may see some signs of that throughout this manuscript? Just a guess. :-)

ABOUT THE AUTHOR

Olivia Dade grew up an undeniable nerd, prone to ignoring the world around her as she read any book she could find. Now she has finally achieved her lifelong goal of wearing pajamas all day as a hermit-like writer and enthusiastic hag. She currently lives outside Stockholm with her patient Swedish husband, their whip-smart daughter, and the family's ever-burgeoning collection of books.

Don't miss Alex and Lauren's unforgettable love story in

SLOW BURN

Coming Summer 2021

"NEXT TIME YOU GET IN A BAR FIGHT, DON'T BOTHER COM-ing back to the set, asshole," Ron shouted. "Do you even *realize* what you've done? That kind of juvenile—"

By this point, the rant had entered—Alex craned his neck to catch a glimpse of Ron's Rolex—its tenth minute. And counting. The amount of blustering tedium the *Gods of the Gates* showrunner could pack into such a short span of time was impressive, truly.

Alex would applaud if he weren't too busy fighting both a yawn and his desire to nut-punch his boss.

Ron's nostrils flared with each harsh exhalation, but he made an attempt to lower his voice. "Legally, given the amount of nega-tive publicity you've generated with your drunken stupidity, we had several avenues of financial and professional recourse avail-able to us, including—"

The showrunner was still speaking, but Alex had stopped lis-tening. Instead, he was studying the woman sitting approximately five feet to Ron's left.

Sharp features, including a beaky, crooked nose. Bright eyes. Very round body with comparatively skinny limbs. Short as hell.

His newfound nanny looked like a bird.

A silent one, though. Not a chirp to be heard despite the advent of dawn.

As soon as Ron got word of the events that had transpired overnight, he'd demanded a meeting first thing in the morning. Even though Alex had left the *Gates* set near midnight and departed the local jail's holding cell maybe an hour ago. He'd barely had time to take a shower and grab an apple by the hotel's front desk before returning to work.

The three of them could have met in a private trailer, but the showrunner preferred public humiliation. So they'd gathered outdoors, near a ragged stockade, where hundreds of Alex's coworkers could conceivably overhear his disgrace, and so could she.

This pale-cheeked stranger. Whoever she was. *What*ever she was.

His eyes were bloodshot, his right eyelid swollen, his vision blurry. If he squinted in the early-morning fog, that lank, ash-brown hair ruffling around the woman's soft jaw might as well be feathers.

Yes, definitely a bird. But what kind, what kind . . .

She was white, so maybe an albatross? It certainly worked on a metaphorical level.

No, albatrosses were too long and narrow for the likes of her.

Once Ron had begun his lecture, she'd perched on a makeshift bench several feet away from both men. Quiet and still, she sat silhouetted before the chaos of their faux-battlefield set as it sprawled along the Spanish shore. Yet somehow, even amid the large-scale staged destruction and ceaseless bustle of extras and crew members, she stood out in sharp relief. Incongruously small in stature, if not circumference. Calm. Avian.

The ocean breeze flipped up the hem of Alex's linen tunic, and he absently batted it back down, wishing he'd brought his woolen cloak to set. A bird-watching guide, too, to help him pinpoint the exact species she resembled.

Also noise-canceling headphones, because Ron was still railing at him—something about *contractual obligation*s and *my cousin Lauren* and *unacceptable conduct for an actor on my show* and *bond company will pull our insurance*, blah blah blah—and, sure, Alex was furious at the reprimand and his allotted punishment and the way no one had asked him what actually happened in that bar, not a single soul, but—

His paid minder, evidently some unfortunate relative of Ron's, looked like a fucking *bird*.

This whole discussion wasn't merely enraging. It was—

"Ridiculous." Alex snorted, sweeping his arm to indicate the woman on the bench. "This bird-woman barely comes up to my chest. How is she supposed to stop me from doing whatever I damn well please? Do you intend for her to cling to my ankle like an oversized bracelet?"

He considered the matter. It would make his workouts challenging, but not impossible.

Ron smirked briefly. "She may be ridiculous, but she's in charge." After casting a sidelong look at his cousin, he turned his attention back to Alex. "You'll do what Lauren says until the series finale airs. Until then, she'll accompany you wherever you—"

Wait. Alex hadn't meant to call *her* ridiculous. More the idea she could effectively keep him out of trouble for months on end.

But Ron was talking, talking, talking, and Alex didn't bother to clarify the matter.

That could wait until later, since he and Lauren would apparently be spending endless, torturous months together starting right . . . now.